Someone Like You

WILD WIDOWS SERIES, BOOK 1

MARIE FORCE

Someone Like You
Wild Widows Series, Book 1
By: Marie Force

Published by HTJB, Inc.
Copyright 2022. HTJB, Inc.
Cover Design by Kristina Brinton
Print Layout: E-book Formatting Fairies
ISBN: 978-1952793295

"Tell me, what is it you plan to do with your one wild and precious life?" —Mary Oliver

One

Roni

Five and a half months ago today, I married Patrick Connolly, the love of my life. During the spring semester of my junior year at the University of Virginia, where he was attending grad school, Patrick stopped by my dorm room with my roommate Sarah's boyfriend and never left. We were a couple from the moment we met. Sarah told me later she'd never witnessed such an immediate connection between two people. After Patrick was shot and killed on October 10, just over two months ago, she told me she's still never known any couple more "meant to be" than we are.

Or I guess I should say than we *were* because we're over now. He's gone at thirty-one, and I'm left to face the rest of my life without him. I'm a widow at twenty-nine, and it's my fault Patrick was killed. I wasn't the one who fired the stray bullet that hit him in the chest and killed him instantly. But I was too lazy to go to the grocery store the night before, which meant we had nothing for him to take for lunch. He left his office on 12th Street to go grab a sandwich and was on his way back when an argument across the street escalated into the shooting that left my husband dead.

Of course, Patrick could've gone to the store, too, but that

1

was something I did for both of us, along with the laundry and the dry-cleaning pickups. As an up-and-coming Drug Enforcement Agency IT agent, Patrick worked a lot more hours than I do as an obituary writer for the *Washington Star*. I can bring work home with me, but due to the sensitive nature of his cases, he couldn't do that. So I took care of the things I could for both of us, including the grocery shopping. For the rest of my life, I'll have to wonder, if I'd gone to the store that night, would Patrick still be alive?

I've shared my guilt about that only once—at a grief group for victims of violent crime that my new friend Sam Holland invited me to attend. She's the lead Homicide detective for the Metro DC police department—and the nation's new first lady. For some reason, she's decided we need to be friends, which is funny because I've had a huge lady crush on her for the longest time. She's a badass cop who happens to be married to our new president, but she doesn't let that stop her from chasing murderers. The day Patrick was killed, she was the one who had to tell me the horrific news.

I'll never forget that day, or how I went from being happily married to my one true love to being widowed in the span of ten unbearable seconds. I can't even think about that day, or I'll put myself right back to the beginning of a lifetime without Patrick. At first, I was surrounded around the clock by people who care, especially my parents, sisters, brother, extended family and close friends. They saw me through the dreadful first week and the beautiful funeral at the National Cathedral. They took care of the massive influx of food, flowers, gifts and sympathy.

One by one, they had no choice but to return to their lives, leaving me alone to pick up the pieces of my shattered existence. My mom held out the longest. She was with me for three weeks and even slept with me many a night, holding me as I cried myself to sleep. Once, she found me on the floor of the bathroom at two in the morning. I have no idea how I got there or how long I was there before she found me shivering violently.

I shook for hours in bed afterward, unable to get warm.

Sometimes I wonder if I'll ever be warm again.

Our bed, which once bore the scent of Patrick on the pillows next to mine, now smells like my mother. I'm left to live alone in the Capitol Hill apartment we chose together and furnished with loving care over countless weekends spent at flea markets and antique sales. We wanted something different, funky and special, not just another living room or bedroom plucked from the floor of a furniture showroom. We wanted our place to reflect us—a little artsy (me), a little nerdy (him), with an emphasis on music (both of us) and cooking (both of us, but mostly me). We also wanted to be able to entertain our friends and family in a warm, comfortable space. Our apartment is gorgeous. Everyone says so. But now, like everywhere else that meant something to us, it's just a place where Patrick will never be again.

For something to do, I've been taking long walks through the neighborhood, getting lost on side streets for hours. Anything to keep me away from the apartment where I see my late husband everywhere I look, and not just in the framed wedding photos in the living room and on the bedside table. I see him on the sofa watching football, hockey and baseball. I see him lounging on the bed, completely naked and erect, a smile on his handsome face as he reaches for me and drags me into bed with him, making me laugh and sigh and then scream from the way he made me feel every time he made love to me.

I miss his hugs, his kisses and the way he had to be touching me if he was anywhere near me. Whether on the sofa, in bed or in the car, he was always touching me. I crave his touch, his scent, his smile, the way he lit up with delight anytime I walked into a room. I fear no one will ever again look at me like that or love me the way Patrick did.

Our life together was perfection, from Ella Fitzgerald Sundays to Moody Blues Mondays to Santana Taco Tuesdays to Bocelli Italian on Wednesdays. Every week, seven different themes chosen by my music aficionado husband from the fifteen hundred records he was collecting since he was fourteen, when his grandfather introduced him to the magic of vinyl.

The first minutes of every new day are the worst, when I wake up, reach for him and have to remember all over again that he's gone forever. He was the most important person in my life. How can he be *gone*? It makes no sense. He was thirty-one years old, with his whole life ahead of him, a dream career, a new wife and more friends than most people make in a lifetime.

One random second of being in the exact wrong place at the wrong time, and it's all over. That's what I think about as I walk for miles through the District, finding myself in places I've never been before even after living here for more than five years. I came to DC right out of college and lived in Patrick's nasty apartment in Shaw for a couple of years before we moved to our dream place on Capitol Hill after Patrick received a huge promotion—and a raise.

Fortunately, he also had awesome life insurance through work, which means I won't have to move. Not right away, anyway. Eventually, I'll probably want to live somewhere else, where the memories of the life I had with him aren't present in every corner of the home we shared.

In addition to the emotional trauma, no one tells you how much *work* death is. The endless forms to be completed, not to mention the number of times you need to produce a death certificate to close an account or change something simple. Every piece of mail comes with someone who needs to be told the news—a credit card company, an alumni association, an insurance agent. It's endless and exhausting and results in a slew of fresh wounds every time someone expresses shock at the news of Patrick's sudden death.

And then there's the criminal element, which is marching forward with hearings that must be attended by the loved ones of the murder victim. That includes the special joy of dealing with the anguished family members of the shooter, who made a tragic mistake and ruined multiple lives in the span of seconds. I feel for his heartbroken mother, sister and girlfriend. I really do, but he took Patrick from me, so my empathy for them goes only so far.

It's all so screwed up, and every day I'm left to wonder how my perfect, beautiful life has evolved into this never-ending nightmare. Thank God for my parents, sisters, brother and a few of my closest friends, who've been so relentlessly there for me. I say *a few* of my closest friends, because some have all but disappeared off the face of the earth since Patrick died.

Sarah, the college roommate who was part of us from the beginning, told a mutual friend who *has* been there for me that she just can't bear it. I know this because I pleaded with the mutual friend to tell me what the hell was going on with Sarah, and she reluctantly told me what Sarah had said. How sad for Sarah that she can't bear the loss of *my* husband. The minute I heard that, a close friend of ten years was dead to me. If she can't put her own needs aside to tend to mine in my darkest hour, then I guess we were never friends to begin with. I'm tempted to cut her out of the wedding party photos.

On top of this already huge mountain of crap, I feel like absolute shit most of the time. I can't eat without wanting to puke. I can't sleep for more than an hour or two at a time. My head hurts, my eyes are probably infected from all the tears, and even my boobs are aching as if they're mourning the loss of Patrick, too. I've lost fifteen pounds I really didn't have to lose, as I'm one of those women you love to hate—the one who struggles to keep weight on while everyone else is trying to lose it.

It's okay to hate me for that. I'm used to it. But losing fifteen pounds is not a good thing for me, and it has my family freaking out and insisting I see a doctor immediately. I have that to look forward to tomorrow.

In the meantime, I walk. It's barely seven in the morning, and I've already been out for an hour when I circle back to Capitol Hill to head home. I'm walking along Seventh Street near Eastern Market when I see a man on the other side of the street. He's moving in the same direction I am, so I can't see his face. He's built like Patrick, with the same lanky frame, and has the fast-paced stride that used to annoy the hell out of me when I tried to keep up with him. We fell into the habit of holding hands whenever we walked somewhere together so I wouldn't get left behind.

I pick up my pace, curious to see where the man is going. I'm not sure why I feel compelled to follow him, but hey, it's something to do. I went back to work two weeks after Patrick died and decided I just wasn't ready to be writing about death, so the *Star* management insisted I take paid bereavement leave for a few more weeks. That's super generous of them, but it leaves me with way too much time with nothing much to do. Following a man who looks like my husband from behind seems like a good use of fifteen or twenty minutes.

When he ducks into one of my favorite coffee shops, I go inside, standing behind him in line. He's wearing gray pants and a black wool coat that I stare at while we wait to order. He also smells good. Really good. What the hell am I doing here? I don't even drink coffee. I hate the taste and smell of it, and Patrick tended to his morning addiction after he left the house most days so I wouldn't have to smell it.

I glance at the menu and see they have hot chocolate and decide to order that and a cinnamon bun because I need the calories, and the pastry looks good to me. I can't recall the last time food of any kind tempted me. My mom bought me those Ensure drinks they give to old people in nursing homes because she's so alarmed by the weight I've lost since Patrick died.

I lean in a little closer so I can listen to the man in front of me order a tall skinny latte and an everything bagel with cream cheese to go.

That's all it takes to send me reeling. Patrick *loved* everything bagels loaded with cream cheese. I used to complain about the garlic breath they gave him after he ate one.

I turn and leave the shop before I can embarrass myself by bursting into tears in a crowd of strangers who just want their coffee before work. They don't need me or my overwhelming grief in the midst of their morning routine. Tears spill down my cheeks as I hustle toward home, feeling sick again. I'm almost there when the need to puke has me leaning over a bush a block from home. Because I've barely eaten anything, it's basically another round of the dry heaves that've been plaguing my days and nights for weeks.

"Gross," a man behind me says. "That's my bush you're puking in."

I can't bring myself to look at him. "I'm sorry. I tried to make it home."

"Have you been drinking?"

"Nope."

"Sure, you haven't. Move along, will you?"

I want to whirl around and tell him my husband was recently *murdered*, and he needs to be kinder to people because you never know what they're dealing with, but I don't waste the breath on someone who probably isn't worth the bother. Instead, I do as he asks and move along, half jogging the remaining block to my building and rushing up the stairs to my third-floor apartment full of memories of my late husband.

There's nowhere to hide from a loss of this magnitude. And now I'm doing weird shit like following men who remind me of Patrick. I'm glad I never saw the guy's face. For now, I can hold on to the illusion that it could've been Patrick, even if I know that's not possible. Maybe me seeing someone who resembled him from behind was a message from him. Sometimes I feel like he's close by, but those moments are fleeting.

For the most part, I feel dreadfully alone even in a room full of people who love me. Bless them for trying to help, but there's nothing they can say or do to soothe the brutal ache that Patrick's death has left me with. I've read that the ache dulls over time, but part of me doesn't want it to. As long as I feel the loss so deeply, it's like he's still here with me in some weird way.

I'm aware that I probably need therapy and professional support of some kind, like what I got from Sam's group for victims of violent crime. It was helpful to know there're others like me whose lives were forever altered by a single second, but again, that support doesn't really change much of anything for me. Patrick is still gone.

Thinking of Sam reminds me I owe her a call to find out if she meant it when she asked me to be her communications director and spokesperson at the White House. A few months ago, a call from the first lady asking me to join her team would've been the biggest thing to ever happen to me. Now I have to remind myself to call or text her or something, but that'll take more energy than I can muster right now.

I remove my coat, hat and gloves, toss them over a chair and head for the sofa where I've all but lived since Patrick died. As I stretch out and pull a blanket over myself, I feel sleepy for the first time in a few days. I hope Sam won't mind if I call her tomorrow. Or maybe the next day. She said she'd hold the job for me until I'm ready. What if I'm never ready? What would being ready for something like that even look like in the context of my tragic loss?

I'm so confused and lost and trying to figure out who I am without Patrick. That's not going to happen overnight. It'll probably take the rest of my life to figure that out.

My eyes close out of sheer exhaustion, and I'm shocked to wake up sometime later to realize I slept for a couple of hours, waking when my mom uses her key to let herself into my apartment.

"Oh, thank goodness you're all right." My mom, Justine, is tall and whip thin, with short gray hair and glasses. "I was worried when you didn't pick up."

While she gets busy in my kitchen making me food I won't eat, I check my phone to see I missed four calls from her. My family is worried I might take my own life, even though I've promised them I wouldn't do that to them. Not that the temptation isn't tantalizing, because it is, but I love life too much to ever consider ending mine prematurely, even if it would mean I could be back with my love sooner rather than decades from now.

Decades—five, six, seven of them. That's how long I'm probably going to have to live without Patrick. The thought of that is so overwhelming, I can't dwell too much on it, or I won't be able to go on.

I never gave much thought to the concept of time when I thought there was plenty of it. Now I know that's not necessarily the case. Why would we think about such a thing when we're in our late twenties or early thirties and just starting our lives? It's not until disaster strikes that we understand that time is the most precious thing we have, and we don't know it until it's too late.

Time used to stretch out before me in an endless ribbon of possibility. Now it's a vast wasteland of nothingness that'll need to be filled with something until I run out of it.

I have no idea what that "something" will be.

Two

Roni

The first thing I do most mornings is check my email. I have to force myself to do it because, as the executor of Patrick's estate, such as it is, it's my "job" to deal with the million forms and questions and inquiries that have to be handled after someone dies. I had no idea what a taxing job it is to basically erase someone's existence, especially when the last thing in the world you want to do is erase that person.

I try not to look at my computer at night because I don't sleep well if my brain is spinning with all the things that need to be done.

Sipping hot chocolate from one of Patrick's DEA mugs, I open a message from an address I don't recognize.

Hey, it's Mia, writing to you from my husband's email.

Oh God, our wedding videographer...

I'm SO SORRY for the delay in getting your video finished. I'm not sure if you heard I went into labor early and our son, Jack, ended up in the NICU for three months. As if that wasn't enough, our house got hit by lightning and fried my laptop, taking all my email contacts with it. Ack! Just waiting for the locusts to arrive next. Anyway, at long last, here is the video of your magnificent wedding, truly one of the most beautiful I've ever attended. You and Patrick are the real deal, and I hope you're enjoying your honeymoon. Please let me know if anything needs to be tweaked or changed. I make edits all the time, so that's no problem. Thank you again for your patience.

Xo

Mia

Beneath Mia's signature is a link to my wedding video.

I stare at that link the way I would a nuclear bomb if I happened to be standing close to one.

I can't. I absolutely *cannot* look at that, or I'll come undone.

Clicking to exit Mail, I get up to change out of pajamas into yoga pants and a sweater, jam my feet into Nikes and grab my coat, phone and keys as I rush out of the apartment like the place is on fire.

The freaking video.

I forgot about it, to be honest.

Mia told me it'd take a month or two for her to get it to me, and I didn't give it a thought since. Funny how the things that were so important to me not that long ago, such as flowers and music and photographers and videographers, are now trivial bits of nonsense from a life I no longer recognize.

I walk for miles with no destination in mind. Anything and anywhere is better than being at home, especially now that the video bomb has landed in my in-box.

Shuddering, I try to block that piece of information from my mind. Maybe if I act like I never saw Mia's email, I can pretend the video doesn't exist. The last thing I need to see right now is my beautiful husband alive and well and beaming with happiness on the best day of our now-ruined lives.

I could tell my sisters to get rid of it, and they'd do it. They'd make it go away until I'm ready to deal with it. If I'm ever ready to deal with it. But I don't call them. I just keep walking in a massive loop that takes me along the National Mall, past monuments and majestic federal office buildings bustling with workers looking forward to the weekend that stretches before me like a nightmare that refuses to end.

Oh shit! The doctor. My appointment is at ten thirty, so I

hook a right toward Capitol Hill, heading for the coffee shop with the cinnamon bun that looked so good to me yesterday before Not-Patrick ordered an everything bagel and sent me running for my life. I do that a lot lately, run away when things are too much to handle.

Before I lost Patrick, I never ran from tough stuff.

Turns out I never really confronted truly tough stuff. I lost grandparents I loved dearly and grieved for them long after they were gone, but that isn't the same as having your beautiful young husband cut down by a stray bullet a few months after your wedding.

Grief is grief, and it all sucks, but there's a difference between the dull ache that comes with the passing of an older family member who lived a good long life and the razor-sharp agony of losing the most important person in your life far too soon.

I'm almost to the coffee shop when I see him—Not-Patrick.

Today he's wearing navy blue dress pants and the same black wool coat. He's on the phone and completely focused on his destination.

Even though I've got somewhere to be, I can't stop myself from following him to the coffee shop and eavesdropping on his conversation.

"I left it with her backpack on the counter." He sounds stressed. "I'm not sure where else it would be. I can come back home if need be." After a pause, he says, "Thank you, Patrice. I appreciate it. Call me if the drop-off doesn't go well. I can pop over before work."

He ends the call with a deep sigh and rolls his shoulders as if the weight of the world is sitting on them.

I want to tell him that whatever is weighing him down isn't the same as having your husband gunned down by someone who doesn't even know him, but I can't say that. Everyone has issues. Just because mine are bigger than some at the moment doesn't make me special.

I'm ready this time for him to order the everything bagel, and it doesn't lacerate me the way it did yesterday.

When he takes his skinny latte and turns away, I keep my eyes averted because I don't want to see his face. The last thing I need is to confirm that he's really Not-Patrick. Keeping the fantasy alive seems critical to keeping me alive. I order hot chocolate and the cinnamon bun, celebrating that today seems slightly better than yesterday was.

Woo-freaking-hoo. Define *better*. I didn't burst into tears when the guy I'm stalking because he reminds me of Patrick ordered the same bagel my late husband liked. Someone get me a badge or a trophy. I'm beating the shit out of this grief game.

Until I remember that damn video is sitting in my in-box, waiting to open all the wounds that have begun to form the thinnest of scabs. I'm proud of those scabs. I've earned every one of them.

As I'm leaving the coffee shop, my mom calls. I take the call only because I don't want her to worry. I hate how my family worries about me.

"Morning."

"Oh, hi." She sounds surprised that I actually answered. "How're you doing?"

"I'm okay. Went out for a walk and stopped for a hot chocolate and cinnamon bun so I won't be forced to drink an Ensure."

"As long as you're eating. That's what matters. You remember the doctor, right?"

"Yep."

My eldest sister, Penelope, got me in with her guy after she called mine and found out she's on vacation for a month. I'm not thrilled about going to a male doctor for anything, but I tell myself a doctor is a doctor.

"Do you want me to go with you?"

"That's okay, Mom. I can handle it."

"I just wish..."

"What?"

"That there was something any of us could do for you. It kills us to see you suffering this way."

"I know, and I appreciate everything you guys have done for me. I'm getting through it one day at a time. I've been reading a lot about young widows online, and I see stories that give me reason to hope that it won't always be this bad."

"That's good to know."

My phone beeps with a call from my sister Rebecca. "Hey, Mom, Rebecca is calling. I'll check in after the appointment, okay?"

"Sounds good. Love you."

"Love you, too." I press the button to take Rebecca's call. "Hey."

"How's it going?"

I repeat this ritual with almost every member of my family just about every day. "I'm okay. How are you?" She recently gave birth to her second child, a girl named Delilah. Once upon a time, we talked about being moms together, but that's another thing that isn't going to happen now.

"My little princess was up all night, but other than that, all good here. You've got the doctor today, right?"

"Yes, and after you talk to me, text Pen to tell her I haven't forgotten. Mom has already checked, too."

"I will. So Jeff and I want to invite you to our friends' place at Lake Moomaw. They've offered it to us for as long as we or you need it."

I feel an instant wave of relief at the possibility of getting away from here for a while. "That sounds good."

"Oh good! I so hoped you'd think so."

It pains me how desperate they are to find a way to make me feel better. I hate that for them and for me. "When can we go?"

"Anytime we want."

"You've got a new baby, Rebecca. You don't need to go. I can go by myself."

"I don't want you there by yourself. Jeff and I talked about it, and he said he'll drive us there and come out on the weekends."

"You guys don't have to do that. You need your husband. I'd be totally fine going by myself. I swear."

"Are you sure?"

"I'm positive, and I'd love the chance to get out of here for a bit."

"I'll talk to our friend Val, who owns the cabin, and let you know the details. Hit me up after the doctor."

"Will do. Love you guys. Thanks for this."

"We love you, too."

When I arrive home, I eat half the cinnamon bun before showering and changing into jeans and a sweater for the appointment. Because the office is across town near Georgetown, and the Metro won't get me close enough, I order an Uber and go outside to wait for it.

The cold December air is such a welcome relief from the warm, cozy vibe of the apartment I once loved so dearly. Everything in the place comes with a story, an outing, a weekend getaway, a memory indelibly tied to Patrick. It took two full years to get the apartment to the point where we considered it "finished," which required champagne with Nat King Cole to celebrate. We had sex right on the living room floor, surrounded by the possessions we collected together.

A stray tear runs down my face that I sweep away with a gloved hand. With the appointment to contend with, I can't lose my composure. Sometimes it takes hours to get it back. When the black Toyota Camry pulls up to the curb outside my building, it takes me a second to snap out of it and realize that's my car.

The heated interior has me untying my coat, loosening my scarf and removing my gloves for the ride across the District.

Everything I do, even simple things like removing my scarf and gloves in the car, feels like it takes effort that I wouldn't have noticed before I lost Patrick. Now it takes effort to breathe, to eat, to shower, even to sleep. Grief is such a weird journey that changes every single aspect of a life, from the simple to the complicated. It's a weight I carry with me every minute of every day, even when I'm asleep and tortured by dreams about the life I used to take for granted.

That part is tough to acknowledge. It simply never occurred to me that I had anything to worry about. Patrick worked in law enforcement, but he had a desk job that kept him safe. We were young, healthy, growing in careers we both loved, making enough money to support a comfortable lifestyle while adding to our healthy savings account. What did I have to worry about?

I'm still thinking about how naïve I was when we pull up to the medical building. I thank the driver, head inside and take the elevator to the third floor. Pen gave me detailed directions that take me right to the door of the office I need. When I step inside, I'm relieved to find only one other woman in the waiting room.

Since I couldn't get an appointment for more than a month with my primary care doctor or hers, she sent me the gynecologist she adores. "A doctor is a doctor," she told me when I said I didn't need a gyno. "You need a doctor, and he's the best."

After I check in, give my ID and the insurance provided by Patrick's agency, I take a seat across the room from the other woman. A week after Patrick died, I received a call from someone in HR at the DEA to discuss my survivor benefits, which included another life insurance policy I didn't know about and three years of health insurance for myself and any immediate family members.

"It's just me," I told the kind woman who made that dreadful call.

"Your husband was very well regarded here. We're all so very sorry for your tragic loss."

Those words are emblazoned upon my heart. Patrick worked so hard to build a sterling professional reputation. The tsunami of accolades about his brilliance at his job overwhelmed me after I lost him. Patrick was heavily recruited coming out of college by private and public-sector companies and agencies. He chose the DEA after interviewing with the FBI, CIA and ATF because he lost a close high school friend to an overdose and wanted to work for the agency confronting the nation's drug crisis. I'm incredibly thankful now for the amazing benefits he had as a federal employee.

I try to flip through a magazine while I wait, but nothing holds my attention. That's another thing that's happened since I lost Patrick—I've developed intense ADD for the first time in my life. My brain refuses to focus on anything for more than a few seconds, which makes reading and watching TV, two of my favorite things to do, impossible.

According to what I've read from other widows online who've suffered the sudden loss of a spouse, the ADD recedes in time, and the ability to concentrate on something other than the tremendous loss returns. I really hope so, because I can't imagine how I'll ever work again in this condition.

Which reminds me, I need to contact Sam.

Ugh, my brain is a disaster area.

I'm called back to the exam room, and when they have me step on the scale, I'm shocked to weigh one hundred and eight pounds, which is down twenty pounds from where I was before Patrick died.

Damn it. That's five pounds worse than I thought.

I'm given a gown and told to take everything off. The room is chilly, and I shiver while I wait for the doctor to come in. When he does, I want to smack my sister. Her Dr. Gordon is ridiculously young, hot and has a kind, sweet smile that immediately puts me at ease.

"Hey, Roni, so sorry to keep you waiting."

Knowing my sister, she's already given him the full lowdown on me to save me from having to go through it all.

He takes a seat on a stool and looks up at me on the exam table. "How're you doing?"

"Oh, just dandy. Never been better."

His small smile is full of compassion. "I'm so sorry about your husband. I read about what happened, and it's such a tragedy."

"Thank you." I never know what to say when people express sympathy. What can be said except *thank you*?

"Penelope mentioned you've lost some weight recently."

"Twenty pounds I didn't have to lose. I just can't seem to make myself eat. I have a lump in my throat that makes me feel like I'm going to vomit all the time."

"Have you been vomiting?"

"Yes."

"How often?"

"Just about every day."

"Well, that's not good. Did you ever have a problem with that before you lost your husband?"

"No, but I've always had to be mindful about keeping weight on, which I know makes me the envy of every other woman out there."

Smiling, he says, "It does make you a bit of a unicorn, but it's good that you're aware of maintaining a healthy weight. When was your last physical?"

"More than two years ago."

"In that case, I'd like to do a full exam, if that's all right."

"You're the doctor."

After he checks my ears and palpates my throat, he has me lie back on the table so he can do a breast exam. It says a lot about my state of mind that a young, hot guy is feeling my breasts, and I honestly couldn't care less. The pelvic exam makes me a little more anxious, but then again, it always does.

"When was your last period?"

I have to think about that because I honestly don't know. "I, ah..."

"More than a month?"

"Maybe two?"

"Are you usually regular?"

"As clockwork." Patrick and I used to joke about how Flo from the Red Sea would show up with relentless attention to the calendar, and if only I could be as punctual as she was, he wouldn't constantly be waiting for me.

The memory has me holding back tears that are always ready whenever I think of something having to do with Patrick and our life together.

After he takes off his gloves and washes his hands, the doctor helps me sit up and then returns to his stool. "I believe you may be pregnant, Roni."

I'm sure I don't hear him correctly. My husband is dead. How can I be pregnant?

"Your uterus is enlarged, and since you've been feeling sick and haven't had a period in a while, I'd like to do a pregnancy test."

I'm shaking my head before he says the word *sick*. "I can't be."

"I think you are," he says gently.

"No." I cannot hear this. I want out of there, but because I'm naked under that stupid paper gown, I need him to leave the room so I can get dressed.

"Roni."

I can't bear his gentle tone or the sympathy I hear in the way he says my name. I don't want his kindness or his sympathy, and I sure as hell don't want to hear any more about being pregnant. I'm *not* pregnant. My husband is *dead*. How would that even happen? Before that thought has two seconds to register, I'm sobbing the way I did when I first heard that Patrick was killed.

I completely lose my shit. I'm not sure if I'm there a minute, an hour or a week, but Dr. Gordon never leaves my side. He even ignores whoever knocks on the door.

"Do you want me to call Penelope?" he asks sometime later.

"No. God, no." I don't want anyone else to know about this. Ever. "How do I find out for sure?"

"Urine test, but that doesn't have to happen today."

"I don't want to have to come back."

"Will you be okay for a minute while I get a nurse to assist with the urine test?"

Accepting the third—or is it the fourth?—tissue he offers me, I nod.

"I'll be right back."

Three

Roni

This cannot be happening.

The same chant that went through my mind over and over and over again during the first week after Patrick died is back and louder than ever. This. *Cannot.* Be. Happening. My heart yearns for him more than it has since I lost him. I can't do this without him. We were supposed to start a family together. This was the year. I went off birth control in June, and we were going to see what happened.

Now he's dead, and I... I'm...

Pregnant.

"No." I break down again as I shiver from shock and the chill of the exam room. My brain races, reviewing recent weeks—relentless nausea I chalked up to grief, sore boobs and missing periods that I attributed to heartbreak. I was so certain that those things were related to my loss. How could they not be?

Tears roll unchecked down my face and onto the thin paper gown. I can't be bothered to mop them up because I know there'll be more right behind them. I'm beginning to realize they're never going to stop. Just when I start to get my legs back under me, I'm kneecapped again by news I never saw coming.

That's further proof of how my sudden widowhood has

completely changed me. Nothing got by me before I lost Patrick. He used to joke that he could never cheat on me because I'd know it before he did it—not that he ever would. One of his many nicknames for me was "Bloodhound." How could I have missed this?

Dr. Gordon returns with a nurse he introduces to me.

I forget her name one second after I hear it.

She gives me an empathetic smile, the kind you'd give to a new widow who's finding out she might be pregnant, and oversees the urine test with a minimum of fuss that makes me grateful.

"When will we know?" I ask the doctor.

"Within thirty minutes. Get dressed and come to my office across the hall. Do you need help?"

"It hasn't come to that," I say with a grim smile. "Yet, anyway."

"I know it seems impossible to believe right now, but you're going to get through this, Roni. Penelope says you're the strongest person she knows."

I shake my head. "I'm not."

"I believe Penelope," he says.

Why does kindness from strangers make me cry?

He leaves the room so I can get dressed, which takes most of the energy I have. I grab my coat, stuff my feet into my running shoes and cross the hall to his office, where he's seated behind the desk.

"It's safe to leave me alone if you have other patients."

"We're on our lunch break."

Cripes, how long have I been here?

"You care if I eat really quick while we wait?"

I gesture for him to go ahead.

As he offers me some of the cut-up fruit he has in a container, I notice the platinum band on his left hand.

"No, thank you." I look down at the floor so he won't feel like I'm watching him eat. "How long have you been married?"

"Just over a year."

"What's her name?"

"Monica."

"How did you meet?"

"Her sister is married to one of my good friends."

"That must be fun." Their life sounds perfect compared to mine. Then again, just about anyone's life looks great next to my new reality.

"Yeah, it is. How did you meet your husband?"

I'm surprised he asks. Most people, including those closest to me, tend to shy away from asking about Patrick, which is upsetting. He's my favorite person to talk about. "We met in college during my junior year. He came to my room with my roommate's boyfriend."

"So you were together a long time."

Nodding, I say, "Almost ten years. We lived together for seven before we got married."

"We lived together for four before we got married. I often wonder why people don't do that. Gets the bugs out before you make it official."

"Yeah, it does." I'm surprised to be talking to him this way. "Patrick and I weren't going to get married. We were perfectly happy the way we were, but our parents wanted it." I shrug. "We did it more for them than for us, but then... The wedding was... It was pretty spectacular, and being married made everything feel different. Did that happen for you guys, too?"

"Totally. We were surprised by that."

"We were, too."

"Were you trying for a baby?" he asks in the gentle tone that makes him so good at his job.

"I was due for a birth control shot in June. We decided to skip it and see what happened. We thought it would take a while." I dab at my eyes with a damp tissue. "How will I do this by myself?"

"You won't be alone. Penelope has told me about your wonderful family, and I'm sure Patrick's family will help, too. You have people who love you, Roni. They'll want to be there for you both."

"I can't do it without Patrick," I whisper. The thought is so huge, so overwhelming, that it wants to drag me under the most relentless wave of grief I've experienced yet.

"You have options," he says softly.

His words settle on my chest like a dead weight of dread. "No, I don't." *Not* having Patrick's child isn't an option.

The chime of his phone or computer grabs his attention.

"Your test came back positive for pregnancy," he says, confirming what we already knew.

I need to get up, leave his office and take this earth-shattering news with me into the stark reality that is my new life, but I can't bring myself to move.

"What can I do for you, Roni?" he asks with sweetness that endears him to me forever.

"There's nothing anyone can do. My husband is dead, and I'm going to have his baby." I'd laugh at how preposterous that sentence was if I didn't hurt so damn much. Every part of me is on fire with the pain of missing Patrick.

"Let me call someone for you," Dr. Gordon says. "You shouldn't be alone with this."

"For whatever reason, that's what I need—to be alone with it. I can't share this with people until I come to terms with it myself." I'm not sure how I know that with such certainty, but the overwhelming need to be completely alone is what finally propels me out of that chair.

He stands to walk me out. "You'll be all right?"

"Yes."

"Do you promise? I don't feel good about letting you leave alone."

"I appreciate your concern and your support over the last..." I check my phone. Jesus. "Two hours. You've been incredible, and I'll never forget it. But I need some space to absorb this without everyone hanging all over me asking what I'm going to do."

"I get that, but I'd like you to check in with me over the next few days. Will you do that?" He hands me a business card. "My cell number is on there. Just a quick text to let me know you're coping will keep me from worrying."

"That's above and beyond the call of duty."

"I'd like to think that maybe we're friends now, and friends check on each other."

I'm filled with gratitude for this kind, generous man. "I'll text you." Glancing up at him, I add, "You'll see me through this, right?"

"You bet."

"Your wife is lucky to have you."

"Your husband was lucky to have you. I have no doubt in my mind that you're going to be a wonderful mother and that you'll make Patrick very proud of you."

"I sure hope so."

His admin sets me up with an ultrasound appointment in a month and a prescription for prenatal vitamins that he wants me to start taking right away.

Dr. Gordon walks me to the door. "If the nausea and vomiting continue, we'll need to address that. For now, focus on eating as much as you can. Whatever appeals to you that you can keep down. Try eating several small meals rather than three big ones. Keeping your stomach full can help with the nausea."

"I'll do what I can."

"I'm here if you need anything. Text me anytime you need me."

"I'm sorry for falling apart and for probably screwing up your schedule."

"Please don't apologize. That's what I'm here for."

"Thank you again. I'll never forget your kindness today."

"Take care of yourself, Roni. Your baby needs you to be strong for him or her."

Nodding, I exit through the door he holds for me and take the elevator to the lobby, where I place a call to Rebecca.

"Hey, how'd it go at the doctor?"

"Fine. Nothing to worry about, but that place in the mountains your friend offered... Would it be okay if I went, like, now?"

"What about Christmas?"

"I can't think about that. Not this year."

I ache when I realize my strong, sassy sister is crying. "I hate this so much for you, for Patrick, for everyone who loves you both. It's so unfair."

"Yes, it is, but since I can't change it, I have to find a way to live with it."

"I'll call my friend. Are you sure you don't want me to come with you?"

"I'm sure. You need to be home with Jeff and your babies. I'll be okay. I promise."

"You wouldn't, you know, do anything that couldn't be undone while you're off by yourself, would you?"

"I swear to God on Patrick's memory I won't do that." It's the best assurance I can give to a question that would've been unthinkable two months ago. "Ever. As much as I hate the idea of living the rest of my life without him, losing him has reminded me that life is a gift to be treasured."

"Thank you for that reassurance. I'd give anything to spare you from this awful pain."

"And I love you for that. I love you all for propping me up, but I have to find a way to do this myself, and I can't do that sitting in our apartment with his records and his clothes and the things we bought together."

"I texted my friend while we were talking, and she said the place is yours for as long as you need it. They never go there in the winter."

The relief at hearing that is immediate and profound. "Thanks, Bec."

"Anything for you. I'll send you the address and directions. When will you go?"

"Tomorrow."

"I could drive down with you. Jeff would come get me."

"I'm fine. I promise."

"Will you text me when you get there and check in every day?"

"I will. I promise." I'll have to set up a group text for all the people who'll need to hear from me daily.

As I emerge into the December chill, forever changed by the information I obtained in that medical building, I'm thankful to have a plan to get away. I've never needed anything more than I need this time to rebuild my life.

THAT AFTERNOON, after I fill the prescription for prenatal vitamins, I walk for miles. I have no idea where I am when I finally look up and realize it's getting dark, and I should head home. I'm heading toward my building on E Street when I see Not-Patrick get out of a dark SUV that's parked at the curb. As he heads toward the gate to a brick-fronted townhome, a child lets out a cry of "Daddy" that has him stopping in his tracks to greet her as she runs into his arms from the other end of the sidewalk.

She's adorable, with blonde curls that escape from the confines of a purple knitted hat. Her cheeks are red from being out in the cold, and she's clearly delighted to see him.

When he swings her into the air, I catch a glimpse of his face for the first time. I'm devastated to discover he's most definitely Not-Patrick. I stop walking to watch him as he chats with a pretty blonde woman who's probably his wife. Whoever he is, I'm glad he has a nice family to come home to. When he spins the little girl in a playful circle, he catches me watching him. His friendly, handsome face hardens in an instant.

I move along before he can ask me why the hell I'm staring at him and his kid like the freak-show voyeur I've become lately.

Shaken by the news about the pregnancy as well as the strange encounter with Not-Patrick, I'm filled with weird energy that has me up way too late packing, or, as Patrick would say, *over*packing. He used to accuse me of taking everything, including the kitchen sink, no matter how long we were going to be away. For Christmas last year, he bought me the biggest suitcase I've ever seen. We named her Big Bertha, which is why even the perfectly routine job of packing is painful.

I expect to sleep in, but I'm up earlier than ever. Adrenaline propels me out of the house at six thirty for a walk. Since I'm not on a schedule, I've decided to wait out DC's notorious rush hour before I leave to head to the cabin. It's also possible that I'm procrastinating a bit because "leaving" will require me to get Patrick's prized silver Audi out of the garage for the first time since he died.

As city dwellers, we have only one car, so it's that or nothing, but I already know that being in his "baby," as he called the car, for the first time without him is going to hurt like hell. So I walk and walk and walk until I find myself back in my neighborhood and standing in front of the coffee shop at a quarter to seven. I pretend I'm not looking for Not-Patrick when I walk in, but I immediately scan the line and see him three people ahead of me, wearing the black wool coat that's become familiar since I began seeing him.

Seeing him seems like a better way of putting it than *stalking* him...

With a few people between us in line, I've got nowhere to hide when he turns to leave, and his gaze crashes into mine. I'm shocked when he takes me by the arm and walks me out of the coffee shop.

His golden-brown eyes are wary as he stares me down. He's very handsome, but in a totally different way than Patrick was. Whereas Patrick was all sunshine and happiness, this guy has a dark, broody look to him that's every bit as attractive. For someone else, of course. Not me. "Who are you, and what do you want?"

Unnerved by his intensity, I pull my arm free. "I don't want anything."

"Then why are you following me and staring at me?"

I'm about to deny I'm doing that, but I find myself saying something else instead. "I thought you were someone I used to know. I'm sorry."

That seems to pacify him somewhat. "Quit following me."

"I'm not. I live nearby, and we're on a similar schedule."

I can tell he's not sure he believes me. "I don't have time for nonsense. Whoever you are, just leave me alone, okay?"

I hold up my hands. "I'm sorry."

He seems a bit contrite once he realizes I pose no threat to him. "My daughter and I have been through a lot. I'm protective. I didn't mean to get weird."

"Neither did I."

"Okay, so I guess I'll see you around."

"Have a good day."

"You, too."

After he walks off, I'm more intrigued than I was before. He and his daughter have been through a lot. What happened to them? Why didn't he mention his wife? He wasn't wearing a wedding ring, but that doesn't mean anything these days. Lots of guys choose not to wear them.

With the daily nausea making its presence known, I've lost interest in the hot chocolate I planned to get at the coffee shop. I walk home with my hands in my pockets and my head down, avoiding the bush that served as the receptacle for my puke yesterday.

I don't need another neighbor thinking I'm weird.

Pre-widow Roni wouldn't have done any of the stuff that makes up my days now. I wouldn't have had the time. I was too busy working and being blissfully happy with my beautiful husband to care about whether a guy who bears a passing resemblance to Patrick is married or what he and his little girl have been through.

I've become someone entirely new since Patrick died, someone I barely recognize. I've been so caught up in my encounter with Not-Patrick that I've forgotten, for a few minutes, that I'm pregnant with my dead husband's child. The reality of that comes rushing back in a whoosh of awareness that has me gasping for breath at the top of the stairs. I give myself a full minute to breathe before I use the key in my door.

This grief shit isn't for the faint of heart, I tell you. It requires a daily commitment of time, energy, emotion and fortitude that run in short supply when you're tapping into the well so regularly. I'm really tired, and now I know it's not just because my husband died, but because he left me with a parting gift that's going to overtake my life for the next twenty years.

The thought of raising this child alone is so huge as to be

paralyzing, so I try not to think too far ahead of the next few minutes as I shower, dry my hair and finish packing. With nothing left to do before I leave, I can't put off my reunion with Patrick's car any longer.

I've put on my coat when there's a knock on my door. I open it to find my mom standing there with a perturbed look on her face. I knew I'd forgotten something.

"Were you going to tell me before you left town?"

"I was planning to call you from the car."

"Honestly, Roni. You can't just go to some cabin in the mountains by yourself when you're in this condition."

Though I fully understand the reason for her concern, I'm stung nonetheless by her reference to my condition. Because she's been as there for me as anyone could be since disaster struck, I bite back my initial reply, which wouldn't have been kind. "I appreciate your concern, Mom, but I need a change of scenery."

"I'll go with you."

"And I need to be alone, to think, to figure out my next steps. I just need some space."

"We've been giving you space, Roni. And if you think it's easy to walk out that door and leave you here alone when you're so fragile, well, let me tell you, it's not."

The waver in my mother's voice tugs at my heart. I hug her tightly. "I'm sorry to make you worry so much."

"Don't apologize. None of this is your fault. This was done *to* you and to poor Patrick."

It is, I realize, the first time I see that she, too, is intensely grieving for the son-in-law she adored. "I'm sorry if I've added to your pain in any way."

"You haven't. This whole thing is just... Watching you suffer this way breaks my heart."

"I'm doing okay. I swear. It's awful and terrible and hard. So very, very hard. But I'm getting through it." I pull back to look up at her. "I have a bit of good news I haven't shared."

"What's that?"

"My new friend Sam?"

Mom's brow rises. "You mean the new first lady?"

"Yep, that's her."

"What about her?"

"She asked me to be her White House communications director."

"Roni! Oh my God. When did this happen?"

"I don't remember exactly when she asked me, but it was recent, of course." Nick became president on Thanksgiving after President Nelson was found dead in the White House residence.

"You didn't say anything!"

"I wanted a minute to sit with it to see how I felt about it."

"And?"

"I feel pretty good about it," I say with a laugh that takes us both by surprise.

When was the last time I laughed? I have no idea, but it's been a while.

"This is wonderful news indeed. It gives you something to look forward to."

"Yes, it does." Although I wonder how I'll ever juggle a job like that with a newborn as a single mother. But I don't have to figure that out today. I want to tell her about the baby, but I can't do that yet. I've been so sick that I need to get further along before I start telling people. I'd hate to get their hopes up only to have them dashed if I can't pull this off. A fresh wave of grief attacks me at the thought of losing this last link to Patrick. That can't happen.

"When will you start the job?"

"After the holidays, so I'm going to take this time away and regroup and get my head together before I begin this new adventure."

"I'm very thankful to her for offering this opportunity to you. It's just what you need."

"I agree. So you see, I'm okay, and I'm looking forward to a little break from all the reminders of Patrick here."

"Are you sure you don't want me to come? I could move some things around..."

"I'm sure."

"Will you check in every day?"

"I promise."

"Okay, then," she says with a deep sigh as she hugs me again. "I love you, and I'm so proud of how you're handling everything."

That makes me laugh again because, if you ask me, I'm not handling anything. "I'm just glad no one is using me as a grief training video. Red-Hot Mess Productions."

"You're not a red-hot mess. You're the epitome of grace under the most devastating of circumstances. Losing Patrick is almost more than I can bear. I don't know how you're doing it, but you're making us all very proud."

"That's nice to hear." Fortunately, the people who love me best can't see beneath the surface. They don't know, for instance, that I've been stalking a guy in my neighborhood who reminds me of Patrick, or how he confronted me this morning for being weird and creepy. I'll just keep that to myself for now and bask in the glow of my mother's pride.

She helps me carry my suitcase down the stairs, and we part company on the sidewalk with another hug.

"I'll be waiting to hear you arrived safely."

"I'll hit you up the minute I get there."

"And if you need anything, even in the middle of the night, call me."

"I will. Thank you for being my rock through this, Mom. I mean it. I couldn't have done it without you."

"That's not true. You, my sweet Veronica, are the strongest person I've ever known. You always have been, and you've shown me that over and over again through this." She kisses my forehead. "Be kind to yourself, my darling. That's what Patrick would've wanted."

Her sweet words bring tears to my eyes as I nod. She's right. Patrick loved me so much. He would've wanted me to be happy and content. I just need to figure out how to make that happen without him.

Four

Roni

The first hour of the drive is rough in the car that smells like him and reminds me of a thousand outings with him at the wheel and me riding shotgun, usually with his hand on my leg when he wasn't shifting the gears. Thankfully, we spent an entire Saturday after he bought the car with him teaching me how to drive a stick. I didn't want to do that, but he insisted, almost as if he knew there'd come a day when he wouldn't be there to drive me around.

I wonder about that sometimes. Did he know his days would be numbered? He was a stickler about things like life insurance and estate planning. What thirty-one-year-old cares about stuff like that? My husband did, and I suspect it was because he had a hunch of some sort, not that he ever shared that with me. That would've freaked me the hell out, and he knew it. But he took care of the details that now take care of me as I mourn his loss.

I love him so damn much for ensuring I'd be all right without him.

My bank account has never been in better shape, with enough to live comfortably for a number of years should I choose to forgo working. Although, that's not an option because I have no idea what I'd do with myself without work to keep me busy.

The money Patrick's insurance provided will help to pay for daycare or a nanny and will make it easier for me to be a single parent to our child. That thought is every bit as overwhelming to me as it was yesterday, even after another vicious bout of nausea has come and gone for the day.

I still can't believe I'm pregnant and had no idea. That's another thing that would've been inconceivable—no pun intended—prior to disaster. I would've noticed that I missed not one but *two* periods. I feel like I'm emerging from some sort of deep fog to find that everything about the life I once treasured has changed. Patrick is gone. I'm pregnant. I've been offered the job of a lifetime at the White House. I'm driving Patrick's car without him. What is this life I'm left with, and what am I supposed to do with it?

That's the burning question that has me pressing on into the Virginia mountains on Interstates 66 and 81, arriving at a gorgeous "cabin" (if that's what you can call this incredible *house*) at Lake Moomaw. I like that name. I keep saying it out loud, putting the emphasis first on Moo and then on Maw, the way Patrick and I would've done if he were here. We joked about everything. Nothing was off-limits, and a name like Moomaw would've been thoroughly dissected.

I miss him desperately. We would've had so much fun here together.

I call the number Rebecca gave me, letting the property manager know I've arrived.

"Be right over," she says in a chipper voice before the line goes dead.

When I get out of the car, I stretch out the stiffness of the four-hour drive and breathe in the cold, crisp mountain air. The house sits right on the shore of the lake, with a dock out front that calls to me. I wander along a stone path that wraps around the house and leads to stairs to the dock. I stand there for a few minutes, staring out at the vast lake, and feel myself relax the way I always have around the water.

When I hear a car door close in the driveway, I make my way

back up the stairs to greet the property manager, a woman named Chelsea Stowe.

"Oh, there you are," she says, smiling when she sees me coming. She has blue eyes and curly brown hair that's covered by a knitted hat with snowflakes on it. I figure she's a couple of years older than me, but mid-thirties tops.

"Couldn't resist the urge to poke around a bit."

"Can't say I blame you. I'm Chelsea."

I shake her outstretched hand. "Roni."

"Come on in. I'll show you around."

I follow her to the front door, where she punches in the code that I was given.

She leads me into a warm, cozy space with a spectacular view of the lake in the back of the house, which is all windows. "I came by earlier to turn up the heat a bit. We keep it warm enough to protect the pipes when there's no one staying here."

"It's beautiful."

"This is one of my favorite houses in the area. The Renfrews were meticulous when they built it and included so many amazing features. Such as..." She walks over to pick up what looks like a remote control for a TV and shows me how to close blinds I didn't even notice on the back windows. "So you won't feel like people can see inside at night, even though there's no one out there."

"There's always a chance the Loch Ness monster will show up."

"That's true," she says, laughing.

I'm relieved to know I can close myself in at night. She shows me how to light the gas stove and gives me the 411 on how to use the wood-burning fireplace before we head upstairs to tour four huge bedrooms. "I set you up in the main bedroom with everything you need—extra blankets, towels, etc. But do let me know if I forgot anything."

"This is great. Thank you, Chelsea."

"Here's my card in case you need anything. It's got my landline and cell. Sometimes cell service can be spotty up here, so make sure your family has the landline number. I left it on the counter in the kitchen. And I also grabbed a few groceries for you, compliments of your sister Rebecca."

"Aw, that's so good of you both. Thank you."

"I just want to say... I'm really sorry for your loss. It's just so heartbreaking."

"Yes, it is, and thank you."

"I hope this getaway will help."

"It already is."

"I have a fun group of friends here in town. We try to get out for a drink at least once a week. If you'd like to join us, we'd love to have you."

"That sounds fun. Let me know when, and I'll see if it's a good day."

"Perfect. I'll be in touch, and please do call me if you have any questions."

"Thanks again."

After Chelsea drives off with a toot and a wave, I retrieve Big Bertha from the car and lock the front door. My footsteps echo in the big house as I move around, making myself as comfortable as I ever am these days. Following the directions Chelsea gave me, I start a fire in the fireplace and sit back to watch it catch.

If Patrick was here, he would've done that, but now I have to do everything myself, which is another thing I'm getting used to. He doted on me, made life as easy for me as he possibly could while I did the same for him in every way I could. As I watch the fire consume the kindling, I wish for the millionth time that I'd made it to the grocery store on the last night we had together. For the rest of my life, I'll have to wonder if he'd still be with me if only I hadn't been lazy at the worst possible time.

Recalling my promises to my mother and sisters, I get up from the thick carpet in front of the hearth and retrieve my phone to send a message to our family group chat along with photos of the view and the fire crackling in the fireplace. *Arrived at the lake. The house is gorgeous. Please pass along my thanks to the Renfrews, Rebecca. I appreciate this getaway so much.*

Penelope responds first. *So glad you got there okay and that it's great. Keep in touch so we don't worry about you!*

Glad to hear from you, Mom says. *Dad says to be careful and have fun.*

I will! Nothing to worry about. Feels good to have a change of scenery. Xoxo

Rebecca responds only to me. *Great to hear the place is nice, and I'll pass along your thanks. I want to talk to you about something else when you get a second. Call me when you can.*

Maybe it's a sign that I've turned some sort of corner with the initial shock of Patrick's death, but Rebecca's message makes me curious about something for the first time in longer than I can remember. I put through a call to her.

"Hey, I didn't mean right now if you have something better to do."

"I don't. I'm sitting in this gorgeous house with a fire going and the sun setting on the lake."

In the background, I hear the baby crying. "I'm green with envy," Rebecca says. "Thank God Jeff is home to deal with them for a minute." She lets out a gasp. "I'm sorry. I shouldn't have said that."

"What? Why? Of course you're happy he's home after being alone with them all day. Don't do that, okay? It's not your fault that Patrick is gone. You have every right to enjoy your husband and family."

"I just don't want to be a jerk about it."

"You're not. Please don't dance around me like that. I can't handle that. Let's keep it real."

"I will. I'm sorry. My hormones are insane, and I find myself crying over everything."

"I get it. No worries. What did you want to tell me?"

"Do you remember my neighbor Iris whose husband was killed in the plane crash a year or so ago?"

"I do." He was traveling for work on a small corporate jet that went down in a storm, killing him, two of his colleagues and the two pilots. "How's she doing?"

"Good days. Bad days. Her kids keep her busy, but it's a lot."

"How old are the kids?"

"Two, four and six."

"Ugh."

"I know, but she called me the other day because she wants to get in touch with you."

"With me?"

"Yes, to tell you about a group she belongs to for young widows that she thought might interest you. She said it's been a godsend to her and has connected her with people who truly understand what she's going through."

"That does sound interesting, although I'm not sure I'm ready for something like that."

"Iris said to tell you it's there for you whenever you need it or not at all. She just wanted to tell you about it in case you thought it might be helpful. She said it's been a lifesaver for her and that she's made a bunch of new friends who truly understand the journey she's on in a way that no one else in her life ever could."

The thought of that appeals to me tremendously, but I need to think about it before I do anything. "Text me her contact info, and I'll reach out to her if I'm feeling it."

"Sounds good."

"Thanks for that, for this getaway and the groceries. You're the best."

"I wish there was more I could do for you. I'd give anything..."

"I know, and that means a lot to me."

"Anything else new that you want to tell me about?"

For a second, I think she means the baby, but how could she know about that? And then I remember I told my mom about Sam and the job offer. "Mom told you about the White House."

"Holy *shit*, Ronald. How have you been sitting on that bombshell?"

"What would've been a big deal before is just another thing now, although that's a pretty good thing."

"She is the coolest. I have the hugest girl crush on her, and her husband is *h-o-t*."

"Is he? I haven't noticed."

"Right... Sexiest president we've ever had. Everyone I know is so excited about them being in the White House, and my *baby sister* is going to work for her! It's crazy. You're going to take the job, right?"

"I am, but not until after the first of the year." That reminds me I need to give my notice to the *Star*, which pains me. My bosses and colleagues have been incredibly good to me since my life imploded. I hate to think of having to tell them I'm leaving.

"This is so cool, and I'll love her forever for giving you something new to focus on."

"I will, too. She's pretty great."

"I can't believe you're *friends* with her."

"Only because Patrick died."

"True, but still... It's cool that you know her and will be working with her."

"Yeah, it is," I say with a sigh.

"What is it?"

"The same old thing. I'm excited about the job, but everything is less exciting than it would've been before."

"As awful as it is right now, I have to think it won't always be this bad," Rebecca says tentatively, as if she's worried about saying the wrong thing.

"I've read that the pain is always there, but it becomes less lacerating over time. I've just got to put in the time to get there." I want so badly to tell her about the baby, to give her and the rest of my family something wonderful to look forward to, but I'm superstitious about sharing it too soon. Maybe after the ultrasound, I'll tell people.

"You're doing great so far. I'd better go rescue Jeff. They're making him their bitch."

That makes me laugh. "Not my precious niece and nephew."

"They're terrorists this time of day. I'll call you tomorrow to check on you."

"I'll look forward to that. Please tell Iris thanks for reaching out to me. I'll be in touch with her at some point."

"I'll do that. Love you, Ronald McDonald."

Hearing my childhood nickname makes me smile. "Love you, too, Becs."

When I end the call, I find a text from my brother, Corey, the

37

eldest of our foursome. He works for a tech startup in San Francisco and is married with two kids. When he got the call about Patrick, he jumped on the first flight he could get to be there for me, and I'll never forget that.

Happy to hear you're getting a break from it all, he wrote just to me. *Think of you and Pat every day. Toni and I send you all our love, kid.*

His heartfelt words bring tears to my eyes. He's twelve years older than me and left for college when I was six, so we didn't really grow up together. But he's always been there for me.

I type out a response. *Thank you! Miss you guys and love you.*

Hoping to get there for a visit during the kids' spring vacation. Will keep you posted. Xo

They have such a busy life in the Bay Area that I doubt they'd be coming home if it wasn't for me and my loss, but I still hope for the chance to see them. His kids are six and eight, and I haven't seen them in a year, since Patrick and I spent a weekend with them last fall during a vacation to California.

The reminder of that trip has me looking at the pictures we took with Corey's family and all the sights we visited in California. We drove down the Pacific Coast Highway in a convertible, with the top down and the radio blasting.

As I zoom in on Patrick's smiling, handsome face, I'm filled with yearning that's every bit as intense here in this new location as it was at home. There are some things a change of scenery simply can't fix.

THAT FIRST NIGHT at the lake, I dream about having sex with Patrick for the first time since he died. It's vivid and real, so real I wake up gasping and on the verge of orgasm. As I stare up at the dark ceiling, breathing hard and reeling from the memories, it occurs to me that Not-Patrick was there, too.

Okay, that's super weird and probably proof I'm losing my mind.

Why would I dream about Not-Patrick being there when I was having sex with real Patrick? And what is even real anymore?

I think about finishing what my dream lovers began, but I can't work up the enthusiasm it would take, so I get up, use the bathroom and go downstairs to get a glass of ice water, taking it with me to stand at the back door that looks out over the lake. The moon leaves a trail of light on the dark water, and a hint of frost has gilded the lawn. Winter stretches out before me as an endless season of frosty mornings and early, dark, lonely nights.

What a depressing thought.

I'm surrounded by a sea of people who'd drop anything for me, but the only one I want is the one I can't have. The dream has me wondering when or if I'll ever have sex again.

Here's a true confession for you—I've only ever been with Patrick.

My college friends used to joke that I was in possession of the last twenty-year-old V card in America. They thought it was hysterical that I hadn't done it by the time we reached our junior year and set out—as a group—to ensure I didn't start my senior year still holding the dreaded card. They were relentless in their efforts to find me a penis, any penis would do, they said.

The memory makes me laugh as I recall the huge bouquet of flowers they sent after Patrick died. They know he was my one and only, but not too many others do.

It took forever for me to go there, but once I did, Patrick and I more than made up for lost time. We were insatiable from the beginning, and the spark between us never waned in the almost ten years we were together. How will I ever do that with anyone but him? Would I rather never do it again than do it with someone other than him?

I'm not even thirty! That's a long time to live without sex, but the thought of any man ever touching me the way Patrick did makes me sick.

When the sun begins to peek through the trees at five o'clock, I'm still there, still contemplating these huge questions and not finding the answers I need.

That's when I decide to reach out to Iris.

If anyone knows the answers to these questions, another young widow would.

I wait until the respectable hour of eight to text her. *Hi, Iris, this is Rebecca's sister Roni. She told me you reached out to her, and I'd love to connect at some point. Thank you for the kind offer of support. I need all I can get right now. Look forward to hearing from you.*

Iris writes back five minutes later. *Are you free for a call in an hour or so? Got to get my kids settled with a movie so I can get a bit of quiet.*

I'm free all day!

Talk soon.

I'm strangely energized knowing I'll be talking to another young widow. I take a shower, make some tea and toast, and after I have something in my stomach, I take a prenatal vitamin, praying it all stays down. While I wait for Iris to call, I check my email for the first time in days, again avoiding the nuclear bomb wedding video message that's still marked as New in my in-box. A message from the managing editor at the *Star* catches my attention.

Hi, Roni,

Hope this finds you doing as well as can be expected. We're all thinking of you and Patrick and sending our love. I hate to have to talk business at a time like this, but I was wondering if you have an estimated date for a return to work. NO RUSH. Mr. Jestings has directed accounting to continue paying your full salary and benefits for as long as you need to be out of work. Whenever you're ready, we're here. Please let me know when you can.

All the best,

Don

The reminder of Ray Jestings's generosity brings tears to my eyes. He took over the ownership of the *Star* after his wife was arrested for orchestrating the murders of two players on the D.C. Feds baseball team that they also own. That was a story and a half when it happened.

Well, no time like the present to share my plans with the boss who's been so good to me since I started at the *Star* two years ago.

Hi, Don,

Thank you so much for your kind note and for checking in.

Please pass along my thanks to Mr. Jestings for his incredible generosity. It has meant so much to me during this difficult time to have your support and his as well as that of my wonderful colleagues. Which is why it pains me to have to give you my notice, although the reason is something positive that has come out of this tragedy. I first met Sam Holland Cappuano when she came to the office to notify me about Patrick's death. Since then, we've forged a new friendship, and to my great astonishment, she's asked me to join her first lady team at the White House.

As you can imagine, I never expected anything like this to happen! I've been deeply torn about leaving the Star *after having had such a wonderful experience there, but please accept this as my notice, effective December 31. Since I'm still out on bereavement leave, I hope you'll forgive me for giving you less than two weeks' notice. I remember a past job telling me that it's better for accounting purposes to leave at the end of a calendar year than to roll over into the new year for only a week.*

Thank you again for your kindness during this difficult time. I'll never forget it.

Sincerely,

Roni

I reread the message twice before I press Send. My belly flutters with butterflies as I make the first major decision in my life without Patrick. Imagining what he'd have to say about me working at the White House makes me smile until I'm reminded that it never would've happened if he hadn't been killed.

Part of me feels sick for being excited about something that's come from his death, but he'd tell me to knock it off and celebrate my new job.

Since I'm giving notice and making it official, I send a text to Sam.

Hi there, thanks for checking on me through Darren. Darren Tabor, my *Star* colleague and friend who covers Sam and her homicide cases, has kept in close touch with me since Patrick died. *Sorry to be out of touch. Things have been a bit crazy, as you can probably imagine. I've given notice to the* Star *as of 12.31, and if you'll still have me, I'd love to join your team in January. I've* been keeping tabs on you guys as you make the transition to the WH, and I'm so proud to say our new first lady is my "shit" friend.

I chuckle as I recall Sam telling me she's a shit friend because she doesn't have time to breathe, let alone make new friends. But she reached out to me anyway, and the friendship of a woman I've long admired has been an unexpected gift in this season of sorrow.

Please let me know what I need to do to make things official, and thanks again for giving me this lifeline. You'll never know what it means to me to have something exciting to look forward to. Happy holidays to you and your family. xoxo Roni

Sam replies a few minutes later. *I'm so happy to hear from you. I've been thinking of you and hoping you're doing okay. January is perfect! I'll have Lilia get in touch about paperwork, security checks and other fun things. We'll be at Camp David (haha—still can't believe I'm saying that!), from the 26th to the 1st, but please feel free to give me a ring to catch up before your start date!*

Will do, I reply. *I also meant to say that I thought you and Nick handled the tragedy in Des Moines with grace and class and empathy. I was so proud of you both. Have the best time at Camp David (so cool) and have a wonderful Christmas with the family. I don't want to bother you while you're with your family, so call me if you get a spare minute. I'm not doing much of anything right now, which is what I need for a few more weeks. I'll have my head together by the time January rolls around. At least I hope so—haha. I'm also thinking of you at the first Christmas without your dad. I know that will be hard for you, but I have to believe he and Patrick are keeping close tabs on us and want all the best things for us in the new year. Your friendship has been such a gift to me in the midst of this tragedy. Thank you again for being you and for reaching out to me the way you have. Hugs.*

I'm surprised when she writes right back. Isn't she the busiest woman in the country with two full-time jobs, one of them being first lady? *Ugh, Des Moines was brutal. How can someone shoot innocent babies lined up to see Santa??? It makes me sick to think of those poor families having to get through Christmas after that. Sigh. I'm so happy to have made a new friend this year. I'm not known for such things, so... LOL! I can't wait to work with you at the WH and to get to know you even better. Thank you for thinking of me and my dad. I sure do miss him. I'll be thinking of you, Patrick and your families this Christmas and hoping for peace for all of you. Hang in there, and I'll definitely try to check in from Camp David (STILL SURREAL—haha).*

I love how real she is, how she hasn't let her lofty new status go to her head. She's exactly the same person she seemed to be when her husband was "only" the vice president. I don't know her all that well, but I followed her career as the commander of the Metro PD's Homicide division long before I had the misfortune of actually meeting her after my husband was killed.

Sam was so caring and empathetic as she broke the life-changing news to me. She's helped me so much in the aftermath of catastrophe, including inviting me to participate in her new grief group for victims of violent crime, that my regard for her has only increased tenfold. Not to mention she's a freaking badass with the shit she does on the job and now as the country's first first lady with a full-time job outside the White House. My friends are going to die when they hear I'm going to work for her.

Five

Roni

I'm rereading the exchange with Sam when my phone rings with a call from Iris.

"Hi there."

"Hey," she says, "is this a good time?"

"Yes, it's perfect."

"Well, hello, and welcome to the worst club you never wanted to join."

I laugh at how she phrases that. "No kidding, right?"

"It's the worst. No sugarcoating it. I hate to even ask this stupid question, but how're you doing?"

"Not terrible days, really bad days, weird days, sad days."

"That sounds about right. It's been two months?"

"Yes, two and a half this week." How have I gotten through *seventy-five* days without Patrick?

"The good news, if there is good news, is the beginning is the absolute worst. The shock, the people, the mourning, the funeral... You're through the worst of it, even if it doesn't seem that way from where you're sitting."

"I can sort of see that, although I'm feeling confused about how I'm supposed to do so many things without him."

"I understand that. I make decisions for myself and our kids

44

every day and think to myself, is this what Mike would want me to do? Would he agree with sending them to that preschool or having them on that soccer team?"

"I can't begin to imagine how much harder it has to be when you have kids old enough to realize something terrible has happened."

"That's been the hardest part for me. Explaining over and over again to my two-, four- and six-year-old kids why Daddy can't come home ever again."

"That has to be brutal."

"It really is. People must be saying the dreaded 'be glad you didn't have kids' thing to you."

"A few have, but I found out yesterday that I'm pregnant."

"Oh wow."

"You're the first person I've told because it doesn't seem real to me, so how can I tell my family or Patrick's?"

"You don't have to tell anyone until you're ready, but I hope you can sort of see this as a gift."

"I can, even if the thought of being a single mother is beyond scary."

"You won't have to do it alone. I know Rebecca well enough to say you have a wonderful, supportive family and friends. And I hope maybe I can convince you to become part of our group, too."

"It's an official group?"

"Yep. We call ourselves the Wild Widows."

The name makes me laugh. "Okay..."

"The name was inspired by the Mary Oliver quote, 'Tell me, what is it you plan to do with your one wild and precious life?'"

"I love that."

"We do, too. It's intended to convey that while we may have lost our partners, we still have a great big wild life left to live. Our goal is to help each other through all the various challenges that only other young widows would understand."

"That sounds like something I need. I had a dream about Patrick last night..."

"The sex dream?"

I'm astounded. "How'd you know?"

"It's happened to quite a few of us."

"Wow, that's interesting. It just made me realize I'm not even thirty, and I'll probably have to do that with someone else at some point, and God, how do you do that, and how do you know you're ready, and... I'm rambling. So many questions."

"We all have them, and it's important to know that the timeline on this is yours and yours alone. We've had people hook up with someone else very soon after their loss just to get that first time out of the way so they don't have to dread it. Okay, so that was me."

"How was it?"

"Every bit as horrible as I expected it to to be. But at least I don't have to dread the first time anymore."

"True." Doing *that* with someone other than Patrick is unfathomable to me.

"Others have been widowed for several years and haven't been on a date yet. We're a judgment-free zone. Everyone has to do what works for them because each widow's journey is unique to that person."

"I really like that. Judgment-free is the way to go."

"You're going to run into tons of judgment as a young widow, because when people think of widows, they picture women with white hair and the best part of their lives behind them. Our experience is different in that we're young enough to potentially have a whole other life with someone else. Often, young widows start looking for that Chapter 2 a lot sooner than people think we should, which is, of course, no one's business but ours. People have trouble wrapping their heads around that."

"I'm having trouble wrapping *my* head around that."

"You will for a while yet, until it sets in that you've got a long life left to live, and there's a very good chance you're going to live that life with someone new."

That's almost too big for me to process at this point. "Have you dated yet?"

"I've been on three dates in the last six months, all of them nice, but there were no second dates. When I have time, I check the online profiles I've set up, but I haven't really gotten serious about it yet."

"How long ago did you lose your husband?"

"Eighteen very long months ago."

"I'm so sorry for you and your kids."

"Thanks. He was one of the good ones. We miss him, especially now that it's Christmas, and with Des Moines on top of it..."

"It's extra horrible."

"It sure is. My friend Taylor and I started the group shortly after we both became widowed and were desperate for some support from people who understood what we were going through. Everyone tries so hard to help, but there's something special about connecting with people who've been where you are."

"I can already see how that will be true."

"It really is. Our core group ranges from twelve to fifteen, with people cycling in and out as their needs change. We meet on Wednesday nights and rotate among our various homes in the DC, Maryland, Northern Virginia area. We also have an Instagram account that I'll send you a link to where you can check out some of the members' stories. We take turns posting there, and it's gained quite a following from people outside of our immediate group."

"It's kind of a shock to realize there're so many young widows."

"It was for me, too. People associate the word 'widow' with older people, but we know all too well how you don't always get lucky enough to grow old with your spouse or partner."

"I was so naïve before this happened. It never occurred to me that something like this could take Patrick from me with no warning."

"I was the same way, blissfully going through my life with my awesome husband and beautiful kids and lovely life with no idea whatsoever how quickly it could all be gone. We've had some great debates in the group about which is harder—seeing a partner through a fatal illness and knowing the end is coming or having it happen suddenly."

"As bad as they both are, the sudden death comes with no warning or chance to say goodbye. But then there's also no long, drawn out suffering for the one you love the most. Actually, I'm not sure which is worse."

"It all sucks, but there're added layers of trauma for people who've been caregivers to terminally ill partners. We also have a woman whose husband has been charged with rape and is going on trial soon. We invited her to join the group because that's like a death of sorts, of the life she thought she was going to have with a man who's not at all who she thought he was."

"Ugh, that's awful."

"She's been through a terrible ordeal, but she's doing a little better now that she's had some time to wrap her head around it. I hate the expression 'time heals all wounds,' because some wounds will never heal, but time does have a way of softening some of the edges and making a loss more bearable."

"I suppose that's true. As bad as I still feel every day, it's not like it was at first."

"I'm glad to hear that. You've still got a long road ahead of you, but deciding to survive your loss is an important first step."

"What choice do I have?"

"I've heard of instances where widows decide they'd rather not continue on after losing the most important person in their lives."

"That's so sad."

"It's terrible, but part of me understands why that path would be tempting. Some days, especially at first, I thought how that would be so much *easier* than going on. I had kids to think about, though, so that path wasn't something I could allow myself to get too enamored with. However, I certainly get why people would want a way out of the awful grief."

"I do, too. I never in a million years would've ever thought that way before I lost Patrick, but for the first few weeks, I thought about it a lot. My family probably suspected where my mind had gone because someone was with me around the clock for weeks."

"My family was the same way. They got me through the worst of it, and by the time they decided I was strong enough to stand on my own two feet again, I'd moved past those grim thoughts."

"I can't tell you what it means to me to speak to someone who truly understands."

"You don't have to tell me. Having that saved me once upon a time, and I try to pay that forward now to people like you, who are just starting this journey. There's one more thing I need to tell you about our group before you decide for sure to join."

"Okay..."

"We have one rule, and that is everyone who joins us has to be open to the idea of what we call a Chapter 2, or a second chance at love. It doesn't have to be something you're actively pursuing when you join, but being open to the possibility is something we all agree to as a general philosophy that keeps us hopeful about the future. I would totally understand if you're not there yet, or if that's too much to even consider at this point—"

"No, it's fine. I think that's a wonderful 'rule' to have, and keeping the focus on hope for the future is something that resonates with me. My husband never would have wanted me to be alone mourning for him for the rest of my life. He'd want me to live with as much joy as I can find."

"Mine was like that, too. He'd tell me, 'Iris, quit your moping and get back to living.' That's sometimes easier said than done."

"For sure."

"You'll always mourn him and the life you planned to have with him. Nothing will ever change that fact of your life, but that doesn't have to mean you're going to be sad and lonely forever."

"That's good to know. I'd love to be part of your group, and thank you again for reaching out to me. It means so much."

"You'll do it for someone else someday and pay it forward. That's how this works."

Iris promises to keep in touch and to send me info about their upcoming meeting early next month.

I end the call feeling optimistic for the first time since Patrick died. To know there's a group of fellow travelers out there who understand my experience is so huge. I send Rebecca a text.

Talked to Iris. She's amazing. Thanks for the connection. I think it will definitely help.

I'm making scrambled eggs and toast when she responds half an hour later. *So glad to hear that! She's awesome. We all admire her so much for her strength and fortitude after losing her husband. Not sure how she does it with THREE kids to care for on her own, but she makes it look easy. Are you going to join their group?*

Yes, I think so. It sounds like a great resource, and Iris was so nice to reach out to me and chat on the phone for an hour.

I'm glad you have that kind of support. It's so hard for everyone who loves you to know how to help.

You help just by being there. I'd be lost without you guys to lean on. And Patrick's family, too. They've been so great, worrying about me during such a hard time for them.

They're good people.

How are things there?

Pretty good except for a baby who won't sleep at night when I want to.

Ugh, that makes for some long days.

Yep. Thankfully, she naps! You going to be okay by yourself tomorrow?? We can come there to hang with you if you want.

I have to think for a second about what tomorrow is. Oh shit. Christmas. *I'll be fine. It's just another day this year. I'll be back to celebrating next year.*

I can't help but think about "normal" years when I'd be running around buying presents for everyone in my life and obsessing about what to get Patrick. Last year, I got him a subscription to a bourbon-of-the-month club that he loved. The last two boxes are sitting unopened on his desk at home.

We'll miss you—and Patrick.

Thank you for including him. It means a lot to me to know he was loved by so many people.

Oh God, he was! I'll never forget his group of friends at the wedding or how much fun they were. Or how heartbroken they were at the funeral.

Yeah, they're great. They check on me all the time. Which reminds me, I need to reply to their texts before they send a search party after me. Hope you have a wonderful day with the fam today and tomorrow.

Can we FaceTime with you tomorrow?

Sure. That sounds good.

See you then. Xoxo

Surprisingly, the eggs and toast taste good to me, and the nausea seems to have given me a day off. Or is it two days off? Yesterday wasn't too bad either. I'm not sure if it's the change of scenery, or if I'm through the worst of the morning sickness, but whatever the cause, I'm thankful to feel better and to be able to eat somewhat normally.

Iris sends me the link to the Wild Widows Instagram account, and I spend half a day immersed in the heart-wrenching stories other widows have shared, along with photos of their lost loved ones. So many of the things they write about resonate with me, such as trying to decide whether they should still wear their wedding rings now that their spouse is gone, or whether they should remove their rings before their first post-loss date, or how to feel okay about having sex with someone new.

They talk about the perils of bringing a new partner into the lives of their children, how to talk to their kids about what happened to their mother or father, how to answer their questions about the cancer, ALS, aortic dissection, brain tumor, accident or whatever it was that killed their parent. I read story after story from widows and widowers alike about close friends, the people you think are ride-or-die, who disappear after a tragedy, never to be seen or heard from again. I sit up straight when I read some of the stupid shit people say to widows, stuff I heard myself in the early days of my loss, such as "at least you didn't have kids," "everything happens for a reason," and my favorite, "You're so young. You'll meet someone else." As if Patrick was a pair of shoes that can be easily replaced with a new pair.

The issues confronted by widows are endless, and it's a huge relief to know that others out there understand my plight.

I lose myself in their various accounts, reading story after story about their grief, their joy, their victories and the defeats that come with rebuilding a shattered life. As I read, I laugh, I cry and I commiserate. These are my people, and I can't wait for the opportunity to get to know them.

Just thinking the words *I can't wait* is a huge improvement from where I was only a few weeks ago when the thought of another day without Patrick, let alone a lifetime, was inconceivable. Now I have a baby on the way, an exciting new job to look forward to and a new group of friends to make. The only thing that dulls my optimism about those things is that I can't share them with Patrick.

With the sun heading toward the horizon, I decide to take a short walk to get some air and exercise before it gets dark. As I walk along the dirt road that circles the huge lake, I can see families inside homes with brightly lit trees celebrating Christmas Eve. I feel strangely removed from my favorite holiday, happy to sit this one out so I don't have to face the empty chair at the table. I'll miss the time with my family, but being here is the right thing for me this year. It's one Christmas out a lifetime of them.

The next day, I'm inundated with texts and emails from family, friends and colleagues letting me know they're thinking of me and hoping I'm doing okay. I respond to every one of them, letting them know I'm doing as well as can be expected and that I appreciate them checking on me.

I receive a lovely note from my boss, Don, congratulating me on my new job and wishing me all the best, which is a huge relief.

I have a long call with Patrick's parents and get to say hello to his brothers and sisters-in-law, all of whom are gathered at his parents' home in Richmond, Virginia. I was invited to join them, and that was one of many invitations I declined.

"We love you so much, sweetheart," Patrick's dad, Pete, says.

"I love you guys, too. Thank you for calling, and Merry Christmas."

One of the text messages I receive is from Sarah, the bridesmaid who couldn't cope with my loss. *I'm thinking of you today more than I do every other day, and I'm sorry for bailing on you when you needed me. I hate myself for not being strong enough to support you through this. I hope you can forgive me. I love you, and I loved Patrick.*

Old Roni would've written right back and told her not to worry about it, that shit happens, etc. New Roni, the one who's going through the hardest time of her life, isn't so forgiving. Hers is the only message I don't respond to right away, even though she can see that I read it. Let her suffer a bit in her selfishness.

Does that make me sound vindictive? I can live with that. She was one of my closest friends since my freshman year of college. That's more than ten years of sharing *everything*. She totally bailed on me in my darkest hour. I have no idea how to go about forgiving her for that.

I love the Maya Angelou quote, "When people show you who they really are, believe them the first time."

I'm not here to make her feel better about being a shit friend, a thought that makes me laugh as I remember Sam describing herself as a shit friend. I met her the day Patrick died, and she's been a better friend to me through this nightmare than Sarah.

I FaceTime with my brother and his family in San Francisco and then my parents and sisters, who are gathered at my parents' home in Alexandria, Virginia, where the four of us grew up. The kids are in high spirits, making it hard for me to talk to the adults, so I just enjoy a little holiday family time.

My mom takes the phone into the kitchen, where I get to watch her stir some stuff on the stove before she returns her attention to me. "You're really all right?"

How long will it be before she stops asking me that every time she sees or talks to me? "I'm really all right and feeling a little better. I actually ate food today, so that's a step in the right direction."

"I hate that you're alone on Christmas."

"I was thinking yesterday that it's one Christmas in a lifetime of them. I'll be back next year. Try not to worry, okay?"

"Easier said than done, my love."

Because I'm tired of talking about myself, I ask, "What did Dad get you for Christmas?"

"Twelve months of massages and facials at my favorite spa."

"Oh, well played, Pops."

"I was very pleased with it. I got him some new waders and flies."

"Which he loved, right?" My dad enjoys nothing more than fly fishing, which he calls his religion. He taught Patrick the fine art, and he loved it as much as my dad does. They bonded over their shared love of fly fishing.

"He did, although he still hasn't been since Patrick died."

"He'll get back to it eventually."

"I'm sure he will, but he's not ready yet."

I'm deeply humbled to realize how Patrick's death has affected so many people, which is a testament to how loved he was.

We talk for another half hour before we say our goodbyes. A few minutes later, the doorbell rings, which makes me nervous for a second before I get up to see who's there.

Six

Roni

I take a quick look outside, am relieved to see Chelsea holding a big basket and open the door. "Hey. Come in."

"Hope I'm not disturbing you."

"Not at all."

Chelsea follows me in and puts the basket on the kitchen counter. "I thought you might enjoy some Christmas dinner. We had tenderloin, potatoes, creamed spinach and some delicious chocolate cake."

The smell of the food makes my mouth water and my stomach rumble with hunger for the first time in longer than I can remember. "That's so sweet of you. Thank you so much."

"No problem at all. I hope you enjoy it."

"I'm sure I will."

"My girls and I are going out for happy hour tomorrow night, our annual thank-God-it's-over after-Christmas celebration."

I laugh at the grimace that accompanies her comment.

"Christmas is a *lot* for the mommies," she says.

"My sisters say that, too." I guess I'm going to find that out for myself.

"Anyway, we'd love to have you join us if you feel up for it."

"I'd love to go, but can I ask a favor?"

"Anything."

"Can you not tell them my situation? It would be nice to be with people who don't know about my tragedy."

"I completely understand. I won't say a word, and I'll ask them to keep the questions to a minimum."

"I'd really appreciate that. Thank you for the invite."

"Of course. Happy to have you join us. I'll text you tomorrow."

"I won't drink, so if you want a designated driver, I'd be happy to pick you up."

"Ohhh, I might take you up on that. My kids were up at four o'clock this morning and have been *nonstop* all day. I'm going to need all the drinks by tomorrow night."

"I gotcha covered." I walk her to the door. "Thank you again for bringing me dinner." The kindness of friends and strangers alike has been astonishing. After the way Patrick died, I needed to have my faith in humanity restored, and people like Chelsea have seen to that.

"My pleasure. I'm right up the road if you need anything." She gives me a quick hug before she departs, leaving my heart full to overflowing with gratitude for her kindness and friendship.

The generosity of others has kept me from descending into despair over the explosion of gun violence that resulted in my husband's death, the murders of innocent children waiting to see Santa and countless others whose lives have been changed forever by guns. Hearing our new president vow to tackle that issue with the full resources of the federal government soothed my broken heart.

Dinner is delicious, and there's enough for two more dinners as well as a massive piece of chocolate cake that'll last me for days. As I settle in to watch HGTV after dinner, I feel better than I expected to feel after having survived my first Christmas as a widow.

"I wish you were here," I whisper to Patrick, hoping that wherever he is, he can still hear me. "Love you more than anything."

. . .

THE DAY AFTER CHRISTMAS, I watch a clip of Sam, Nick and their family walking across the lawn at the White House to board *Marine One*, which will transport them to Camp David. "After spending their first Christmas at the White House, the president and his family are headed to Camp David for the first time to spend the holiday week at the presidential retreat in Catoctin Mountain Park in Maryland," the news anchor says.

Sam, wearing a long red wool coat, walks next to her husband, holding hands with Aubrey while Aubrey's twin brother, Alden, runs ahead, eager for the ride on the helicopter. Eli and Scotty bring up the rear, with Scotty's dog, Skippy, on a leash. Sam's issues with infertility have been well documented, so it's a thrill to see her and Nick surrounded by the children they've acquired through adoption and guardianship.

I spend a week in total at the cabin and enjoy a fun night out with Chelsea and her friends, during which, for the first time in months, I'm not the victim of a senseless tragedy. That's a huge relief.

A few days after Christmas, I finally reply to Sarah. *Thanks for getting in touch. It's nice to hear from you.* Since I don't know what else to say, I leave it at that.

I'm not surprised when she calls me a few minutes later.

After an initial hesitation, I take the call, summoning the deep inner well of strength I've discovered inside me the last few months. "Hey."

"Hey. Thanks for taking my call."

"Sure."

A long, uncomfortable silence follows my one-word reply. Old Roni would've filled the silence with chatter in an effort to smooth the awkward edges. New Roni refuses to make that effort.

"I know you're angry with me."

"I'm not angry. That would take emotional energy I don't have right now."

"I'm sorry, Roni," she says, sounding tearful. "I fucked up, and I'm very, very sorry. Tell me how I can make this right."

"You can't, Sarah. I'm sorry to be harsh, but I don't feel like I can ever again count on you to be there for me in a time of need. Friends are there for each other, and you chose not to be there for me at the most difficult time of my life." Credit to the Wild Widows on Instagram for giving me the courage and the words to speak my truth, even if it hurts.

After another long pause, she says, "Fair enough. I hate that this has happened to Patrick—and to you."

"Thank you. That means a lot."

"Would it be okay if I checked in once in a while?"

"Sure." It'll take some time for her to realize we'll never again be the friends we once were.

"I'm thinking of you, Roni. All the time."

"Thank you." We've never been so polite with each other, not even the day we met when we had no idea if we were going to be good roommates.

"Well, I, uh, I'll let you go."

"Thanks for calling."

"Take care of yourself."

"I will." I press the red button to end the call, thankful to have gotten through that without tears. I ought to feel bad for being hard on her, but I don't. She was one of my closest friends, and she fell off the face of the earth after my husband died. I owe her nothing.

On New Year's Day, I strip the bed and wash the sheets and towels before I hit the road for home, feeling rested and somewhat restored by the time away.

Four hours later, as I cross the 14th Street Bridge that takes me from Northern Virginia into the District, I experience a feeling of elation that reminds me of the time, about two years ago, when I drove home from a conference in Richmond. I was away from Patrick for four nights, the longest we'd been apart since college, and I was so excited to see him. We were silly that way, dramatic about having to spend any time apart and always so damned glad to be back together.

He was waiting outside our place when I drove up in the old Toyota Camry we shared before he bought the Audi. I can still remember his big smile, the way he opened the driver's door and pulled me into the tightest hug, so tight I couldn't breathe, not that I cared. He kissed me right there on the street and told me I was never allowed to leave again. We spent the rest of that day and night in bed making up for lost time. I don't think we even ate dinner that night.

With that memory close to my heart, I find myself looking for him as I approach our block, hoping against hope that he might be waiting the way he was that time. But there's no one there.

I knew there wouldn't be, but the powerful feeling of disappointment threatens to undo the progress I made while I was away. I knew he wouldn't be there, and yet I let myself hope. I've got to stop doing this shit to myself. This situation is rough enough without me making it worse than it needs to be.

After stowing the car in the parking garage, I trudge toward home, dragging my suitcase behind me. I'm almost there when I see Not-Patrick across the street, walking hand in hand with his little girl, who skips alongside him. I try not to stare, but I can't help it.

Thankfully, he's completely absorbed in her and doesn't see me. I figure I'm about one encounter away from him calling the police on me. While I drag my heavy suitcase up the stairs, I laugh to myself as I imagine Sam, the cop, getting that phone call about me. "There's a weirdo following me around," he'd say. "She says I remind her of someone, which is fine, but she's creeping me out."

I need to stop being a freaking weirdo and get back to some semblance of normal, whatever that might be in the aftermath of calamity. That's the only resolution I've brought into this new year. Get back to "normal."

If only I could figure out what the hell that means.

ON JANUARY 3, I meet with Lilia Van Nostrand, chief of staff at the White House, at the coffee shop that's served as the host to my non-relationship with Not-Patrick, to complete paperwork and discuss the role of communications director to the first lady. I still want to pinch myself over that title and that I'll be working in the White House! Because Patrick was required to have a top-secret security clearance as a DEA agent, we both were fully vetted, which will expedite my employment.

I'm not required to have a security clearance to work with the first lady, who also doesn't have one, but I would've been subjected to a lengthy review process that won't be necessary now. *Thank you, Patrick.*

I looked Lilia up on the White House website so I'd recognize her. When she comes through the door, I wave to her from the table I grabbed for us. She's gorgeous, with shiny dark hair cut in a cute bob and luminous brown eyes that light up when she smiles. "It's so nice to finally meet you," she says, shaking my hand.

"You as well. Sam speaks so highly of you."

"Aw, thank you." She removes her red wool coat and black scarf. "She thinks the world of you, as well. Let me grab a coffee, and we'll chat. Can I get you anything?"

"I'm all set. Thank you."

While I wait for her, I sip my hot chocolate and scan the other patrons, wondering if Not-Patrick only comes in first thing in the morning or if he does meetings here during the workday. And why do I care about a man who bears a passing resemblance to my late husband and who thinks I'm a weirdo stalker?

I don't care. I'm just wondering if I'll see him. That's all it is.

Keep telling yourself that, girl. I'm just curious about him. Nothing more than that. It makes me feel queasy to even think about "liking" another man the way I liked Patrick. Not to mention, I'm pregnant, which is a sobering reminder of what my immediate future is going to look like. When I try to imagine "dating" while pregnant, I have to laugh to myself. Who'd want to take on the red-hot mess of my life?

I have no business being curious about any man, let alone one who's a single encounter away from reporting me to the police.

Lilia returns with a steaming cup and sits across from me. "Thanks for taking the time to meet. I thought it would be easier to do it here before your official start date at the White House. Getting in there can be a hassle before you're officially on board."

"I still can't believe I'm going to work there."

"It's surreal at first. I first started working with Mrs. Gooding when her husband was still in the Senate. She was involved in a number of initiatives involving military families and child welfare reforms. When they became the vice president and second lady, we moved to the White House and continued that work. Then after he resigned due to illness, I was retained by Mrs. Cappuano when her husband became the vice president, and now here I am working for the first lady."

"Your career has mirrored, in a way, the new president's." He went from chief of staff to a senator to vice president and then to president in two years.

"Indeed it has. It's been a bit of a whirlwind, but I'm delighted to work for her, to know them both and to consider them friends."

"I haven't known them long, but they seem like great people. She's been very good to me since..." Damn it.

Lilia reaches across the table and places her hand on mine. "I'm so sorry for your loss, Roni."

"Thank you. I was hoping to get through one thing without bringing that into it, but alas..."

"It's totally understandable. What happened to your husband was so tragic, and I can't begin to know what you've been through since."

"It's been pretty brutal, but I'm still here." I force a smile. "And possibly doing a tiny bit better than I was at the beginning. That said, I don't want you to think I can't do the job. I'm very excited to get started and to support Sam any way that I can."

We spend the next hour going over the duties of my new position, which include crafting statements for the first lady on a wide range of issues and subjects, managing the FLOTUS social media accounts and handling press inquiries.

"Everyone wants an interview with her." Lilia hands over a very full file folder. "I printed the first hundred. There are, like, five hundred other requests from media outlets all over the world. It'll be up to you to go through them all, narrow them down to a few that might interest her and then work with her to decide whether she's willing or able. As you know, she has a full-time job on top of this, not to mention three children, so her time is at a premium. After you get started, I'm going to talk to her about trying to set up a once-a-day call so we can stay on the same page with her."

"That's a good idea."

"The most important thing, obviously, is that we have to clear everything we do on her behalf with her. And that can mean having to hold things until she's available."

"I understand. I'd never want to speak for her without her approval."

"She's lovely to work with, but is the busiest person I've ever met."

"I really admire what she's doing, juggling both jobs and motherhood."

"She's a wonder, and a lovely, lovely person, as you certainly know."

"She's been very good to me since we met under the worst of circumstances."

"That sounds like her. She introduced me to my fiancé, Harry, who's a longtime friend of the president."

"I was going to say that's a gorgeous sparkler you've got there."

Her pretty face flames with embarrassment. "Thank you." She gazes at the ring for a second. "He did good."

"How long have you been engaged?"

"Just over a week. He proposed at the first family's Christmas Eve party."

"That's really cool. Congratulations."

"Thanks, and I'm sorry to be going on about it. I don't mean to be insensitive."

"Please don't do that. You're entitled to your happiness, and I can't wait to meet your guy. It's all good."

Lilia smiles as she fiddles with her pearls. "I can see why Sam likes you so much."

"Likewise."

We talk for another half hour about the daily routine at the

White House, where to park, how she'll meet me on my first day next Monday to walk me through getting a badge and parking pass to use if I need to drive to work and to give me a tour of the East and West Wing offices. By the time we part company with a quick hug on the sidewalk, I feel like I've made another new friend. She's sweet, kind, smart and stylish.

So stylish, in fact, that it occurs to me I have nothing to wear to work in the White House. I wore leggings and hoodies to the *Star*, and clearly, that won't work at my new job. As I walk home, I call my mom. When she answers, I ask, "You want to go shopping with me?"

I BARELY SLEEP the night before my first day at the freaking White House. I got together yesterday with my parents, sisters and their families to celebrate my new job. They're so excited for me to have this opportunity. I almost told them about the baby, but I'm sticking it out until my next appointment with Dr. Gordon on Wednesday afternoon.

Over the weekend, I texted Lilia to ask what I need to do to get out of work for the appointment. She said there's no problem with taking time for outside appointments and promised to walk me through the scheduling system that she uses to keep tabs on everyone. After the ultrasound appointment, I'll attend my first meeting of the Wild Widows, which I'm also looking forward to.

I've chatted a few times by text with Iris. She introduced me to Brielle, who lost her husband while she was expecting their first child. We've played text tag the last few days, but I'm hoping to chat with her tonight after work.

Wearing a black suit with a pink silk blouse, I put new black heels in a tote bag and slip on sneakers for the walk to the Eastern Market Metro station. I take the blue line to Metro Center, which is a mad house during rush hour. After a short walk, I'm at the gate to the White House, where I show my driver's license to the guard.

"I'm starting as the communications director to the first lady today." I hold back the giggle that's dying to bust loose at the preposterousness of that sentence. This has to be the most surreal experience of my life.

He checks a list and makes a phone call that brings Lilia to meet me at the checkpoint.

"Welcome to the White House team," she says with a warm, welcoming smile that puts me immediately at ease.

The next few hours pass in a blur of more paperwork, a tour of the East and West Wings and a meeting with the rest of the first lady's staff.

We're wrapping things up when Sam comes rushing in, her face flushed from the cold and her curly dirty-blonde hair down around her shoulders. She's wearing a black turtleneck sweater with camel-colored wool pants and black boots. Her blue eyes light up with pleasure when she sees me.

I stand to greet her with a hug.

"It's so good to see you." She stands back to take a good look at me, keeping her hands on my shoulders. "How're you doing?"

"I'm still here," I tell her, aware of my new colleagues watching us with curiosity. I decide to address the elephant in every room I'm in. "I lost my husband of three and a half months, who was my boyfriend for almost ten years before that, in October when he was struck by a random bullet on 12th Street. I met Sam, er, Mrs. Cappuano, when she had the misfortune of having to inform me of what happened to Patrick. She's been a very good friend to me since then and has honored me greatly by asking me to join this amazing team."

"My name is *Sam*," she says emphatically. "Just Sam."

"We're so sorry for your loss, Roni," Lilia says as the others weigh in with their condolences.

"Thank you," I say, touched by their kind words, "but I'm okay, excited to be here and to have this new challenge."

"I was hoping to be here to greet you first thing," Sam says, "but I got called out on a new case earlier this morning and got here as soon as I could."

"Thanks for coming in. I know how busy you are."

"I wanted the chance to talk to you guys about how we should be managing Skippy's Instagram account and growing fan club," Sam says, rolling her eyes, "and yes, I can't believe we have to worry about managing the first dog's account, but alas, she gets more mail than the president does. Scotty started the account for her, but it's gotten way bigger than he could've imagined, and now it needs more attention than any of us have time to give it."

"I'm on it," I tell her, delighted by the idea of managing an Insta account for the first dog. "Would it be possible to meet with Scotty and Skippy to get to know them a little better?" I've met Scotty once before, the night I attended the grief group meeting at Metro PD headquarters. But I haven't met Skippy.

"We'll make that happen." Sam checks the time on the wall clock. "We have the first meeting of Nick's new task force to address the issue of mental health and guns. Lilia and Roni, why don't you join me for that, but only if you feel like you're strong enough to address that topic, Roni."

"I'm fine, and I'd love to be involved in that issue." What better way can I make something positive come of Patrick's senseless death than by being involved in an effort to address the gun violence that has become so commonplace in our society? It's not acceptable, and we need to do something about it. The man who fired the shot that killed Patrick had well-documented mental health issues that should've precluded him from having a gun in the first place.

I tell myself I can handle this meeting. I hope I'm right.

Seven

Roni

I walk with Sam and Lilia to a conference room in the West Wing.

The handsome young president is standing outside the door, shaking hands with people as they arrive for the meeting. He lights up with pleasure when he sees his wife coming toward him. They're crazy about each other and don't care who knows it.

He greets her with a kiss to the cheek. "How's your day going so far?"

"Not too bad. You remember Roni, right?"

"Of course." He shakes my hand and offers me a warm smile. "It's great to see you again. Welcome to the team."

"Thank you, Mr. President."

"Roni has agreed to work with us on the task force," Sam says.

"I appreciate you bringing your unique perspective to this challenging issue," he says.

"I think it'll be helpful to feel like I'm doing something to help prevent what happened to me and Patrick and our families from happening to other people."

"We're very happy to have you."

He's gorgeous, charming, sweet, sincere and madly in love with his beautiful wife.

I'm truly honored to have the chance to work with and for both of them.

The task force is chaired by Dr. Anthony Trulo, the resident psychiatrist for the Metropolitan Police Department, a close friend and colleague of Sam's. They've brought in people from all walks of life to form this task force—doctors, educators, scientists, weapons manufacturers, social media executives, citizen gun owners and law enforcement representatives.

Nick—*am I allowed to think of him as Nick?*—opens the meeting by thanking everyone for agreeing to work on one of the most vexing issues of our time. "We all know someone who's been touched by gun violence. My family has been touched by gun violence. My father-in-law, retired MPD Deputy Chief Skip Holland, succumbed in October to injuries he suffered in a shooting four years ago last month that left him a quadriplegic. Our friend lost her young husband to a stray bullet fired during an argument on a city street.

"The proliferation of guns in our society has reached a crisis level, especially when they end up in the hands of someone who'd shoot innocent children waiting in line to see Santa. It has to stop. I understand this issue is fraught with intense emotions, not to mention political peril for anyone who dares to address it. Let me say right here and right now that if my political career is ruined by trying to make our schools, churches, movie theaters and other public spaces safer for everyone, then so be it. That's a hit I'm willing to take if it means we can make real, meaningful progress in addressing the connection between mental health and gun violence. I have no interest in taking guns from responsible gun owners, but I'm asking them to help with this important effort. I believe all Americans support meaningful progress toward making our country safer for everyone. I look forward to working with all of you toward that goal."

I'm moved nearly to tears by his passionate commitment and thrilled to be part of such an ambitious effort. Over the next two hours, a robust conversation is held on the various issues, the scope of the task force and a punch list of issues and concerns to be addressed. As the meeting comes to an end, I realize it's the most engaged I've been in anything since I lost Patrick, and it's a huge relief to get a break from the relentless grief that's overtaken everything.

Lilia remains in the room after the meeting, so I make my way back to the East Wing by myself, hoping I'll remember how to get there. As I round a corner, I come face-to-face with Not-Patrick and suppress a gasp of surprise.

His expression registers shock and then anger. "What the hell are you doing here?"

I'M SO stunned to see him here, of all places, that my brain goes completely blank for a second.

"Come in here." He opens a door and gestures for me to go ahead of him into the room. He's wearing a lilac dress shirt with a matching tie. His light brown hair is combed straight back, making his unsmiling face look even more stern and unwavering.

For a second, I can't bring myself to move. Is it safe to go into a room alone with a guy who's clearly angry with me? But then I remember this is the White House, and it's not like he's going to physically attack me, so I step into the room.

He closes the door and leans against it, which is when I notice he has a White House staff ID hanging around his neck like I do. "Who are you, and what are you doing here?"

"I'm Roni Connolly, and I... I work here."

His brow furrows. "Since when?"

"Ah, about six hours ago."

"What's your job?"

"Communications director to the first lady. What's yours?"

"Deputy chief of staff to the president."

Oh damn. Well...

"I'm trying to be fair here, but it's really weird that I caught you basically stalking me, and now you show up at my workplace."

"I had no idea you work here! And I wasn't stalking you. I

happened to see you a couple of times in the neighborhood where we both live."

He crosses his arms as he stares at me without blinking. "We both know it was more than that."

"I told you that you reminded me of someone I used to know."

"Who?"

I want to tell him it's none of his business, but he's not the one who made this weird. That was all me. "My husband."

His posture immediately relaxes somewhat. "You said you used to know him. What does that mean?"

"He's dead."

After a long moment of silence, he says, "I'm sorry. What happened to him?"

"He was hit by a stray bullet on 12th Street."

Wincing, he says, "How long ago?"

"October."

"I'm so sorry that happened to you both."

"Thank you. I'm really not a weirdo. Well, I'm usually not. You reminded me of him from behind, but of course you're not him, and you actually don't even look like him. It was just an odd new-widow thing. I hope you'll accept my apology for making this strange."

"I do. I accept your apology, and I understand new-widow weirdness better than you might think. My wife was murdered eighteen months ago."

I gasp. So the woman I saw him with on the street wasn't his wife. "I'm sorry for your loss."

"Thank you, and when you read up on what happened to her, which of course you will, because I already know that's how you are, you'll see why I might've overreacted to someone following me."

He thinks he's got me figured out. How cheeky. "I'm sorry I freaked you out."

"I'm sorry I overreacted." He releases a weary-sounding sigh and runs his fingers through his hair, leaving it standing on end. "It's just been really rough since I lost my wife, and the circumstances of her death have made me extremely paranoid, and... I'm rambling."

"I understand. Say no more."

"How do you know the first lady?"

"She was the one who told me what happened to my husband, and we've kind of become unlikely friends. When she offered me the job, it was just... Well, it's a lifeline of sorts. How do you know the president?"

"We've been friends for fifteen years, since we both came to Washington as junior staffers to congresspeople. I worked for Nelson, and when he died, Nick... er, the president, asked me to stay on his team."

Which means he's also friends with Sam. "How old is your daughter?"

He smiles. "Maeve is two and a half."

"She's adorable."

"Yes, she is, and she saved my life after Vic died." He straightens as if he suddenly realizes he's supposed to be doing something else. "I'm, ah... sorry if I was a jerk."

"You weren't. I was weird. I had it coming."

He cracks a small grin that softens his countenance. Having the chance to look closely, I notice he's every bit as handsome as Patrick was, but in his own way. "I should get back to work."

"Me, too. They've probably sent out a search party for me."

"It was nice to officially meet you, Roni."

"You never told me your name."

"It's Derek. Derek Kavanaugh, with a K for when you google me."

That makes me laugh. "Thanks for the clarification."

"Have a good rest of your first day."

"Thanks."

He opens the door, and when we step out of the room, he heads west while I go east, dying to get to my computer so I can do exactly what he predicted I would. When I return to the first lady's suite, there's no one else around, so I duck into the office I was assigned and fire up the laptop I was given to use for all White House-related work.

Maybe I shouldn't google a colleague on that computer... I reach for my cell phone and call up the browser to search for him.

Thirty minutes later, when Lilia comes to the door, I'm sitting at my desk with tears running down my face.

"Roni! Are you all right?"

Nothing like getting caught crying in the office on the first day on the job. I wipe away the tears and force a smile for my new boss. "I'm fine. I was just reading something sad."

"Why're you doing that?"

"Just a little research after the meeting." She doesn't need to know I'm cyberstalking one of our colleagues.

Derek's wife wasn't just murdered. I remember reading about former presidential candidate Arnie Patterson and his sons plotting for years to get insight into the Nelson camp, going so far as to plant a woman close to a member of Nelson's team and then murdering her when she stopped providing the information they wanted. The Kavanaughs' daughter went missing for days after her mother was found dead in their home in what had to be a complete nightmare for poor Derek.

No wonder he's so suspicious and protective of himself and his daughter. He has good reason to suspect the worst of people. I have so many questions, but I can't think about that now when my new boss is in my office, and I have a job to do.

"If the task force work is too much for you after what you've been through, please feel free to say so," Lilia says.

I so appreciate her offering me an out. "I'm really fine. Just a little extra emotional these days." For reasons I'll have to tell her eventually, but not now. Not yet.

"I want you to promise me that you'll tell me if something is too much for you or strikes too close to home. We have a wonderful staff that supports each other in every way we can. There's no need to suffer needlessly when you've had enough suffering already."

"That's very nice of you. Thank you for being so kind and understanding. It means a lot to me."

Sam appears behind Lilia. "Knock, knock."

Lilia steps aside to allow the first lady to join our conversation.

"Thank you both for being at that meeting," she says. "It means a lot to both of us to have you working with us on this issue."

"It's long overdue," Lilia says.

"I couldn't agree more," I add.

"Could I have one minute with Roni?" Sam asks.

"Of course," Lilia says as she leaves the room.

Sam closes my office door. "You're settling in okay?"

"Yes, it's been great. Everyone is so nice."

"I'm glad to hear it. You know how to reach me if you need anything."

"I do, and I was thinking that I'll end each day with an email summary to you with ideas that you can approve or disapprove as I figure out how best to speak for you. Would that work?"

"That sounds great, and I'll commit to answering that daily email on the same day it was sent so you can do this job while I'm off doing my other job—or I guess I should say *jobs*, plural, including being a mother to three kiddos."

"I'm here to help in any way that I can. If you need something with one of the kids, ask me. If you need help crafting a response on a case, ask me. I'm willing to do whatever you need."

"I appreciate that more than you know. In the second month of this new situation, the shock has worn off a bit, and gritty reality is setting in." She stops, and her expression turns to one of horror. "My God, I lost my mind for a second there. The shock of my husband suddenly becoming president is no comparison to what you've been through."

"Shock is shock, Sam. Or, I mean, Mrs. Cappuano."

She scowls. "Don't do that. I'm Sam to you. And yes, I guess you're right about shock. But you're doing okay? I was worried about you when you fell off the map for a while there."

"I'm doing better than I was. I spent some time away by myself, got through the holidays, got my head together a bit, and now I'm super excited to be starting this incredible new job you gave me. It's been nice to have something new to look forward to."

"I'm glad to hear you're okay. If you're ever not, I'm here for that, too, as your favorite new shit friend who has no time to breathe, let alone make new friends."

I laugh at the memory of her describing herself that way to me the first time she said it. "In the legion of shit friends I've had, you're the best."

"Aw, I'm honored."

"I met your friend Derek Kavanaugh."

"Oh good. He's great, and sadly, you two have a lot in common." As she says that, she tips her head and gives me a more penetrating look.

"Whatever you're thinking, knock it off," I say, laughing.

"I'm only thinking that you two have a lot in common. Unfortunately."

"Yes, we do."

"He's one of Nick's closest friends. Has been for years."

"We've met a few times—we live in the same neighborhood—but I had no idea who he was." She doesn't need to know that I borderline stalked him. "Until I saw him here today."

"Ah, I see. Remember the thing that got Arnie Patterson locked up?"

"Yes, I already know it was Derek's wife who was killed."

"It was horrible. I worked that case. Total nightmare, especially the several days it took us to find Maeve."

"God, poor Derek."

"It was awful for him, but it helped a bit for him to find out later that Vic protected him and that she really loved him, despite how it began."

"How did he find that out?"

"In a letter that came from her attorney, something she did in the event that the worst happened."

"Wow, that's amazing." My heart aches for someone I barely know. "He must've been so relieved to hear that."

"He was, but it didn't change the fact that she was still gone, you know?"

"Yeah, for sure."

"If you're interested in getting to know him better, down the road, of course..."

"Of course," I murmur, amused by her.

"I can help with that. My track record is somewhat legendary when it comes to matchmaking."

"That's good to know, but I'm hardly in a position to be thinking about such things. Not yet, anyway."

"I don't mean to be disrespectful."

"You're not. Not at all. It's already registered with me that at some point, I'm probably going to have to face the reality of starting over with someone new."

"That doesn't have to happen any time soon."

"I'm taking it one day at a time and keeping my mind open to everything that comes my way."

"I give you so much credit for getting through this with so much grace."

That makes me laugh. "Don't look below the surface. It's ugly in there."

"Be nice to my new friend. She's amazing and brave, and I admire her very much for showing us all how to get through the worst kind of adversity."

"Wow, I like the way I look to you."

"You should. Well, I'd better get back to the grind. Call me if you need anything at all."

"I will. Thank you again for this. I'll never have the words to tell you what it means to me."

"It means just as much to me to have someone I trust watching my back in the shark pit that is my life these days."

"I gotcha covered."

"Then I shall sleep well at night. Enjoy the rest of your first day."

"Will do. Watch for that email later."

"I'm on it." She departs with a smile and a wave that leave me with the warm feeling that comes with having made a new friend of someone I admired long before I got to know her. To find out she's even more than I ever could've hoped for is a gift in the middle of unrelenting grief.

I take the time to unpack the few personal things I brought from home—my degree from UVA that I hang on a nail that the previous tenant left in the wall, a silver-framed picture from our wedding that I put on my desk and the leather Day-Timer that my parents gave me as a college graduation gift that has a brand-new calendar loaded and ready to record the events of this coming year.

My husband and colleagues at the *Star* used to poke fun of my old-school Day-Timer, but I spend enough time staring at a screen all day. I prefer to write things down and to keep a written record of what I do every day. Patrick couldn't have survived without his iPhone reminding him of every commitment. But he worked in the tech world and was super savvy with computers, phones, tablets or any such device. That's another thing I'll miss—having someone who can fix those things for me and everyone else in our lives.

"What would you think if you could see me now in my office in the *White House*?" I whisper to his smiling face in the photo from the best day of our lives. "I hate that it only happened because I lost you, but maybe you sent Sam to me, knowing I'd need a fresh start to survive losing you."

That possibility is something I cling to as I dive into the details of the FLOTUS social media accounts, Skippy's Instagram account and the mountain of interviews and speaking requests that've been submitted for Sam. Everyone wants her in any way they can get her, and it's my job to determine who should receive the limited amount of time she has to give to being first lady.

By the time I leave work on my first day, I've made a good list of interview requests for Sam to consider and come up with a dozen potential social media posts to keep her engaged as the first lady. I send the promised email, copy Lilia, and then shut down the laptop.

I remove my heels, stash them under my desk and slide on the sneakers for the walk to the Metro.

"Good first day?" Lilia asks when I stop to tell her I'm leaving. Should I be leaving before her? She doesn't seem to care, so I guess I shouldn't either.

"Very good. Thanks for making me feel so welcome."

"We're happy to have you. *I'm* happy to have you. Doing your job and mine has been a challenge."

"Roni to the rescue."

"Indeed. Have a good night."

"You, too."

Eight

Roni

As I walk toward the East Wing lobby, I wonder if I'll see Derek again, although why would I when he works in the West Wing? I can't stop thinking about his story and how awful it must've been for him after his wife died and his little girl was missing. As bad as what happened to Patrick was, I can't imagine how awful that had to have been for Derek. And then to learn that the woman who became his wife was planted in his life to get intel on Nelson... I shudder in the January chill as I walk to the Metro station.

Total nightmare.

Tears fill my eyes as I walk. Life can be so very cruel. People can be so very cruel. Imagine Arnie Patterson wanting to be president badly enough to plant a woman close to Nelson, to get her to pretend to fall in love with a man all as part of a diabolical conspiracy. How did someone go on after a thing like that? Even after Derek found out his wife really did fall in love with him and stopped cooperating with Patterson and his thugs, how did he cope with everything he learned?

I'm thankful to know that there are no skeletons lurking in Patrick's closet. No, just clothing that smells like him and a lifetime of possessions I'll have to contend with eventually. Not yet, though. And while the thought of being a single parent is completely overwhelming, I'm deeply grateful that part of him will live on in our child. After the ultrasound on Wednesday, when we confirm the baby is healthy, I'll tell our families the good news.

A spark of excitement grows in me as I think about our baby, even as the excitement is weighted by heartache. Patrick would've been a wonderful father, and the thought of our child never knowing him is unbearable.

On the subway, I send a text to my family to tell them my first day at the White House was awesome and that I'm working on the president's new gun-control initiative.

The responses flood in.

Rebecca: *I still can't believe you're actually working there! So glad to hear it was a great first day.*

Penelope: *So proud of you, kid.*

Mom: *That's wonderful, Roni. Dad and I are so proud! Are you feeling okay about working on the gun-control issue?*

I think it will be good for me to feel like I'm doing something to help keep what happened to us from happening to someone else. Both Sam and Lilia, her chief of staff, told me to speak up if it's too much for me. They're both great, and I'd feel very comfortable telling them if I can't handle it.

Mom: *That sounds good. I'm so glad you have this grand new adventure to look forward to and are working with and for such good people.*

Rebecca: *Agreed. Total #girlcrush on the FLOTUS. She's the bomb!*

She really is. I hope you can meet her one of these days.

Rebecca: *FAINTS!*

Their enthusiasm and excitement make me smile. I'm glad to be giving them something positive to think about rather than worrying incessantly about me. And there's more good news coming, at least I hope so. It's weird how I'm refusing to let myself get too invested in the baby until I'm sure it's actually in there, although the lack of a period, relentless nausea and sore boobs are pretty good signs that I missed before the test popped positive.

When I get home, I make a salad with grilled chicken that I force myself to eat, even though I'm not at all hungry. Both the baby and I need the nutrition, and I'm determined to stay healthy.

I'm snuggled under a blanket on the sofa watching HGTV when Brielle, the woman from Iris's group with whom I've been playing text tag, calls me at eight. "Hi there."

"Is it too late for you?"

"Not at all. It's nice to finally catch up."

"I'm so sorry it took so long. My son is teething, and it's absolute hell."

"I've heard that from my sisters."

"Bourbon to the rescue. For Mommy, that is."

She has me laughing in under a minute. "I'll keep that in mind."

"How are you feeling about the pregnancy after having had some time to wrap your head around the news?"

"It still doesn't seem real. How can I be pregnant when Patrick is dead?"

"I know that feeling so well. We'd been trying for *years*, and we finally succeed, and then he didn't live to meet our child? It just made a horrible loss that much more so."

"God, that must've been so hard." Her husband died in a skiing accident while on a trip to celebrate his brother's upcoming wedding.

"It was surreal. I was so angry about it for the longest time. Like, how could God or the universe or whoever think this was a good idea do this to me and expect me to raise this child without Mark? I kept thinking of ways to end it all for both of us so I wouldn't have to raise him alone, and he wouldn't have to grow up without a father."

"I'm so sorry you went through such an awful time."

"It was pretty awful, but it doesn't stay that way forever. Eventually, you begin to accept that this was the hand you were dealt, especially after the baby arrives and gives you no choice but to pull yourself together. I'll always be heartbroken that Mark isn't here to help raise Charlie. He would've been the best father, and it kills me that Charlie will only know him through photos, videos and stories from the people who knew him. That's the part that doesn't get better, no matter how much time goes by."

"I'm sure it doesn't," I say, saddened to realize once again that's how our child will know Patrick.

"I've come around to understanding that having this part of Mark live on in our son is actually an amazing gift. Of course, on days when he's teething, it doesn't seem like a gift," she adds with a laugh.

I laugh along with her. "I'm sure it doesn't, but it's great to think of having part of Mark and Patrick live on in our children. If only the idea of raising this baby on my own didn't seem so daunting."

"Oh, honey, you won't be on your own. Iris told me your sisters live nearby and your parents. Your friends will step up. I'll be there for you because I know what it's like to bring that little bundle of joy home by yourself. There's so much joy mixed in with a fresh wave of grief, coupled with all the postpartum hormones."

"Ah, so much to look forward to."

Laughing, Brielle says, "You'll get through it, and that little person is going to bring you so much happiness. I look at my little guy, even when he's having a fit, and I just can't believe he's mine. As unbelievable as it may seem right now, it's going to be okay. I promise."

"This is so incredibly helpful, and it's so generous of you to share your experience with me."

"That's what we do in our group. We help each other through the challenges of widow life. We laugh, we cry, we commiserate, we celebrate, we support, we never judge, and we get it. We just simply get it."

"And, of course, you know how huge that is."

"I do. People who've never been through this have no idea how to help, even if their intentions are so pure and beautiful. How can they know what it's like to lose the person you thought you were going to grow old with and to have to live decades without the one you loved the most?"

"They can't know."

"No, they can't, and they often make a ham-handed mess of trying to help. That used to make me really mad in the beginning, until I realized it's not their fault they don't know what to do or say. Lucky for them, they haven't been where we are, so they don't possess the language needed to truly support us in the way we need. I've learned to pick and choose the parts that are useful and to try to ignore the things that hurt me."

"I have one close friend who's seriously disappointed me. I'm wrestling with what to do about her."

"You're lucky it's only one. When you get to know our group, you'll hear so many stories of people who've disappointed us. One thing I've learned is that it takes a lot of energy to carry around that anger, and you're going to need all your energy to deal with the grief while you're growing a new human."

"That's true. Part of me wants to let it go, but the other part..."

"I get it. Believe me. My sister was weird after Mark died. She disappeared for a while. When I asked her why, she said she didn't know how to manage my grief while dealing with hers. I was like, wait, *what*?"

"Yes! Exactly that. Like, WTF? How is this about you?"

"But you do come to see that the loss of your Patrick has an impact on everyone in your life who loved him."

"I'm seeing that. He and my dad loved to fly-fish together, and my dad hasn't been once since we lost him."

"Their grief matters, too, but not as much as ours. That's my line in the sand. You can grieve him all you want, but you have to be there for me, and you need to keep your grief far away from mine."

"I want you to be my new best friend."

Brielle's cackle of laughter makes me smile. "I'm happy to be your new best friend, one of many you'll make when you join our group."

"I'm looking forward to the meeting on Wednesday."

"We're excited to meet you in person, even if we hate the reason that brings you to us."

"I'm getting the feeling that contrast is a big part of widowhood. The joy in new things, new friends, new adventures, but the pervasive feeling that someone is always missing."

"Yes, for sure. It does get easier in time, but you never 'recover' from this kind of loss. You just learn to live within it."

"I really appreciate you taking the time to talk to me and to text with me and to support me."

"There's comfort for me in helping others going through this. You'll find that to be true when you reach back to give a hand to someone just starting this journey. Paying forward the wisdom you gain is very satisfying."

"Well, thank you for sharing yours."

"My pleasure. I'll see you Wednesday."

"See you then."

I end the call feeling buoyed by her support and the knowledge that I'm certainly not the first woman to have a baby after being widowed. And it's good to know I'll most likely survive the challenges that lie ahead, as big as they might seem now.

As I crawl into our king-sized bed alone a short time later, I miss Patrick so much. I wish I could talk to him about the baby, my new job, how weird Sarah has been and so many other things. I lie on my side, facing the empty half of the bed, remembering so many nights wrapped up in him. All these weeks later, it still seems impossible to believe I'll never see him again, that I will live the rest of my life without the man who was at the center of it for most of a decade. During the first days after he died, that was the hardest part, to imagine a life that didn't include him.

But so much has happened since he died, and I'm already living my life without him. I'm doing what seemed so impossible then, and from deep inside the pit of grief, I have no choice but to acknowledge that progress.

Derek

I CAN'T STOP THINKING about Roni Connolly and what happened to her husband. As I pour myself a drink after tucking Maeve into bed, I stare out the window into the dark as I contemplate the woman who now works at the same place I do. Since Vic died, I've barely noticed any other woman. I haven't wanted to date or let any of my well-meaning friends fix me up with someone new. I've had two meaningless sexual encounters that made me feel worse after the fact, so I'm avoiding that for the time being.

I don't want someone new.

I want the life I used to have with Vic, even though that's not possible.

I know it's time to get back to living for more than my job and my daughter, but the thought of starting over with someone new is so unsettling that I avoid it rather than even consider it.

But now I find myself thinking about the gorgeous young woman who seemed to be stalking me, and let me tell you, that scared the crap out of me. After what I learned about Vic and Arnie Patterson after she died, I'm paranoid about people and their intentions.

Yes, I've had therapy. Months of it after Vic died, and it helped me accept what happened—as much as anyone can ever accept such a thing—and to focus on the letter Vic left for me in case something ever happened to her. That letter is my lifeline. It's my proof that what we had was real and true.

Regardless of how we began, she loved me.

That's the only thing that matters to me, but trust is going to be hard to come by in any future relationship. How in the hell will I *ever* trust *anyone* after the ruse that was perpetrated on me?

Hearing about what happened to Roni in October hung over the rest of my day. I went back to my office, looked up the stories about her husband's death and felt profound grief on her behalf. I know all too well how it feels to suffer through such a loss and how difficult it is to rebuild your life afterward. That they were married for such a short time when she lost him absolutely gutted me. They never had a chance.

Was it weird that she followed me? Sure, but when she

explained it, I understood. I did strange things after Vic died, too. Once in the grocery store, I saw a woman with long dark hair who reminded me of her. I followed her through the entire store, stood behind her in the checkout line and waited in breathless anticipation until I finally saw her face and had to accept that she wasn't my wife come back to life. Because that's not possible. But try telling that to someone attempting to acclimate to life as a widower.

God, I hate that freaking word.

Widower.

My grandfather is a widower, but he's eighty-two.

I'm thirty-eight, and let me tell you, there's a big freaking difference between being a widower at eighty-something versus thirty-something.

I've been lucky to have the help of my wonderful parents, who've quite simply kept me and Maeve alive with their love and support, as well as wonderful friends, such as our new president, Nick Cappuano, and his wife, Sam. Nick and I go way back to the beginning of both our careers in Washington, and he saved me after President Nelson died and left me without a job. Nick asked me to stay on as deputy chief of staff, which is a huge honor—and a relief to know I can keep doing the job that makes it possible to manage the rest of my life. Not that I couldn't have found something else if I had to, but staying in the job I already had was the best possible outcome.

It took quite a bit of time and effort after Vic died to set up a new routine that works for Maeve and me. We have a wonderful nanny, Patrice, who drops Maeve at the nearby daycare that gives her time with other kids. Patrice collects her after her nap and entertains her until I get home from work. Maeve loves her, and she's been a godsend to me.

For a while after she started, I suspected Patrice was hoping she might be more than just Maeve's nanny, but I shut that down right away so things wouldn't get weird between us. Sometimes I still catch her eyeing me with that look women get when they're interested in a man, but I need her too much to ever cross that line with her.

Besides, as lovely as she is, I'm not into her.

But I could be into Roni Connolly, and that strikes me as so damn crazy, especially since I was immediately attracted to her even when I thought she was stalking me. Why her and not the many women I've come in contact with since Vic died? Why her and not Patrice, who's obviously into me, loves my daughter and vice versa?

Because life is bizarre that way. That's why. I should be annoyed by how weird Roni was when we first encountered each other, but after hearing about her loss, I just want to know more about her. I want to know if she's okay, if she's coping and if she needs... well, anything. Which is bizarre. I know it is, but everything about widowhood is bizarre until you get used to it, and then it just hurts. All the time, like an unrelenting ache that nothing can soothe.

It sucks.

But life is so relentless in the way it marches forward like nothing has happened, expecting you to show up—to work, to take care of your kid and to do all the things you did before—only now without the only person who made life worth living. Not that Maeve doesn't make my life worth living, because she does. But it's different. Everything is different without Vic, and not in a good way.

I'll tell you another thing about being a widower—it's exhausting to feel like absolute shit all the time. That gets old really fast, not to mention it's contrary to my nature. I'm an overall positive, upbeat kind of guy, and being hideously depressed and heartbroken has worn me out. I'm tired of being tired and sad and often pathetic. I'm ready to get back out there and maybe try again with someone else. Sam and others have offered to fix me up with a wide variety of women, but I hate the idea of that, so I've declined their kind offers.

I'd rather it happen organically, such as when a gorgeous, newly widowed woman seems to be stalking me because I remind her of her dead husband from behind. What could go wrong there? That thought makes me laugh as I finish my drink, check the locks for the second time, arm the security system I installed after my wife was murdered in our home and head upstairs to bed.

I stop outside Maeve's room and tiptoe inside to check my little girl, who's sound asleep with her thumb firmly planted in her mouth. We're working on breaking her of that habit, and clearly, it's not going well. Vic would've had her weaned a long time ago. She knew how to take care of our child in a way that was ingrained in her, despite having been parentless for a big part of her life. Bending at the waist, I give Maeve a kiss on the forehead and brush the blonde curls back from her sweet face.

She's an absolute angel, and I'm so blessed to have her. When I think about the days she was missing... Shaking off those hideous thoughts so I'll have a prayer of sleeping, I leave her room, propping the door open so I can hear her if she wakes up, and head into the master bedroom that my mother encouraged me to redecorate after Vic died.

I took her advice, and I'm glad I did. I probably should've sold this place after what happened in the kitchen, but with so much upheaval in our life at that time, the thought of packing and moving—or finding another place when this one was so hard to come by—was inconceivable. Vic and I searched for months for a place in the Capitol Hill neighborhood and bought this house the day we looked at it so we wouldn't miss out.

I simply couldn't bear to go through that again, even if I see her lying in a bloody pool every time I walk into the kitchen, which was also redecorated in an attempt to rid the room of horrible memories. But some things can't be forgotten no matter how hard we try.

We should've moved. I realized that shortly after my awesome mom oversaw the renovations when I told her I wasn't up for moving. I never told her the renovations haven't helped, but I think she knows. I unbutton the dress shirt I wore to work and toss it in the dry-cleaning pile that I'll deal with on the weekend. I go through the motions of changing into pajama pants and a T-shirt.

Vic and I slept naked, which was another thing that had to

change after she died. I can't have my little girl waking up in the middle of the night and finding me in the buff.

This is the part of the day that's the most difficult for me, crawling into a big, empty bed and longing for a time when I wasn't here alone. I miss my beautiful, sweet, funny wife and how much fun we always had together no matter what we were doing. It's been hard to reconcile that she was deceiving me at the beginning, that our magical connection was really a big fat lie. At first. What started out as a deception became a love match, which Vic confirmed in the letter she left for me.

That letter is everything to me. I bought a special fireproof safe to keep it in so there's no way anything can ever happen to it. When Maeve someday hears the story of how her mother died, I want her to have that letter to know who her mother really was. It'll be just as important to her to have that information as it's been for me. Poor Vic never stood a chance in life once the Patterson family "took her in" after her parents' tragic deaths, which were later tied to Arnie and his diabolical sons.

As I stare up at the dark ceiling, reliving the darkest days of my life, I realize it's been a while since I thought about this stuff. Meeting Roni and hearing about what happened to her and her husband has brought back my crap, which is probably a sign that I need to stay away from her. The fact that she has the same dark-haired, brown-eyed coloring as Vic is another oddity, although she honestly doesn't look anything like my late wife.

Wallowing in this shit isn't good for me or Maeve, and I need to keep myself strong and balanced for her. Thinking about Vic and what happened to her—and why—isn't healthy for me. Just like having inappropriate thoughts about a new colleague, who also happens to be a friend of the first lady and a recent widow, also isn't productive.

She's recently suffered the most devasting loss of her life, which means she's in no way available to me or anyone else. I could barely tie my shoes three months after Vic died. That she's even functioning is admirable.

Allowing my mind to wander down any path that leads to Roni is a waste of time that could be better spent on taking care of my daughter and helping one of my best friends have the most successful presidency in history.

I don't have time to be thinking about a new widow, or how pretty she is, or how sad I felt when I heard what happened to her husband, or how cute she was while telling me why she was following me, or how she fully took the blame for being a weirdo, all of which was rather adorable.

I just can't go there.

Nine

Roni

I arrive at Dr. Gordon's office shortly before my four o'clock appointment, my nerves shredded by worries about how the ultrasound will go and whether my baby is okay and how I'm going to have to tell people after this if everything checks out. I'm not sure how I feel about sharing this secret with those closest to me. Part of me wants to keep the news to myself for a while longer, because once I tell my family and Patrick's, the baby won't be just mine any longer.

Not that I want the baby to belong just to me once it's here. No, I definitely don't want that. I'm going to need all the help I can get, but for right now, while the baby is the size of a little peanut (I read that online), part of me wants to keep him or her all to myself.

And that is *so* not me. Pre-disaster Roni would be telling everyone about the baby by now. She couldn't keep anything to herself. I told Patrick everything, and my mom and sisters heard most of it, too. It's weird that I haven't told them about the baby yet, but I've already proven I'm weird by the way I behaved with Derek Kavanaugh.

Ugh.

I was such a dork Monday telling him he reminded me of

Patrick from behind and apologizing for following him. I cringe every time I recall that conversation, and now I have to work with the guy, although hopefully, our paths won't cross often at the White House.

I didn't see him yesterday or today, not that I was looking. I wasn't!

If I could make one little confession, however... I'll just say that meeting him and finding out he's widowed, too, has given my spirits an odd lift that I can't really explain. There's no way I'm interested in him as a man, because it's way too soon, but knowing he's out there and that he gets what I'm going through has made me feel better.

It's not lost on me that I'm getting weirder with every day that goes by. One of the widows I follow on Instagram wrote that after you lose your person, you become a whole new version of yourself without them. That's definitely happening to me, and apparently, this new version of me is going to be a total weirdo who follows strange men around because they look like my late husband from behind.

Where in the hell is the doctor, anyway? The gown the nurse gave me isn't enough to keep me from shivering in the exam room while I wait for him. I take the time to check my first posts on the FLOTUS Facebook and Instagram accounts, where "Sam" wrote about her kids going back to school after their winter break and how she hopes all of America's schoolchildren are off to a great start back to school in the new year.

We went with a fairly innocuous message for our first post, and as I skim through the responses, I realize there's no such thing as innocuous when it comes to the first lady. One person commented that it must be nice to be able to send your kids to a fancy, expensive private school, which is annoying. The twins still attend the school they went to when their parents were alive, which was in their best interest since they had enough changes in their lives. Scotty attends a public middle school, but no one bothers to mention that.

I dash off a text to Sam. *We're getting some pushback on the twins being in a swanky private school. Do you want me to respond to that?*

Dr. Gordon knocks on the door and enters the room. "Hi, Roni, so sorry to keep you waiting. I had an unexpected delivery first thing this morning that's thrown off my whole day."

I toss my phone into my purse on the chair next to the exam table. "Babies are unpredictable that way."

"You have no idea how unpredictable they are. How're you feeling?"

"Better than I was. The nausea seems to have let up some, which is a relief."

"That's good news. You're eating for two, and we've got to keep you healthy. I'm glad to see you're up two pounds since your last visit." He types something into the computer and then looks up at me. "Are you ready to see your baby?"

"Before I do... If there's anything wrong, you'll tell me, right?"

"I will. That's one of the reasons we do ultrasounds."

Part of me doesn't want to know if there's anything wrong. I can't take any more bad or sad news, but I also have to keep things real. I'm going to be a mother to this child, and as such, I need to know everything about him or her. Speaking of that... "Will you be able to tell the sex?"

"Probably not yet. That's usually a bit later, like fourteen to eighteen weeks along."

"Oh, okay."

"Are you ready to take a look?"

"I think so."

"I'm surprised you didn't bring someone with you for this."

"I haven't told anyone."

"Why not?"

"I wanted to do the ultrasound first."

"Well, then, let's get that taken care of for you. I'll be back in a few."

A nurse comes into the room to prep me by placing a sheet over my bottom half and folding my gown up to reveal my abdomen.

She explains how the doctor will put gel on my stomach and then run a wand over me. If he can't get a good look at the fetus, he may need to do the exam vaginally.

I swallow hard at the thought of that. "That sounds pleasant."

"It doesn't hurt at all."

"Oh, good."

She pats my shoulder. "Just relax and try not to worry. The ultrasound is painless and often very exciting, as you'll get to hear your baby's heartbeat for the first time."

I'm on pins and needles at the thought of hearing my baby's heartbeat.

The doctor returns a few minutes later and goes right to the sink to wash his hands before donning gloves. "All set?" he asks me.

"I think so."

"Just try to relax. All of this is perfectly routine."

"To you."

That makes him laugh. "Here we go." He squirts a big glob of gel onto my belly and then runs the wand back and forth, all while intently watching the screen.

All of a sudden, I hear it... The thudding sound of my baby's heartbeat.

"There we go." He smiles as he points to an image on the screen that doesn't really look like much of anything to me, until he begins to narrate what I'm seeing. "The head is there, an arm, hand, leg and foot."

I can barely see it through my tears. There's really a baby in there. Patrick's baby. "Is he or she... Are they... Okay?"

"Everything looks good. I'd say you're right around thirteen weeks."

"How could I be that pregnant and have no idea until you told me?"

"Your mind has been otherwise occupied, Roni. Trauma does strange things to us, and it doesn't surprise me at all that you hadn't put this together until I told you."

While he finishes the exam, I start thinking back to where we were three months ago. Oh my God. That was the early October weekend we went to the beach in Rehoboth, Delaware, with two couples we're friends with from college, the last weekend we had together before Patrick died. It was so unseasonably cold that we couldn't stand to be outside, so we hunkered down in the house we rented with the fireplace and our books and some movies. It was a fun, relaxing weekend, during which our baby was conceived.

Tears roll unchecked down my face as I stare at the screen, watching its little heart flutter frantically. Every aspect of my life has changed since that weekend at the beach. I barely recognize myself in a life that no longer includes Patrick.

"Is there someone I can call for you, Roni?" Dr. Gordon asks gently.

"No, thank you. I'm okay. It's just a lot on top of a lot."

"I know, but the good news about babies is they give you lots of time to prepare for their arrival."

All the time in the world wouldn't be enough to prepare myself to raise this child without its father. "That is good news," I tell the doctor, mostly so he won't worry about whether he should let me leave here on my own.

He wipes the gel off my belly and helps me sit up. "Based on the info we have and the size of the fetus, I'd put your due date around June 25."

I breathe a sigh of relief at realizing he's right. I do have time to prepare myself for this.

"I know it seems really overwhelming right now, Roni, but I have every faith that you're going to be a wonderful mother to this little one."

"Thank you," I say softly. "I hope so."

"We'll see you back here once a month until we get close to your due date, when I'll want to see you weekly."

"Okay."

He hands me a printout from the ultrasound. "I'll leave you to get dressed."

When I'm alone, I stare at the black-and-white image with the white thing in the middle that is my baby.

I'm having a baby.

By myself.

I break down into deep but silent sobs at the sheer unfairness of Patrick missing this, all because two idiots fought over a woman, and one pulled a gun. I cry so hard, I can't breathe. I'd give everything I have for Patrick to wrap his arms around me and tell me everything is going to be all right, the way only he could.

As much as I love my new job and the people I've met since I lost him, I'd go back to before I lost him in a heartbeat if it meant more time with him, if it meant he'd get to meet his child.

It's just so sad and unfair. It's ridiculously unfair.

I grab some tissues from a box on the counter and dry my face before removing the gown and getting dressed in the leggings and long T-shirt I brought to wear to the Wild Widows' meeting. I fold my work clothes, stuff them into my tote bag and run a brush through my hair. When I'm as pulled together as I ever am these days, I emerge from the exam room to find Dr. Gordon waiting for me in the hallway.

"Are you okay?" he asks with that kind expression that makes me want to hug him.

"I will be. Eventually."

"Have you found a good therapist?"

"Not yet."

"Might not be a bad idea. You've had a lot to contend with. I can give you some names if that would help."

"I'll take the names."

"If you give me an email address, I'll send them to you."

I take the prescription pad and pen he hands me and write down my Gmail address.

"I'll be in touch in the next day or two."

"Thanks."

As his receptionist hands me an appointment card for my next visit, she gives me a sympathetic smile. I'm sure he didn't tell her about my loss, but somehow she knows. Maybe she read about it in the paper or heard about it on the local news. The story got a lot of attention when it first happened.

I leave the doctor's office shortly after five and step into frosty darkness outside. I think about skipping the widows' meeting, but I need the support more than ever after seeing my baby on the ultrasound, so I summon an Uber for a ride to the garage to get the car.

I'm nervous about driving at night, but determined to get to Fairfax to meet this group of people who've already been so good to me. Traffic is, as always, a bitch on the way out of the District. I'm stopped for fifteen minutes on the 14th Street Bridge, which gives me time to check my messages. The one from Sam in response to my earlier query makes me laugh.

Fuck no, I don't want you to respond to those idiots. We're not giving them any of our energy. Although don't quote me on the "fuck no" part.

God, I love her. She's so funny and real and cares so much about the people in her life.

You got it, and for what it's worth, I agree. People need to mind their own business.

It's worth a lot, and yes, please with the MYOB. I'm probably in the wrong marriage if I hope other people aren't going to mind my business.

That, too, makes me laugh. *Probably so.*

Thank goodness he's worth it, because if he wasn't...

LOL

How did your second and third days at the WH go?

Very well. Everyone is super nice and helpful.

Sorry I haven't been around. Work is crazy, as always. I'm here if you need me for anything.

All good. We've got you covered.

That's a huge relief to me, Roni. Seriously.

Glad to be able to help. I'll check in tomorrow.

I'll be here.

I send her a thumbs-up when I really want to ask her about Derek Kavanaugh, but I never would. That's just too weird, and I'm weird enough these days without making it worse. Besides, judging from the meltdown at the doctor's office, it's far too soon for me to be asking anyone about any guy. The thought of dating someone else is preposterous to me, even as I recall Iris telling me it's perfectly normal to be having such thoughts as reality sets in, reminding me I have a very long life left to live without Patrick. It doesn't feel normal to me at all, and I can't fathom a time when it ever will.

"Oh, by the way," I say out loud, "I'm pregnant with my dead husband's child, but other than that, I've got no baggage."

I giggle to myself at the ridiculousness of it all. I'm sure guys would line up to take on me and my unborn child and all the mess that goes along with someone who'll forever be in love with someone else. I wonder if there's a special category on the dating apps for widows still in love with the person they lost. I need to ask the group about that.

Widowhood is so freaking bizarre. One minute you're on the bathroom floor sobbing your heart out over your lost love and the next you're wondering about a guy you met who seems interesting. However, you have no space in your life to accommodate an interest in anything other than getting through the next five minutes. I've read accounts from many young widows who talk about this strange new world of coping with life-altering grief while keeping one eye on a future that will most likely involve a new love at some point.

It's overwhelming and depressing because the only love I want is the one I lost. And I'm right back around in the never-ending circle of grief that makes me feel like a stranger inside my own mind.

I'm about thirty minutes late by the time I finally arrive at Iris's two-story home in Fairfax. Since there are quite a few cars parked outside, I find a spot farther down the street and grab the bottle of wine I brought from home for this meeting. Since I can't drink it, I may as well share it with others. I stop a little short at the realization that I planned ahead to that extent. As far as I can recall, this is the first time I've done something like that since Patrick died. For a while there, I wondered if my brain had simply stopped functioning at that level. A bottle of wine proves otherwise.

Look at me, making tiny bits of progress that are juxtaposed with the ongoing grief. The incident in the doctor's office proves

I'm a long way from healed, but hey, I remembered to bring wine for the widow meeting, so I'll take the progress where I can find it.

I'm suddenly nervous as I take the steps to Iris's front door and ring the bell.

Iris smiles widely as she opens the storm door for me. I recognize her from her Instagram profile. She's petite, with light brown skin, luminous brown eyes and curly hair contained by a colorful headband. She hugs me like we're old friends, which puts me immediately at ease about coming into a room full of strangers. "I'm so glad you came," she whispers when she finally releases me.

"I told you I would."

"A lot of people say that, and then when the time comes, they don't show, which is totally fine. I was just hoping you'd make it so we could meet in person."

"Your home is lovely."

"Oh, thanks. If there's one saving grace of widowhood, it's life insurance. Mike's was exceptional, and it's allowing me to stay in our home and not have to work until my kids are all in school. That's a huge blessing."

"That's great. Patrick's was good, too. It helps not to have to think about that."

"Indeed. Not everyone in our group is so fortunate." She hangs my coat on a hook by the door and then takes my hand. "Come in. Let me introduce you to everyone."

In the living room, I recognize Brielle from her profile and return the warm hug she gives me. She's curvy and pretty with dark hair and eyes and a smile emboldened by bright red lipstick.

"So nice to meet you in person," she says.

"You, too."

I meet several other people in the living room before I follow Iris into the kitchen and nearly stop breathing when I see Derek there.

"No way," he says with a small grin. "This officially counts as stalking."

Ten

Roni

"I didn't know you'd be here!"

His laughter makes his already handsome face even more so.

"I take it you've met Derek," Iris says, smiling.

"She's stalking me," he says.

"I am not! Well, not anymore."

"I sense a story here," Iris says, offering me a drink.

I hand her the wine I brought, which I suddenly want to drink straight from the bottle. "I'll just have ice water, please." That's when I notice the spread of food and desserts on her kitchen table that spills over onto a counter. "You forgot to tell me to bring food."

"Next time." She hands me a glass of water. "We never ask new people to bring food, but help yourself."

Since I'm actually hungry for once, I fix a plate of two kinds of salad, some pasta and a chicken dish that smells delicious.

Derek makes room for me to stand next to him as I eat.

"I swear I didn't know you'd be here," I tell him between bites.

"Sure you didn't," he says with a teasing grin. "I'm glad you

98

heard about this group, though. It's been a godsend to me. I hope it will be for you, too."

"How long have you been coming?"

"More than a year, I guess. Since shortly after I lost my wife. A friend of my mom's through yoga was a member. She reached out to me about it. At first, I resisted it, thinking I didn't need something like this, but after a rough few months, I was desperate enough for some relief that I decided to come to a meeting. I've made some great friends in this group."

Several of the women he was talking to when I came in are still hovering close by, as if maybe they're hoping for the chance to talk to him some more. One of them eyes me with a hint of hostility that has me focusing on my food. I'll bet he's prime property in widow circles—young, hot, successful and the single dad to a gorgeous daughter. I no sooner have that thought than I feel small and petty for even thinking it.

What do I care if he's catnip to the other widows? It's not like I have any space in my life to be interested in him or any other man. They can have him.

Except... I don't like that either.

Jesus, Roni, eat your dinner and shut the hell up already.

"How's the new job treating you?" Derek asks.

"I love it so far. Everyone in our office is so nice and helpful, and of course, working for Sam is just awesome." I glance at him. "It is okay to call her Sam, right?"

"Hell yes. I call him Nick when I'm alone with him. He insists on it. With everyone calling him Mr. President these days, he's desperate to keep it real. I'm sure she is, too."

"They seem pretty great."

"They are, and they're an incredible couple. He's never been happier since they got together two years ago."

"They're the ultimate power couple, but with such a sweet way about them with each other. It's such an honor to be part of their administration."

"Yes, it is. I worked for Nelson, so when he died, I was worried about what I was going to do, but then Nick asked me to stay on in the same role in his administration, which was a huge relief. Single fatherhood isn't easy, so having a schedule I can count on is key."

"Derek, are you going to introduce us to your friend?" asks one of the women, a cool blonde with gorgeous blue eyes and large breasts I would've killed for before my sweet husband told me less is more.

That memory takes my breath away for a second, but thankfully, Derek is busy introducing me to her, so no one notices.

"Roni, this is Aurora, Naomi and Kinsley. Ladies, this is Roni. Let's make her feel welcome."

He gives Aurora, the blonde, a meaningful look as he says that last part, which has me wondering if he might have some sort of history with her. Naomi has red hair and a bubbly personality, while Kinsley, who has light brown, shoulder-length hair and light blue eyes, is more reserved but still friendly.

"How do you two know each other?" Aurora asks.

"We work together," Derek says.

"Oh, so you work at the White House, too?"

"Yes, I work for the first lady."

"She's *so* cool," Naomi says. "And her husband is just..." She fans her face. "Smoking hot."

I laugh at the face Naomi makes.

"Sorry, it's been a while," she says with a sheepish grin. "A girl has to have her fantasies, and he makes for a good one."

"Ew," Derek says in a teasing tone. "That's my friend you're talking about."

"I know," Naomi says, "and yet I have no shame. Your friend is hot."

I immediately like her and have immediate reservations about Aurora, who's gone quiet since she heard I work for Sam.

"Come on, everyone," Iris calls from the living room. "Let's get this party started."

When I follow the others into the living room, I see that chairs have been arranged in a big circle. I take the seat next to Derek's because that's the closest one to me, not because I feel the need to sit with him.

You're being weird again, Roni. Knock it off.

This time, my inner thoughts come to me in Patrick's voice rather than my own. He was so good at redirecting me when my thoughts got out of control or went in counterproductive directions. He could bring me back with a few well-chosen words that always returned me to an even keel. To hear his voice, even if it's only in my head, is such a gift.

When everyone is settled, Iris calls the meeting to order. "Before we introduce ourselves, I want to welcome our new member, Roni Connolly, to the club no one ever wants to join."

"Thank you so much for having me."

"We don't like to put new members on the spot," Iris says, "but if you want to say anything, you're more than welcome to."

I sort of expected that I'd have to introduce myself, so I'm somewhat prepared for this. "I lost my husband, Patrick, in October when he was out for lunch and was killed by a stray bullet on 12th Street in the District. We'd been together for almost ten years, but only married for three and a half months."

"Oh Lord," one of the women I haven't met yet says. "That's so sad. I'm sorry for your loss."

As the others pass along their sympathies, I feel comforted to be in a room full of people who understand this particular loss.

"I want to thank Iris for inviting me to come tonight and Brielle for reaching out to me ahead of the meeting. I've enjoyed your Instagram account and have gotten to know a few of you through that. I'm looking forward to the chance to get to know you better and to soak up the support and friendship you've so generously offered me."

"We're happy to have you, Roni," Brielle says, "although we wish you didn't need what we have to offer."

I return her warm smile. "Me, too. I'm still pretty new to all this, so go easy on me."

The others laugh, and I breathe a little easier after having gotten the introduction out of the way.

"Let's introduce ourselves to Roni and go from there," Iris says, gesturing for Derek to go first.

"I'm Derek. My wife, Victoria, was murdered as part of a sinister plot you've all read about, so I won't expound upon it. I have a two-year-old daughter, Maeve, who is my sunshine, and I just survived my second Christmas without Vic. Life has gone on, but it's a very different and less exciting life than it was with her. But Maeve and I are muddling through, and this group has been great. I'm very thankful for you guys."

"We're thankful for you, too, Derek, and your darling Maeve," Iris says. "You already know me, Roni. My husband, Mike, was killed in a plane crash almost nineteen months ago. I have three kids who are six, four and two. Thankfully, they're with my parents tonight so I can have some time off to wallow with my widows." She holds up her wineglass. "Cheers to nights off and to wallowing."

"Cheers to both," Brielle says. "My husband, Mark, died in a skiing accident nine months ago, which was two months before our son, Charlie, was born. It's been rough. Really, *really* rough, but I'm doing better than I was and getting used to single parenthood."

"You're doing great, Bri," Naomi says. For my sake, she adds, "I lost my fiancé, David, to lymphoma two years ago after a brutal battle and have the distinction of not being an actual widow. Yes, people have actually said that to me, but I still lost the love of my life, the person I expected to be with forever, so damn it, I'm a fucking widow."

"Absolutely," Iris says. "You sure as hell are."

"Why do people have to say stupid things to people going through such an awful loss?" one of the men asks. He's Black, muscular and handsome, but with an aura of sadness about him that I can certainly understand. "Oh, sorry, I'm Adrian, and I lost my wife, Sadie, when she hemorrhaged after giving birth to our son six months ago."

Oh my God. I know that can happen, but I've never heard of it happening to anyone I know, and it's the last thing I need to hear after seeing my baby for the first time today. My entire body goes cold with fear and anxiety.

"Needless to say, my life has been a bit of a mess since then, but I'm starting to get my shit together and figuring out how to care for a newborn. It's just so hard doing it without her. She would've been such a wonderful mother, and it kills me that she never got the chance to hold him."

My eyes flood with tears that I desperately try to contain.

Derek hands me a tissue that I press to my eyes. He surprises me when he pats me on the back.

That small gesture means so much to me, which is silly. He's just being nice, but still... He's being nice to *me*.

I catch Aurora giving me a hateful look that makes me want to shrivel up and make myself invisible.

"We're all so proud of you, Adrian," another woman says. She's probably in her mid-thirties with shoulder-length brown hair and green eyes. "You're such a great dad to Xavier." For my benefit, she adds, "I'm Christy. My husband, Wes, suffered an aortic dissection, which means his aorta basically broke open. He was dead before I realized something was wrong. He's been gone three years, and I'm doing much better than I was, but my kids, who are ten and twelve, have had a rough time since we lost him. They witnessed it, and managing their trauma and grief on top of my own has been a struggle."

"Christy is our patron saint," Iris says. "She's been at this the longest and is such a tremendous source of support to the rest of us."

"Aw, thanks," Christy says. "It helps me to help others. I'm glad you found us, Roni."

"Me, too. Thank you."

"I'm Aurora, but you already know that. I'm not technically a widow, but I lost my husband when he was arrested for rape."

Even though I've heard about that, I still struggle to hold back the gasp that is at the tip of my tongue over the blunt way she puts it right out there.

"At first, I didn't believe that was possible, but the evidence is irrefutable, so I've had to accept that the man I lived with and loved and slept next to for five years is actually a vicious monster. The only blessing is that we didn't have kids who would grow up knowing what their father is. My loss is not the same as the rest of yours—"

"It is, though," I say. "You lost the life you expected to live with him, and you have every right to grieve that."

Aurora seems surprised by my generosity. Hell, I'm surprised after her thinly veiled hostility toward me simply because I already knew Derek, but her grief is no less painful than mine. Plus, she has to live with the fact that she never really knew the man she married. That has to be its own special form of hell.

"Thank you," she says in the softest tone I've heard yet from her. "There've been people in widow circles who refused to welcome me into their ranks, as my husband is, unfortunately, still alive. But this group has been a lifeline. I hope it is for you, too."

"It already is," I reply.

"I'm Lexi, and I recently lost my husband to ALS after a four-year battle with the most hideous disease." She has brown skin and long, curly, dark hair. "I'm still recovering from losing him and reclaiming my life after being a full-time caregiver. Jim didn't have life insurance, and I was out of the workforce for years while he was sick, so that's been a real struggle on top of the grief issues. I've had to move back in with my parents, which is no one's idea of a good time at thirty-four." She takes a deep breath and releases it. "It's all so difficult, but it was worth the sacrifices to have that time with him and to be there when he needed me. I'm just so sad that we never got to have kids. I'd love to have something of him left now, but I suppose it's for the best since his illness devastated us financially."

"You are a warrior, Lex," Adrian says. "You're going to get back on your feet and figure out a new life for yourself. I know it."

"From your lips to God's ears," she says with a smile. "So far, He's not hearing my request for a new job with a big enough salary that I can pay off our massive debt and get out of my parents' basement."

"We're all praying for that," Kinsley says. "Soon enough, He'll hear us."

"I hope so, but in the meantime, I continue to play Powerball every week," she says to laughter.

Lexi's perspective makes me extra thankful for the baby I'm carrying. If I can put aside all the worries about how hard it will be, I can celebrate that I'll have part of Patrick with me to carry on his legacy.

"You already know I'm Kinsley. My husband, Rory, had pancreatic cancer and died just over a year ago, forty-two days after his diagnosis. He was thirty-eight, and we'd been together fifteen years. We have two kids—Christian is six and Maisy is four. So it's been rough, to say the least, but we're doing okay." She offers a small, tired smile. "One day at a time."

"You're doing great," Brielle says.

Kinsley smiles at her. "Thanks to all of you."

"I'm Gage, the group's elder statesman at forty," he says, grinning at the others. He's got dark hair and eyes and a hard edge to him that keeps him from being classically good-looking. "Just over two years ago, I lost my wife, Natasha, and eight-year-old twin daughters in a drunk-driving accident. Only it wasn't really an accident, because the man who hit them made the choice to drink and drive. He took everything from me, and the rebuilding of my life is an act in progress with a *long* way to go. Christy brought me into this group, and I'll be forever thankful to her and the others here who've helped to piece me back together."

The magnitude of his loss is unbearable. His wife and *both* his daughters... My God.

"You're our hero, Gage," Lexi says. "Keep being awesome and inspirational." To me, she says, "If you're not following him on Insta, his daily posts are must-reads for those of us on this journey."

"Aw, thanks," he says. "I appreciate that."

"What's the account name?" I ask.

He recites it for me, and I immediately give his account a follow. "Thank you."

"Gage is a hard act to follow," the next woman says. "I'm Hallie, and I lost my wife, Gwen, to suicide."

I've been fascinated by her colorful sleeve tattoos since we first sat down. Her blonde hair is cut into a bob with a hot-pink streak in the front.

"Being a suicide widow is a strange place to be since my spouse chose to leave our life, or that's what the ignorant masses think. In reality, she battled her demons for years before she succumbed to their lure. I just never thought she'd actually leave me, so that's been the hard part. Well, it's all hard, but that's what I struggle with along with the memories from the day it happened. I was the one who found her, so..." She shrugs. "I, too, am a work in progress."

"Aren't we all?" Iris asks. "We're all in this boat together, Hallie. Don't you ever forget that."

"I won't." She takes a tissue from Gage and wipes her eyes. "You all are keeping me going. There's no one else in my life who understands the way you do."

"We're here for you forever, kid," Gage says. "You can't get rid of us."

"Thank God for that," Hallie says.

The last person must be the youngest of us all. Her jet-black hair is cut in a buzz on one side with the longer side falling over half her face. She's got piercings up one whole ear and has a ring through her lip. "I'm Wynter. I lost my husband, Jaden, to bone cancer in November. We were only married a week when he died. We knew he was dying because they'd told us there was nothing more they could do for him after years of treatments didn't work. We had one of those sadly uplifting hospital weddings you read about in *People* magazine. My mom heard about this group, and she made me come. This is my third time, and I still don't want to be here, but I've decided not to hate you guys, so that's progress."

Everyone laughs when she says that.

"None of us want to be here, Wynter," Iris says gently, "but there's no sense in going through it alone, is there?"

Wynter shrugs as if she doesn't care, but I'm sure she probably cares far too much. I can't imagine going through such a searing loss at her young age. "I'm not interested in meeting someone else, so I don't even qualify for membership."

"We still want you here," Kinsley says.

"That's a dumb rule anyway," Wynter says. "It's effed up to

expect people to want to fall in love again after what we've been through. I never want to put myself through that shit again."

"I can totally understand why you feel that way." I speak up before I lose my nerve. "You lost your husband shortly after I lost mine, which means it's way too soon for either of us to be thinking about a Chapter 2, or anything much beyond getting through today. But for me, the rules of this group have given me a tiny kernel of hope to cling to that I won't always feel as bad as I do now and that there might be a chance for happiness again in the future. Granted, it won't be the same as it was. Nothing could be the same for me without Patrick or for you without your Jaden. But it could be a different kind of happy. Maybe." I shrug because I've run out of words, but I hope I said something she finds helpful.

"I guess," Wynter says, "but that isn't something I want."

"Which is perfectly okay," Iris says. "We're all on our own journeys, but the point of the group is to be on those journeys together. While we're on the subject, does anyone have any Chapter 2 news they want to share?"

Kinsley raises her hand. "I went on a date."

The others congratulate her with a round of applause, which has poor Kinsley blushing and holding up her hands.

"It was just that—a date. I don't think there'll be a second one with him, but I got the first one out of the way."

"That's so huge," Brielle says. "I did it recently just so I wouldn't have to think about what it would be like to go out with someone else. It sucked, but I'm still glad I did it to get it out of the way."

"Don't you feel like you're cheating?" Wynter asks.

"Nah," Brielle says. "Mark would be the first to tell me to get back out there and find someone who makes me happy. He loved me, and he wanted me to be happy. We never got the chance to talk about this stuff, because who does that when they're twenty-seven and twenty-eight and think they have their whole lives ahead of them? But I know he'd want this for me. I *know* it."

I nod because I feel the same way about what Patrick would want for me. I have absolutely no doubts about that, even though

we never talked about it either. He put me first in his life
—*always.*

"If Jaden were still here, you'd never have given anyone else a
second thought for the rest of your life, hopefully," Iris says. "But
since he's not here, now you have to put yourself first and figure
out who Wynter is without him."

Wynter blinks furiously. "I have no idea who she is."

"You're going to figure that out, sweetheart," Gage says. "And
when you do, I can't wait to get to know her."

I think that might be one of the kindest things I've ever heard
anyone say.

"I made a huge mistake posting that I'd broken the seal and
gone on a date," Kinsley adds. "Someone I don't even know
commented, 'Boy, that was fast.'"

"Stop it," Adrian says. "That's such bullshit, and you know
it. Tell me you know that."

"I do," Kinsley says. "But it still hurt to think that people are
judging me when it required every ounce of courage I have to
take this step."

"Don't let some asshole who has no idea what you've been
through do that to you," Derek says fiercely. "They don't pay rent
for space in your head, so don't give it to them for free."

I can't help but glance at him, stunned by his powerful and
thought-provoking words.

"Thank you," Kinsley says softly. "I needed to hear that."

"So sorry I'm late," a woman says as she comes bursting in the
front door. "Freaking traffic!" She's tall, mixed race, strikingly
pretty and wearing a power suit and heels so high, I wonder how
she can even walk. But she struts into the room like a badass on
those four-inch heels, bringing a rush of cold air with her.

"Joy, this is Roni," Iris says. "She's new tonight."

She comes right over and bends to hug me. "I'm so sorry
you're here."

Bowled over by her, I return her embrace. "Thank you."

When she stands upright, she says, "I brought the chicken
wings you savages devoured last time."

As they offer an enthusiastic round of applause, she takes a dramatic bow.

I love her instantly.

She takes her bag into the kitchen and returns with a glass of wine, taking a seat next to Lexi. "What'd I miss?"

Eleven

Roni

The others take turns filling Joy in on my story, which I appreciate. Telling it once was hard enough.

"I really am so, so sorry, honey," she says softly. "I know what it's like to have your entire world suddenly tipped upside down. My thirty-four-year-old husband, Craig, went to bed one night and never woke up. The autopsy was inconclusive. Natural causes, they said. I've since learned it happens far more often than anyone realizes and to people too young to die that way."

"I'm so sorry for your loss, too." I'm touched by the change in her when she speaks of her late husband. She's gone from high as a kite when she came in to wilted like a balloon that's lost all its air.

"Thank you. It was a couple of years ago now, but some days, it's like it just happened. Other days, I have trouble remembering the sound of his voice, which is the worst. How can I not remember that?"

"That happens to me, too," Derek says. "Sometimes I have to really stop and think about what her voice sounded like, which sends me to the videos, which sends me into a tailspin."

Before I take one second to think about what I'm doing, my hand is on his arm, offering support and friendship.

He sends me a small smile in response, and I remove my hand, lest it get weird—again.

His last comment reminds me of my wedding video. Perhaps these amazing people will know what I'm supposed to do with that. "Speaking of videos, my wedding video recently arrived in my in-box, where it's sitting like a nuclear bomb waiting to detonate. What the hell do I do with that?"

"Forward it to someone you trust, one of your bridesmaids maybe, and ask them to hold on to it for you until you're ready to see it," Iris suggests.

"And then delete it from your in-box so it won't be taunting you every time you check your email," Adrian adds.

"When you're ready to see it, you can go to the person you entrusted with it and watch it together," Kinsley says.

"I like that plan. I could send it to my sister and ask her to hold it for me." I look around at the faces of people who were strangers to me an hour ago and wonder how it's possible they already feel like old friends. "Is it strange that in my old life, pre-disaster, I wouldn't have needed advice on how to handle anything?"

"Nah, baby," Joy says. "We've all been there. Grief does crazy shit to your brain."

"Widow brain," Lexi says. "It's a thing."

"The grief takes up a lot of space, a lot of emotion," Brielle says. "It doesn't leave much room for anything else."

"It messes with your sense of time, too," Derek says. "You ever notice how when you're doing something fun, the time just flies, but when you're running on the treadmill, thirty minutes goes so slowly, you think you'll never get there? Grief time is like being on the treadmill. It moves *so* slowly. Days feel like weeks. Months feel like years. Everything moves in slow motion."

"Yes," Gage says. "That was so well said. I dream about being underwater, trying to find the surface and gasping for air when I finally break free of the depths."

"The dreams are the worst," Hallie says. "Especially the sex dreams."

Everyone groans in agreement.

"Why do we gotta dream about what we can't have?" Iris asks. "It's almost cruel."

"It is cruel," Wynter says.

We all look to her, hoping she'll say more.

After a long pause, she says, "The whole goddamned thing is cruel." Every word she says drips with rage.

"Yes, it is," I whisper. "It's the cruelest thing ever."

"But we're still here," Gage says. "We're still here, and it's a decision we have to make to carry on, to make them proud of us by living lives full of meaning and possibly even joy again some-day. We have to go on. We have no choice."

"Yes, we do," Wynter says. "We can check the eff out and stop feeling like shit all the time. And before you call my mother and tell her I'm suicidal, I'm not. I'm just saying... It's an option."

"Please don't consider that an option," Hallie says gently. "You mentioned how cruel this is, and it is. But that... It's an incredibly cruel thing to do to the people who love you."

"I'm sorry," Wynter mumbles. "I shouldn't have said that."

"It's fine that you said it," Hallie says. "Of course, it's an option for all of us."

"If you feel that way," Iris says to Wynter, "please talk to someone. We need you to stay with us, no matter how bad it gets. We'll be here for you as long as you need us."

"I swear I'm okay," Wynter says tearfully. "I was just venting. And I'm sorry if I was insensitive, Hallie."

"Don't be. I understand."

"I think it's time for dessert," Iris says.

As the others stand and head for the kitchen, Derek and I hang back. "That got intense," he says.

"She's so, *so* young to be dealing with something so heavy."

"She is."

"How old is she?"

"Nineteen, I think."

"I was only a year older when I met Patrick. I can't for the life of me imagine what it would've been like to go through a loss like this at her age."

"I know. Same. It was bad enough at thirty-six." He looks

down at me with gorgeous golden-brown eyes that are nothing like Patrick's baby blues. Now that I've gotten to know Derek, he doesn't remind me of my husband at all. "The group is helpful, no?"

"Oh God, yes. It's like I've found my people."

"That's how I felt the first time, too. It was such a relief to be with people who truly understand."

"I loved what you said to Kinsley about giving people rent-free space in her head."

"That's been one of my favorite sayings since long before I was widowed, but it applies liberally to our situation. People say the most screwed-up shit to other people going through immense loss. A lot of the members say it helps them to share their thoughts on social media, but that's not for me. I don't need people judging me, especially after how public my loss was."

"I think you're wise to protect yourself from that."

"Who needs the extra drama? I've got enough without asking for more. Every time there's a development in the Patterson case, I get calls from the media looking for comments. I've never commented. I'm never going to, and even though I tell them that every time, they still call me."

"Jeez, that sucks. Maybe you should issue a statement that says that while you understand the intense interest in the Patterson case as it winds through the courts, the loss of your wife was a very personal thing for you and your daughter. You could say that you'll never comment publicly on the case now or in the future, so please stop asking me. 'My daughter and I request privacy as we continue to mourn the loss of our wife and mother.'"

He rubs at the late-day stubble on his jaw. "I suppose I could do that, but I'd hate to draw any more attention to myself."

"It might shut it down for good if you issue a blanket statement asking for privacy. Anyone who hits you up after that is just a dick."

His snort of laughter pleases me. I get the feeling he doesn't do that very often.

"Do you think maybe you could write that down for me?"

"Sure, I can do that."

He reaches for his wallet, withdraws a business card and hands it to me. "My work email is on there. It's the only one I have."

"I'll send you something in the morning."

"Put it on Sam's tab."

Laughing, I say, "Will do. Now I need some sugar."

"Lead the way."

We end up walking out together when the group disbands half an hour later. The night is cold and clear, with an abundance of stars overhead.

"Where'd you park?" he asks.

I point to the left. "That way."

"Me, too."

As we walk down the quiet street together, I wonder what he's thinking, but I don't want to pry. I feel like we've traveled a million miles since he thought I was a stalker. I'm beginning to seriously value our fragile new friendship.

"It's good that you came here so soon after your loss," he says, breaking the silence. "I wish I'd done it sooner than I did. I had to be talked into it."

"Who invited you to come?"

"A woman named Taylor, who's since remarried. Like I said earlier, my mom knew her from yoga, and when she heard about Vic's murder, she told my mom about the group. It took a lot of persuasion to get me to go, which turned out to be the best thing I could've done for myself."

"Self-care doesn't always come easily to people, but it's so important."

"I've learned that. Before I lost Vic, I was so focused on external things—my job, the president, Congress, the daily grind of managing work, marriage, fatherhood. I was like a robot in some ways, going through all the expected motions. Except for when Vic and I were alone together. That's when I truly came alive." He gives me a side-eyed look. "Which is probably TMI."

"Nah, I get it. It was like that with me and Patrick, too. We worked hard, but the minute we got home, it was all about us until we had to leave again. That's a difficult void to fill."

"Yeah, that's the toughest part of the day for me, after Maeve is in bed, and it's too early for me to go to bed. I usually just drown myself in work that could've waited until the next day. If there's any upside to widowhood, I've never been more on top of the rest of my life than I am now."

"I'm still working on that."

"You're probably in the thick of the estate shit and the death certificates and all that."

"Yep. Just when I think I've told everyone, here comes the alumni association, or the fraternity brother who was working in Egypt just heard the news, or the registration on his car needs to be renewed, which means I have to switch it into my name, which apparently takes an act of God. It never ends."

"It does, eventually, but it takes a while. It was easier for me because Vic didn't have any family of her own or much in the way of stuff outside our marriage."

"Patrick belonged to six different professional organizations for IT professionals, not to mention three for law enforcement professionals. It's been a lot."

"Sounds like it. I read he was with the DEA."

He read about me? Or, I should say, he read about Patrick? "Yes, and one of the most overwhelming things that's happened since he died was finding out just how well-respected he was in his field. The outpouring was nothing short of a tsunami."

"That's really nice."

I'm still trying to process that Derek read about us.

"Listen, I know you're still in the early days of this, and I'm further down the road, even if at times it feels like I'm still at square one, but..."

I wait with breathless anticipation for what he'll say next.

"Do you want to get a drink and talk some more?"

"Like now? Don't you have to get home to Maeve?"

"My parents are sleeping over, so I can do it now if you want to."

I'm extremely torn between wanting more of his comforting

presence and feeling disloyal to the husband I lost three months ago for even talking to another man—even if we're talking mostly about grief and everything that goes with it. "There's something I need to tell you."

Derek

THE MORE TIME I spend with Roni, the more I enjoy talking to her. Not to mention she's so damn pretty. It's way too soon after her loss for me to ask her for anything, but I like being with her, and I get the sense she feels the same way. Since I'm so sick and bloody tired of feeling like total shit, I grab the lifelines where I can find them.

And then she says the dreaded words *there's something I need to tell you* that make me want to plead with her not to do anything that will mess with the nice new groove we've found together.

She steps up to a sleek silver Audi and leans against it, her breath making a crystal cloud in the cold.

"Whatever you want to say, Roni, just put it out there. I've learned from the Wild Widows that it's so much easier to air out the stuff that's weighing us down rather than trying to cope with it on our own."

"I can definitely see how that's true, but this is kinda big."

"Isn't everything these days?"

Her soft laugh touches me in a place deep inside that's been walled off from the outside world since I lost Vic. Roni touches me with her sweetness, her obvious love for her late husband, her determination to press on despite her grief. "Yeah, I guess it is. So, I found out recently that I'm pregnant."

I didn't see that coming. "Oh. Wow. That is big. How're you feeling about it?"

"Name an emotion. I've had every one of them since I got this news. I've gone from denial to elation to despair to joy to fear and back to despair, and that was the first five minutes."

I smile at how lovely and funny she is, despite having all the reason in the world to be bitter and angry.

"I'm really scared I won't be able to handle being a single parent to this child."

"If I can handle it, *anyone* can. Granted, I have tons of help, but I'm sure you will, too."

"I will. My family is close by, and I know they'll be there for me."

"I'll share my nanny with you if you need one."

Roni looks stunned. "You'd do that?"

"Sure, she's great, and Maeve would love having a baby around. She asks me all the time when she can have a baby sister."

"Aw, that's so sweet."

"I'm not ready to explain to her that a daddy can't have a baby sister without a mommy because I'm afraid she'll ask me when we're getting a new mommy."

"She's very cute."

"And she knows it. She has me wrapped firmly around all her chubby little fingers. My mom is always saying, 'Honestly, Derek, you're going to spoil her rotten.' And she's not wrong. I've had to start being more mindful of what I'm letting her get away with as she gets older. I'm constantly overcompensating for her having to grow up without her mother."

"She's very lucky to have you, and I'm sure she'll grow up to be a wonderful person."

"I hope so. Making sure of that is the most important thing in my life, and it will be for you, too, when your little one arrives."

"Is it weird that the baby seems like something that's happening to someone else? Even though I saw it on the ultrasound today and had to accept that it's very real."

"I don't think that's any weirder than following a random dude around your neighborhood because he reminds you of your late husband from behind."

That makes her laugh—hard. "Am I ever going to hear the end of that?"

"Nope. Never."

"Good to know."

"So a drink? Yes or no?"

"Nonalcoholic counts?"

"Whatever you want."

"Where should we go?"

"Follow me. I grew up out here. I know a place."

Twelve

Roni

Derek clicks a button on his key fob that lights up a black SUV across the street.

"Sounds good."

He starts to walk away but turns back, withdrawing his phone from his pocket. "Give me your number in case we get separated."

As I recite it for him, my heart starts to beat faster, and my face feels warm, even though it's freezing.

"I sent you a text so you have mine, but I'll do my best not to lose you."

"That would be good."

He heads to his car while I fumble my way into mine, dropping the keys on the floor and nearly smacking my head on the wheel when I reach for them. "Sheesh, girl, stop acting like an idiot. He asked you for a drink. Don't make it weird."

I do a U-turn and follow him out of Iris's subdivision. After a few turns, we end up on a busy highway that leads into a retail area. I have no idea where we are, so I make sure not to lose him. We end up at a twenty-four-hour restaurant that's close to an exit for Interstate 66.

"Is this okay?" he asks when we meet outside our cars.

"Works for me."

We grab a table inside, and a waitress named Judy comes to take our drink orders.

"I'm going to do a bourbon on the rocks with lemon, please," he says.

"Just decaf tea with lemon for me, please."

"Any food?"

"You want anything?" he asks.

"No, thanks, I'm stuffed."

"Just the drinks, please."

"You got it. Be right back."

"This is a cute place." I check out the long counter with red vinyl-topped stools and the black-and-white checkerboard flooring.

"We used to come here after games in high school."

Judy returns with our drinks. "Let me know if I can get you anything else."

"Thank you," Derek says for both of us.

I watch as he stirs his drink and note that there's a faint white line on his left ring finger where a wedding band used to be. "Can I ask a personal question?"

"Anything you want."

"How long ago did you take off your ring?"

"Not that long ago, actually. Maybe October?"

"How did you know it was time to do that?"

"When I stopped feeling like I was still married."

"And that took more than a year?"

"Less than that, but I didn't take off the ring until Maeve asked me about it. I told her it was the ring Mommy gave me when we got married. She asked if she could have it, and I said she could. So I took it off, put it on one of Vic's old necklaces, and now Maeve wears it when she plays dress-up. She says it's the ring she's going to give her prince someday."

"I love that story."

"I was glad she gave me a good reason to take it off, and Vic would've appreciated it, too. She was all about things not going to waste. She would've liked that we found a way to repurpose it."

"Maeve may not remember the specifics of things like that, but she'll remember you were always there for her."

"I hope so."

"She will."

"She's a special kid. I'm lucky that she sorta rolls with it all, but then again, she doesn't realize her dad is a bit of a mess."

"No, you're not. She's obviously very well loved and cared for."

"She is, but I'm still finding my groove when it comes to being both Mom and Dad. Like when do I put her in dance class, and how soon should she be in preschool? Vic knew that stuff instinctively, and I'm clueless."

I smile as I lean in. "You could ask someone those questions."

Smiling back, he says, "I do, but you know what I mean. What if I'm not asking the right questions? That's the stuff that keeps me awake at night."

"Surely you must know someone who has kids roughly the same age who can tell you what to do?"

"My two sisters-in-law have been awesome, but they don't live here, so it's sort of distance coaching."

"Where do they live?"

"One in Denver and the other in Vegas."

"They're your brothers' wives?"

"Right."

"Are you close to your brothers?"

"Very. I wish they lived closer, but thankfully, my parents still live in the house where we grew up a few miles from here. I don't know what I'd do without them close by. They're always willing to help with whatever I need."

"Mine are great, too. My whole family was so there for me in those first early days."

"You have siblings?"

"Two sisters and a brother, all of them married with kids and all local except my brother, who lives in the San Fran area."

"I'm glad you have that kind of support close by. You'll need it when the baby comes. They must be excited about it."

"I haven't told them yet."

He seems shocked to hear that. "How come?"

"I'm not sure exactly. Mostly I wanted to see it to believe it, which I did earlier today. That made it very real."

"Maybe you also wanted it to belong to you and Patrick for a while before everyone else found out."

"I suppose so."

"If he was still here, you might not have told people yet. We waited until Vic was in her fourth month to tell anyone."

"Was she superstitious about losing it?"

"A little, I guess. But with hindsight, I realized she was terrified of Patterson's people finding out that she was having a baby. Apparently, that wasn't part of their sinister plan."

"I'm so sorry that was done to you, Derek. It's obscene."

"It sure was."

"Do you ever feel like... like it's just not physically possible to be this sad all the time?"

"I definitely do. It's unsustainable long term, and you'll find as you go forward that it does get a little easier once you're further removed from the shock of what happened. That's not to say you forget or you don't love him anymore or anything like that. But joy starts to creep back in, and you start to have more okay days than dreadful days, and you start to notice the sun and the moon and the stars again."

I prop my chin on my hand as I listen to him. "That's really lovely."

He scoffs. "Whatever. It's true."

"No, it is. It's a comfort for me to know it gets a bit easier as time goes on."

"It does, even if the wound never fully heals."

"Are people in the group serious about dating and stuff?"

"Some more than others." He leans in. "You want some scoop?"

"Duh. Of course I do."

"One of them slept with a guy a month after her husband

died because she was afraid she'd never do it if she didn't get it over with."

"Iris told me about that."

"She cried the whole time and didn't hear from the guy again."

"Poor thing."

"She said it was awful, but she said she stands by her decision because now she doesn't have to be thinking about what it will be like with someone else."

"That's true."

"Another one went all in with a new guy really fast. We were urging her to slow down a bit."

"Oh my gosh. What happened?"

"It crashed and burned because the guy realized she was in no way ready for it. She was devastated all over again, only it was worse this time because she was still coping with losing her husband, too."

"That breaks my heart for her."

"She went through a really rough time, but she's better now and taking things slower. Everyone reacts differently to dating after loss. Some people dive right in, and others want nothing to do with it. But there's so much freaking judgment from people who have no clue what it's like to be us."

"I felt so bad for Kinsley that someone she doesn't even know said something so hurtful."

"It's gross, but I wish some of them shared a bit less on social media. When you put yourself out there, you're opening yourself up to the bad and the good."

"So what's the deal with Aurora who looks at you like she wants to eat you up?"

He cringes. "Ew. Stop it."

"Well, she does!"

"She's sort of a lot."

I try not to laugh at the pained face he makes. "I could see that."

"She's not a bad person, and she'd tell you herself that what her husband did has completely ruined her life, too."

"Of course it has."

"We had to vote about letting her into the group since she's not technically a widow, but she still 'lost' her husband in a sudden and shocking way, so we agreed to let her in. A few times since then, I've regretted my vote in favor."

"She's totally hot for you."

His scowl makes me laugh. "I've had a hard time letting her know I'm just not interested in her that way."

"That's uncomfortable."

"It sure is. I've been tempted to leave the group because of her, but I love the others so much, and it's such an amazing source of support."

"Don't leave the group because of her."

"I won't, but she drives me a little crazy."

"When she figured out that we knew each other, I worried for my life."

"I saw that, and I'm sorry. She has absolutely no claim on me, and she knows it."

"Roni?"

I look up to see my sister Penelope's mother- and father-in-law staring at me, clearly shocked to see me sitting with a *man* in public. *Shit.* "Hey!" I force a smile for them.

"We thought that was you." Rita glances at Derek before she returns her gaze to me. Speaking of judgmental...

"Rita and Lou, this is my friend Derek. Derek, these are my sister Penelope's in-laws, Rita and Lou."

"Nice to meet you both," he says.

"You as well." Rita takes a good long look at him, as if to memorize every detail for when she runs home to tell Pen I was with *a man*. My sister can't stand her. "What're you doing out our way?"

"Derek and I were at a meeting with other widows and widowers." I give her a pointed look that I hope instills a little shame into her.

"Oh, well. That's very nice."

"Actually, it totally sucks, but what're you going to do?"

Derek focuses on his drink, probably so he won't laugh out loud.

"We were out at Charlotte's lacrosse game. Did you hear she's been offered athletic scholarships at six different colleges?"

Did you hear my husband died, and I don't give a flying fuck about your grandchildren who aren't my sister's kids? "I hadn't heard that. Congratulations."

"We're so proud of her."

"Let's let Roni get back to her friend, Rita." Lou earns my eternal gratitude for ending this awkward encounter. "It was really nice to see you, sweetheart. We think of you so often."

"It's nice to see you getting back on the horse," Rita adds with a knowing little grin.

The comment shocks me to my core. "*What?* I'm not back on any horses. I'm having a drink with a *friend.*"

Lou takes ahold of Rita's arm and steers her away. "Take care, Roni."

"Oh my God," I whisper the second they walk away. "What were you saying about judgmental people?"

"She's a piece of work."

"My sister often wants to have her killed."

"I can see why."

"I'm sorry, but I need to text Penelope before she does."

"Of course. Go ahead."

I type in my code, see the text from him from before and leave it unread so I'll remember to add him to my contacts later. After opening a new message to Pen, I start typing. *I'm out for a drink with a fellow widow (a man) and ran into Lou and Rita, who thinks she's stumbled upon the scoop of the century and is glad to see me 'back on the horse.' Just a heads-up if she reports in.*

Pen writes back a few minutes later. *Ugh, she's such a jackass. I'm so sorry she said that to you. I'll make sure Luke talks to her and tells her to keep her fat yap shut.*

I respond with two thumbs-up emojis.

How was the widow meeting?

Really good. Will tell you more tomorrow. Oh, and save Saturday night. I want to have everyone over for dinner.

No way! We'll have YOU over.

I want to do this. Spread the word.

Are you sure??

Yep.

Okay, then... Love you so much, Ronald McDonald. Thinking of you all the time. Xoxo

Love you, too.

"Sorry about that," I say to Derek after returning my phone to my purse.

"No worries. I understand the need for damage control."

"Why would anyone want to do more damage to someone who's contending with a tragedy like what happened to me?"

"Isn't that a question for the ages? People don't think about what they're saying or the harm it can do."

"I couldn't believe she said that about me getting back on the horse!"

"I guess I'm the horse in that metaphor?" he asks, laughing.

"I'm sorry. She was so far out of line as to not even be funny."

"Yes, she was, but another thing I've learned is how desperately the people in our lives want to fix what's broken for us. They want to put the pieces back together the way they were before so they can get back the person we were then. It takes a while for them to figure out that's never going to happen, but I'm trying to be a little more forgiving of their good intentions than I was at the beginning."

"Wow, yes, I hadn't really thought of it that way before, but you're right. I've seen some of that among my family members in particular. 'Tell us what we can do for you, Roni,' they'll say. I wish there was something anyone could do, but there isn't. Sometimes I want to say, 'Bring Patrick back, and everything will be fine,' so they'll see how impossible that question is."

"They love you, and they hate that you're hurting. Even good old Rita probably feels that way. You've probably known her awhile, right?"

"Penelope and Luke have been married for twelve years."

"So, there you have it. Rita, in her own ham-handed way, just wants to see you happy again."

"I suppose, but we both know it's not as simple as getting back on a horse."

"No, it isn't, but you're doing all the right things. You've joined a supportive community, you're making friends who've had similar experiences, you've given up stalking men who look slightly like your late husband."

I sputter with laughter. "It was a *man*, singular, not men, and I wasn't stalking you!"

"So you say. From my point of view, it was full-on stalking."

As I laugh with him, I realize this is the "lightest" I've felt since disaster struck. I enjoy being with him, even when he's calling me a stalker. "Are you ever going to stop calling me your stalker?"

"Probably not."

"Good to know."

He rests his elbows on the table and leans in. "I understand it's way too soon for you to be thinking about anything other than getting through each new day, but I just want you to know... I've decided to forgive you for stalking me."

I release a deep breath full of laughter. I wasn't sure where he was going with that. "Gee, thanks. You're a pal."

"I'd like to be. Your pal, that is. If you could use an extra one."

"I need all the friends I can get right now. A few of the people I would've thought were ride-or-die have disappeared, leaving me with some openings in the friend department."

"That happens," he says. "People can't handle it."

"How sad for them."

"Right? That's a topic that comes up a lot in the group. People we thought would be there for us who've been strangely absent."

"Who was it for you?"

"One of my best friends since childhood. Dave and I went to St. George's School in Rhode Island, which is a boarding school. We lived together for three years. He came to Vic's funeral, said and did all the right things, and I haven't heard from him since."

"Oh wow. That hurts, huh?"

"Yeah, it does, and the thing I don't get is why he wouldn't even reach out to check in. We talked all the time before, and now, there's just silence where he used to be." He takes a sip from his drink and then uses the stirrer to mix it up. "Who is it for you?"

"My college friend Sarah. Like your friend, she was there at first, but since then, she's mostly disappeared. She told one of our mutual friends that she simply couldn't bear it."

"Poor love," Derek says, his tone dripping with sarcasm that I appreciate.

"Exactly! What happened to *her*?"

"Nothing, but your tragedy is a reminder that it *can* happen to her, and that's what she can't deal with."

"I never would've suspected she would cut and run when life got hard." I glance up at him. "She texted me to apologize."

"What did you say?"

"That I wasn't available to help her through my loss. I got that line from one of the Wild Widow posts on Instagram, and it was just what I needed to sum things up with her."

"Good for you for telling her the truth."

"Old Roni would've smoothed it over with her. I hate drama and angst with the people in my life. I would've gone out of my way to fix things, but this... This is different, and new Roni isn't so quick to try to fix things with people who can't do the bare minimum for me."

"While I totally get that, I think you should consider forgiving her."

That surprises me. "You do?"

"Yeah, because being angry with her is taking energy you need for other things."

"I guess that's true. Would you forgive Dave?"

"If he asked me to, I suppose I would, but I'm not going to make the first move. That's up to him. Your friend has admitted that she sucks, so that's something anyway."

"Yes, I suppose it is."

"Think about it. You don't have to do anything about it until you're ready to, but it was big of her to reach out and own her shit. That probably wasn't easy for her. People, even really good people, often don't know how to deal with a loss of this magnitude. Hell, it happened to us and we don't know how to deal with it."

"That's true. You've definitely given me something to think about."

"Excellent, then my work here is finished."

I glance at the big wall clock over the counter, and I'm shocked to see it's already ten thirty. "We should go. It's a school night."

"This was fun. We should do it again sometime."

"I'd like that." I'm not exactly sure what I'm agreeing to, but I refuse to pick it apart after the best night I've had in a while.

Derek insists on paying, and we walk out together.

"Where do you park the car?" he asks.

"A few blocks from my place."

"I'll follow you there and give you a ride home."

"You don't have to do that!"

"I know, but I'll sleep better knowing you got home safely."

"I could text you."

"Or you could let me follow you and give you a ride home."

"If you insist."

"I do."

"All righty, then."

"Lead the way."

As I drive back to the District, I pick over the parts and pieces of this momentous day, from the ultrasound to the widows' meeting to the time alone with Derek. The competition between joy and sorrow is ever present in this new life of mine. No matter what I'm doing or how much I'm enjoying something, grief is part of the mix. I wonder if it'll always be that way, and I assume it will, since my love for Patrick will never die. He'll be with me forever, but I simply can't spend the rest of my life counting the days until I'll get to see him again in the afterlife. I'm just not wired that way.

I went through a particularly devastating breakup in high school. My boyfriend, Connor, who I honestly thought I'd be with forever, suddenly decided we were done and didn't even have the decency to tell me that himself. He got one of his friends to do it for him. I've never forgotten how dreadful that felt or how I was sure that I'd never feel that bad again. How funny that seems now. But then, like now, I had a hard time remaining in that low, devastated space indefinitely.

Not that I didn't ache for a long time from the loss of that relationship, not to mention the cowardly way he ended it, because I did. But my optimistic nature prevailed, and within a few weeks, I was back to feeling more or less like my old self, albeit with a few new internal scars.

I'm finding that happening now, too. I ache all the time over the loss of Patrick, what was taken from him, from us, from our child. I can't bear to think of that awful day or the dark weeks that followed, but I'm finding that with each new day that passes, I'm settling into a place of acceptance. I never would've chosen to create a life without him, but what choice do I have?

The new job is helping, as are the new friends I've made through the Wild Widows. But more than anything, the baby growing inside me is giving me a reason to go on. On Saturday night, I'll have my family over to tell them the news, and I'm already looking forward to how they'll respond. After that, I'll go see Patrick's parents to share the news with them, too.

I can't wait to tell them, to give them a reason to look forward to the future.

Back in the District, I park in our assigned space in the garage that does, in fact, give me the creeps. When I emerge onto the street, Derek is parked in his black Lexus SUV at the curb, waiting for me. I get into the passenger seat and direct him to my building.

"You shouldn't be walking alone from the garage at night."

"It's fine. No one ever bothers me."

"Still, Roni, it's dark, and you're alone, so you should call me any time you need a ride from the garage."

"I'm not going to do that, but thank you for the concern."

"How do you get to work?"

"On the Metro."

"I'll pick you up."

"You don't have to do that!"

"I know I don't, but I will. Seven thirty work for you?"

Since a ride in his warm SUV beats the Metro any day, I say, "Uh, sure."

"What do you get at the coffee shop?"

"Hot chocolate and a cinnamon bun. Why?"

"I was just wondering."

I give him a side-eyed look. "What're you doing, Kavanaugh?"

"Hanging with my new friend, Roni. What're you doing?"

"Getting through another day."

"You're doing great."

"If you say so."

"I do, and I'm somewhat of an expert on these things."

"Thanks for the ride and the drink and for understanding."

"Available whenever you need it."

"Good to know. See you in the morning."

"See you then."

Thirteen

Roni

I get out of the car, go up the stairs to my building and use my key in the door. When I look back, he's still there, waiting to make sure I'm inside before he waves and drives off. As I go up the stairs to my apartment, I'm a mixed-up jumble of emotions regarding Derek Kavanaugh, which makes me feel unfaithful to Patrick.

That's ridiculous, and I know it, but it's there, nonetheless.

Patrick would tell me to live, to love, to be happy and to remember him. That last part will be the easiest, as I'll always remember him with so much love and gratitude for the wonderful years we spent together.

Which is why I hate that I'm a tiny bit attracted to Derek.

There. I said it. And I hate myself for it.

It's too soon to be attracted to anyone. Patrick isn't even gone four months yet. But those months feel like an eternity of emptiness and loneliness. And no, I'm not that woman who can't be alone and needs a man to make her feel complete. I've never been that woman. After Connor, I didn't date anyone until Patrick, almost three years later. Not that I didn't have the opportunity to date others. I just chose not to.

I waited for someone special, and almost the minute I met

Patrick, I knew he was different from the other guys who'd asked me out in the years between Connor and him.

Derek is like that, too. He's special, and not just because he gets what I'm going through, although that doesn't hurt anything. But even when he was accusing me of being a stalker, I felt a spark of that special something I've experienced only twice before.

The timing is horrendous with me a few months out from a brutal loss and expecting my late husband's baby. What man in his right mind would want to take that on?

"He's probably just being nice to the new widow, and you're reading all sorts of nonsense into it," I tell my reflection in the mirror. "Don't go getting carried away on some crazy trip when you have enough on your plate as it is."

After having this talk with myself, I brush my teeth and get into bed with my laptop to check my personal email. I immediately forward the wedding video to Rebecca and tell her to keep it for me until I'm ready to look at it.

Once I see that the message has sent, I delete it out of my inbox so I won't be tempted to reopen my wounds by watching it. I'm definitely not ready for that, and it's possible I may never be, even if I'll be glad to have it for our child to watch someday.

I have yet another email from yet another company that requires a copy of Patrick's death certificate before they can close his account. I attach the scanned copy in PDF format and hit Send, hoping this will be the last time I'll have to do that. I'm quite certain it won't be. Shutting down a life isn't simple business.

That's been one of the hardest parts for me—erasing the life Patrick built for himself over his thirty-one years on earth. Eventually, I'll have to donate the clothing in his side of our closet. I'll have to give away the things that made up his life, including his baseball card and record collections, although he'd tell me to sell them because they're valuable. I can't imagine selling or giving away the things, such as the multiple computers, that made him who he was. That doesn't have to happen any time soon, but eventually, I'll have to deal with that and figure out what to do with it all. Some of it I'll put away for our child to have someday. I want him or her to have things that were Patrick's since they won't have him.

The very idea of dealing with his stuff is so formidable as to be nauseating, so I try not to think about that as I settle in to sleep. My thoughts wander back to Derek, who was so sweet and kind tonight. I'm not sure what's going on there, but whatever it is, I'm relieved to have something else to think about other than the relentless march of grief.

Derek

WHAT AM I DOING? That is the question of the morning as I wait in line for my usual breakfast order, adding a medium hot chocolate and a cinnamon bun, which seems to shock the woman behind the register. So I'm a creature of habit. What can I say?

That brings me back to my original question: What am I doing buying Roni breakfast or offering to drive her to work?

I tell myself it's all about supporting a new friend going through the same awful loss I suffered, but I can't deny it's more than that. For the first time since Vic died, I'm legitimately attracted to someone. For so long, I've wondered if that would ever happen, and now that it has, it's almost a surprise to feel something I thought I lost forever.

Because I can't do anything the simple way, I have to be attracted to a woman who is in no way ready to start over again. So I have two choices: move on from this attraction comforted by the fact that I *can* feel that way about someone other than my late wife, or wait until Roni is ready.

The logical thing would be to move on, taking the new information with me as I continue to work and take care of my daughter and hope that lightning will strike again sometime. But I've lived long enough by now to know that lightning doesn't strike very often, and when it does, it's something that needs to be treated like the special event that it is.

These are the thoughts in my mind as I pull up to Roni's building at seven thirty.

When I see her coming, my heart starts to beat a little faster. This isn't good at all, and yet it feels better than anything has since before I lost Vic.

I lean over to open the passenger door for her, and she gets in, sighing with pleasure at the seat I heated for her.

"This is some excellent service you provide, Mr. Kavanaugh."

"Nothing but the best for you, Mrs. Connolly. There's your breakfast."

"Derek! Come on. You didn't have to do that."

"I wanted to."

"You're very sweet," she says with a deep sigh. "But I hope you know, I'm just not... I mean, I can't..."

I reach over and place my hand on top of hers, which I immediately realize was a mistake. Her skin is so soft, and it's been so long since I touched a woman. "It's fine, Roni. I understand where you are and what you're dealing with."

She surprises me when she turns her hand and wraps it around mine.

Shit. I can't have a predictable response to her touching me, but that's what happens.

"I like you, Derek. I really do. And not because I thought you resembled Patrick at first. I like you for you."

"I like you, too."

"I'm very conflicted about the fact that I like you."

Her honesty is so incredibly refreshing, but then again, everything about her is refreshing.

"I understand that, better than just about anyone else ever could. It's the strangest thing, isn't it? To be forever in love with someone who isn't here anymore and to be thinking about someone new, too."

"Yes," she says on a long exhale as she squeezes my hand. "That's exactly it."

"The beautiful thing is that we're allowed to be forever in love with the people we lost, and we're allowed to entertain the possibility of new people in our lives, too. It's this bizarre dichotomy of grief and joy all mixed into one big pot of emotion that makes sense only to those of us who've traveled this path."

"Sometimes, when you say that stuff, it feels like you're inside my head and can see my thoughts."

"It's because I get it, Roni. I freaking *get it.*"

"I'm not ready for something new."

"I totally understand." And I already know I'm going to wait for her to be ready for whatever this could be. All it took was ten more minutes with her to convince me that I don't want to go looking for lightning anywhere else. Not when she's around.

"I shouldn't be holding your hand."

"Does it bring you comfort?"

"Yeah."

"Then don't let go."

She holds on all the way to the White House, where she's forced to let go so we can get out of the car to go to work.

"Thank you for the ride and for breakfast. I'll buy tomorrow."

"No, you won't."

"Yes, I will!"

"No, you won't. Text me when you're ready to go home. If I can break free, I'll give you a ride."

"I can get myself home."

"I know that, but why take the Metro when you can ride in heated seats with a new friend?"

"You drive a hard bargain, Kavanaugh."

"Have a good day, Connolly."

"You, too, and thanks again for the ride and the breakfast."

"My pleasure."

We're about to part company, her to go to the East Wing and me to go to the West Wing, when Sam appears in the foyer, seeming startled to see us together.

"Children," she says in a teasing tone as her eyes dart between us. "What's going on?"

"Nothing, Mom." I leave them with a grin and head to work.

Best ride to work ever.

Roni

"HOLY BOMBSHELL, BATMAN," Sam says after Derek walks away. "I haven't seen him smile like that in a very long time." She's wearing a plum-colored top and black dress pants, and her dark blonde hair has been straightened into waves that fall to her shoulders.

"He's very nice."

"Yes, he is." She uses her shrewd detective stare to try to see inside me to get to the real story. "Quit looking at me like that." And yes, I am talking to the first lady of the United States that way. But right now, she's not the first lady, she's my friend, and I need one.

She takes me by the arm and steers me toward a staircase carpeted in bright red. "Come with me."

"Where are we going?"

"Upstairs."

"Don't you have to go to work?"

"Yep, but it can wait."

Anyone who knows her even a little knows her work doesn't wait for anything, so I'm honored that she's giving me some time when she has more important things to do. We end up in a sitting room in the residence. "Wow, this is really nice." I put my cup of hot chocolate and the bag that presumably contains a cinnamon roll on a coffee table and sit on the sofa.

She sits next to me. "It's amazing, but I don't want to talk about the residence. I want to talk about you. And Derek."

"There is no me and Derek." The statement sounds weak, even to me. If I want her to believe that's true—hell, if I want *myself* to believe that's true—I need to be more convincing. "There can't be anything like that. Not now, anyway."

"But do you *want* it to be something?"

"I can't think about that, Sam. Patrick has only been gone for three months. It wouldn't be right to be thinking about someone else. Not yet." The tears that fill my eyes infuriate me. I'm so sick of crying. I've cried more since Patrick died than in my entire life beforehand.

Sam hands me a tissue. "I haven't been where you are, and I pray to God every day that I never will be. My heart aches for you, Roni, for Patrick, for everyone who loved him. It's so incredibly unfair that he was taken so suddenly from you."

"Thank you. It is so unfair."

"I've only known you without him, but I don't need to see you with him to feel your love for him. It's so much a part of who you are, who you'll always be."

Her words are so sweet and kind and exactly what I needed to hear.

"That said," she adds with a small smile, "you have a very long life to live, and you should be free to feel and do whatever makes you happy or provides you comfort. As the first lady of the United States, I give you permission to be happy, Roni."

I laugh through my tears as I lean into the one-armed hug she gives me.

"I'm so, so sorry you're going through such a rough time, but seeing you becoming friends with our beloved Derek makes me happier than anything has in a long time. And you should know, I used to hate when my world and Nick's would collide, like it did when Gonzo and Christina got together or Terry and Lindsey— his people dating my people. Cringe."

She's nothing if not irreverent and funny.

"But you and Derek... If those two worlds collided, no one would be happier about that than I would be. I just want you to know that."

"You're very sweet to say so, but there's no colliding going on. Just a friendship borne out of mutual understanding of tragic loss."

"Which is lovely, and I'm so glad you both have that kind of support."

"It's mostly been him supporting me so far."

"I'm sure it helps him to pay forward the things he's learned, having been on the journey longer than you."

"Maybe."

"Roni, I've known him well for more than two years, and in all the dreadful months since he lost Vic, I've never seen him look the way he did this morning, except for when he's with Maeve. Don't think you aren't helping him, too."

"What would people say if I started hanging out with someone new a few months after Patrick died?"

"Who gives a crap what people say?"

"Um, well, everyone does, except for you, of course."

"You can't care about that shit, Roni. You need to live your life in a way that makes sense to you. As long as you aren't hurting anyone else, you should do what feels good to you."

"It would hurt Patrick's parents if I dated someone new."

"Would it, though? I assume they loved you as much as he did."

"We've always had a nice relationship, and they've been lovely to me since he died."

"Then I feel pretty confident they'd tell you the same thing I am—do what feels good to you, and don't worry about what other people say."

"Last night, we went for a drink after we attended a meeting for the Wild Widows—"

"Wait. What? The Wild Widows? That's a thing?"

Laughing at the stunned face she makes, I tell her, "It's a group for young widows with only one rule for members—we have to be open to the possibility of falling in love again."

"Oh, that's incredible," she says on a deep sigh. "I love that such a thing exists."

"It's an amazing group made up of such strong, resilient people. Anyway, Derek and I went for a drink after the meeting, and I saw my sister's in-laws there. They were shocked to see me with him, even though I told them we were friends."

"It's really hard to not care what other people think of you and your choices, Roni, but you simply can't let people who've never suffered through what you have make you feel that anything you do is wrong."

"I want to be you when I grow up. You're such a badass."

"So are you. Everyone who knows you probably admires the

way you've handled such a devastating loss. That makes you the baddest of badasses."

"Is 'baddest' a word?"

Snorting out a laugh, she says, "If it isn't, it should be, with your name next to it."

"Thank you for this. It helps."

"I wish there was more I could do for you."

"Are you *kidding*? You've given me a job that's made me the envy of everyone I know, and you're sitting here with me in the *residence* of the *White House* when we're both supposed to be at work. You're the best shit friend I've ever had."

We share a laugh that makes me feel infinitely better than I did before she brought me up to the private area she shares with her family.

While we have this moment, I want to tell her about the baby. "There's something else I should probably tell you..."

"What's that?"

"Well, it seems that I'm pregnant."

"Oh, Roni. That's amazing news. Right?"

"Yes, of course it is. I'm thrilled and sad and, you know, generally a disastrous mess over it. But I get that it's a tremendous gift to have part of Patrick living on in our child, even if I'm scared shitless of single parenthood."

She hugs me tightly. "You'll be a wonderful mother. I have no doubt about that."

"I'm glad you don't."

"Are you feeling okay?"

"I'm better than I was. I'd assumed the nonstop nausea was a side effect of widowhood, but I found out otherwise right before Christmas."

"I want you to let me know if there's anything at all we can do to support you through this. After the baby is born, you can bring him or her to work. I'm sure Shelby would be happy to share her nanny with you. They're on the third floor when Shelby is here."

"You're like my fairy godmother," I say, my eyes filling, "fixing everything for me."

"Nah, I'm just a friend doing what any friend would do for another."

"Not just any friend. An extraordinary one. I hate to say I got lucky in any way the day Patrick died, because that would be morbid, but I'm thankful to have you in my life."

"Likewise. And I'm just saying... Derek certainly understands single parenthood if you need someone to talk to about it."

I roll my eyes at her shameless matchmaking. "Duly noted." I take a long look around at the beautiful room. "I can't believe you live here."

"How do you think I feel? Want to see the rest of the residence?"

"Is that a yes-or-no question?"

Laughing, she helps me up and links her arm through mine as she gives me a guided tour of the residence. By the time we head downstairs, I'm half an hour late for work, but since I was with the boss, I hope that won't be held against me.

Sam walks me to the East Wing offices and pops her head into Lilia's office. "I waylaid Roni on the way in, so don't dock her for being late."

"We'll let it slide this one time," Lilia replies, her dark eyes alight with amusement.

"I've got to get to my day job," Sam says. "I'll check in with you ladies later on."

"Have a good day, Mom," Lilia says.

"You, too."

After Sam walks away, Lilia gestures for me to come into her office. "Everything okay?"

"Yes, of course. I just have to say how much I adore our boss, however. She's the best."

"She really is. I feel very blessed to not only work for her, but to have her as a friend."

"Same." I take a sip of my hot chocolate, which isn't so hot anymore, but it still tastes good. "What's on our docket for today?"

We spend the next half hour sorting through yet another massive stack of interview and speaking requests that've come in

141

for Sam. Because her time is at such a premium, we once again narrow it down to a few that we think will best suit her. Lilia asks me to compose an email that outlines what we've come up with to send to Sam for her thoughts.

The day passes in a flurry of activity, meetings and planning. The German chancellor is coming to the White House in two weeks, and the president and first lady are hosting their first state dinner. Lilia and I meet with Shelby Hill, the social secretary, to go over the details of that event and the various demands that will be required of the first lady while the chancellor and his wife are in town.

My favorite meeting of the day happens at four o'clock, when Scotty Cappuano and his dog, Skippy, come to the office to, as he puts it, "take a meeting."

He's a handsome fourteen-year-old adopted by Sam and Nick out of state custody in Virginia, after having met Nick during a campaign stop at the group home where he lived. Skippy is an adorable, full-of-energy golden retriever puppy.

"Ladies, I apologize in advance for anything she does while she's here," Scotty says. "She's incorrigible." Stopping, he glances at me and says, "Did I use that word right? It was one of our vocabulary words last year, but that was a lifetime ago."

"If you mean you can't do a thing with her, then yep, you used it right."

"Excellent," he says, grinning. He has dark hair and eyes and bears a faint resemblance to Nick. The first time I met him, I noticed how he's affected his father's expressions and mannerisms, which is so sweet. "My mom tells me you guys can help me deal with her exploding social media accounts. Dad says I'm going to start an international incident if I make the wrong kind of comment there, so I need all the help I can get. Not to mention the mail. She gets more than my dad does!"

"We heard that," Lilia says. "Let's see what we can do to help you manage that."

We spend a delightful hour with Scotty and Skippy, who is indeed incorrigible, but so damn cute, too. Lilia and I are both covered in blonde dog hair by the time Scotty says he must head upstairs to the residence so he can get a jump on his dreaded algebra homework.

Before he leaves, he solemnly shakes hands with both of us. "Thank you so much for being willing to help us."

"It's a pleasure," I tell him, and I mean it. Running an Instagram account for the first dog sounds like the most fun anyone could ever have at a job. "I'll be in touch with some thoughts about how we can show the two of you together, and with the twins, as we go forward. People love the narrative of a boy and his first dog."

"Especially a boy who was adopted himself," Scotty says.

"Absolutely."

"Excellent. You know where to find us if you need me and the superstar."

"Good luck with the algebra," I tell him.

He scowls as he heads for the door to our suite. "My dad is going to outlaw it."

"What an awesome kid," I say to Lilia after he leaves.

"He really is. We all adore him, and Skippy is beyond cute. I love how he named her for Sam's late dad."

"It's all so sweet. Running that account is going to be a blast."

"I agree, but we'd better see about a lint brush for the office."

I crack up laughing and head back to my own office. With my day winding down, I take a second to text my parents, Pen and Rebecca about dinner on Saturday night. I end the message with, *I'm looking forward to hosting you guys, and don't worry about bringing anything.*

I no sooner send that message than my phone vibrates with a text from Derek. *Can you bust loose yet? I'm heading home soon.*

Since the temperature is expected to dip into single digits tonight, I decide to take him and his heated seats up on the offer of a ride home. *Meet you in the foyer in ten?*

I'll be there.

The quickening of excitement that occurs when he texts those three little words has me on guard against the crush I feel forming. While I know there's nothing wrong with that, it still seems wrong to me.

Don't be ridiculous, Ron. I hear Patrick's voice as if he's right next to me. I stand perfectly still, hoping he'll have more to say. *I loved you so much. You know that. And everyone knows how much you loved me.* My eyes dart around the room, a place Patrick has never been. Where's it coming from? *I want you to be happy. You do whatever it takes to be happy, you hear me?*

Tears slide down my cheeks, but I still don't move, hoping there might be more. I have no idea how long I stand there, barely breathing, waiting for something that doesn't come.

Fourteen

Roni

Derek appears in the doorway to my office. "Hey, did you get sucked into something?" He takes a closer look, sees my tears and comes in, closing the door. "What happened?"

I've only recently managed to convince him I'm not crazy. How can I share this with him or anyone?

"Roni? Tell me what's wrong."

"I heard his voice. Patrick's voice. It was like he was right here."

"Maybe he was."

The possibility of that breaks me wide open inside.

Derek rounds my desk and puts his arms around me, holding me close while I sob all over him. "Shhh, it's okay." He rubs my back with just the right amount of pressure to be comforting. "I believe they're always close by, keeping an eye on us from the other side of the veil."

"You do? Really?"

"Yes, of course. Where else would Victoria want to be but watching over Maeve and me? I'm sure your Patrick is the same. He wants to be wherever you are."

"His voice was so clear to me."

"That's a wonderful gift."

"Except I want more of it."

"I know." After another long moment of silence, he says, "Do you want to talk about what he had to say?"

"He said how much he loved me, how everyone knew I loved him, and I should do whatever it takes to be happy. He was quite insistent about that last part. He even called me Ron, which was one of his many names for me."

"It sounds like he really wanted you to know how he felt."

"Where would that have come from? I mean, it's not possible for it to have been him."

"How do we know that's not possible?"

"He's dead, Derek."

"I know, but how do we really know what happens after someone dies?"

"We don't, I guess."

"As long as we don't know for sure, anything is possible."

We're there for quite some time before I emerge from my grief state to realize my face is resting against his suit coat, and his arms are still around me. When I start to pull back, he releases me.

I wipe my face with the tissue I take from the box on my desk. "I'm sorry for the meltdown."

"Please don't apologize. There's no need for that."

"Thank you for... for understanding."

"I do."

"Have you ever heard Vic's voice like that?"

"No, I haven't, but I know what she would say if she were here. And I have proof of it in the letter she left for me. That letter set me free in so many ways."

"You're lucky to have that."

"And I know it. Widow groups often debate which is worse —the sudden death or the lingering disease. They're both horrible, but with the disease, at least you have warning that the loss is coming. The shock of what happened to us, of having the person we love the most ripped out of our lives suddenly and without warning... That's not something I'd wish on anyone."

"Me either."

"I hate to say it, but I have to get home. My nanny has class tonight."

"Oh gosh." I take a deep breath. "I'm so sorry."

His warm smile lights up his eyes. "You're not apologizing to me, remember?"

"In that case, then, I'll just say thank you for being there for me."

"I'm happy to be there for you."

We walk out together, and as he holds the passenger door for me, I wonder if I'm setting off a White House scandal by being seen with him.

"Will people be talking about the two widows coming and going together?"

"Let them talk. I don't give a flying fuck what anyone has to say about it, and you shouldn't either."

"Well, all righty then."

"I don't mean to discount your valid concerns." He waves to the Secret Service agent working the gate we drive through to leave the White House grounds. "It's just that when you've been through what we have, you stop giving a shit about what other people think of you. At least I have."

"I'm still working on building up that immunity."

"Understood. If you'd rather not be seen together at work, that's fine with me."

"I don't care about being seen together or people knowing we're friends. I'm just not sure I'm ready to be the target of work-place gossip."

"I'll shut down anything I hear. As the number two staffer in the building, people tend to do what I ask, so don't worry."

His no-nonsense protectiveness sends a jolt of awareness through me that has my full attention as he drives us home to Capitol Hill. The traffic is intense as always, and what should be a five-minute ride stretches into twenty minutes, but I enjoy every second of his heated seats and his company.

I respond to texts from my family asking what they can bring on Saturday with *absolutely nothing*.

"Do you want to have dinner with Maeve and me? I'm

making pasta with meatballs for her and shrimp for me. I've got plenty of both, and we'd love to have you join us."

I have no idea whether it's a good idea to encourage this friendship—or whatever it is—but all I know is I don't want to be alone tonight, and his invitation perks me up. "Sure, that'd be nice. Thanks for asking me."

"No problem. Do you want to stop at home first?"

"I'd love to change, but only if it won't make you late for your nanny."

"I've got time."

A few minutes later, he brings the car to a stop outside my building. "I'll be quick."

"I'll be here."

I dash upstairs and change into leggings and a sweater and look around for something I can take to contribute to dinner. The only thing I can find is a bottle of white wine that I hope he'll like. I grab my down parka out of the closet, put sheepskin-lined boots on in anticipation of the walk home and am back downstairs within five minutes.

"That was quick," he says as he pulls away from the curb.

"I told you I would be."

"My research has shown that the female version of quick often differs from the male version."

"Well, Patrick's research has shown that I was forever making him late for everything, which drove him bananas because he was super punctual and hated being late."

"I'm the same way, and Vic was like you. I'd be in the car for ten minutes before she'd come breezing out like she had all the time in the world to get where she was going."

"Maybe I'm getting better about that. Five minutes in and out just now."

"I'm impressed."

"What else did she do that you didn't like?"

"She was secretive about her past. At the time, I figured it was painful for her to think about losing her parents so young, but later I realized she was intentionally secretive. What about you? What else did he do that you didn't like?"

"He was messy. Always leaving his crap around. He'd come in from playing basketball, softball or touch football and leave his dirty shoes in the living room and his equipment right inside the door for *days* until I had to say something about it. I'm a neatnik, so that drove me crazy."

"Did he mind when you said something about it?"

"Oh, no, never. He was always so good-natured. He'd just say, 'Whoops, sorry, babe. Keep reminding me. I'll grow up eventually.'" I'm sad that he never got the chance to finish growing up. "I used to chalk his messiness up to his brilliance. Like there wasn't enough space in his brain for all the stuff he knew how to do and to clean up, too. I met a lot of people he worked with after he died, and they all said the same thing—smartest guy they'd ever met."

"That must've been nice to hear."

"It was, but I already knew it. I used to be intimidated sometimes by how smart he was about *everything*."

"I was intimidated by Vic's easy way with people. She was so warm and friendly. You felt like you'd known her forever after a few minutes with her."

"You're like that, too."

"I never used to be. I was much more remote and closed off to new people than I am since she died, and I found out quickly that keeping myself closed off was going to make for a very lonely existence."

"So you feel like you've changed a lot since you lost her?"

"I doubt she'd recognize the person I am now."

I have so many questions about what he means by that, but we've arrived at his house, so I don't get the chance to ask. He parks the SUV in a driveway that makes me envious. I'd love to have a driveway. I follow him to the back door that opens into a mudroom, where I kick off my boots and hang my coat on one of the open hooks.

"Come in," he says, leading the way into the kitchen, where we're greeted by the shriek of a little girl happy to see her daddy after a long day apart.

She runs to him, and he picks her up, giving her a tight hug that makes her squeak.

"How's my baby girl?"

"Good," she says, glancing at me over his shoulder.

I waggle my fingers at her, and she hides her face in the crook of his neck.

"Say hi to my friend Roni."

Maeve raises her head and says, "Hi," before burying her face again.

"Patrice, this is Roni. Roni, Patrice."

The nanny is in her early twenties, blonde, pretty and in a big hurry.

"Hey," I say, "nice to meet you."

"You, too," Patrice says while managing to avoid looking at me. "I have to run to class."

"Say bye-bye to Patrice," Derek says.

"Bye-bye."

"See you tomorrow, pumpkin," Patrice says as she hustles out of there.

"Thanks, Patrice," Derek calls after her as he puts down Maeve.

She runs off to play in an adjoining room.

"Was it something I said?" I ask Derek after the door slams shut behind Patrice.

He pulls a pained expression. "She's been different since I had to make it clear that our relationship is never going to be personal."

"Yikes."

"Maeve adores her and vice versa, and I pay her really well, so thankfully, she didn't quit, but ugh... Messy."

"Does she think that I'm... That we're... Uh..."

"Don't worry about that. I have a right to bring friends home." As he says that, he pulls off his tie and releases the top two buttons on his dress shirt. "Ah, that's always such a relief." He tosses the tie over a kitchen chair. "What're you doing, Maeve?"

His daughter comes dashing into the kitchen, arms laden with stuffed animals.

"Why don't you introduce Roni to your friends while I make dinner?"

I sit right on the kitchen floor and am treated to a delightful recitation of each animal's name, some of which are words Maeve has clearly made up, because I've never heard them before. She speaks with a combination of actual words and gibberish, but I can understand most of what she's trying to tell me.

"So this guy is that guy's daddy?" I ask her, holding up a bunny and a bear.

She nods, her expression serious. "His mommy go to heben."

"Ah, I see." I glance at Derek in time to see his jaw tighten with tension as he stirs something on the stove.

Maeve moves right on past the moment as if it was nothing to her, which is a bit of a relief, actually. I shudder to think of this precious child's mother being murdered and her being abducted. I want to put my arms around her and hug her tightly, but since I don't want to frighten her, I resist that urge.

"Let's wash your hands for dinner, Miss Priss," Derek says, lifting her off the floor and hurling her over his shoulder with a kind of practiced ease that impresses me. He's great with her, and she obviously adores him. While I listen to their chatter in the bathroom, I arrange the stuffed animals in the corner of the kitchen.

Maeve lights up with a smile when she sees where I've put her babies.

Derek puts her into the high chair, ties a plastic bib around her neck and brings her dinner to her on a special plate that has sections that he's filled with spiral pasta with no sauce, cut up meatball and peaches. He tops off the presentation with a sippy cup full of milk.

"Now to cook for the adults," he says, drizzling olive oil into a pan and adding precut peppers and onions. When they've cooked some, he adds shrimp.

"Do you actually prep for meals ahead of time?"

"I do it on Sundays for the whole week."

"That's incredibly impressive."

He shrugs off the compliment. "It's out of necessity. She's ready to eat the minute I come home, so by having things prepared ahead of time, I save myself from dinnertime melt-downs while she waits for me to cook. Trust me, I've learned every parenting lesson the hard way."

"You're like the Yoda of single dads."

"Oh my God, please," he says, laughing. "I'm so far from that, it's not even funny." He glances over at Maeve. "Are you eating or playing?"

"Eating," she replies with a big grin.

When he smiles at her, I melt on the inside.

He's sweet, kind, thoughtful, compassionate, smart, successful and obviously a wonderful father. If I'm not careful, my low-burn crush is going to turn into a wildfire I'm not ready for.

The dinner he serves to me is simple but delicious. He's tossed the shrimp, onions and peppers over linguine with a light butter sauce.

He retrieves the parmesan cheese from the fridge and puts it on the table next to me. "That's the secret ingredient."

"Ah, gotcha." I shake some on top of my food and take a bite. "Wow, that's really good."

Derek brings his plate and a glass of ice water for me to the table.

"I brought wine for you," I suddenly recall. "I left it in the mudroom."

"I'll grab it."

He brings a wineglass and corkscrew with him when he finally sits at the table.

"Maeve done."

"Maeve can wait until Daddy eats to get up."

"No."

"Yes."

"No."

"That's her all-time favorite word."

He manages to take a few bites before she starts to seriously fuss about getting out of her seat.

"Sorry, this is her cranky time of day. It's almost bedtime."

"No need to apologize. I get cranky at bedtime, too." The words are no sooner out of my mouth than I'm wondering if I should've said them. It's so strange to be with someone new, even if he's just a new friend, and have to worry about everything I say and do. Although, with Derek, I don't worry too much.

He gets up to fix her a tiny bowl of ice cream and brings it to her, buying himself a few more minutes to wolf down his dinner.

"Straight to the tub with you, my grubby little girl," he says when he finally lifts her from the high chair. "We'll be quick."

"Take your time. I'll clean up."

"Don't worry about it. I can do it later."

"I've got it."

"Say night-night to Roni."

"Night," Maeve says, popping her thumb in her mouth, her eyes heavy and ready for sleep.

"I'll be back in a few."

He carries her upstairs, the sound of his chatter and her giggles following them. As I clean up the kitchen, I can hear water running and more happy conversation between the two of them. I wasn't kidding before when I told him I'm super impressed with how good he is with Maeve and how efficiently he runs their lives. I try to picture Patrick doing what Derek does, and I can't. For all his smarts and his endless capabilities, I don't think he would've handled single fatherhood as smoothly as Derek seems to. Although, I'm sure he didn't get to where he is now overnight.

I find storage containers for the leftovers, load the dishwasher, scrub the pans and wipe up the countertop, stove, table and high chair.

When he comes back downstairs a few minutes after I finish, his eyes widen with surprise. "Wow, thanks. You really didn't have to do all that."

"You didn't have to make me dinner."

"I was happy to do it."

"Likewise. And by the way, your daughter is adorable."

"She really is. I'm not at all objective. She's the cutest baby girl ever."

"She's tied for first place with my nieces."

"I'll allow that." He pours himself another glass of wine. "She likes you."

"How do you know?"

"She told me you're her new friend."

"Aw, that's so sweet. I'm happy to be her new friend."

He brings his wine and sits next to me at the table. "It's nice to have someone to talk to after she goes to bed. The nights are long and quiet."

"It's a big adjustment to go from living with your spouse to living alone or with a small child."

"Sure is."

"You probably can't see it because it's your normal routine, but you really are slaying the single-father gig."

"You think so?"

"Hell yes. Anyone would think so. You *meal-prep* on the weekends, Derek."

He laughs. "Out of pure necessity. Maeve got her mother's propensity for extreme crankiness when she's hangry, as Vic called it. By the time I get home from work, she's on the brink of meltdown. I quickly discovered that planning ahead makes for more peaceful evenings."

"Hella impressive."

"I do laundry, too," he says with a boyish grin as he props his head on an upturned hand. "I can even iron if I have to."

I fan my face dramatically. "You're one hell of a catch, Kavanaugh."

"That's what my mom says, too, but she kinda has to."

"No, she doesn't. She says it because it's true."

His expression becomes more serious. "I want Vic to be proud of me."

"She's up there bragging to all the other moms about how great her man is at being a single dad."

"You think so?"

154

"Oh, for sure."

"When she was here... I spent too much time at work because I thought that was what I was supposed to do. She took care of Maeve and the stuff at home, and I worked. A lot. I regret that now. I'm deputy chief of staff to the president. The coolest job of anyone I know, and it wasn't enough. I had to put in the hours to prove myself or some such bullshit. I don't do that anymore. I leave on time these days. I had to find out the hard way that the most important things in life were right here in this house."

"I'm sure Victoria would say you were a wonderful husband and father."

"Vic never said a bad word about me. I found that out from her friends after she died. They told me that when they would launch into husband bashing, she never participated."

"There you have it."

"Just because she didn't trash me to her friends doesn't mean I couldn't have been a better husband and father. If I ever get married again, I'm going to do it differently."

"How so?"

"I'm going to be around more, for one thing. There's no job worth sacrificing time with your family. In this dog-eat-dog town, it's easy to get so caught up in the rat race that you can't see the forest for the trees. I hate that it took losing Vic and nearly losing Maeve, too, for me to wake up to what mattered."

"You knew what mattered before that, Derek. You just value it more now."

"Yeah, I guess so." He glances toward the stove area. "She was there, on the floor, when I came in from a weekend at Camp David with Nelson and his team."

"I can't begin to imagine what that was like for you."

"Worst thing I've ever seen."

"How do you stand to stay here after that?"

"It's Maeve's home. I didn't want to disrupt her life any more than it already was by moving on top of everything else. I redecorated the kitchen and our bedroom. But it took me a full year not to see her there every time I walk into this room and not to recall my frantic search for Maeve."

I reach out to him and curl my hand around his arm, wishing there was more I could do to comfort him.

"Anyway," he says, releasing a long breath. "Enough about that. Not sure why I even brought it up."

"Because you wanted me to know what happened and how you feel about it."

He stares at me, his expression wistful, as if he sees something he can't have. "Yeah, I did want you to know."

"I should, um, get going home."

"Let me get an Uber for you."

"It's two blocks. I can walk."

"I don't want you to walk, Roni. It's cold and dark, and I'd feel better if you let me get you an Uber."

"I can get my own Uber."

"I'll do it."

Because it seems to matter so much to him, I nod and pull my hand back from his arm so he can get his phone out to summon the car.

"Thank you for dinner and for letting me spend time with Maeve. She's delightful."

"Thanks for coming. I'm glad you got to meet her."

When the car is a minute away, I go into the mudroom to put on my boots and coat.

Derek walks me out to greet the car and hands the driver a twenty. "I know it's a short ride, but I appreciate you getting my friend home safe."

"Thanks, man," the driver says, pocketing the bill.

"Thanks again for dinner."

"Thanks for the company. Pick you up at seven thirty?"

"Only if I can get breakfast."

He gives me a side-eye like he's going to object.

I give him my most mulish expression.

"Fine."

"Fine."

He holds the back door for me. "Text me to let me know you got home."

"I will." Neither of us will ever again take simple safety for granted. "See you in the morning."

"See you then."

He waves as the car drives off, and when I look back, I see that he's still there, watching us drive away.

"Nice guy you got there," the driver says, glancing at me in the mirror.

"Oh, he's not... We're not..." *Shut up, Roni.* After spending the evening with him and his daughter, I'm more conflicted than ever about what exactly he is to me. We've fallen into this easy routine of friendship, commiseration, empathy, sympathy and the sort of deep conversations that are the hallmark of any enduring friendship.

But that's all it is, or so I tell myself as I arrive at my building, thank the driver and head inside. Once I'm in my apartment, I text Derek. *I'm home. Thanks again for dinner and a lovely evening.*

He writes right back. *Entirely my pleasure. Sleep well.*

You, too.

I'm wound up about him and what it all means. Because it's only nine thirty, I reach out to Iris. *Are you awake?*

I am. You want to call?

Yes, please...

Fifteen

Roni

I make the call, and she answers on the first ring. "What's wrong?"

"Ugh, nothing. It's just that I've made a new *friend*, I have no idea what any of it means, and I'm spinning."

"Is it Derek?"

I'm dumbfounded. "How do you know that?"

"A few of us noticed a spark or two flying between you guys."

"No! There're no sparks flying."

"None at all?"

"Iris!"

She laughs. "What?"

"I can't have sparks with another guy so soon after losing the love of my life."

"You ready for some tough love?"

"I'm not sure..."

"Well, here it is anyway. Have you considered the possibility that Patrick might be your first love and that you haven't met the love of your life yet? Or you've met him, and you don't know yet that he's going to be your great love?"

"Stop. I can't hear that. Patrick was my great love."

"Patrick is gone, sweetie." She says that in the gentlest

possible tone, but it's devastating nonetheless. "And you've got a great big, long life to live without him."

"I don't want to live without him."

"I know." After a long pause, she says, "If I can just add... I've gotten to know Derek fairly well, and he's a truly wonderful man, not to mention handsome as can be."

"Is he? I hadn't noticed that."

Iris howls with laughter. "Now you're just lying, girl."

"Is it weird that I have no problem telling you about this... whatever it is... with Derek, but I'd be mortified to tell my family or friends out of fear they wouldn't understand it?"

"It's not weird at all. You're telling someone who's been where you are and who truly gets the conflict that comes with developing feelings for someone who isn't your late spouse."

"I don't have *feelings* for him. I just like being with him."

"Isn't that how these things begin?"

"Are you trying to piss me off?"

"Nope," she says, laughing again. "I'm just trying to make you see that whatever you're feeling is normal. You may not be ready to see that yet, but it is normal."

"Nothing is normal anymore."

"It's the new normal."

"I don't like the new normal."

"None of us do, sweetie. But what choice do we have but to embrace what *is* while honoring what *was*?"

The question is so profoundly moving that it takes my breath away for a full minute.

"Roni? Are you there?"

"I'm here. What you said..."

"It's the crux of our dilemma as widows."

"I'm going to write that down."

"I'm honored that you want to remember something I said."

"I do want to remember it."

"While you're busy remembering it, how about you live it, too? Embrace whatever this is with Derek while continuing to honor Patrick with every breath you take."

"You're like a widow whisperer."

"Haha, whatever you say. I'm all about every one of us doing whatever we can to move forward with hope and optimism."

"I want to do that. I really do."

"Then do it, Roni. Do it with your whole heart and soul and with your arms wide open to anything that might come your way. Anyone who matters knows you would've been with Patrick for the rest of your life if he hadn't been so cruelly taken from you. Please don't feel like you have to explain *anything* you do next to *anyone*."

"I feel like I say thank you every other minute lately."

"You're welcome, and if you're saying thank you a lot, it's because you're surrounded by people who want to help."

"And I'm grateful for every one of you. How are things with you?"

"I'm having a somewhat chaotic week with two of my kids sick with strep throat as of this afternoon, and the countdown on to the third one getting it."

"Ack, that's awful. Is there anything I can do for you?"

"No, thanks. I'm fine. I got a grocery delivery yesterday. We're hunkering down until the storm passes. I just hope I didn't expose you guys to the crud when you were here last night."

"I'm sure we'll be fine."

"I sure hope so."

"I'll check on you tomorrow to see if there's anything you need," I tell her.

"You're a sweetheart. Thanks."

"Please. I appreciate you more than you'll ever know."

We say good night, and I go into the bathroom to shower. As I'm blow-drying my hair, I think about what she said about embracing what is while honoring what was. That's what it's all about now, I suppose. I can be friends with Derek without that friendship taking anything away from the love I'll always have for Patrick.

The widows I've met so far are full of hard-earned wisdom and so willing to share what they've learned with those of us just beginning this journey.

I put on my warmest flannel pajamas and get into bed,

glancing as I always do at Patrick's side of our bed and wishing with all my heart that I could go back to that last night with him. I'd plead with him to call in sick, to stay home with me, to not be walking on that sidewalk at the exact wrong moment.

Turning to face his side of the bed, I reach for him and find only the empty space he used to occupy so fully.

Eventually, I drift off to sleep, and as I do, my last thoughts are of Derek.

I WAKE to a text from him. *Ugh, I'm freaking SICK with a crazy sore throat and fever. Just texted Terry to let him know I won't be in today.*

Oh crap, I respond. *I talked to Iris last night, and two of her kids have strep.*

Greatttttt... At least I know where it came from.

Is Maeve okay?

So far so good, but I won't be surprised if she gets it, too. It pains me to keep her home today bc I feel like SHIT, but I can't send her to daycare when she's been exposed to this.

What can I do for you?

We're fine. Got an appointment at my primary care doc at noon.

I'll check on you later.

Hope you don't get it. He adds the fingers-crossed emoji.

Crap, I hope I don't get it either. As I schlep my way to work on the Metro, I miss Derek's heated seats and his company more than I probably should.

Lilia and I spend the morning strategizing social media posts for Sam to make on her FLOTUS accounts, supporting issues she's passionate about, such as law enforcement, learning issues, infertility and spinal cord research in honor of her late father, who was a quadriplegic after being shot on the job.

The goal of our efforts is to show the world she's an active, engaged first lady even as she holds a full-time job outside the White House.

At one thirty, I send a text to Derek. *How are you feeling? What did the doc say?*

I feel like death, and it's strep. He gave me an antibiotic. My mom came and got Maeve *THANK GOD* even if I feel guilty about exposing them.

So sorry you feel so lousy. Can I bring you anything after work?

No, I'm good, and I don't want you exposed any further even if I'd love to see you.

My heart does this weird little boogie skip when he says he'd love to see me. *I hope you feel better soon. I'll check on you later.*

Will look forward to that.

Again with the little jolt to my battered heart. *Get some rest!*

That's about all I feel like doing.

I feel so bad for him and wish there was something I could do for him. On the Metro home from work, I decide there is something I can do. I pop into a pharmacy near my house and pick up throat lozenges and spray, a couple of magazines and some Popsicles and ice cream. I spend an inordinate amount of time trying to decide if he's a Chunky Monkey or Cherry Garcia kind of guy. I grab one of each and head for the checkout.

As I walk the short distance to his house, I'm elated in a way I haven't been in months. And I'm not even going to get to see Derek.

I hang the bag from the store on his back door and text him. *Are you awake? Brought you a care package that requires refrigeration.*

Be right down.

Only out of concern for my unborn child do I take a step back from his stoop to keep some distance between us when that's the last thing I want to do.

He comes to the door, and I immediately note that his hair is standing on end, his jaw is covered with whiskers, and he in no way resembles the pressed, polished work-day professional I've come to know. If possible, he's even handsomer when he's disheveled.

He takes a look inside the bag. "This is very nice of you."

Shrugging, I say, "I wish I could do more. Are you feeling any better?"

"A tiny bit. My throat is the worst. Like I'm swallowing razor blades."

"Ouch."

"Sucks."

"I won't keep you. Just wanted to say hi."

"I'm so glad you did. You're feeling okay, right?"

"So far." I hold up crossed fingers.

"I hope you stay that way. This is the worst." He pauses, seeming to catch himself. "Well, we both know it can be worse than this, but it's damned unpleasant. My mom says I haven't had this since I was in fifth grade, and funnily enough, I remember that."

"I used to be prone to it when I was a kid. If it was anywhere near me, I got it."

"I sure hope you've outgrown that."

"Me, too. Call me if you need anything?"

"I will. Thanks again for this. You got my favorite."

"Which one?"

"Cherry Garcia for the win."

I pump my fist into the air. "Yes! The Chunky Monkey is my favorite."

"Good to know."

An actual shiver goes through me when he says that. "All right, mister. Back to bed with you. Talk to you later."

"Thanks again, Roni. I really appreciate this."

"It's payback for your heated seats."

Smiling, he waves as I turn to leave. I feel him watching me until I'm out of sight, which is when I release the deep breath I've been holding. I've got a red-hot crush on Derek Kavanaugh three short months after my husband died.

I'm going straight to hell, but what a way to go.

Derek

I'M TOTALLY DIGGING Roni Connolly, and it feels better than anything has in a very long time. It was so sweet of her to bring me a care package. The orange-flavored throat lozenges she brought are awesome and give me the first bit of relief I've had all day.

Naturally, I text her to tell her that. *These throat lozenges are magic.*

Yay! So glad to hear they're helping.

I can actually swallow after a very long day of resenting my own spit.

LOL, it's the little things, right?

Definitely. Did I miss anything at the WH today?

Didn't hear much from the West Wing today. We worked on Sam's social media and the planning for some appearances and interviews.

I hope she can juggle all that on top of her day gig.

We're trying to keep it as manageable as possible for her. I've been spending an hour or two a day dealing with Skippy the dog's Instagram account!

How much is she paying you for that?

She pays in dog biscuits. I told her I like the chocolate ones.

I send the laughing and dog emojis. *It sure is cool to have one of my best friends and his wife as our new POTUS and FLOTUS. They're awesome people, and our country is so lucky to have them. Nick may be young, but he's smart, savvy and really wants to make a difference.*

Has he said any more about whether he'll run for reelection?

As of right now, the answer is no. He doesn't want to be away from his family to campaign.

I don't blame him. What a grind that must be.

It is. I did it with Nelson the first time around, and it was brutal. Nonstop travel, events, demands. And it goes on for months.

Ugh, that sounds awful.

It is, and I'm with Nick. I don't want to be away from Maeve like that, which was why I sat out the traveling for Nelson's most recent reelection campaign.

Did you know about the affair? The former president's affair with an ex-campaign staffer had come to light shortly before the woman was murdered, plunging the Nelson administration into yet another scandal.

The senior staff suspected something was going on... It was all so sordid, especially because we knew his wife was undergoing cancer treatment at the time. It was infuriating to those of us who truly adored her.

She seems like a lovely person.

She's the best, and I feel so bad for her that he died when they were estranged. Ah, enough about that. Tell me more about you— and I'd call you if it didn't hurt to talk.

Let's see... I grew up in Alexandria, went to UVA, met Patrick, moved to the District for work after college, lived together for years before bowing to parental pressure to tie the knot.

Why do parents care so much about that?

No idea. We were happy to stay as we were, but I do have to say... The wedding and the vows and all that... It made something great even better, but don't ever tell my mom (or his) that I said that.

Haha, your secret is safe with me.

What about you? How did you meet Vic? Or is that a painful subject?

It's not as painful to think about as it used to be... We met at the gym. Nick, Andy and Harry used to work out with me, and they were the ones who had to clue me in that she was into me. I thought she was a goddess. I was afraid to even talk to her. LOL

Aw, that's so cute.

I was a mess. They had to shove me toward her before I could work up the nerve to talk to her. Later, when I found out the truth about her and why she happened to show up at my gym... I questioned everything. But I have her letter, and that's the truth I hold on to.

I can't imagine how much worse all that made losing her.

It was brutal, but enough about the sad stuff. We've both had enough of that.

Yes, we have.

Tell me something else about you.

You want to hear a confession?

Uh, yeah?!?

I feel kind of guilty.

About?

Talking to you this way. (Now I'm going to hide in the closet because I feel so stupid.)

Aw, don't feel guilty or stupid. This stuff is so hard for people like us. We all struggle with it.

"This stuff." What is "this stuff" to you?

Does it need a label? Can't we just be friends and enjoy spending time together without guilt or judgment from ourselves when we'll get enough of that from others?

We can. It's just that... I'm not ready for it to be anything more than friends.

I know that, Roni. Even if you freaked me out by stalking me at first (haha), I'm so happy we've become friends. I don't want you to worry about anything.

Thank you for understanding.

I do. I get it, and I mean it when I say don't worry. Things will work out the way they're meant to, and we've both had enough heartache to have earned the right to be happy in whatever way we can.

She gives that text a thumbs-up. *I'm happy we've become friends, too. I should let you get some sleep. Talk to you tomorrow?*

Sounds good. Thanks for keeping me company.

Anytime.

Sleep well.

You, too.

Sixteen

Roni

For a long time after I put down my phone, I think about Derek and how nice he is, how normal—which, according to my single friends, isn't as easy to find as one might think—and how great it is to be able to talk to someone who understands the many pitfalls of widow life. Anything I'm dealing with, he's already experienced, and there's comfort in that.

When I'm brushing my teeth, I notice my throat feels funny. "Ugh, do not do this to me," I tell my reflection in the mirror. "I have no time for this, so you can just skip right over me and go give your plague to someone else."

I find vitamin C in Patrick's jammed medicine cabinet, which is a reminder of something else I need to deal with, and take two, hoping it will stave off any potential sickness. I should've taken it the second I heard Derek was sick.

Crap, I really hope I don't get it.

That turns out to be wishful thinking. I wake up at two in the morning in a blaze of heat so intense, I worry for a second that my apartment is on fire. The apartment isn't, but I am. I stumble from the bed, my head spinning and my stomach churning with nausea. Then I make the mistake of trying to swallow and instantly regret it.

Son of a bitch.

I find the thermometer and take my temperature. When it registers as one hundred and five, I figure the thing has to be broken. I take it again and get the same result. Shit, that's bad, and I'm so dizzy, I can barely remain standing.

All I can think about is the baby.

This can't be good for him. Or her. I sit on the bed, hoping that will keep my head from spinning. It doesn't. I'm scared. I'm not sure what, if anything, I can take for the fever, and I'm certain one-oh-five is dangerous. I've never had a fever anywhere close to that. I want to call my parents, but if I call in the middle of the night, they'll panic.

I find my phone in the damp bedclothes and open my messages. The first one I see is the recent message from Derek. Of all my friends and family, he lives the closest to me, so I text him. *Are you awake by any chance?*

I release a sigh of relief when I see him responding.

What's up?

I'm sick. Like, really sick. 105 fever. Scared. Do you think I should I call 911?

I'll come get you and take you to the ER.

No! You're sick, too. You don't have to do that!

Get ready. I'm coming. He texts again a few minutes later. *Can you get downstairs by yourself, or do you need help?*

I can do it.

Be there in two min.

When he pulls up outside, I'm waiting at the door.

He jumps out of the car and rushes up the stairs to the front door of my building to help me down the stairs.

"This is way above and beyond the call of new friendship."

"It's no problem. Hold on to me. I've got you." He helps me into the car and leans over me to put the seat belt on. "Christ, Roni, you're burning up."

"Worried about the baby."

"Just hang on. I'll get you to the ER in a few minutes."

I'm comforted by his assurances, his presence and, of course, his heated seats as I shiver from the fever. Everything hurts, especially my jaw from trying to control my chattering teeth.

Derek places his hand over mine. "You're going to be okay, and so will the baby."

"H-how do you know?"

"I just know it. Try not to worry."

The next thing I know, he's shaking me awake to tell me we've arrived at the George Washington University Hospital Emergency entrance. I really hope this isn't going to be an actual emergency.

Derek opens the passenger door, helps me out and keeps an arm around me as we walk inside. Thankfully, there are only a few people waiting at this time of night, or I guess it's morning.

"She's been exposed to strep, has a one-oh-five fever and is pregnant," Derek says to the triage nurse.

"Right this way," she says, leading me to a cubicle.

"I'm going to park," Derek says. "Be right back."

I'm incredibly thankful not to have to sit in a chair in the waiting room for God knows how long. The nurse helps to get me settled in a bed and brings in a warm blanket that is the best thing I've ever experienced.

My throat is so sore, I can barely swallow, and talking is incredibly painful, so I keep my words to a minimum. "Baby," I whisper.

"We're going to check you both," she says, patting my shoulder.

Relieved, I close my eyes and wake up again to a female doctor with a stethoscope leaning over me as monitors beep. Looking around, I find Derek leaning against the wall, looking pale and wan himself. I want to tell him to go home, but I suspect he won't leave until he hears I'm okay.

"We're going to put you on a fetal monitor, Roni," the doctor says, "and start an IV."

"You don't look so good either," the nurse says to Derek.

"I'm almost twenty-four hours on an antibiotic for the same thing."

"Have a seat." She gestures to the visitor chair. "Your wife is going to be here awhile."

"Oh, she's not... We're not..." He looks at me with wide eyes that would've made me laugh at any other time.

The nurse leaves the small room before he can set her straight.

Naturally, she assumed we're married because I'm still wearing my wedding rings, and he has the same thing I have. "Sorry," I whisper to him.

"Don't be. It's fine."

I have no idea how long we're there. I sleep for most of it, coming to only when the nurse starts the IV in the back of my hand, which hurts like hell.

Derek is there the whole time, holding my other hand and dozing in the chair as doctors and nurses come and go.

All I want to know is if the baby is okay, and when the fetal monitor records a strong heartbeat, I'm so relieved. I close my eyes tight against the instant rush of tears that slide down my cheeks anyway. I feel Derek wiping them away with a tissue, but my eyelids are so heavy, I can't open them or find the energy to thank him.

Time becomes this odd never-never land of beeping and people in and out and sleep and murmured voices. I'm hot and then cold in extremes I've never experienced so acutely before. All the while, I'm aware of Derek there the entire time, but I can't keep my eyes open long enough to talk to him or thank him or tell him to go home.

The next time I come to, I'm in a different room, and sunlight is streaming through the window.

Every part of me aches, and my throat is on fire. I try to turn my head to see if Derek is still there, and I wince from the pain of moving.

"Hey," he says, standing to take my hand.

His skin is so cool next to mine.

"How're you feeling?" he asks.

"Like I got run over by a bus." My mouth is so dry. "Is there water?"

He pours ice water from a pitcher into a plastic cup with a straw that he holds up to my mouth.

That sip of water is the best thing I've ever tasted, until it hits my throat, causing me to wince.

Derek puts the cup down and turns to do something. He holds up the packet of throat lozenges that I bought for him. "Want one?"

"God, yes."

"You can't choke on this, do you hear me?"

"I won't."

He hands one to me, and I pop it into my mouth.

The relief is nearly immediate. "Thank you."

"You're the one who bought them. They're the best."

"Mmmm." I force my eyes open to look at him—handsome, a bit disheveled and clearly exhausted. "You should go home and get some sleep."

"I'm not leaving you here alone."

"I can text my parents. They'll come."

"If you want to do that, I'll wait until they get here."

My first thought is how I'll explain him to them, but I want him to go home to get some rest, so I take my phone from him and send the text to my mother.

Hey—don't panic, but I'm at GW with a high fever.

"Did they say if I tested positive for strep?" I ask him.

"Yep, you did."

I add that info to the text. *Nothing to worry about, but just wanted you to know. They've got me on an IV. Probably going to be here for a while.*

My mom responds right away. *Oh my goodness! Dad and I will be right there! What room are you in?*

"She's asking what room."

"Five twelve."

I text that info to my mother.

See you shortly.

"They'll be here soon. You really don't have to wait. You've been such a trouper."

"It's no problem, and I'll wait."

171

"Are you always this stubborn?"

He smiles. "When I need to be."

"How do you feel?"

"Much better today, thank goodness. I texted my mom, and she said Maeve is fine and not to worry about her."

"That's good news. I'd hate for her to get this."

"Me, too. I'm sorry you did."

"I blame Iris and her kids."

"Yes, it's all their fault."

Sleep pulls me under once again, and when I wake the next time, my parents are standing by my bed, wearing masks and looking pinched and worried the way they did after Patrick first died.

I realize that's the first time I've thought of him in hours, and I'm not sure what that means.

"How're you feeling, sweetie?" Mom asks.

"I've been better." I glance to the left to see that Derek is still there. "Did you meet my friend Derek?"

"We did."

"He gave me a ride over here and refuses to leave."

Derek smiles. "I'll go now that you're in good hands, but I'll check on you later?"

"I'll be here."

As he walks around the bed, my dad extends a hand to him. Dad is tall and burly from years of working in construction. He has snow-white hair—he says from raising three daughters—and a weathered complexion. What you can't see from the outside is the heart of gold. He would do anything for anyone. He survived lymphoma five years ago and has a compromised immune system, thus the masks. They shouldn't even be here.

Derek shakes his hand.

"Thank you for helping my daughter, Derek."

"No problem. It was nice to meet you both. Feel better, Roni."

"Thank you, Derek," Mom calls after him. "What a nice young man," she says after he's gone.

"Yes, he is."

"How do you know him?" she asks, because she can't help herself.

"We work together."

Mom adjusts my blanket, which doesn't need adjusting. "So he works at the White House, too?"

"Yes, he's the deputy chief of staff to the president."

Her eyes go wide over the top of her mask. "Oh my goodness. And you're already close enough to him, after just a few days on the job, to call him when you're sick?"

"I met him before I started at the White House. It's a long story." Which involves a certain amount of stalking that I'd prefer my parents never know about. Speaking of things they need to know... "So, guys, when I asked you to come for dinner tonight..." I pause and reach for the water.

Mom holds the cup and straw for me. "I assume that's off."

"Yeah," I say with a grimace, "it's off. But there was something I wanted to tell you."

"Is everything all right, honey?" Dad asks, his brows coming together into the expression he wore for weeks after we lost Patrick.

"It is... Well, as all right as anything is these days, but it's actually very good news, or at least I'm trying to see it that way." I look up at them, both so dear to me, my rocks after the tragic loss of my husband. "It seems I'm pregnant."

Mom gasps. "Oh, oh... Roni... That's... Oh, honey." Tears fill her eyes. "How far along are you?"

"Almost four months."

My dad seems to sag a bit. "That's wonderful news, honey, but I'm sure you must have very mixed feelings."

"So many emotions," I say, attempting to swallow. That's when I notice that Derek left one of the trays of lozenges on the table next to my bed. I reach for them, and my mom saves me the trouble, handing them to me. After I put another one in my mouth and revel in the sweet numbness and relief it brings, I look up at them again. "I'm thrilled to know Patrick will live on in our child."

Dad's eyes flood with tears, and he turns away from me.

"Is this why you've been so nauseated?" Mom asks.

"Apparently so. I thought it was grief, but that wasn't it."

"And the baby is okay?"

"Yes, they've had me on a monitor since I came in, and the heartbeat is very strong."

"Thank goodness." She sighs, wipes away tears with a tissue and reaches out to brush the hair back from my face. "My strong, brave girl. We're so proud of you already, and now... You're going to be a mom."

"I'm going to need tons and tons of help."

"You'll have all the help you need," Dad says gruffly. "Whatever you need."

"Thanks, guys. Love you both so much. I never would've survived all this without you."

"Yes, you would have," Dad says in the same uncharacteristically gruff tone. "You're tough as nails. We've always said that about you, and you've proven it to us again in the last few months."

His sweet words make my chin quiver as I try to contain the overload of emotion. "Thank you, Daddy, but you guys ought to go. This place is full of germs."

"We'll go in a little bit," he says.

The day passes in a strange state of sleep and people. I wake up to my sisters having relieved my parents, who've ceded to my request that they go home and get my dad out of the germy hospital.

"Girl, you've been keeping some secrets," Rebecca says. Her dark hair is up in a bun that makes her look glamorous. The same look on me would make me look dumpy.

"Mom told you about the baby?"

"Yes," Pen says on a long exhale. Her hair is lighter than ours, but we share the same brown eyes. "We're so excited about it, but, Ron, you have to be, well..."

"My emotions are all over the place. I'm so sad Patrick is missing this, and the thought of doing it alone is just..."

"You will *not* be alone," Rebecca says adamantly. "You will *never* be alone."

I squeeze her hand and smile up at the sisters who've always been there for me.

"Mom also told us about the 'friend' who was here with you when they got here," Pen says.

Of course she did. "Oh. Derek."

"The same guy you were with the other night, right?"

"That's him."

"Derek, who's the number two staffer to the president," Rebecca adds in case I didn't know what he does for a living. "And wait, you were with him the other night?"

"We're *friends*. He's a widower."

"Oh wow," Pen says on a long exhale. "That sucks."

"Remember the thing that got Arnie Patterson arrested?"

"What about it?" Rebecca asks, her brows furrowed.

"Derek's wife was the one they murdered."

"Holy crap," Pen says. "I remember all that. That poor guy. His kid was missing, too, right?"

"Yes, for several days. But thankfully, they found her. My new boss, Sam, was the one who led that investigation."

"You mean your new boss, Sam, the first lady," Pen says, smiling.

"It's all coming back to me now," Rebecca says. "Well, this is an interesting development."

"We're friends. That's it."

"If it was more than that, no one would judge you, Ronald McDonald," Pen says gently.

"Yes, they would. Rita did the other night when she and Lou saw us together."

"Wait, what?" Rebecca says, looking between us. "Where did they see you?"

Penelope spares me from having to repeat the story by filling her in. "And for what it's worth, Rita's judgment doesn't count because she's a boob and has no sense. Do not let *her* or people like her dictate how you live your life going forward."

"Still," I say, moved by Pen's emotional outburst. "It's too soon."

"Is there a rule book about these things?" Rebecca asks.

"No, but there's common decency and respect for my husband's memory."

"For which you have tons of respect," Pen says. "If you're not ready, you're not ready. But if you are... Don't get caught up in what other people expect. You do you."

"I'm sure I'll be in hot demand out on the dating scene, especially since I'm pregnant with my late husband's baby. That's some kind of sexy."

"Mom says Derek is very handsome," Rebecca says.

I roll my eyes, which hurts my head. "Mom needs to take a chill pill, and so do you."

"How long are you going to be here?" Pen asks.

"They haven't said yet."

"You can come to my house when you get released," Pen adds.

"No, that's okay. You don't need me bringing whatever this is into your house. I'll be fine at home."

Much later, I wake from yet another nap and find Derek sitting next to my bed. At first I wonder if the fever is back and I'm seeing things, but no, it's really him, and he looks much better than he did earlier. I suppose that's to be expected since it's no longer the middle of the night. "Hey."

"Hey, yourself," he says. "How're you feeling?"

"A little better, but still not ready to climb mountains or scale tall buildings."

"You'll be back to that in no time."

"If you say so. Thanks for leaving the magic throat pills earlier."

"I figured they might come in handy. You want one?"

"More than anything."

Smiling, he stands to retrieve the tray of lozenges from my bedside table and pops one into my outstretched hand.

The relief is immediate and intense. "That's the best thing since ice cream."

"Sure is. Iris has it now, too, and she's super upset that your first meeting with the Wild Widows put you in the hospital."

"Not her fault."

"Still, she feels bad."

"I hope she has help with the kids while she's sick."

"Her mom is there."

"That's good. How's Maeve?"

"She's having fun with her grandparents, who spoil her rotten. They're keeping her until Monday after work."

"You must miss her."

"I do, but I was feeling so shitty until earlier today that it was a relief to know they were taking care of her."

"I hope she doesn't get this."

"I hope so, too, and that she doesn't give it to my parents."

"You should go home and rest while you can."

"I'd rather hang out here with you."

"Because I'm such great company right now. And I must look like I took a trip down Ugly Street and hit every bump."

His laughter makes me smile. "No, you don't, and you're very good company, even when you're sick."

"Does this mean you've forgiven me for the alleged stalking?"

"Not quite yet, so you need to let me hang out so you have more time to redeem yourself."

He's cute, funny, thoughtful, handsome, a wonderful father... He's the full package, and I'm starting to look forward to our time together in a way that leaves me unsettled. Would Patrick be "moving on" to someone new this quickly if I'd been the one to die? I no sooner ask myself that question than I stop that train of thought from leaving the station. Every grief journey is different. That's one of many things I've learned since I was plunged into this situation.

I'm not doing anything wrong by enjoying the time I spend with Derek.

Maybe if I keep repeating that to myself, over and over and over again, I might start to believe it.

"Unless you'd rather be alone, that is," he says after a long moment of silence.

"No, I wouldn't rather be alone, and that's kind of the problem."

"I didn't realize we had a problem."

"We don't. It's just..."

"What, Roni?"

"Confusing."

"What is?"

"This. You."

"Ah, I see what you mean now. I don't need to be here if it makes you uncomfortable, and I'm sure you had to answer some questions with your folks earlier when they found me here with you."

"A few."

"Were they upset about it?"

"No, not at all. Just curious." I turn my head so I can look at him. "I'm struggling with this. With you..."

"I'll go."

Seventeen

Roni

"No! I don't want you to go, and that's the part I'm struggling with. I like having you here. I like being with you, and... It's just... I don't know how I'm supposed to feel about that."

"I totally understand. You know I do. Like, how can I still be in love with Vic, forever in love with her, and have feelings for you, too?"

"You... You have feelings for me?"

"I do, but that doesn't have to make things weird between us."

I snort out a laugh that makes my throat hurt. "Because why would that make anything weird?"

His smile lights up his handsome face. "Exactly."

"Is literally everything a screwed-up mess after your spouse dies?"

"Every single thing."

"So it's not just me, then."

"Nope." After another pause, he says, "Should I have kept that info to myself?"

I suddenly feel shy for the first time in years. "No."

"Does it make things harder for you?"

"No." I take the opportunity to swallow while my throat is still numb. "It's not your feelings that upset me. It's mine. I have them, too. For you. And I just wonder what kind of wife that makes me—"

He covers my hand with his. "Stop that, Roni. After hearing you talk about Patrick and your life with him, I have no doubt in my mind that you were a wonderful, devoted wife. It's not your fault that he was killed or that you have to go on without him. It's not your fault, and it's not his. If he hadn't died, you never would've left him. You two would've been together for sixty years and had a wonderful, full life together."

His sweet words bring tears to my eyes. "We would've. We were so happy together."

"I know you were, and you know the truth. That's what you have to hold on to—your truth. Not anyone else's ideas of what's acceptable or how things should go or what you should do with this new life you're forced to live without the man you love."

"It's just so soon to be looking beyond him."

"You're not doing that. It's not like you went out and joined a dating service looking to replace your dead husband as fast as you possibly could. Not that there's anything wrong with that if someone chooses to do that."

"Do you know people who've done that?"

"I do, and so do you. Members of our group have done it because that's what they needed, and I refuse to find fault with whatever people do to get through the day after a loss like we've suffered. But you didn't do that. You met someone organically—even if there was stalking involved."

Derek's golden eyes dance with amusement as he says that. "What matters, Roni... The only thing that matters, is how *you* feel and what *you* want. You're the boss of your life now. Just you. No one else. I know it's too soon for 'feelings' between us. I understand that some of those 'feelings' are due to our shared journey and might fade in time."

The thought of that happening sends a pang of angst through me. "I hope that doesn't happen, because I like feeling something for you. It's better than feeling nothing but agony all the time."

"Yes, it is."

"You know what else I like?"

"What's that?"

"How widowhood causes us to put our cards on the table and be honest about stuff in a way we wouldn't have before."

"That's very true. Especially for me. I was so closed off and remote before I lost Vic."

"Even with her?"

"Yeah," he says, looking pained. "In all the years we were together, I never had a conversation with her like this one with you. I told her I loved her—often—and I did love her, but I didn't get into the nitty-gritty of it with her. I just left it at the I-love-you level, and that's one of my regrets. I never came right out and told her all the many ways I admired her or appreciated her. I just assumed she knew."

"I'm sure she was very happy with you."

"I think she was, but I'm just saying... I could've done better. I *want* to do better going forward, and that's why I'm being kind of blunt with you. New Derek puts it out there so people know how he feels about them. He's more open with his emotions and understands that time is all we have to give to the people we care about. There's none to waste."

How could I not have feelings for this man? "You're not being fair."

"Huh?" he asks, seeming genuinely surprised.

"I'm trying *not* to have feelings for you, and then you go and give me *more* reasons to have them."

His low chuckle amuses me. "Don't let me stop you."

"I'm being serious."

"I know you are, and here's the good news. We're both allowed to have whatever feelings we want to have, and we're allowed to not do anything about it until we're both in a place where it feels right to act on it."

"What if one of us never gets there?"

"Then one of us never gets there."

"What happens to the other one?"

"He—or she—goes on with their life with a lovely new friend that will support and encourage them always."

I'm not sure if it's the illness or pregnancy hormones or widowhood that has my eyes filling to overflowing, but whatever it is, Derek is ready to mop up the waterworks with a tissue.

"Don't do that. Girl tears freak me out."

"That's a guy thing." I laugh through my tears. "Patrick was the same way."

"I think I would've liked him."

"*Everyone* liked him."

"I don't want you to worry about anything. I'm here. I'm not going anywhere unless you tell me to get lost, and I'm not looking to make anything worse for you. Only better. Okay?"

"Okay. And, Derek?"

"Yes, Roni?"

"I'm not going to tell you to get lost."

Derek

I FALL asleep in the recliner chair next to Roni's bed. At some point during the night, a nurse must've put a blanket over me, because I wake up warm and toasty. I didn't plan to stay, but after she said she wasn't going to tell me to get lost, I got comfortable. I can't believe how open and blunt I was with her last night.

If you'd known me before I lost my wife, you'd ask, who is this guy who shares his feelings so freely? I barely recognize this new version of myself, but I'm wise enough to know that he's a much better version of me than Vic got.

It took me a lot of therapy to deal with the realization that I could've been a better husband to her than I was. Maybe if I'd been more emotionally available, she would've told me about the mess she was in with the Pattersons, and I could've done something about it before they did.

I'll regret for the rest of my life that she didn't feel she could tell me. I would've gone to the president himself, if that's what was needed, to get her free of the nightmare they perpetrated upon her.

I'm truly determined to be a better version of myself going forward, which is why I put my cards on the table with Roni, even if I feared the truth might drive her away.

I really like her.

Really, *really* like her.

I look over at her sleeping peacefully in the hospital bed, attached to an IV drip, and all I want is to spend more time with her. As much as she'll allow, even if we're firmly in the friend zone until she's ready for it to be more. Being friends with Roni is the most fun I've had since I lost Vic, and for the first time in a very long time, I feel like I'm doing more than just surviving each day.

She's a breath of fresh air that I badly needed, but of course I couldn't be falling for someone who's free and clear and ready to pursue a relationship. Nope, I have to keep things complicated, but it's okay. I already know that Roni is worth taking my time with and doing the work to bring her—and her child—into my life and Maeve's.

And no, it doesn't faze me in the least that she's expecting her late husband's child. I want to be a source of support to her as she faces an uncertain future, because I know all too well how difficult that road is going to be for her. I want to be there for her. It's that simple—and that complicated.

Roni stirs to life, blinking with disbelief when she sees me there. "You stayed."

"I did, although not intentionally. I guess I fell asleep."

"I'm glad you're here," she says with the small, sweet smile that just does it for me.

"I'm glad I am, too."

A nurse comes in a short time later, followed by the doctor on rounds, who declares Roni well enough to be sent home.

While they get her up and showered and ready to go, I go downstairs to the gift shop to buy a toothbrush and toothpaste and then to the cafeteria for a coffee for me and a hot chocolate for her.

When I return, she's seated on the bed wearing the sweats and T-shirt she had on when I brought her in the other night. Her hair has been brushed into a high ponytail that leaves her pretty—but pale—face on full display. "You look good."

"I look like roadkill."

"No, you don't," I say, laughing as I hand her the hot chocolate.

"Thank you."

"Welcome."

She takes a sip of the hot chocolate. "Mmm, that's good."

"How's your throat?"

"Much better than it was."

"IV antibiotics to the rescue. They probably saved you a couple of days of suffering."

"Probably so."

The nurse returns with discharge paperwork, a prescription to continue the antibiotics and orders to take it easy for the next few days.

"No choice there," Roni says as she signs where directed. "I feel like a newborn kitten."

"Let your husband wait on you hand and foot," the nurse says, grinning at me. "That's what he's there for."

"Oh, um…" Roni gives me a worried look as her pale face flushes with embarrassment that is adorable on her.

"I'll take good care of her," I tell the nurse. "Don't worry."

"You got yourself a good one, honey," the nurse says as she helps Roni up for the wheelchair. She chatters to us all the way to the main door of the hospital.

I run out to get my car and return to hear her saying, "And that baby of yours will be beautiful with you two as its parents."

Because Roni looks like a deer in headlights, I step in. "Thank you so much. I can take it from here."

After I help Roni into the passenger side of my SUV, the nurse says, "Have a nice day." She takes off with the wheelchair, blissfully unaware of the bomb she just dropped on us.

I go around the SUV to get into the driver's side and glance at

Roni. She's staring straight ahead, her eyes bright with unshed tears.

"Sorry about that," she says.

"Don't be. You're still wearing your rings. She leapt to the logical conclusion."

Out of the corner of my eye, I see her gazing down at her rings.

"I love my rings so much. I can't bear the thought of not wearing them anymore."

"Some people move them to their right hand so they can still wear them but not send the 'married' message."

"That's a good idea. Maybe I'll do that."

"You don't have to do anything if you don't want to."

"I know, but I can see how it's confusing to people."

"They don't matter. Only you do."

"I'll have to take them off eventually, I suppose."

"You don't have to do it today or tomorrow or next week or next month. Everything about this journey is on your timetable."

"Except for one thing. The baby."

"True. Soon enough, you'll be on his or her timetable, so you need to enjoy the next few months of setting your own rules."

"I'll get right on that as soon as I can hold my head up straight again." With her head back against the seat, she turns toward me. "What did you do with Victoria's rings?"

"I have them in a safe. I thought Maeve might want them someday."

"I'm sure she will. I don't know what to do with Patrick's ring. I wore it on a chain for a while, but the clasp broke, and I haven't gotten it fixed yet."

"You should hang on to it for the baby. If it's a boy, maybe he'll want to wear it someday. If it's a girl, she can give it to her future husband."

"I like that."

"Someday those symbols will mean something to our kids."

"I'm going to have a *kid*. I still can't wrap my head around that."

"That's why pregnancy lasts so long. Vic and I used to say it's so you have time to get ready for a bomb to go off in your life."

"Is it really a bomb?"

"Uh, you want the truth, or should I sugarcoat it?"

"Forget I asked. I'm in no condition today for bombs."

"Good call." I pull up outside her building, put the SUV in Park and shut it off, intending to at least walk her in and make sure she has what she needs. "Oh crap. We forgot to drop off your prescription. I'll go do that after I get you settled inside."

"You don't have to do that. I can call my sister."

"I don't mind doing it." I offer her a hand to help her out of the car.

She takes it, and when she stands, she sways precariously, forcing me to put my arms around her to keep her from falling.

"Go slow."

"No choice. Haven't felt this shitty in years. Well, except for... you know."

"Yeah, I know." I keep an arm around her as we walk up the stairs to her front door, where she hands me the key that gets us inside. As we're heading up the first flight of stairs, an older woman is coming down the stairs and stops short at the sight of us.

"Roni."

"Oh, hi, Mrs. Eastwood."

"Are you all right?" the woman, obviously a neighbor, asks.

The question is directed to Roni, but all her attention is focused on me.

"I've got strep and was in the hospital. My friend gave me a ride home."

"Oh my goodness. If you need anything, give me a call."

"I will. Thanks."

I fear I'm going to have to ask her to move to let us by, but she steps aside before I have to say anything.

Roni is so weak that I almost have to carry her up the stairs, which would be no hardship. She's already told me how she lost weight she didn't have to lose after Patrick died, and even through her winter coat, I can feel how fragile she is.

I use her key in the door of her apartment and walk her straight to a gorgeous leather sofa, where she sits to take off her coat.

"Why do I feel like I just ran a marathon when all I did was walk upstairs, and with your help, I might add?"

"You've had the legs knocked out from under you, but you'll feel better in a couple of days."

"Ugh, I'm going to have to call in sick to my new job."

"Text Sam and tell her what's up. She'll totally understand."

"Lilia is technically my boss."

"Then text her. She's awesome, too. She's marrying one of my best friends."

"Ah, yes, her Dr. Flynn is a lovely guy. I met him when he came by the office."

"Yes, he is." I find the prescription form in the pile of papers she put on the coffee table. "Where do you go?"

"Grubbs."

"Got it."

"This is above and beyond the call of new friendship, Derek."

"I'm sure you'd do the same for me, Roni." I pause and give her a playful look. "Wouldn't you?"

"Of course I would."

"Well, then, there you have it. You need anything else?"

"Not that I can think of."

"What kind of soup do you like?"

"Is there any other kind besides chicken noodle?"

"Got it. Do you mind if I take your keys so I can get back in without disturbing you?"

"Sure, go ahead."

"I'll be right back." I shut the door, make sure it's locked and head down the stairs, eager to get her what she needs and return to her as soon as I can.

Yes, I know that's crazy. Yes, I know she's in no way ready for me to be eager to get back to her, and yes, I know I have to take it easy with her and give her the time she needs to cope with her loss and her grief. I remember all too well what the first few months were like, how lost she feels without her anchor and how long it will be before she feels strong enough to take on a new relationship.

I'm willing to be patient because I also know how rare it is to feel this way about anyone. In my entire life, I've only ever felt this kind of spark with someone once before.

At the pharmacy, I give them Roni's script and have to text her for her date of birth, which is a reminder that whatever is happening between us is in its infancy, and I need to slow my roll.

July 12.

Got it. I pass the info along to the woman working the counter, and she tells me it'll be twenty minutes. So I spend the time gathering soup, crackers, cookies, more of the magic throat lozenges in multiple flavors and some of the same throat spray she got for me that worked pretty well. In the magazine aisle, I grab *Vanity Fair* and *Rolling Stone* as well as one of the fashion magazines, hoping she likes such things.

Add that to the list of things I don't know about her.

I wait until nineteen minutes have gone by before I add some Chunky Monkey to the basket and return to the pharmacy counter.

"Two more minutes," the woman says.

I use that time to text my mom to check on my daughter.

She's doing great. Dad took her sledding at the high school, and she loved it. She's taking a little nap now, but she requested spaghetti for dinner.

She'd eat that three meals a day if she could.

I think so. How are you feeling?

Much better, but now one of my good friends has it, too, so I'm helping her out.

Her?

A friend, Mother.

Can't blame a mom for hoping her precious son might find someone new to love someday.

I don't blame you for that, and you'll be the first to know if there's news in that department.

"All set for Connolly," the pharmacy tech says.

Gotta run, I tell my mom. *Have Maeve call me at bedtime.*

Will do.

Thanks again for having her.

Our pleasure always.

Thank God for them. I say it a hundred times a day, but it's so true. I never would've survived losing Vic without them. I'm glad to know Roni has a strong family supporting her, too. Not all the Wild Widows are lucky that way, and I can see how much harder it is for them without that support system.

"I notice there's one pending for Mr. Connolly, as well. Do you want to pick that up, too?"

I have no idea what to say. "I, uh, sure. I'll take them both."

"Very good."

She rings me up, I pay for the two prescriptions as well as the items I got for Roni, and head back to her place. If there's one good thing about weekends in the District, street parking tends to be slightly easier than it is during the week. I find a spot and am about to use the key in the door to her building when Mrs. Eastwood opens it.

"I was hoping to see you again, young man," she says. "I'm not sure if you're aware of what our Roni has been through, but she's not ready to have men visiting her."

"With all due respect, ma'am, I'm a friend and colleague of hers. I did her a favor because she's been sick. I don't think she'd appreciate you speaking for her."

The woman doesn't like that. "We care about her. What she's been through is just awful."

"Yes, it is, and a lot of people care about her. I'm sure she appreciates your concern, but I need to get back upstairs. She's waiting for her medicine."

"Young man?"

"Yes, ma'am?"

"Take good care of her."

"I will."

I continue up the stairs, feeling the heat of her stare on my back. I know she means well, but Jesus, do the words *mind your own business* mean anything to her? Although, she's just looking out for Roni, and I can't blame her for that.

She's asleep on the sofa when I get back, so I quietly stash the ice cream in her freezer and put the other things on the counter for her to find later. I'm not sure if I should stay or go, but I want to hear from her that she's okay before I leave. So I stretch out on the other sofa, find the remote, turn on the TV and mute it with the Washington game on.

As I look around at her apartment, I'm struck by how unique and eclectic it is, a mix of modern and antique that works together in perfect harmony that I could've never achieved. Either Roni or her husband, perhaps both, had a flair for decorating.

I notice the framed wedding picture on the table next to the sofa where she's sleeping and move in for a closer look at two happy people on the best day of their lives. Patrick was handsome, smiling, thrilled with his life and his bride. But Roni... She's a stunning bride, but that's not what really sticks out to me. I realize I've never seen her look like she does in that picture, full of the kind of unfettered joy that hasn't been touched by unspeakable tragedy. I hope that maybe someday she'll again look as happy as she did on her wedding day.

I return to the other sofa, finding myself unbearably sad for two people I never knew as a couple, and especially for the one who's left to put her life back together into some new version that she never wanted.

I close my eyes, just for a minute or so, I tell myself...

Eighteen

Roni

When I wake up, the room has gone dim with late-afternoon light, and I'm surprised to see Derek out cold on the other sofa. I sit up slowly, wait for my head to quit spinning and get up slowly to use the bathroom. I go to the kitchen to get a glass of water and see the bag that Derek left on the counter, full of treats, medicine, magazines and soup.

He's too sweet.

I open the box of cherry-flavored lozenges and pop one in my mouth for instant relief from an intensely sore throat. In the bag from the pharmacy, I find my prescription and another one for... Oh my God, it's for Patrick.

My brain races to recall what it was for, and then I remember the rash on his back that erupted two days before he died. He'd been to the doctor the day before but hadn't yet picked up the prescription.

I stare at that bottle for the longest time, stunned that a prescription can bring on such a wave of grief. In our last days together, Patrick complained incessantly about how itchy the rash was. I ran him an Epsom salt bath and put cortisone on it for him, but when nothing helped, he went to the doctor. I completely forgot about that until now, and I'm gutted by the reminders of those last moments of normalcy.

"They told me there was one for him, too." Derek's voice startles me out of the memories. "I wasn't sure if I should get it or not."

"He had a rash before he died and was miserable. I didn't know he hadn't picked up the prescription."

"I wasn't sure what to do."

"It's okay. Just brings back memories of those last minutes of normal life, you know?"

"I do. For me, it was the laundry I discovered in the washer several days after Maeve and I were back in the house. It had gone smelly after days of sitting there wet, but it was a slap in the face to realize what Vic had been doing right before disaster struck. Just normal, everyday things."

"It's so strange how the most innocuous things can bring it all back."

"You just never know what it's going to be." He puts his hands on the counter and stretches. "How're you feeling?"

"A little better. My throat is still super sore, and my head is all fuzzy."

"I wanted to stay to make sure you're okay before I go. Hope that's okay."

"Of course. You can stay as long as you want to. I like the company."

"You feel like something to eat?"

"What do you want?"

"Pizza?"

"That sounds good to me." She gasps. "I never gave you my card to pay for the prescriptions!"

"Don't worry about it."

"I will worry about it. I'm paying for the pizza for you and soup for me."

"If you insist."

"I do."

We order the pizza and soup and settle on the sofa to watch the game, and it all feels easy, like we've been hanging out together for years. As soon as I acknowledge that comfort, I feel guilty to be sitting in the home I created with Patrick, enjoying the company of another man. Grief is such a bitch that way. She gives you a moment of contentment and then sprinkles some guilt on top to make sure you can't fully enjoy it.

Each of my family members checks on me, all of them offering to come stay with me. I decline their offers and assure them I'm okay.

Rebecca wants to know if my friend Derek is with me.

I don't respond to that text, and I'm not sure why. We're not doing anything wrong, but it still feels strange to admit, even to my sister, that he's here.

After Washington loses badly to the Saints, we end up watching *An Officer and a Gentleman* until we're both yawning our heads off.

"I should go," he says, stretching.

"Thanks for hanging out."

"It was fun."

"Yes, it was."

"You want to hear a true confession?"

"Sure."

"I really enjoyed a few days off from fatherhood, and I feel like a jerk for even saying that."

"You shouldn't feel bad about that. I'm sure it's very intense."

"She's a delight. I'd never say otherwise."

"I know."

"As much as I enjoy just about every minute with her, I also enjoy the breaks my parents are always willing to give me."

"Thank goodness for them."

"You know it. Yours will be the same, I'm sure."

I get up to walk him to the door, feeling a little steadier on my feet than I did earlier. "They will. They love being grandparents."

"You should take every break you're offered. You'll need it."

"That I'll be raising a child alone still feels too big for my brain to process."

"That's just it, though. You won't be alone. You'll be surrounded by a village, and that will make all the difference."

"Sam told me I can bring the baby to work. Her friend Shelby has a nanny that we can share, if the nanny agrees, that is."

"That's amazing. It'll be great to have him or her close by, especially the first year. Maeve and I will show you all the best playgrounds. We've done a ton of research and have our favorites."

"I'll look forward to that."

As smoothly as can be, he kisses me on the cheek. "Call me if you need anything during the night."

"I'll be okay."

"If you're not, call me."

"I will. Thanks again for everything."

"My pleasure."

After he leaves, I lock up, noticing how quiet the apartment is now that I'm alone again. On the way to my room, I stop to flip on the light in the guest bedroom we lovingly put together for Patrick's parents and siblings. We wanted them to be able to visit us whenever they wanted to. I suppose I'll need to transform that room into a nursery for the baby, a task that seems so big to me that I quickly turn off the light and save that thought for when I'm not feeling like shit.

I get in bed and send a text to Lilia, telling her about my weekend stay in the hospital and how I'm not ready to come back to work.

Oh my goodness, she says. *Take good care of yourself and let me know if you need anything.*

What a sweetheart she is. *Thank you*, I reply, *but I'm okay. Just feel like I got hit by a bus!*

Take as much time as you need. I'll check on you tomorrow.

Thanks again.

I make sure the alarm on my phone is off and snuggle into bed, looking forward to sleeping in on a workday. For a long time, I'm awake, thinking about what used to be, what is and what's to come. My dreams are a scattered mess of Patrick, Derek, babies, Maeve, the White House. When I wake in the middle of the night, sweating and gasping, it occurs to me that my new life shows up in dreams much more often than my "old" life these days.

That makes me sad.

I'm moving away from Patrick.

I never wanted to do that. Not ever.

But that choice was taken from me in the most random way possible, and now... God, it's just so hard to look forward to a future that doesn't include him. It's hard to have made this new friend in Derek and to have to feel guilty about enjoying his company because I still feel married to a man who's gone forever.

Ah, yes, widow brain. I remember that coming up at the meeting. Not only does widow brain make you feel scattered and forgetful, it also spins you into these never-ending circles of despair followed by a burst of optimism, followed by an even deeper pit of despair topped off with a dollop of joy. And that's all in five minutes. It's no wonder that people experiencing deep grief often feel like they're losing what's left of their minds as they take an out-of-control roller-coaster ride that no one would sign on for willingly.

My friendship with Derek has helped. I can't deny that. I can talk to him about things others in my life wouldn't understand, such as the conundrum over wedding rings. He gives me hope that I'm going to get through this unbearable loss and figure out a new life for myself and my child.

It won't happen overnight, but Derek is proof that it *will* happen.

I had no idea how much I needed that proof in my life until he became part of it.

The simmering attraction between us adds another level to the mix, one I'm not ready to explore yet, but it's nice to know I can feel a spark for someone other than the only man I've ever loved. I've just got to put that spark on ice for right now. It wouldn't be fair to either of us to let that happen when I know I'm not ready.

I spend the next day lying around, watching TV, napping and not doing much of anything else. My brain refuses to engage in anything other than mindless tasks.

Derek texts after work to see if I need anything.

I'm good thanks to you and the soup run. What did I miss today at work?

Another day in paradise spent trying to get fighting members of Congress to work together. Good times as always.

Better you than me.

You know it! People say I'm good at dealing with them, but some days I want to tell them to grow up and stop acting more immature than my toddler.

I'd pay to see that show.

Haha, it's a SHIT show ninety percent of the time.

How's Maeve?

Perfectly fine. I guess her immune system is far more robust than ours.

Glad to hear it. I'd hate to think of her having this. It's miserable.

Is your throat still bad?

Better than it was, but still not great.

So another day off tomorrow?

I think so. I'm still like a newborn kitten over here. Can't do much of anything. This plague hit me hard.

Take it easy.

No choice about that.

I'll check on you tomorrow. Call me if you need anything.

Thank you.

Sure thing. Driving to work is less fun without you. Get well soon.

I respond with a smiley-face emoji as my heart flutters from his sweet words. I'm so lucky to have made such a lovely new friend, and I hope he'll still be around if and when I get to the point where I might be ready for my Chapter 2.

Nineteen

Roni

Winter finally gives way to spring...

In late April, Derek, Maeve and I spend a Sunday in Ocean City with Iris and her kids. Derek drives Iris's minivan so we can all go together. The day is unseasonably warm, allowing us to spend a relaxing afternoon on the beach. While Iris and I laze in the sun in beach chairs, Derek and the kids build an elaborate sandcastle. He's great about including each of the kids by giving them age-appropriate tasks to complete.

Iris's kids hang on his every word and light up with pleasure when he praises them.

"They're like sponges for paternal love," Iris comments. "They're like that with Mike's brother, too. All over him like ants at a picnic. Bless his heart. He comes almost every Saturday and spends the entire day with them. I'm so thankful to him for the commitment he's made to them."

"It's lovely of him to do that."

"He and Mike were soul mates. Losing him has been as hard on his brother as it's been on me. Rob was supposed to be on the flight with Mike that day, but bailed at the last minute because he'd met a woman he really liked. That guilt has eaten him up ever since."

"But he would've died, too."

"There are times when I think he'd prefer that to having to go on without Mike. They were eleven months apart in age and did everything together."

"That's so sad. Did he stay with the woman?"

Iris shakes her head. "He said he couldn't look at her after Mike died."

"God, why does life have to be so unbearably hard sometimes?"

"I don't know, but it's also wonderful." She gestures to Derek, who's now being buried by four enthusiastic kids. "The friends I've made since Mike died are some of the best I've ever had."

"Same for me since Patrick died. Brielle checks on me every day. Joy has brought me dinner a few times and then stayed with me so I wouldn't have to eat alone. She makes me laugh so hard."

"She's an awesome friend."

"Yes, she is. All the Wild Widows are wonderful."

"Even Aurora?" Iris asks, brow raised.

"She'd grown on me before she stopped coming to the meetings."

"The poor thing had her heart set on Derek, even though he never gave her any reason to think that way." Iris glances my way. "He never looked at her the way he does you."

"Stop."

"I'm serious. He's into you big-time."

I shift my gaze to where he's playing with the kids, having busted out of the sand to chase them around. Iris's youngest child, two-year-old Laney, is screaming with delight as he catches her and swings her up in the air while the others trail behind, waiting for their turn.

My heart can't handle the surge of emotion I experience as I watch him with Maeve and Iris's three fatherless children.

"He's a special guy," Iris says softly.

"Yes, he is."

"What're you going to do about him?"

"I don't know yet. It feels too soon to be thinking about questions like that."

"Even if you see him every day?"

"Even if."

"I think he has his heart set on you, Roni."

"I think so, too, and I adore him. I really do. I'm just not ready for it to be more than close friendship."

"Can I ask one favor?"

"Of course."

"If you think it's not going to happen for you—ever—will you tell him sooner rather than later? I couldn't stand to see him hurt."

"I promise I will, but the last thing I want is for him to not be in my life."

"That's telling."

"I think so, too. He never puts any pressure on me for it to be anything more than what it is right now, and I so appreciate that."

"But you know he wants more."

She says that as a statement and not a question. "Yes, I do." With my hand on the curve of my pregnant belly, I look over at her. "I'm focused on growing this tiny human and preparing for the birth while holding down a busy, demanding, high-profile job. That's all I'm capable of now. Derek understands that."

"Have you talked about it?"

"Not in so many words, but I feel like we understand each other."

"Maybe you should talk about it. If you want him there when you decide you're ready for more, it might not hurt to tell him that."

"We'll see if I get the chance."

When the little ones start to tire, we clean them up as best we can using the showers at the beach and then take them to a seafood restaurant on the boardwalk. I have broiled scallops that give me heartburn, but then again, everything gives me heartburn as my pregnancy progresses.

I'm suffering in silence on the way home when Iris gasps in the back seat. "What?" I ask her.

"Oh my God. Adrian's mother-in-law died of a massive heart attack today."

"Oh no." Derek sounds as distressed as I feel. "He relies on her for everything with Xavier."

Iris gets busy on her phone, and a few minutes later, she says, "The Wild Widows are going there to see what they can do. I contacted my sitter, and she's willing to stay with the kids tonight if you guys want to leave Maeve at my place for a bit."

Derek looks over at me. "Do you feel up to that?"

He knows how tired I am as I move into the third trimester. I don't feel up to it, but I wouldn't miss the chance to support Adrian. "I'm fine."

"All right, then. I'll put Maeve down at your house and pick her up after we see Adrian."

That's going to get us home wicked late on a work night, but that's what we do for each other in our group. We show up. Adrian would do it for me. I have no doubt in my mind about that.

We swing through the District to pick up Derek's SUV so we'll have a way to get home. I stay in Iris's car in case Maeve wakes up.

"This sucks so bad for poor Adrian," Iris says as we head toward Fairfax. Thankfully, the traffic is light at this time on a Sunday night. "It's too much on top of too much. Sadie and her mom were really close. I bet she died of a broken heart, the poor thing."

"It's awful. What'll he do?"

"I guess he'll have to hire someone. He'd just settled into a bit of a routine after a rough few months, and now this. He really loved Alyssa, his mother-in-law."

"I've heard him say how lost he'd be without her."

When we arrive at Iris's house, we get the kids settled and tuck Maeve in with Laney. Both girls are sound asleep, and the older two are so tired, they go down without a fight. We leave them with Iris's sitter and head to Adrian's in Arlington in Derek's SUV.

The three of us are quiet as we contemplate yet another terrible loss for one of our sweet friends, who's already been to hell and back after losing his wife from complications of childbirth. I can't even think about what happened to Sadie without breaking out in a cold sweat of fear. It's chilling to know perfectly healthy women still die in childbirth.

I force my thoughts away from that distressing topic to focus on the equally distressing topic of Adrian's beloved mother-in-law's sudden death. My heart aches for him and for Xavier and the rest of a family that's already had enough tragic loss to last a lifetime.

When we arrive at Adrian's townhouse in Arlington, the street outside is lined with cars.

Derek parks a couple of blocks away, and as we're walking toward Adrian's house, he says, "We should've brought food or something."

"I'm sure they've got more than they can eat in a month by now," Iris says.

"True," he says.

My emotions are all over the place as we climb the stairs to Adrian's home.

Gage is working the door and hugs each of us as we go by him.

"How is he?" Derek asks.

"Not good at all," Gage says, his expression somber. "Adrian's sister came to get Xavier a while ago and is keeping him at her house for the next few days."

"I guess that's for the best," Derek says.

"He's in no condition to care for a baby," Gage says bluntly.

I want to turn around and run from the sadness that permeates this place, but Adrian is my friend, and it's important to me to be there for him.

Derek's hand on my back helps to calm and center me. I'm not sure why he has that effect on me, but he does, and I appreciate that he knows I need the support.

Another facet of grief is how other people's tragedies can resurrect the memories of our own, taking us back to that first awful day when our lives changed forever. That's exactly what happens to me as I walk into Adrian's latest disaster.

He's on the sofa, surrounded by people trying to comfort him. When he sees us, he stands to hug each of us. His eyes are red and swollen, his face haggard with grief. "Thanks for coming."

"I wish there was something we could say," Derek says for all of us.

"I know," Adrian says. "It's unbelievable. Not sure who I pissed off."

"We're here for you, friend," Iris says. "Whatever you need."

"Thank you."

Others have come in behind us, so we yield to them so they can say something that won't matter to Adrian. I feel like I'm going to be sick as we go into a kitchen that's laden with food, as Iris predicted it would be.

Wynter is ferociously stirring something in a metal bowl. She's so consumed by what she's doing that she doesn't notice us at first.

"What're you making, Wynter?" Iris asks her.

She looks up and seems startled to see us. "Pancakes. It's the only thing I know how to make, and I wanted to do something."

"That's very sweet of you," Iris says.

Wynter shrugs, her expression full of devastation. "What the eff is wrong with this world?"

"So many things," Iris tells her, "but the one thing that's right is friends who show up for each other at the best and worst of times. It's good of you to be here."

"I'm so sad for him," she says softly. "How could this have happened after what he's already going through?"

"I don't know, honey," Iris says. "It's terribly unfair."

"What's he going to *do*? She helped him with *everything*."

"He'll figure it out," Derek assures her. "And we'll be there to help him."

Wynter wipes the tears off her face and goes back to stirring her pancake batter, albeit with less intensity than before.

Because it gives me something to do, I find a skillet and get the stove ready for Wynter.

She and I make two dozen pancakes over the next half hour without exchanging a single word. What is there to say?

We're almost finished when she looks over at me. "Are you banging Derek?"

"What? No!"

"Huh, that's surprising. I would've bet my life that you were."

"Well, I'm not, so don't go gambling with your life."

"You ought to. He's into you."

"In case you haven't noticed, I'm quite pregnant with my late husband's child."

"I hear pregnancy makes you horny as fuck. Is that true?"

"Honestly, Wynter. You need to get a filter."

"My mom says that, too, but it's probably not going to happen. Does it make you horny?"

Yes, I want to say. *Hornier than hell.* But I'm not telling her that. "Not so much. I'm not really thinking about that at the moment."

"You're a terrible liar."

"And you're a terrible snoop."

She laughs, which is so rare for her that it has the other Wild Widows coming to see it for themselves. Wynter is *laughing*. The joyful sound is just what we all needed.

"Is Wynter laughing?" Adrian asks as he joins us in the kitchen.

"I'm sorry," Wynter says. "This isn't the time for laughter."

"Sure it is," Adrian responds. "What would we do if we couldn't laugh at the sheer madness that is our lives?"

"That's true," Brielle says as Kinsley nods in agreement.

"What did Roni say that was so funny?" Joy asks.

"Never mind," I say with a pointed look for Wynter.

"We were talking about how pregnancy makes her horny, and she has no outlet for that."

"Oh my God! *That is not what I said!*"

"Your face, though," Wynter says, losing it all over again as the others join in.

Even Adrian manages a chuckle.

I shake my head at her. "You're outrageous."

"I'd rather be outrageous than horny."

"Stop!" I'm mortified, but willing to take one for the team if it provides some relief from the latest disaster to befall our group.

Wynter passes around the plate of warm pancakes like they're an appetizer.

I take one and roll it up before taking a bite. "Hey, that's really good, Wynter."

"Thanks."

"What's that I taste?" Joy asks.

"Almond extract. That's how my grandma made them."

"They're really good," Adrian says. "Thanks, Wynter."

"You're welcome. I wish there was more I could do."

"We all do," Kinsley says as she takes a sip of wine.

"It means a lot to me that you guys are here," Adrian says.

"We're here, and we're gonna be here for the long haul," Joy assures him.

Adrian, who is overcome with emotion, just nods and leans his head on top of Iris's when she puts her arm around him.

I hate that this has happened to Adrian, but I'm so thankful for this group of people and how we have one another's backs.

AFTER WE DROP Iris at her house and pick up a sleeping Maeve, Derek drives us back to the District. It's almost midnight by the time we cross the 14th Street Bridge. I'm going to be an absolute wreck at work in the morning.

"Do you want to stay with us tonight so you don't have to be alone?" Derek asks.

I'm so stunned by his offer that I'm temporarily speechless. Is he thinking about what Wynter said?

"I know you were upset at Adrian's," he adds.

"I was, but I'm okay."

"I've got a lovely guest room that's all yours whenever you don't want to be alone."

"Thank you for that and so many other things too numerous for me to ever be able to list."

He pulls up outside my building. "Every minute we spend together is my pleasure." He leans over to kiss my cheek. "See you in the morning?"

"Ugh, bright and early."

"Get some rest."

"You, too." I glance back at Maeve, sleeping soundly in her car seat, her sweet cheeks pink from being in the sun all day even though we reapplied sunscreen numerous times. "Tell her I said I'll see her soon."

"I will."

"Night." I get out of the SUV and go up the stairs, waving to him when I'm inside the main door to my building. He always waits until he sees the lights go on in my apartment before he leaves. That's the sort of thing that has endeared him to me since we became friends. He takes care of me, even though I'm certainly not his responsibility.

I can barely stand to admit that Wynter's teasing struck a chord for me. Pregnancy has made me "horny," as she so inelegantly put it, and when I'm alone in my bed at night, it's not my sweet husband I think about.

No, it's Derek Kavanaugh I want, and the guilt threatens to consume me. Intellectually, I know there's nothing wrong with wanting him, but emotionally... It still feels wrong to want anyone other than Patrick. I wonder if a bell will suddenly ring one day, giving me permission to act on the feelings I have for Derek.

I'm not sure how I'll know if or when the time is right. All I know for sure is I'm not ready for that. Not yet, anyway.

ONE MONTH LATER...

Roni

It's Memorial Day weekend, and we're going to a cookout at Iris's home with the Wild Widows, who've become a wonderful part of my life. I'm round with pregnancy and starting to count down to my end-of-June delivery date. The fog of early widowhood has begun to lift as I've carved out a new life for myself.

And much of that new life revolves around Derek and Maeve.

We see each other every day. I've even relieved Patrice a few times when Derek had to work late, making dinner for Maeve, bathing her and tucking her into bed for him. I love her so much. She's the most adorable little girl, and she's completely obsessed with the baby in my belly. I've decided not to find out the gender of the baby ahead of time, but I think Maeve wants to know more than anyone else.

We take her to movies, to the playground, to McDonald's for the chicken nuggets Derek says she'd eat every day if he let her, and I've even been with them to dinner at his parents' home a few times.

He and Maeve came with me to a get-together my parents hosted when my brother and his family came home for spring break. My parents love Derek, and they adore Maeve, and it's all so...effortless.

I suppose that's the way it should be, two people who were lucky enough to find each other in this crazy world, fitting into each other's lives and families with ease and comfort. We still have the occasional uncomfortable moment when we're out with Maeve, and people assume we're married with our second child on the way.

We've never come right out and discussed our plan of attack for when that happens. Rather, we both nod and smile at the person and move on with our day as if the comment hasn't lacerated two recovering broken hearts.

Other than an occasional peck on the cheek or one-armed hug, our relationship is completely platonic, even if the sparks that were there at the beginning are still very present, simmering on slow burn until some undeclared date in the future when things will presumably change between us.

I've begun to wonder lately when or if that's going to happen. Although, it's sort of difficult to tell the guy you've been crushing on for quite some time now that you might be ready for a little more than a peck on the cheek when you're super pregnant with your late husband's child.

So yeah, that's where we are.

Derek and Maeve are picking me up in thirty minutes to drive to Iris's house. I'm putting the finishing touches on the coleslaw I made, along with chocolate chip cookies that will be Derek's contribution. He does things to make life easier for me, such as drive me to and from work most days, so I do what I can for him, the way I did for Patrick.

I experience a pang when I recall that fateful last night and how my failure to go to the grocery store led him to being out on the street where he was hit by a stray bullet. A while ago, I brought that up again with the Wild Widows and talked about how it continued to haunt me. Turns out many of them had similar woulda-coulda-shoulda stories that have stuck with them long after losing their spouse or significant other. It continues to help to know I'm not alone with the thoughts and feelings that come with profound grief.

As promised, Dr. Gordon sent me a list of possible therapists, but I've found that I get the therapy I need from the Wild Widows' weekly meetings and frequent get-togethers like the one today, where I'll be surrounded by people who understand me like no one else ever could—even the best of therapists.

The one area of my life that's not what I'd like it to be is my relationship with my in-laws. They were elated when I called to tell them about the baby, but when I tried to explain my friend-ship with Derek and Maeve to them, they got upset, even when I assured them it isn't romantic in nature. "We're just friends," I said, but even that, apparently, is too much for them to handle.

Iris tried to explain to me that I can have my Chapter 2 with someone new, but they can't find a new son.

"That's not what I'm doing, though," I protested. "I'm not replacing Patrick."

"You and I know that, and we understand the complicated

dynamics of this situation, but it's harder for them. They want everything to be the way it was before they lost Patrick, and you moving forward with someone new is a reminder to them that nothing will ever be the same."

"I can't bear to be at odds with them," I said.

"Then don't be. Make them part of everything with the baby and your life, and eventually they'll come around. Or they won't. That won't be up to you."

Gah, it's the worst to wonder if they're angry with me for getting on with my life. What choice do I have? I keep coming back to that question. If Patrick hadn't been killed, I would've spent the rest of my life with him. I know that, and so do they.

I've made a point to include them in every development with the baby, texting when I felt it move for the first time, first kicks, my thoughts about names, etc. Last Sunday, they threw a lovely shower for me with their family and friends, and for a while there, it felt like old times, but with one very important person missing.

After everyone left, my mother-in-law, Susan, asked me if Derek was my boyfriend.

"No," I said. "He's not. We're just very good friends who have been through a similar ordeal."

"And that's all it's ever going to be?"

I was flabbergasted by the question. "I... I don't know."

"I see."

No! I wanted to say. *You don't see anything! You still have your husband of forty years by your side. I lost mine. You don't get to judge me!*

Patrick's sister-in-law, Clara, was the one to tip me off that they'd heard about me and Derek. A random friend of theirs saw us at the grocery store with Maeve, looking "like a happy little family," which immediately got back to them. I guess they were especially perturbed that I didn't tell them myself that I'm seeing someone new.

Except I'm not *seeing someone new*. I have a *friend* who is a *man*. It's all so terribly uncomfortable, and it's caused me a few sleepless nights that I can ill afford, as the third trimester has wiped me out.

However... The reason I couldn't answer Susan's question is that I *do* want more with Derek, and I know he wants more with me, but we're stuck firmly in the friend zone for now. I suspect he might be waiting until after the baby arrives to bring up what exactly we're doing here.

In the meantime, we're together every chance we get, and our friendship is a tremendous source of comfort to me. I refuse to give that up, even if it makes Patrick's parents uncomfortable.

I haven't told anyone about what's going on with them—not my family or Derek. I've kept it to myself in the hope that it'll work itself out eventually. The last thing I need is everyone who loves me resenting them for making things harder for me. If I've learned anything in the last almost eight months, it's how brutal grief is. I'm the last person who'd ever judge anyone, even my in-laws, for how they choose to handle a loss as egregious as what happened to their only son.

I miss the warm relationship I shared with Susan, in particular, and her husband, Pete, and I hope against hope we might regain some of our former closeness after the baby arrives. My child will tie our two families together forever, and I want Susan and Pete, as well as Patrick's brothers and their families, to be a big part of his or her life.

I try to push the worrisome thoughts about my in-laws to the back burner so I can enjoy the day with my friends. Tomorrow, May 28, is Patrick's birthday. The Connollys asked me to come to their house for dinner, but I told them I'm planning to spend the day alone at home. I even scheduled the day off from work, knowing I wouldn't be able to focus on anything productive that day. I've decided I'm ready to watch the wedding video, and that's how I plan to honor him on what would've been his thirty-second birthday.

In my bedroom, I pack a tote bag with sunscreen, a hat, my maternity bathing suit in case I get brave enough to take a dip in Iris's pool and one of Patrick's DEA T-shirts. His clothes have become an essential part of my wardrobe as I explode out of everything else.

The one good thing about pregnancy is that I've put on a

little weight that has filled out my cheeks and made me look healthy again, even if my ankles are so swollen, I can barely see my feet. Dr. Gordon says that's perfectly normal, especially this time of year when it starts to get hot again, but he's keeping a close eye on me to make sure it doesn't turn into preeclampsia.

I read up on what that is and then immediately regretted it.

I'm fine, my baby is fine, and that's how it's going to stay.

Iris told me I have nothing to worry about because I've already had my big tragedy, so the rest of my life ought to be smooth sailing. If only I could believe that. Anxiety was never part of my life until I lost Patrick and discovered how everything you hold dear can be lost in an instant. Now I worry about everything—and everyone.

My phone chimes with a text from Derek. *Here.*

Coming!

Yesterday, at my checkup with Dr. Gordon, he advised me to remove my rings in case my hands swell like my feet have. "You don't want to wait and have to have them cut off," he said. I should've done it when I got home yesterday, but I didn't, and I know I should since it's warm outside, and the heat doesn't help with the swelling.

As I gaze down at my gorgeous rings on my left hand, I decide to do it quickly before it can become "a thing" that'll ruin my day. I work them off my finger, which is harder than I expect it to be, indicating the swelling is already affecting my hands. I place them in my jewelry box, grab my bags and head downstairs to meet Derek and Maeve.

It's no big deal that I'm not wearing my rings. I can always put them back on after the baby comes. The last thing I want is to have them cut off, so it's the right thing to remove them now. I would've had to do that even if Patrick was still here.

Like everything, however, it's harder because he isn't.

Twenty

Roni

Derek gets out of the running car to take my bags from me and stashes them in the back. Then he's there to help me into the passenger seat. "How're you feeling today?"

He asks me that every day. "Bigger than a whale."

"Cutest whale I've ever seen," he says with a wink.

See how he does that? Makes me feel special with five little words that mean the world to me because I don't have my husband to tell me I'm a cute preggo? How could anyone not fall for a man who's handsome, sexy, kind, thoughtful, sweet and always thinking of ways to make your life easier? I'm definitely falling for him, if I haven't already fallen, that is.

"If you say so."

"I do. I say so."

"Ron!"

I turn to smile at the little girl buckled into her car seat. "Hi, Maeve."

"Party!"

"Yes, we're going to a party."

"She's very excited to swim in Miss Iris's pool," Derek says. "We had a long talk about staying away from the pool unless Daddy is there, didn't we, pumpkin?"

"No pool, Daddy."

"That's right." He glances at me. "Are all little girls as cute as mine is?"

"Nope. None of them are."

"I'm glad you agree. If you didn't, that might've been a deal breaker."

"Do we have a deal?" I ask casually, as if our deal is no big deal.

"I sort of thought we did."

"We should probably talk about that at some point, huh?"

"Probably so. I'll look forward to that."

Even though the idea of actually discussing with Derek what we're doing makes me nervous, I also feel silly and lighthearted, the way I did when I first met Patrick, and everything seemed possible. It's a welcome relief from the months of heavy grief, but it's not without the ever-present gray space that sits between joy and sorrow.

When we arrive at Iris's house, we're surrounded by our Wild Widows, who've become like a second family to me. Especially Iris, who is one of my new best friends. Her kids, Tyler, Sophia and Laney are as excited about my baby as I am, or so it seems. They can't wait to "babysit" for me and have promised to teach the baby everything he or she needs to know to survive in the world.

Iris and Derek set me up by the pool with my swollen feet propped on a footstool Iris brings out from her living room. "You're too good to me," I tell her.

"You're the most adorable pregnant lady I've ever seen," she says for the umpteenth time. She's taken it upon herself to say all the things my late husband would've said to me as my body bloomed with pregnancy.

"I don't know about that, but I'll be damned glad when it's over."

"We all say that. It's supposed to be the most natural thing, but try telling that to lungs being squeezed, a bladder being sat upon and skin that feels like it's going to burst at any second."

"Right? I'm stuck between wanting the pregnancy to be over and being terrified to have the baby."

"It's all going to be fine. Try not to worry."

I want to soak up the assurances of a mother with three children, but as the birth has gotten closer, I'm increasingly more anxious about the actual delivery. The childbirth classes I took with Rebecca, who will be my coach, didn't help allay those fears. Rather, they only made the fear more intense. In the last month, I've had to stop reading the what-to-expect books and stay offline when it comes to childbirth.

Derek brings me an ice water with lemon and a plate of appetizers.

"Thank you," I say, smiling up at him. How blessed am I to have these new friends who understand my journey to share this new uncharted season with?

"Welcome."

Naomi, Kinsley and Brielle, carrying her little Charlie, join me on lounges by the pool where we while away a lovely afternoon of sun, fun and friends. Aurora, the one who had her sights set on Derek, still hasn't come back to our group. Iris has reached out to check on her again, but hasn't heard anything from her. While I'm glad not to have her glaring at me at every get-together, I do worry about whether she's okay. Her ex-husband's trial is coming up, so it's been in the news a lot lately.

Derek spends much of the afternoon in the pool with Maeve as well as Adrian and his son, Xavier. Maeve adores Xavier and talks about him all the time, so she's thrilled to be swimming with him, Iris's kids and Wynter, who has come so far out of her shell since I first met her as to barely resemble the person she was then. We're all so proud of her and the progress she's made since losing her young husband to bone cancer.

The Wild Widows are a lovely group of people, and they've been one of the greatest blessings of this difficult time for me. I'm so thankful as I sit among these special friends who feel like family and enjoy this beautiful late spring day. Just like the buds on the trees and the flowers in the garden, I feel myself emerging from a dark winter to all the possibilities that come with spring.

As usual lately, I have to pee urgently. When I start to get up, everyone is there to offer hands to help me, making me feel like a little old lady. I start to say so when a gush of fluid between my legs has me wondering with horror if I've just peed my pants. I'm still staring at the puddle at my feet when Iris speaks up.

"Honey, I think your water just broke."

THIS CANNOT BE HAPPENING! It's a month early! The baby isn't ready, and neither am I! My emotions border on pure hysteria as everyone scrambles to figure out what to do with me. "Oh my God, Rebecca is in Colorado this weekend visiting her in-laws. My parents are away, and so is my other sister!"

My parents are spending the weekend in Chincoteague Island with old friends, and Pen is at a family reunion in Texas for Luke's family. They were uncomfortable about leaving me home alone so close to the baby's due date, but I assured them that with a month to go, it was safe for them to go out of town.

"Don't worry," Derek says. "I'll go with you. I've done this before."

His reassurance and his presence help to calm me somewhat, but I still feel like my heart is about to burst from my chest at any second.

"I'll have my parents come get Maeve," Derek says to Iris. "Is that okay?"

"Of course. Leave her with me and go."

Derek takes a minute to explain what's happening to Maeve, who's thankfully familiar enough with Iris and her kids that she's fine about us leaving. She comes over to hug me, her sweet chubby little arms encircling my neck in a death grip.

"Baby," she whispers.

"Love you," I respond.

"Love."

I don't want to let her go, but the tightening ache in my abdomen is a sign that my water breaking was the start of things to come. I'm so scared that I tremble uncontrollably as Derek leads Maeve over to Brielle, who will watch her while Iris helps him get me to the car.

In the background, I hear Maeve crying as we walk away. I want to go back to her, to assure her that everything is all right, but I can't do that right now.

"Don't worry," Iris says. "She'll be playing and laughing again in no time."

When I'm seat-belted into the front seat of Derek's car with my beach towel under me, Iris squats to look me in the eye. "Just keep breathing. You're fine. The baby is fine."

My eyes flood with tears. "I'm scared."

"Breathe. I promise you can do this."

As I nod to reassure her that I'm okay when I'm anything but, I want Patrick so fiercely that the need for him threatens to consume me.

She leans in to hug me before she shuts the door and waves us off.

Derek is on the phone with his parents making arrangements for Maeve as I sob softly.

The emotional tsunami was to be expected, I suppose. Of course I want Patrick as I'm about to have our child. And then I recall the date. It's one day before his birthday. Will the baby be born today or tomorrow, on Patrick's birthday? I should notify my parents and Patrick's, but I don't want to worry them if this is a false alarm.

Derek ends the call with his parents and reaches for my hand. "How you doing?"

"Okay. I guess."

"You should call to let them know you're coming."

What does it say about me as a mother that it never occurred to me to call ahead to the hospital? That maybe I'm not at all ready for any of this. "Oh, good idea." I make the call to the number we were given in the birthing class and let them know I'm coming.

"We'll meet you at the main entrance," the nurse says.

"All set," I tell Derek. "They're going to meet us."

He reaches for my hand. "Hold on to me. I'm right here."

I curl my hand around his and hold on tight as the pain becomes a bit more intense. "Thank you."

He drives faster than he probably should to get me back to the District and the George Washington University Hospital.

I'm so scared and nervous. The sight of the hospital makes it real, and everything in me recoils from going in there.

"Are you breathing?" Derek asks.

I realize I'm holding my breath, and his question spurs me to release it slowly.

"Keep breathing. It'll help."

A nurse wearing pink scrubs is waiting at the main door with a wheelchair. She tells Derek where to find me after he parks and whisks me inside and upstairs to the OB ward that I toured during my class. The team up there is so efficient that they have me changed into a gown and attached to a fetal heartrate monitor before Derek arrives fifteen minutes later.

"You can come right over here, Mr. Connolly," the nurse says.

The words are an arrow to my heart. "He's Mr. Kavanaugh," I tell the nurse. "Mr. Connolly died almost eight months ago."

"I'm so sorry."

"It's okay," I say, even if it isn't okay at all. I requested that information be included in my patient record, but they probably didn't have time to delve into that before I arrived a month early. "Will the baby be okay coming this early?"

"Any time after thirty-six weeks, you're in the zone, but we'll see what the doctor says when he arrives."

The next few hours pass in a flurry of activity, examinations, monitors and people in and out.

"Looks like we're having a baby today or tomorrow," Dr. Gordon declares after he thoroughly examines me. His presence helps to calm me.

Derek offers to leave the room for the exam, but I want him right there with me. I just hope he doesn't see anything that can't be unseen.

It's such a strange mix of sadness, joy, anxiety and excitement. I'm so happy Derek is there with me. That feels right even if everything about it is wrong. Patrick ought to be standing beside me, feeding me ice chips, running cold cloths over my face and telling me I'm doing great. I'm weepy for him in a way I haven't been for a while now, which makes me feel guilty. Why haven't I been weepy for him the way I was at first? What's wrong with me that I'm not still crying for the love of my life every day?

"Roni."

Derek's voice snaps me out of the spiral my thoughts have taken me on.

I look up at him.

He takes hold of my hand, the one without the IV. If I never have to have another IV needle in my hand, that'll be fine with me. "Breathe and stop doing whatever it is you're doing to yourself. You've got enough to deal with today without whatever you're adding to the mix."

"Patrick should be here."

"I bet he is. I bet he's right here watching over you and your baby and making sure you're both safe."

"Do you really think so?"

"I do. I'm sure there's nowhere else he'd rather be than wherever you are." With his free hand, he uses a tissue to wipe up my tears.

"It's so unfair that he has to miss this. That he'll miss everything."

"I know."

"Is it unfair for me to be talking about him with you?"

"What? No, of course not."

"Oh," I say on a long exhale. "Okay. Good."

"You never have to worry about talking about him with me, Roni. He's such a big part of you, and he always will be. He's welcome in whatever relationship you and I have, just as I hope Victoria is, too."

"Yes, she is. For sure." I think of the photos of his gorgeous wife that I've seen around his house and feel sad for him, for both of us.

"Don't worry about stuff that you don't need to."

"I'm an emotional disaster area today."

He wipes away more of my tears. "Nah, you're about to

become a mom for the first time. You're allowed to feel all the things."

"Was Victoria like this when she had Maeve?"

"Yep. It's perfectly normal."

"I know how much you hate girl tears," I say, smiling at him.

He makes a comically stern face that's wildly out of character for him. "I'll make an exception for today and tomorrow, and then we're back to business as usual with no girl tears allowed."

I wouldn't have expected to laugh right then, but leave it to Derek. "We never got to have that conversation we had planned."

"We will. We've got all the time in the world to have every conversation we need to have. For now, let's focus on bringing your little one into the world."

"Thanks for being here with me. It's not what you signed on for—"

"I'm here for all of it, sweetheart. Don't worry about me. Focus on you and the baby. It's all good."

His calm demeanor and reassurances have me releasing a deep breath.

"Would you rather have a girlfriend here with you for this?"

At some point, he's become my touchstone, my true north, the one I want by my side for the biggest moment of my life. "I'd rather have you, unless you want to get back to Maeve."

"She's fine with my parents, and I'm right where I want to be." He tucks a strand of my hair behind my ear. "Do you want me to have someone grab your bag from your place?"

"I hadn't packed anything yet," I say, feeling sheepish. "I thought I had time."

"The baby had other plans."

The words are stolen from me by the sharpest pain I've had yet. *Crap*, that hurt. Within an hour, I'm begging for an epidural.

"I've called the anesthesiologist," the nurse says, "but they're backed up. They'll be here soon."

Things go downhill fast from there. My sisters and friends with kids told me I wouldn't remember much about giving birth. They said I'd be so happy to have the baby that the pain wouldn't matter. I've already decided that's a bunch of bullshit, and I'm nowhere near ready to push yet. I'm so out of my mind with the pain that I barely care when the anesthesiologist finally shows up and sticks a needle in my back that provides instant relief.

Thank God for modern medicine.

I'm so exhausted from the last few hours that I immediately crash into dream-riddled sleep, in which Patrick is there, whole and healthy and vibrantly alive even as I'm aware that he's still dead.

The craziness continues when I come to, awakened by intense pressure between my legs and a flurry of activity happening around me.

I look up at Derek.

He holds my gaze. "You got this, Roni. You're so strong. You're almost there."

Behind him, the sky is dark. Have we been here that long? "What time is it?"

"Just after midnight."

Jesus. "Patrick's birthday."

Derek gasps. "Is it?"

Nodding, I grimace from the pressure as my legs are lifted and spread obscenely in front of a room full of people I've never met. That I don't even care who's seeing me spread wide open is an indication of my current state of mind. I have zero effs to give for anything other than getting this baby out right now.

Turns out, the first part was easy compared to pushing. Even with the epidural, I feel like I'm being split in half as the baby fights to make its way into the world. I push for two hours before I hear the doctor mention something about a cesarean.

"No, I don't want that." I double down on the pushing, giving it everything I've got until the baby finally arrives at four thirty-two.

"You have a son," Dr. Gordon announces.

I can't see through my tears. Everything hurts. But I have a *son*.

Patrick and I have a son.

"Is he..." I gaze up at Derek, feeling frantic. "Shouldn't he be crying?"

"He's doing great," another doctor says from across the room, where she's examining the baby. "Six pounds, two ounces, nineteen inches." She brings him to me, wrapped in a receiving blanket with a little cap on his head. Dr. Gordon is still doing something between my legs, but I can't be bothered with that when my son wants to meet me.

"He's beautiful, Roni," Derek says, subtly swiping at a tear of his own. "You were amazing."

I can't stop staring at the perfection that is my son's face. "He's so small. My God. No one tells you how small they'll be!"

Derek laughs. "That won't last for long, so enjoy it while you can."

It takes about two full seconds for me to see that he looks exactly like his father, right down to the tiny dimples in his cheeks.

"What's his name?" Derek asks.

"Dylan Patrick Connolly." I decided on that name for a boy or a girl. "Named for Patrick and his favorite musician of all time."

"I love that. Hi, Dylan. So nice to meet you."

"Dylan, this is Derek. He's been a very good friend to Mommy while she was expecting you, and I suspect he's going to be a very good friend to you, too. And wait until you meet his sweet daughter, Maeve. She's so excited to meet you."

"I'm going to be there for you, Dylan." Derek leans in to kiss the baby on the forehead. Then he kisses my cheek. "And your mom."

Twenty-One

Derek

I'm wrecked from the emotional overload of being with Roni while she gave birth to Dylan. She was a warrior, and I'm so proud of her and already in love with her little guy. He's absolutely adorable. And that he was born on Patrick's birthday... It's all too much. I haven't left her side in hours, except to pee twice. I'm hungry, tired and need a shower, but none of that matters.

What's really odd is I feel exactly the same way I did when Maeve was born—elated, terrified, thrilled, madly in love and looking forward to everything with this new little boy.

I have no idea if I should allow myself to go there, but I'm already there without having given it much thought. Everything with Roni has been so organic from the beginning. We've fallen into this sweet friendship that could be so much more than that if we allowed it to be. I'm ready for that, but I'm on her timetable. I wish we'd gotten to have "the conversation" before Dylan arrived, but we'll get there. I hope sooner rather than later, because I want to be part of their lives. I want Maeve and Dylan to grow up together. I want us to be a family, but only if that's what Roni wants, too.

Roni is with the lactation nurse as she tries to figure out breastfeeding, which seems like a good time to take a break and get a coffee. I'd give anything for a toothbrush, but that'll have to wait until the gift shop opens at nine.

I take a second in the cafeteria to send a text to Terry and Nick. *Roni had her baby at 4:32 a.m.—a month early, a boy named Dylan Patrick who was born on his father's birthday. Since we were together when shit got real, I ended up being her coach (most useless position in the game). I'm going to take a personal day tomorrow and maybe Tuesday, too. Not sure what she's going to need. Anyway... That's my situation.*

I'm not surprised when Nick replies right away in a private message just to me. His insomnia is a thing of legend, never more so than since he suddenly became president last November. *Congratulations to Roni on the arrival of Dylan. And on his dad's bday. My heart.*

I know. Mine, too. It's amazing.

How are you?

I'm fine. She's the one who did all the hard work.

But how are YOU?

Leave it to my old friend to home in on the question of the hour. *I'm in this weird place of wishing I knew for sure I was going to get to raise this little guy as my son. Any other questions?*

Well, there you have it. What do you think she'd say to that?

I think I know, but not for certain, which is making me crazy. We were going to talk last night, but Dylan had other plans for us.

For what it's worth, I think it's a big deal that she wanted you with her when she probably has a lot of other people she could've asked to be there.

I tend to agree, but I'm trying not to get ahead of myself.

Sam and I love you two together and hope something comes of it. You've been wise to take it slow and give her the space she needs for her grief.

I love the way this has happened with her, how we've kind of just eased into this super comfortable friendship that has so much potential. She's incredible with Maeve, who absolutely adores her, and the best part is that there's room for Vic and her husband, Patrick, in our relationship. We both get what the other has lost. It's perfect in every way. I'm just not sure if it's ever going to be more than what it is.

You need to be patient. It hasn't even been a year since she lost him.

I know. Sigh. I'm all about the patience.

But you're ready to move forward, too.

Yeah.

It's going to matter to her that you gave her the space to come around to this in her own time, that you didn't rush her or make her feel obligated. It will matter to her that you've been there for her through the roughest time in her life and that you'll be there for her and Dylan. I have to believe all of that will add up to what you want it to be.

I really hope so. How much do you charge for middle-of-the-night counseling from POTUS?

Free for you, my great friend. I'm so, so happy to see you coming back from your own horrible loss. Sam said the same thing recently —how she feels like we're getting Derek back lately.

That's nice to hear. It's been a journey for sure, and I tell myself that Roni has the right to travel her own path to get to a place where she's ready for what's next.

I've seen the two of you together. She's on her way to you. She might not have arrived yet, but she's coming.

You really think so?

Absolutely.

That makes me feel better. Thanks for the pep talk.

Keep doing what you're doing. Sam will want to visit Roni later.

I'm sure she'd love that.

Hang in there, brother.

Will do. Thanks again, Nick. Really. This helped.

You got it.

As I take the elevator back to the maternity floor, I think about what Nick said and summon the patience I need to see this through to the point where Roni is ready to talk about *us* and whether there's going to be an *us*. If that's not what she wants, I'm still prepared to continue a friendship that's brought me comfort, solace, joy, laughter and so many other things, it would be impossible to name them all.

I love her.

I have for quite some time. I first suspected it way back in March, on a freezing cold Friday night when we watched *Frozen* with Maeve for the nine hundredth time. Roni sang along to the songs, which delighted Maeve. She loves her, too. She talks about Roni and the baby all the time. I've wondered whether it was wise to allow her to get so attached to Roni when I have no idea where this is headed.

I worry about Roni waking up from her grief to realize I'm not what she wants for the next part of her life. I'll be completely crushed if that happens. I've allowed my mind to wander pretty far down the road to a life that includes her and Dylan. It's nice to be able to assign a name to him beyond "the baby."

Dylan.

His name is Dylan Patrick Connolly.

And I already love him with all my heart.

When I return to Roni's room, she's out cold, and Dylan is in the bassinette next to her, wide awake. Despite being swaddled, he's moving around like he's ready to try life on the outside. I debate for a second whether Roni would mind if I pick him up and decide of course she wouldn't. After I put down my coffee, I lift him carefully from the bassinette and take him with me to the recliner chair in the corner.

"Hey, buddy, it's me, Derek," I whisper to him. "I'm your mommy's friend, and we've been so looking forward to meeting you." I adjust the knitted cap on his head back off his forehead.

He studies me carefully, even though I recall from when Maeve was born that newborns can't see much at first. Dylan seems to be an exception. Wanting to test my theory, I raise my index finger over his face, and his eyes follow it from left to right. "You're brilliant like your daddy was. I knew it."

I rock him for a long time, and he stares at me almost without blinking.

"I'm not the guy who should be welcoming you to this world. I didn't get a chance to meet your dad, but from what everyone tells me, he was a heck of a guy. He was smart and kind, and he loved your mom very much. Even though I didn't get to meet him, you can take my word for it when I tell you he'd want to be here with you and your mom more than anywhere else. And you were born on his birthday, which is so cool. I don't believe in coincidences, buddy. You came a month early because your daddy wanted you to have his birthday."

He listens intently to me while continuing to squirm inside the confines of the blanket.

"But since he can't be here, I want you to know that I am. I'm here, buddy, and I'm not going anywhere. Whatever you need, I'll make sure you get it. No matter what. Okay? I'll show you everything you need to know about being a guy, like how to throw the perfect curve ball and spiral and how to talk to girls— or boys—no judgment. I'll show you how to drive and how to skateboard and anything else you want to do. We'll do it all. I can't wait for you to meet my Maeve. She already loves you so much. We both do."

I decide to free him from the blanket because that seems to be what he wants. I hold out my hand to him, and he wraps a strong little hand around my index finger.

"It's very nice to meet you, too, Dylan," I say, my voice heavy with emotion.

Roni

I WAKE to the sound of Derek's voice as he speaks softly to Dylan. His sweet words bring tears to my eyes. How can there be more tears? These tears, however, are tears of joy. I have a *son*, and I have Derek. And I have Maeve. As I listen to Derek pledge to be there for Dylan, to teach him guy things and tell him he already loves him, I can no longer deny I'm in love with Derek Kavanaugh.

My emotions are a series of soaring highs and crushing lows. Patrick should be the one holding his newborn son, but since that's not possible, Derek is here. He's been right here with me almost since the day we met, and despite the weirdness of our initial meetings, he's been steadfast in his friendship and support ever since.

I want him in my life—and Dylan's. I want to be in his life—and Maeve's. This wasn't the path I planned for myself, but it's the one I'm on, and I'm so very thankful that he's walking beside me.

"Hey," I say when I've gotten myself as together as I'm going to get today.

"Mommy's awake," Derek tells Dylan. "You want to go see her?"

The baby's arms and legs are in constant motion.

Derek stands and brings the baby to me. "I think he's going to be a star soccer player. He never stops moving. He wanted out of the swaddle."

As he passes the baby to me, Derek's hand brushes against my arm, setting off a reaction that zings through my entire body. "I love that he's already showing us his personality."

"He's so perfect and alert. I swear he can already see, even though they say that's not possible."

"Clearly, he's brilliant like his daddy was."

"I couldn't agree more. Iris texted to check on you, so I shared the news with her. Hope that's okay."

"Of course it is."

"She said she'll tell the other Wild Widows and ask them to sit on the news until you get the chance to tell everyone."

I need to tell my family and Patrick's that Dylan has arrived, but for a little while longer, I want to share him only with Derek. I look up at him. "Thank you so much for being here with us."

"I wouldn't have wanted to be anywhere else."

He looks at me in a way that tells me his feelings are every bit as strong as mine are. There's so much I want to say to him, but I'm so tired and drained that now isn't the time.

"You should go home to Maeve."

"She's very happy with Grandma and Grandpa."

"Are you sure? You must be so tired."

"I'm fine. Don't worry about me."

"We need to have that conversation..."

"We will. I promise. In the meantime, I'm not going anywhere. Unless you want me to."

"No, don't go."

His sweet smile lights up tired eyes. He takes hold of my free hand and kisses the back of it. "Thanks for letting me be part of Dylan's first day."

"We're very happy you're here." I move my tired, aching body over to the far side of the bed. "Come be with us."

"Are you sure?" he asks.

"I'm very sure."

WE SPEND that entire night snuggled up in my hospital bed, marveling at the miracle that is Dylan, caring for him together like two first-time parents, except one of us is experienced. Derek changes his diaper like a champ and laughs when he gets peed on in the middle of the night. "I forgot that boys have skills that girls don't," he says, wiping pee from the side of his face.

"Oh my goodness, Dylan! Don't pee on Derek!" I can't stop laughing, even though it hurts to breathe, let alone laugh.

"Y'all are having way too much fun," a new nurse says when she comes into the room to find us cracking up.

"The baby peed on Derek," I tell her.

"All the new daddies with boys have to find that one out the hard way," she says, chuckling. "You'd think they'd know what that thing is capable of at this point."

Her comments set us off all over again, and I don't worry about correcting her comment about Derek being a new daddy.

"As long as you can laugh, you're going to slay this parenthood thing," she adds after she checks my vitals. "Are you comfortable, honey?"

"Define 'comfortable.'"

"You're going to be sore for a few days, but you'll bounce back quickly." Lowering her voice, she adds, "And you've got a handsome man to make it all better. You go, girl."

It's all so wonderful and awful at the same time. Where's

Patrick? He should be here. My heart soars with love for Dylan and Derek even as it breaks with sorrow for Patrick.

In the morning, I text my family and Patrick's to share the big news and to marvel that Dylan was born on Patrick's birthday. I include a photo of me holding Dylan that Derek took on my phone.

The responses are instantaneous.

Holy crap, Rebecca says. *I missed it! I'm so sorry, Ronald!*

He's beautiful, Pen says. *Congrats, Ron!*

Welcome to the world, Dylan Patrick, my brother says. *We can't wait to meet you.*

My parents reply with excitement and joy over their new grandson and ask if they can come see us.

I'm probably going home later today. I'll let you know.

Do you need a ride? Dad asks.

Derek is here. I'll let you know when we're home.

Dad replies with a thumbs-up.

"Is it weird that no one from Patrick's family has responded?" I ask Derek half an hour later.

"I'm sure they're processing the news. It has to be bittersweet for them, like it is for you."

"I guess." While that may be true, I'm still disappointed not to hear back from them. "Do you think they're mad that I texted rather than called?"

"Roni, you just had a baby. You don't owe anyone anything more than you've already given them. Besides, wouldn't they want to see a photo of the baby?"

"I suppose so."

Though I'm determined to focus on Dylan and preparing to take him home, the silence from Patrick's family casts a pall over the day. The same nurse we had yesterday is back to walk me through the basics of bathing the baby and tending to his umbilical cord. My milk has come in with a vengeance, and thankfully, Dylan is breastfeeding like a champ. While I practice bathing and feeding, Derek runs to my place to get the infant car seat I bought in anticipation of this day.

He's back for a few minutes when he accepts a FaceTime call

from his mother, and Maeve's cute little face pops up on the screen. "Wanna see him."

He smiles at her bossy tone. "Roni is feeding him right now, but I'll show you as soon as they're done."

Maeve has a million questions about the baby, about when she can see him and whether he can be her baby brother.

Derek looks at me with wide eyes when she asks that.

"Of course he can," I say. "He'll be very lucky to have you as his big sister, Maeve." When he finishes feeding, he's knocked out. I adjust my gown to cover my breast and situate him so she can easily see his face.

"He so *tiny*," she says on a long exhale.

"Yes, he is," I respond. "We have to be very gentle with him for a while, but soon enough, he'll be chasing you around."

"I take care of him," she says solemnly.

I swallow the huge lump that forms in my throat. "He'll like that, sweetie."

"How're you feeling, Roni?" Derek's mom asks me.

"Like I got hit by a bus, but I'm told that's normal."

"It is, and thankfully, it doesn't last too long."

"That's good to know."

"They're about ready to discharge Roni and Dylan," Derek says. "We'll check in with you later."

"Daddy come home!"

"Tomorrow, pumpkin. One more night with Grandma and Grandpa, and then you can come home, okay?"

"Okay."

"Love you."

"Love you," she says, pointing at him.

"Be good for Grandma and Grandpa."

"I be good."

They say their goodbyes, and he ends the call. "She's so excited."

"She's adorable. I can't wait for her to meet Dylan tomorrow."

"What she said about him being her little brother... I didn't expect her to say that."

"I love that she said that. How lucky will Dylan be to have Maeve as his big sister?"

"I'm feeling all the feels here, Veronica," he confesses with an adorably shy smile.

"Me, too. All the feels."

"And that's okay? Are you ready for that?"

"Yes and no. It's such a strange place to be. It's wonderful and terrible at the same time."

"I know, sweetheart. I know."

"That helps. That you get it."

"I do. And what I know for certain is that we're both still here for some reason, and we found each other for a reason."

"Are we having that conversation?" I ask, smiling.

"We're starting it. To be continued after we get your little guy home."

I tingle in anticipation. Among all the terrible things, a kernel of hope blossoms within me even as I continue to intensely grieve the loss of my Patrick. It's like trying to walk on a teeter-totter while balancing the hope and the grief and the overabundance of love for people who are here and one who isn't. It's a tricky task, but one I have no choice but to undertake.

I didn't go looking for a new relationship. Well, I didn't intend for that to happen when I started following Derek in the neighborhood. Our friendship has evolved organically into something more, even if that wasn't something I would've thought I wanted until I had it.

People who don't understand are going to judge. The secondary losses are almost as painful as the loss of Patrick was— friends I thought would never leave my side have all but disappeared. People who were there in the beginning have gone back to their own lives, having done what they could to help me through my tragedy. I don't blame them for that. I really don't, but I also know now that the future is mine to chart as I see fit. No one else can decide that course for me and Dylan. Only I can.

I have a whole new group of people in my life, due to of our shared experiences, and I'm ever more thankful to them.

All this is on my mind as Derek drives us home. I'm in the

back seat with Dylan, who is sound asleep and missing his first car ride.

I love Derek. I still love Patrick, and I always will.

Who am I now? A mother to a fatherless child, a wife to a man who's no longer physically present and now in a relationship with another man and his daughter, who've become the center of my new life.

I glance at my phone and see no response from any of Patrick's family, which hurts me more than I care to admit. Aren't they happy to hear Patrick's son has arrived, not to mention on his birthday? Sure, the date of his arrival probably made it hurt a little more for them as it did for me, too, but I'm so confused by their lack of response and have no idea how to interpret their silence.

Twenty-Two

Roni

Derek carries the baby seat up the stairs to my apartment. By the time I get there, I'm completely exhausted. My legs feel like rubber noodles, and my boobs are already bursting with the need to feed Dylan again.

When I'm settled on the sofa with a baby who's still sound asleep, I take advantage of the opportunity to text the photo to Sam and Lilia. *Dylan Patrick Connolly arrived a month early yesterday, on his father's birthday. I'm sorry for the short notice, but I guess I'm on maternity leave.*

Sam responds right away. *Oh, Roni! He's beautiful. And born on Patrick's birthday? That's so amazing. Nick and I are delighted for you and can't wait to meet Dylan!*

Congratulations, Roni! Lilia says. *Harry and I are thrilled to hear Dylan Patrick is here, and on his dad's birthday. Please don't worry about work. Enjoy every minute with your bundle of joy.*

I send a similar text to a bunch of other friends of mine and Patrick's and am flooded with responses from everyone.

Except his family.

"I don't know what to do," I tell Derek. "Should I call them?"

"Why don't you call his parents? You'll feel better after you talk to them."

Before I can overthink it to death, I put through the call to Patrick's mother. It rings four times before she picks up. "Roni."

"Hi there. I was just making sure you got my text about the baby coming early—and on Patrick's birthday."

"We did. Congratulations."

I want to ask her why she didn't reply to the text, but the words are stuck in my throat.

"We wondered why we didn't hear from you on Patrick's birthday."

I'm stricken by those words. "I was... I was having a baby."

"Yes, I realize that now."

Her cool tone is so far removed from the way she used to speak to me that I barely recognize her. "Are you angry with me, Susan?"

"Of course not."

"Why does it seem as if you are?"

"I'm not. This is all just very hard for us."

"It is for me, too. I just had my dead husband's baby on his birthday without him there to share in the joy with me. I think I understand how hard this is."

"But you have someone new now."

"I have many new friends who've traveled this same journey and have helped me through it."

"And one of them is extra special to you."

"That has nothing to do with the grief I feel for Patrick every minute of every day!"

"It seems soon to us for you to move on with someone new."

I'm so flabbergasted that I don't know how to respond. "I haven't moved on from him, Susan. If you knew how much I've suffered over his loss, you'd never say such a cruel thing to me."

"It's just how we see it."

"Well, that's good to know. I'm going to go take care of my son now."

"We'd like to see him."

I want to tell her to go to hell. She's not coming near me or my son, but out of respect for Patrick—and only him—I don't do that. "I, ah, sure."

"We'll be in touch."

"Okay."

I end the call without saying goodbye or anything else. What more is there to say?

Derek sits in front of me, on the coffee table Patrick and I bought at an estate sale five years ago. "Whatever she said, you know the truth. She doesn't know. *You* do. You're the only one who's been inside this journey, Roni. Only you."

"She says it's too soon for me to move on with someone else."

His expression hardens. "She doesn't get to decide that for you or for anyone, and you were right when you told her it was cruel for her to say such a thing to you. You haven't moved on from Patrick. You've moved forward because you had no choice but to do that, and you've brought him with you every step of the way."

"Yes, I have," I say softly. "I haven't done anything wrong."

"No, you certainly haven't. You've been respectful of him, his memory, them. They have no right to do this to you. I have to think, from what you've shared about them, that this might be *her* grief talking."

"It's not fair."

"No, it certainly isn't, but you can't take this on. You can't let it be a setback for you. Not when you have Dylan to care for. He needs you." He wraps both his hands around mine. "When she's had some time to think about what she just said, I'm sure she's going to be very sorry."

"Even if that's how she really feels?"

"Even if. Her feelings are not your responsibility. You were a wonderful, loving, devoted partner to her son for years. You made him very happy, and she had to have seen that. You honor Patrick's memory every single day with the way you're courageously living your life when it would've been so much easier to curl up in a ball and give up."

"It would've been easier, but that's not who I am."

"No, it isn't. You're full of optimism and joy, and nothing, not even the worst tragedy imaginable, can dim the light that shines in you."

"I feel like all I ever do is thank you."

"You don't need to thank me."

"Yes, I really do, because if you hadn't been here to tell me what I needed to hear, what she said would've taken me off the deep end."

"I'm here any time you need a reality check."

I crook my finger at him to bring him closer.

He barely breathes as he leans in.

I wrap my free hand around his neck and kiss him. Just a soft, sweet, simple kiss on the lips that's been an awfully long time coming—and is actually anything but simple. "I've wanted to do that for a while now."

"Me, too." He rests his forehead against mine. "I'm sorry she upset you. She had no right to do that."

My phone rings, which ends the moment between us. "It's my mom. Hey."

"Are you guys home?"

"We are. What about you?"

"Just got here and were going to come see you, if that's okay."

"Yes, come on over. I'm sorry you had to cut your trip short."

"We're not sorry. We can't wait to meet our grandson. Do you need anything?"

"I have no idea." I can't seem to remember past yesterday and don't have a clue what I've got for food in the house.

She laughs. "We'll stop at the store on the way. Be there shortly."

"Thanks, Mom. See you soon." I end the call and look down at my son, who's sleeping through everything on his first day out of the hospital. "Does this mean he's going to be up all night?"

"Probably."

"I was afraid you might say that." I feel shy around him now, after the way I brazenly kissed him. But I'm not sorry I did it.

"How about I run and get us some lunch?"

"I am kind of hungry."

"I'll hit the deli down the street. What do you feel like?"

"Some soup maybe?"

"You got it. I'll be right back."

Derek

I'm FUCKING *FUMING*. I can't believe Roni's mother-in-law would say such an awful thing to her after everything she's been through—and especially after she just had her late husband's baby. Does the woman have any concept of what an ordeal Roni has endured? Or how strong she is? I want to punch something, I'm so pissed.

She was so happy after Dylan arrived and so excited to bring him home. How dare anyone do anything to take that away from her?

I'm so spun up that I decide to take an extra minute to calm down by sitting outside the deli and breathing in the fresh air.

A waiter comes over. "Hi there. I'm Justin. What can I get you to drink?"

"I'm actually interested in takeout."

"Sure, I can help with that."

I order a roast beef sandwich for myself along with a bowl of chicken noodle and a grilled cheese for Roni. "Can you also toss in a couple of chocolate chip cookies?"

"You got it. Can I get you something to drink while you wait?"

"I'd love a coffee with cream. Thanks."

"Coming right up."

While I wait for the food, I decide I need someone to talk to about how I'm feeling before I actually act on the desire to punch something, so I call Iris.

"Hi there! How's our girl?"

"She's doing great. She and Dylan are home and resting."

"I'm so glad he's here, and it all went well."

"Me, too. But you won't believe how her mother-in-law is behaving." I fill her in on how Roni sent the text that went unanswered and then what happened when she called the woman.

"Oh gosh," Iris says with a sigh. "I hate that she said that."

"I know! Me, too. I'm so pissed. Roni was having such a great day. She's so happy about the baby, and he's just adorable. Now she's all upset about what her mother-in-law said, and the worst part is that nothing has even happened between us."

"Hasn't it, though?"

Those three little words cut straight to the chase. I huff out a laugh. "Leave it to you to get right to the point."

"Who among us has time for bullshit?"

"None of us."

"You love her."

"Yes."

"She loves you."

"I think she might."

"You were the one she wanted with her when her son was born, Derek."

"Yes," I say gruffly. "It was an incredible experience."

"Trust me. She loves you, or you wouldn't have been there. And I think it's wonderful you were there."

"This is all so..."

"Amazing and difficult?"

I drop my head into my hands. "Both those things."

"But so, so worth it, right? To feel that way again?"

"Yeah."

"I think you two will make for a fantastic couple. We all do. You both glow when you're together. The other day, Brielle said you look at Roni the way Brielle's husband looked at her."

I'm so choked up to hear that, I can barely breathe.

"What matters, Derek, is the two of you and what you're building together and with your children. I think it's beautiful."

"Thanks, Iris. I really needed to hear that."

"Stay the course. You both know you haven't done anything wrong. You've found comfort and hope in each other, and that's a very special thing after what you've both endured."

"Yes, it is."

Justin returns with my coffee and takeout bag.

I hand him my credit card. "I'd better get back to Roni and Dylan," I say to Iris.

"I *love* his name."

"I do, too. It suits him."

"Give Roni my love and take some for you, too, my friend."

"Back atcha, Iris. You're the best."

"I'm here if you guys need anything."

"Thanks again."

I end the call, thankful for the special friends I've made in the widow community. While I've leaned heavily on my parents, brothers and close friends like Nick, Andy and Harry, my widowed friends have formed the foundation on top of which I've built a new life for myself and Maeve.

As I'm walking back to Roni's, I receive a text from Adrian. *Heard the baby arrived. Congrats to Roni—and to you. I predict you're going to play an important role in young Dylan's life, and I wish you all the best.*

Thanks so much, friend. Dylan can't wait to meet you and Xavier.

Adrian's message touches me deeply. That our friends are rallying not only around Roni but around me, too, is so sweet.

My love for Roni has only grown over these last few months of close friendship, of shared dinners, of gatherings with friends and family, of creating something from the ashes of both our lives and building something new and important. When she kissed me earlier, I let go of all the worries I've carried about whether she and I are in the same place, or if this is going to turn into something more.

I've suspected for quite some time that she wants the same things I do, but she's taking the time she needs to be sure she's ready to move forward with me. In the meantime, I've tried to be patient. I've given her the space to cope with the first year without her husband while preparing to have their child.

Off in the distance was the baby's due date, and I've sort of hoped that once we got past that milestone, we might have time to breathe and figure out the answers to the unasked questions. Everything between us is so good, so easy, so perfect.

I just hope Roni's mother-in-law hasn't ruined that for her—and for me.

As I'm approaching Roni's front stairs, a black SUV comes to a stop outside. A man I recognize from the White House staff emerges, holding a huge bouquet of flowers and a box.

"Hi there. I'm Derek Kavanaugh. Are you looking for Roni Connolly?"

"Ah, yes, of course, Mr. Kavanaugh. Yes, I'm looking for Mrs. Connolly. The president and first lady asked me to deliver these gifts to celebrate the birth of her son."

"I'd be happy to take them up to her."

"Oh, thank you very much, sir. Please give her the best regards of the entire staff and our sincere congratulations." He hands me the flowers, the box and another card. "We all signed that."

"She'll love it. Thank you so much for delivering."

"My pleasure, sir."

Juggling bags, flowers and the box, I manage to get back inside the building and up the stairs to Roni's place. From outside the door, I can hear the baby crying. Inside, I find Roni walking him around the apartment, patting his back and trying to calm him.

I put the stuff on the counter and go to them.

"I don't know what's wrong," she says, her eyes big with emotion and exhaustion. "I fed him and changed him."

"Did he burp?"

"I think so."

"Want me to try?"

"Sure. Thanks." She hands him over to me.

"Hey, buddy, what's all this racket about?" I bounce him while giving him some brisk pats on the back that yield a very loud burp a few minutes later. "There it is."

"How'd you do that?"

"It's all in the wrist," I tell her, grinning.

The baby immediately stops crying and settles into my arms for a nap.

"I suck at this," she says, frowning.

"No, you don't. Everyone goes through the first few days flying blind. Soon enough, you'll be able to predict what he needs before he needs it."

"Are you sure?"

"I'm positive."

"How can they just send us home with him when we have no idea what we're doing?"

My lips quiver with the start of laughter that I know she won't appreciate.

"Are you trying not to laugh at me?"

"Would I do that?"

"Yes, I think you would."

She's so freaking adorable all the time, but even more so when she's indignant.

"Figures you're some kind of baby whisperer or something. Look at how you knocked him right out."

"I wasn't like that with Maeve." As I look down at Dylan's sleeping face, it pains me to admit that. "I left most of it to Vic. I wish I had that to do over again."

"You've more than made up for anything you were lacking at first."

"My wife had to *die* for me to get a clue about what I was missing out on, to discover there's more to life than work. I never want to make that kind of mistake again."

"You won't, Derek."

"I want to be part of his life. And yours. I want us to..." I stop myself before I can say something while running on adrenaline and emotion that can't be unsaid.

"What?" she asks, sounding breathless.

I shake my head. "Not now."

"Yes, now. I'm tired of dancing around this conversation. It's long overdue. Say whatever it is you want to say to me. I'm ready to hear it, Derek. I promise you."

"Even after what your mother-in-law said?"

"Even after that. What is it we're always saying? This isn't her journey. It's mine. She's on her own, and I respect that the things she's feeling in her grief are not in line with what I want them to be, but I can't control that. I'm the only one who knows the truth about how deeply I've grieved the loss of Patrick and the life we planned."

While I cradle Dylan, I reach out to tuck a strand of her hair behind her ear and run my finger over her face. "You've been nothing but respectful of him and his memory."

"I always will be. I'll love him for as long as I live, and nothing could ever change that."

"No, it won't."

"That said..." She looks up at me with her heart in her eyes. "I also love you. And Maeve."

"We love you, too. And Dylan."

She swallows and licks her lips with a delicate dab of her tongue. "I... I love you differently than I love Maeve."

I can barely breathe as she says things I've wanted to hear for so long. "I love you differently than I love Dylan," I say, smiling down at her, "and what I want more than anything is for the four of us to be a family. I want you to help me raise Maeve, and I want to help you raise Dylan. I want them to grow up together as siblings. I want to be there for you both every day."

"I want those things, too."

"You do? Really?"

She nods. "But..."

I hold my breath, waiting to hear what she'll say.

"I want to wait until after the first anniversary of Patrick's death in October to make anything official. I just feel it's important to me to stay focused on him and Dylan in this first year, not that I want anything to change between us. I just... I feel like I need..."

I place my index finger on her lips. "Say no more. I understand completely."

"You always do, and that means so much to me."

"Everything we just said to each other will still be there in October." I put Dylan in the bassinette and face Roni, holding my arms out to her.

She steps into my embrace. "I probably smell like curdled milk."

My low rumble of laughter rocks us both. "No, you don't." I pull back to look down at her sweet face and can't resist a chaste kiss now that I know for certain she feels the same way I do. I can be patient if it means a lifetime with her. "How about that lunch I promised you?"

"I could definitely eat."

"Sam and Nick sent you presents."

"They did?"

"You want to see?"

"Hell yes."

"Let's do it, then."

Twenty-Three

Roni

I'm overwhelmed by the flowers and baby clothes from my friend the first lady and her husband the president. After I dash off a quick text to thank Sam for the gifts, I sit next to Derek on the sofa, our food on the coffee table. I find myself taking surreptitious glances at him the way I have for months now. I've gotten so used to having him around, so comfortable with him that the conversation we just had didn't feel awkward at all.

"I can see you looking at me," he says around a bite of roast beef sandwich.

"I do that a lot."

"Trust me, I know."

"In all fairness, you knew I was a weirdo from the get-go. The stalking and all that."

His smile is a thing of beauty, and it's one of the things I love best about him. I've noticed he smiles a lot more than he did when we first knew each other, and I like to think I'm partially responsible for that. "Yes, I know you're a weirdo, but why are you staring at me?"

"I like to look at you."

He freezes for a second before he resumes chewing, chasing the bite with a swig of the lemon-flavored seltzer I started buying for him to have at my house. "That works out rather well, because I like to look at you, too."

I snort with laughter. "I've been a *whole lot* to look at lately." I've never been bigger in my life than I was the last few months of my pregnancy. "If you're into the hot air balloons at the Macy's Thanksgiving parade."

"Stop," he says as he tries not to crack up. "You were beautiful pregnant, and you're beautiful as a mother."

"Can I say one other thing about the topic we're not talking about until October?"

"Whatever you want."

"Anything that happens... Physically... Between us... It can't happen here. Not that I am in any way thinking about that today or any time soon."

His lips quiver with amusement. "Understood."

"Or at your house."

"Also understood."

"Turns out I have one more thing to say."

He wipes his mouth with a paper napkin that came with the food and turns to face me. "Lay it on me."

"You know what I love best about you?"

His golden eyes glitter with equal parts affection and amusement. "I can't wait to hear."

"That you always understand. Whatever it is I'm dealing with or going through or obsessing about... You get it, and you don't make me feel stupid or overwrought for wallowing in my grief the way some people would and do. That's a tremendous gift to me as I rebuild my life."

"Your feelings about losing Patrick are never stupid or overwrought. It's hopefully the biggest loss you'll ever experience, and you should fully expect to experience grief over the loss of him for the rest of your life. It's not like we just 'move on' from losing people like Patrick and Vic. We move forward, but they come with us."

"Yes, they do, and it means everything to me that you get that."

"You want to know what I love best about you?"

I give him a playful shove. "Hello, have you met me? Of course I want to know!"

"I love that despite everything you've endured since October you've never lost your optimism or your joy."

"Neither are quite what they used to be."

"Maybe not, but they're still very present and very admirable. Tied for first place for the thing I love best about you is how great you are with Maeve."

"I adore her."

"And she adores you right back. I first knew I was truly falling for you that night I had to work late, and I came home to you two snuggled up in her bed reading stories."

"That was the night she made me read *five* books. I was easily manipulated by her cuteness."

"Seeing you two together like that..." He places his hand over his heart. "I was a goner."

I could talk to him all day about the things we love about each other, but our lovely conversation is interrupted by the door buzzer.

"I'll get that," he says.

"Probably my parents."

As Derek crosses the room, I watch him go, caught up in the bubble we've built around ourselves and our relationship. I'm amazed by what a difference it makes to have shared my feelings with him. It's a huge relief to know for certain we both feel the same way, even though I've been pretty sure about that for quite some time now.

He waits at the door to admit my parents, who come in with grocery bags, more flowers, gifts and excitement over their new grandson.

They hug Derek on their way to me and stop short of where I'm sitting on the sofa so they can take their first look at Dylan.

"Oh, look at him," Mom says with tears in her eyes. "He's absolutely beautiful."

"I think so, too, but I'm kinda partial."

"How about you, going off and having a baby all by yourself!" Mom adds as she comes to the sofa to carefully hug me while Dad continues to gaze at Dylan.

"I wasn't by myself." I look up at Derek. "Derek was with me when I went into labor at our friend Iris's house. He stayed with me through the whole thing."

"Thank you for being there for our Roni," Dad says.

I've noticed before that Dad treats Derek almost the same way he did Patrick, as if they're old friends. Today it's even more than that. There is genuine affection in the way he looks at the man who has slowly but surely become the center of my life.

"I'm glad I was able to be with her," Derek says with a warm smile for me as he cleans up the remains of our lunch. "My mom texted that they're almost to my place, so I'm going to go get Maeve. I'll bring her back to meet Dylan, if that's okay."

"Sure, that sounds good."

"Okay, I'll see you in a bit, then. Nice to see you, Justine and Roy. Congratulations on your new grandson."

"Thank you," Mom says for both of them. "And thank you for being there for Roni."

"That's always a pleasure." To me, he says, "Text if you need anything."

"I will. Thanks." I wish I could hug and kiss him and tell him I love him again before he leaves. I never want to part company with him without telling him how I feel, because you don't know when you might not see someone again. But I'm not ready to do any of those things in front of my parents, so I stay seated on the sofa and give him a look that I hope conveys everything I want him to know.

After the door closes behind Derek, my dad moves to sit on the other side of me.

"How're you holding up, sweetheart?" Dad asks.

"So far so good. I mean, it's a lot... He was born on Patrick's birthday, and I think he looks like him."

"I think so, too," Mom says.

"It's unbearable that he's not here to meet his son, to raise him, to show him how to be a good man."

"Call me crazy, but it seems like there might be another man here to help with those things," Dad says with a teasing glint in his eyes.

"If you mean Derek, then yes, he's here, and he's going to be there for Dylan. And for me." I look down at my hands because I'm not sure where else to look as I say this next part. "I know it's too soon and all that—"

"Who says it's too soon?" Dad asks, frowning.

"Susan, for one."

Mom stares at me, her expression completely blank. "She actually *said* that?"

"She did. Her exact words were, 'It seems soon to us for you to move on with someone new.'"

"How dare she say such a thing to you?" Mom asks, outraged. "You were a wonderful, loving wife to her son, and she knows that. She *saw* it the same way we did."

"I understand it's her grief talking."

Mom shakes her head. "I hope with all my heart I never have to experience that kind of grief, but it doesn't give her the right to be unkind to you, especially after you've just given her a grandson."

"I'm going to try really hard not to take it personally. All I can do is live my life in the best way possible and hope everyone I love will support me in that. If they don't, I can't take that on."

"My God, you amaze me," Dad says, his eyes bright with tears. "Your strength and resilience are awe-inspiring."

"I don't know about that."

"It is, Roni. Listen to your father. We've all been amazed by how you've pressed forward after an unimaginable loss."

"Thanks to a lot of help and support from you guys and many others."

"That may be true," Dad says, "but it's due in large part to the inner toughness that's always been such a big part of who you are."

"I've had no choice but to be tough. I'm the youngest of four kids!"

"And you always held your own with them," Mom says.

Dylan wakes with a snort and a cry.

"Allow me." Mom gets up to retrieve him from the bassinette. "Hello, handsome. I'm your Grandma Justine, and I'm going to spoil you rotten. Grandpa Roy is going to help me."

"You bet I am," Dad says, sounding choked up.

Mom puts a blanket right on the coffee table and changes him with professional efficiency before handing him over to me to be fed. She drapes a receiving blanket over us to protect my privacy.

"You're good at this," I tell her.

"Four children and now seven grandchildren. I've had a lot of practice."

"How long does it take to feel like you sort of know what you're doing?"

Mom glances at Dad. "Thirty years?"

"That's about right," he says.

The three of us share a laugh. "Gee, thanks for that."

"We're here for you, pal," Dad says with a laugh.

Derek returns an hour later with a very excited Maeve, who wants to hold Dylan. We set her up on the sofa, and I carefully place the baby in her arms while Derek records the moment on his phone.

"Hi, baby. I wuv you," she whispers, running her hand gently over the wispy blond hair on his head. "You be my baby, 'k?"

"He'd like that very much," I tell Maeve as I wipe away tears. Could she be any sweeter?

Mom makes dinner for all of us, and we're cleaning up when my phone buzzes with a text from Susan.

We're coming into the District in an hour or so and were hoping to see the baby. Is this a good time?

It's not. We've had a long day, and I'm exhausted. She's the last person I want to see after what she said to me earlier, but I won't refuse Patrick's parents access to his son. Ever. I respond and tell her it's fine if they want to come by.

"Who is it, Roni?" Mom asks.

"Susan. They want to see the baby."

"We'll get out of here before they come," Derek says. "You'll be here?" he asks my parents.

"We're not going anywhere," Mom says fiercely.

I'm incredibly relieved to know they're going to stay, at least until after Susan and Pete leave. My dad might think I'm strong, but the thought of facing them on my own has my knees knocking.

Derek nods to my mom and picks up Maeve.

"Say good night to Mr. and Mrs. Fletcher," Derek says to Maeve.

She gives my parents a shy smile and a wave.

"Good night, Maeve," Mom says, blowing her a kiss.

I want to wail and beg Derek not to go. Not yet, anyway, but it's probably for the best if they aren't here when the Connollys come. Besides, Maeve is rubbing her eyes and acting ready for bed. I give them both a hug. "Sleep tight, pumpkin."

"I see baby tomorrow?"

I kiss her on the cheek. "Any time you want."

"Oh jeez," Derek says. "Don't tell her that. We'll be here all the time."

"That's fine with Dylan and me." While Mom and Dad finish cleaning the kitchen, I walk Derek and Maeve to the door.

"Call me later?" he asks.

"I'll try."

He kisses my cheek. "Sleep while he does."

"He's gonna be up all night after sleeping all day."

"Maybe. I'll check in after a bit." He starts to walk away, but then turns back. "Don't let her hurt you, do you hear me?"

Smiling, I nod. "I hear you."

I watch them go down the stairs until they're out of sight before going back into my apartment and closing the door. I'm dreading seeing Susan and Pete, now that I know what they really think of me.

While I wait, I receive a text from Darren Tabor, my friend and former colleague at the *Star*. *Heard the baby arrived. Congratulations! Can't wait to meet him.*

Thank you, Darren! He can't wait to meet you, too.

Darren has been a good friend to me since I lost Patrick. He's one of the people who has surprised me in a good way, unlike many others who've surprised me by keeping their distance.

"Mom, will you watch him for a minute while I take a quick shower?"

"Of course, honey. Take your time."

Even though I'm so sore I can barely breathe, I rush through a shower, blow-dry my hair and put on a bit of makeup so I won't look too awful when they come. I dress for comfort in a pair of Patrick's sweats and one of his T-shirts.

Since I've taken a tiny bit of care with my appearance, I ask my mom to take a picture of Dylan and me that I post to Instagram and Facebook, tagging Patrick's still-open accounts with this caption: *Welcome to the world, Dylan Patrick Connolly, born on your daddy's 32nd birthday and weighing in at six pounds, two ounces and nineteen inches long. We are so in love with you, Dylan.*

For a long moment, I stare at the words that will come as a shock to ninety percent of the people we know, most of whom have no idea I was even pregnant before I attach the picture and post it to both platforms. "You're Facebook and Insta official now," I tell my son, who looks up at me with big eyes that remind me so much of his father's.

The flood of comments is immediate and full of surprise and congratulations.

I get a text from Sarah. *Oh my God! You had a baby!?!? Way to keep secrets! Congratulations! I love that he was born on Patrick's birthday.*

Me, too, and thanks.

I change and feed him so he'll be ready to meet his other grandparents. By the time they arrive, he's sitting with his back against my thighs, gurgling and gnawing on his own fingers.

My mom lets in the Connollys, who greet my parents like they're old friends. I give my parents credit for keeping things cordial, even though they're angry about what Susan said to me.

"Come in." They both look stricken to be walking into Patrick's home for the first time since the dreadful week that followed his death. "Come meet Dylan."

Susan sits next to me while Pete bends over the back of the sofa for a closer look at his grandson.

"Oh my," Susan says softly. "He looks just like Patrick did as a baby. Doesn't he, Pete?"

"He sure does."

Mom comes to sit on the arm of the sofa, next to me. "Isn't he beautiful?"

"Yes, he is," Susan says as she contends with a waterfall of tears. "I'm sorry. It's just… It's so hard to meet Patrick's son when he isn't here."

"It sure is," I say. "But I feel like he's close by, keeping an eye on us."

"Do you?" Susan asks. "I never feel him around me."

"It's more a sense of his presence than anything concrete."

"You're lucky to have that and to have his son as a daily reminder of him."

"We're all lucky to have Dylan," Mom says. "He's a lovely gift in this difficult time."

I feel like I should hold my breath as I anticipate an explosion from one or both of my parents if Susan so much as hints at Derek and me being inappropriate in any way. That she could even say a thing like that is appalling.

He and I haven't been in any way inappropriate, but there's no way I can convince her of that. She's going to believe what she wants to, regardless of the truth. As these thoughts cycle through my mind, I'm as angry as I've been in a very long time.

Dylan begins to fuss, so I take him from her and get up to move around with him.

Words are burning on the tip of my tongue, words that once spoken can never be taken back. Old Roni would've kept the peace at all costs. Widowed Roni isn't quite so willing to accommodate the feelings of others at her own expense.

"I need to say something."

Twenty-Four

Roni

All four of them look at me. Before I can lose my courage, I look directly at Susan. "What you said earlier hurt me very deeply. You made it seem like I've been behaving inappropriately as I mourned the tragic and sudden loss of my husband. The truth is every single day I have to force myself to get out of bed, to keep breathing, to keep moving forward, to find joy anywhere I can and to remain hopeful despite the aching absence of the person I love best in the whole world. I had to go through an entire pregnancy without the father of my child to hold my hand, to rub my back, to indulge my cravings, to tell me I'm beautiful even when I felt horrible."

I look Susan directly in the eye. "Your loss is unbearable. I've had one day with Dylan, and I already know that if anything ever happened to him, it would break me in a way that even losing Patrick didn't. But for you to judge how I or any other widow or widower chooses to handle the loss of the person we expected to spend the rest of our lives with is just grossly unfair, especially as you sit by your husband of thirty-something years, having never experienced widowhood."

My dad, who's standing off to the side where the others can't see him, raises his fist in support of me.

"I have loved your family like my own for all the years I spent with Patrick. I want you to play a huge role in the life of our son, but you'll never again judge me for the choices I make for myself as I try to rebuild my life without my husband. Are we clear on that?"

"Yes," Pete says while Susan weeps silently. "We've always loved you, too, Roni, and we very much want to be part of Dylan's life."

"To be part of Dylan's life, you have to be part of mine, which means accepting my choices. If Patrick hadn't died, I never would've looked at another man for the rest of my life, and you know that."

"Yes, we do," Pete says. "We know that."

"Susan, tell me you know that."

She nods as she wipes away tears. "I'm sorry if I hurt you, but it hurts *me* to see you with someone else."

"I understand, and I'm sorry it hurts you. But having Derek's support through the worst year of my life has been instrumental in me surviving it. He's been where I am. He knows what it's like, and his friendship, and that of all the other widows and widowers I've met, has been a lifeline to me."

"Are you two... Are you together?"

"Not yet, officially, but we will be eventually. We're taking things very slowly. I still have significant healing to do."

"You know for certain you're going to be with him?"

"Yes. I know it the same way I did when I met Patrick. Some things are just that simple, Susan, and that complicated. I certainly didn't go looking for a new relationship. What I have with Derek has grown from a place of intense grief and sorrow and has given me hope that not every day for the rest of my life is going to hurt the way the last eight months have." A surge of emotion threatens to cut me off at the knees, but I'm determined to get through this without losing my composure. "No matter what happens with Derek, or anyone else, for that matter, nothing will ever change or diminish the love I have for Patrick. I'll take him with me everywhere I go forever. I'll never stop saying his name or honoring his memory. You have my word on that."

"Thank you," she says softly. "Thank you for remembering him."

"Always."

"About his things..."

I've avoided going through anything of Patrick's because I just haven't had it in me. "What about them?"

"There are a few things we'd like to have. Kristy would love to have some of his records, and Kelsey wants one of his shirts." They're his older brother's daughters. "The boys would probably like his some of the baseball cards."

"I'm sorry I haven't gotten to dealing with his things before now. Why don't we pick a Saturday in the next few weeks and go through everything together? Would that work?"

"Yes, that would be good. Thank you."

I sit next to her with Dylan cradled in one arm and put my free hand on top of hers. "Let's keep talking, okay? There's no need for us to be on opposite sides of this awful loss. Patrick wouldn't want that for any of us."

"No, he wouldn't."

I FEEL SO MUCH BETTER after clearing the air with them, and over the next few weeks, I talk to Susan more often than I have since the first week Patrick died. The Wild Widows are proud of me when I tell them how I stood up to my mother-in-law and called her out for judging me.

"I just want to say that without you guys, I never would've had the language I needed or the courage to tell her how much it hurt me," I convey to them when I return to a meeting for the first time since Dylan was born. Most of them have been to visit us, however.

"We're so proud of you, Roni," Joy says. "That's the way to set your boundaries and let people know your expectations."

"It felt good to speak my truth."

"You're amazing, Roni," Brielle says. "It takes a lot of guts to speak up like that."

"My knees were shaking the whole time, but I didn't cry. That was important to me."

We move on to other people after that, but I bask in the glow of their approval. I'm totally slaying this widow game, which is a sentence I never expected I'd say or think, but alas, here I am, getting it done and even figuring out single motherhood. It's easier at the moment because I'm on maternity leave until Labor Day. The real test will be when I go back to work full time, but Shelby Hill's nanny has agreed to care for Dylan, too—with a nice pay raise. I'm thrilled that Dylan will be upstairs while I'm at work and will have Shelby's kids to play with.

That night is the first I hear of the Wild Widows retreat weekend in Bethany Beach, Delaware, that Iris and Brielle are planning for late October. They've rented two houses next door to each other right on the beach, and everyone is excited about the prospect of getting away together.

I glance at Derek and find him looking at me. I wonder if he's thinking the same thing I am—a weekend away, perhaps kid-free...

I squash that thought into the back of my mind where all such thoughts about him will reside until October 10 has come and gone, marking a full year without my beloved husband.

On a gorgeous late-June Saturday, Patrick's family comes to help me go through his things, to take what they want and to help me complete the dreaded task of packing up a life that ended far too soon. I went through everything before they came and boxed up the things I wanted for myself and Dylan, so I tell them they can have anything that's left. Derek and Maeve have been in Vegas with his parents visiting his brother's family this week and are due home later today. My parents have taken Dylan for a few hours so I can devote myself to my in-laws.

Patrick's younger niece Kristy is in tears as she meticulously packs the record collection into special boxes she bought. "He'd have slapped my hand if I ever touched his records," Kristy says, smiling through her tears.

"Oh, me, too," I tell her. "I always did it wrong. I put him in charge of all record handling so I wouldn't have to hear his critique of how disrespectful I was."

"That sounds about right," Kristy says.

Kelsey comes out of the bedroom wearing one of Patrick's favorite flannel shirts. "Remember the time he showed up to the black-tie fundraiser wearing this shirt?" Kelsey asks.

"As if I could ever forget," Susan says. "I was *mortified*."

"'No one told me it was formal!'" we all say together before dissolving into laughter that's followed quickly by tears.

"Tell me it's going to get easier someday," Kelsey says as she hugs me.

"I wish I could promise you that. I think there's always going to be a sharp ache where he used to be."

"Yeah, probably so."

We force ourselves to go through everything, and when we're done, there are twenty boxes stacked in my dining room that'll be picked up by a local charity on Monday. Susan orders pizza, and we end up telling funny stories about Patrick that cap off our day with laughter and more tears.

"Thank you for this," Susan says when she hugs me goodbye. "It meant so much to us to have this time in the home Patrick loved so much, with the woman he loved so much."

"I appreciate the help with a task I've been putting off."

"Understandably so." Susan glances at the boxes in the dining room. "I remember when we did this after my mother died, how I felt then as I do now, like we're erasing someone's life like it never happened."

"As long as we continue to talk about him, he lives on in all of us."

"That's very true," Susan says with a sad sigh.

"I admire how you've handled yourself this year, Roni," Pete says. "It can't have been easy."

"Thank you. I've had a lot of wonderful support that's been critical. The new job has helped, too."

"We'll see you for Kelsey's shower, if not before?" Susan asks.

"I'll be there." I was dreading Kelsey's wedding in November, but after being with them today, I feel better about a lot of things.

My parents bring Dylan back, and I've just finished nursing him when Derek arrives an hour later.

I rush into his arms, thrilled and relieved to see him after a seemingly endless week apart. "Missed you guys so much."

He hugs me tighter than he ever has before, and I can tell he's dying to kiss me. "We missed you guys, too. Longest week ever. Next time, you and Dylan have to come with us."

"We'd love that. Where's Maeve?"

"My parents wanted to see her, and I wasn't sure how you'd feel after the job today. How'd it go?"

"Not bad, all things considered. It's amazing what I can do in months nine and ten that would've been inconceivable in months one through six."

"Grief is like fitness—the more you do, the better you get at it."

"That's an interesting metaphor."

"It's true, isn't it?"

"I guess it is."

"I remember my mom and I packing up Vic's things. It was brutal—and far too soon for me to be doing it, but I just wanted it all gone so I didn't have to see it every day. With hindsight, that was a mistake. I wasn't ready."

"I'm sorry that was hard for you. I'm glad I waited. It felt right to do it now."

"Have you given any more thought to what we talked about the other night?"

"Refresh my memory," I say, smiling, as if I've thought of anything else since he first pitched the idea of us getting a place together for the four of us when we were on one of the marathon phone calls that got us through this week apart.

"It went something like this—your lease is up at the end of the year. I'd like to move out of the place where my wife was murdered. Maeve and I would like to live with you and Dylan so I don't have to constantly hear how she wants to go to Ron's to see Dyl. It'd be so much easier if we all lived together. Oh, and I love you and want to be with you every minute that I can."

I feel the same way I did the first time he pitched this idea to me—excited, happy, optimistic and a little bit afraid because loving someone means worrying about losing him. Since it's happened before.

"Earth to Roni. Come in, Roni. Are you with me?"

"I'm with you, and I think we should look around and see what's available."

"You do? Really?"

"Yes, really." I smile at the excitement I hear in his voice even as I ache at the thought of leaving the home Patrick and I made together. "But we need to stay in the Capitol Hill neighborhood. I love it here."

"I do, too. We'll find something close that works for all of us."

"Will you bring your meal-planning skills to our new home?" I ask him. He's been making dinner for all of us for months, usually at my house to accommodate Dylan's erratic schedule.

"Do I have to?"

"Oh yeah, you've got me spoiled."

With a deep, overly dramatic sigh, he says, "All right, then. I'll do that and the grocery shopping if you'll do the laundry."

I hold out my hand to him. "Deal."

He takes my hand and kisses the back of it, sending a zing of sensation all the way through me. "Deal."

"Are we really doing this?"

"We really are."

"What if..." I bite my lip as I try to find the courage to ask the question that's been on my mind a lot since we began stumbling our way toward a more permanent arrangement.

"What? You can ask me anything. You know that."

I do know that. He's so easy to talk to, which is one of many things I love about him. "What if things between us don't work out? We haven't even slept together, and we're talking about moving in. What if we're a bust in the bedroom?"

His cackle of laughter is the best thing ever because it takes a lot to get him to really laugh, although he laughs more than he used to.

"I'm serious!"

"We're not going to be a bust in the bedroom, Veronica."

"How do you know that, Derek?"

"You're just going to have to trust me on this one. How many more months until we can find out?"

"Three, or is it four?"

"I'm going to spontaneously combust before then. That's how I know we're going to be fine."

"In case I forget to tell you, I appreciate that you're giving me this time and waiting for me to be ready."

"In case I forget to tell you, I have a feeling that waiting for you is going to be the smartest thing I ever did."

Derek

I'M GOING to die from wanting her long before October rolls around. I've never been a guy who was led around by his dick until I had to put my feelings for Roni on ice so she could see through her year of mourning for Patrick. I totally get why that's important to her. I waited for more than a year after I lost Vic before I went out one night looking to get laid and got exactly what I wanted, even if I was heartsick for days afterward.

Having random sex after being married to a woman you loved and lost to murder is about as horrible as it sounds. But I was glad to get that first time out of the way so I wouldn't have to wonder just how horrible it would be. I've done it one other time, after a blind date with a friend of my sister-in-law's who I actually liked and wanted to see again. But she said that as much as she liked me, too, she wasn't up for dating a widower with a kid. It was all too much for her to take on.

Fair enough.

It is a lot. We're a lot, Maeve and me and the baggage we bring with us. I'm glad I waited for someone like Roni, who fully understands what she's getting. As do I. And what I'm getting is a beautiful, joyful, funny, sweet, sexy woman who is incredible with my daughter and who has a son I adore.

I'm working late on a Tuesday night in July, the week after we celebrated Roni's thirtieth birthday with her family. Patrice dropped Maeve off with Roni for dinner and bath time while I work the phones trying to get the votes we need for Nick's landmark gun-control legislation. Everyone knows we need to do something, but the bill has still been a tough sell, and we're running out of time before the August recess to get something done. The more time that passes since the shooting last December in Des Moines, the less likely it is that we'll be able to make it happen. People forget, they move on, but the lives of people touched by violence are forever changed.

This bill is personal to me—and to Nick due to the loss of his father-in-law to gun violence.

Speaking of the man himself, he pops into my office, looking the same as he did fifteen years ago when we met as young, fresh-faced congressional staffers just starting out in the political racket. His shirtsleeves are rolled up, his tie is loosened, and his top button was probably released hours ago.

I stand to greet him. "Mr. President."

Twenty-Five

Derek

"Sit your ass down, Derek."

"Yes, sir." I hold back a laugh, knowing how he hates when his closest friends treat him like he's the shit, even though he is.

"Where are we?"

"Three short in the house and two in the Senate."

"Son of a bitch. Any cracks in the armor?"

"Possibly. I'm working it from a parental standpoint. Don't they want their kids and grandkids to be safer? To be able to go to a meet-Santa event without having to worry about some mentally ill person showing up with an assault weapon?"

"I'll never understand how everyone doesn't want that."

"It's more about what their donors want, as you know."

"Which is total bullshit."

"We could talk all night on that topic."

"Yeah."

"I think we'll get it done in the end. They're just going to make us work for it."

"You should go home to Maeve. It's late."

"She's with Roni and Dylan, who are her favorite people in the world. Daddy has been completely replaced."

"Aw, that's so sweet, though."

"It is."

"You two seem great together. Are you, you know, making plans?"

"We're talking about moving in together, even though we're not yet officially an actual couple."

His brow furrows with confusion. "You're not?"

I shake my head. "She's taking the year after losing Patrick, which I totally understand, but we're committed to each other. It's just all platonic thus far."

"Ah, well, that's interesting."

"And frustrating."

We share a laugh that reminds me of old times, before my wife was murdered, and he became the most important man on earth.

"But it's all good. I certainly get where she's coming from, and she's worth waiting for."

"Sam and I are so happy for both of you. We love the two of you together."

"Thanks. It's nice to feel good again after feeling like shit for so long. Maeve is just crazy about her and Dylan, and vice versa." I fiddle with a pen as I try to push back the one thing that has me afraid of this new life I'm making with Roni.

"If you're so happy, why are you doing that thing with your eyebrows that you do when something is bugging you?"

"Quit acting like you know me so well. Mr. President."

His laughter rocks his entire body. "I do know you so well, so what gives?"

"I really love her. And Dylan."

"I can see that. So what's wrong?"

"Absolutely nothing."

"And that's a bad thing?"

"I worry about..." I force myself to look up at one of my best friends. "If something ever happened to her—"

"Stop, Derek. Don't do that to yourself. What happened to Vic was outrageous and horrible, but you can't go into this with Roni thinking something like that will happen again."

"We both know all too well that it's possible. Look at how her husband was killed minding his own business."

"Still... I get how hard it is not to worry about the worst happening. Every day when I see Sam off to work, I fear I might never see her again."

"How do you stand that?"

"Sometimes I can't, but I tell myself the good times—and any time with her is the best I've ever spent with anyone—is worth the worry that comes with loving her. Love is worth the risk, Derek. You know that."

"Yeah, I do, and I'm excited about the future with Roni. I'm trying not to let what happened in the past color the future. It's just hard sometimes not to fear the worst."

"I get it, but all we have is right now, and we have to live that to the fullest."

"You're right. That's very true."

"I hope you know I'm here if you ever need a friend."

"I do. It helped to air it out. Thanks for listening."

"Anytime. And now I must get upstairs to see my kids before they go to bed. You should go home and see yours, too. That's an order," he adds with a smile. "Tomorrow is another day."

"Yes, sir, Mr. President."

"Stuff it," he says over his shoulder as he walks out of my office.

Since the president himself told me to go home, I'm outta here. On the drive home, I dart in and out of traffic, eager to see my little family after an endless day apart. I'm so lucky that Roni was willing to take Maeve for me after she and Dylan got home so I could work a little later tonight, but I try not to make a habit out of missing dinner with them. I like to think I've learned that lesson, but with this bill so close to having the support it needs, I wanted to give it a few more hours since members of Congress are easier to reach later in the day.

As I park a block from Roni's apartment, I shut off the lingering concerns and stress of the workday to focus exclusively on the people I love the most in this world. We exchanged keys quite some time ago, so I let myself in and take the stairs two at a time. From outside her door, I can hear Dylan crying, Maeve chattering and the low tone of Roni's voice as she holds court with both of them.

I'm smiling before I even put the key in the door. I do that a lot these days, and I have Roni to thank for giving me a Chapter 2 that far exceeds my wildest dreams—and I haven't even kissed her yet. Not really.

I love that the physical side of our relationship has had nothing to do with getting us to where we are now. We were friends—best friends—long before we were anything else, and I have faith that foundation will stand strong against whatever may come our way in the future.

Maeve lets out a bloodcurdling scream when she sees me and comes running, launching herself into my arms and hugging me like she hasn't seen me in weeks. She knows how to make her daddy's day complete. I hug her and kiss her and swing her around, which makes her laugh hysterically.

"Careful, she had spaghetti for dinner, and that'll be colorful coming back up."

"Oh, Roni makes a good point. How was your day, pumpkin?"

"Good." She places her pudgy hands on my face and squeezes my cheeks before planting a noisy kiss on my lips. Could she be any cuter? In the next second, she's squirming to get free of me so she can go play. I put her down, and she scampers off, stopping to kiss Dylan on the forehead before moving to the toys Roni got for her to have at her place.

I plop down on the sofa next to Roni. "Hi, honey, I'm home."

Dylan immediately reaches for me, and I take him from her.

"It's not fair that he likes you better than me. I gave birth to him."

I love being Dylan's favorite and happily snuggle the baby into my right arm before I lean in to kiss Roni chastely even as I yearn for so much more. "He loves you best because you're running the milk bar. I can't compete with that."

"If that's true, why does he always want you over me?"

"For the same reason Maeve wants you over me."

"And what is that reason?"

"Our kids have good taste in people."

Her smile lights up her gorgeous face and makes my life complete. There are times, such as right now, when things between us are so perfect that I wonder how I survived before she stalked her way into my life. I'll be forever thankful to the passing resemblance she saw to her late husband at first, which she now says was wishful thinking. In reality, she doesn't think I look anything like him, which was somewhat of a relief to hear.

"Are you hungry?" she asks.

"Starving."

"I left the dinner you made in the oven for you," she says with a cheeky grin that makes me laugh.

"You're very good to me."

"Likewise."

"I hope you think so."

"I really do."

I have an idea right then... A big idea that takes root over the next few days and weeks, as we count down to October and the weekend away with the Wild Widows. We're taking Dylan with us because she's still breastfeeding him, but Maeve will be with my parents, and Roni and I will have an entire weekend to ourselves—and our closest friends. But we'll have lots of time alone, too, and I plan to make the most of that time.

Roni

ON OCTOBER 10, I take the day off and stay home with Dylan. Everyone in my life asked me if I wanted to do something special today, but what I want to do is something I've put off so many times now, it's almost comical.

I'm going to watch our wedding video, and I'm going to fully wallow in love and grief and every other emotion that the video is certain to stir up.

I asked Rebecca to send it to me a week ago, promising to call her if I wanted her to come watch it with me.

I don't call her or anyone. I put Dylan down for his morning nap, make my cup of hot chocolate and cue up the video on my laptop, fully aware that I'm opening a healing wound and that it's going to hurt like hell.

But a funny thing has happened over the last year... I've gotten used to Patrick being gone, and as I watch the video of our beautiful day, I see only the happiness, the joy, the excitement and the fun.

Patrick is beautiful, sweet, sentimental, emotional... The vows he spoke from his heart touch me all over again, reminding me that I was once deeply and perfectly loved. Watching his face, hearing his voice... It's as overwhelming as I expected it to be, but I'm also able to see this video as yet another gift that will someday mean everything to my son.

I cry as I watch our first dance to "Yellow" by Coldplay, which we danced to the first time we ever went out and had been our song ever since. I haven't allowed myself to listen to it this year, and hearing it now brings back a million beautiful memories.

I'll never forget the toasts, the dancing, the sweetness of the day.

For a long time after the video ends, I lie on the sofa, looking up at the ceiling as the movie of the life Patrick and I had together runs through my mind. I hope I never forget the little things that made us who we were together. I want to someday share them with Dylan, which is why I've started writing stories in a journal that may turn into a book at some point.

Who knows? I've learned anything is possible and that I'm capable of things I never would've imagined I could do before this day last year.

I did it.

I survived a year as a widow.

I started a new job.

I made wonderful new friends and mourned the loss of others I thought would be part of my life forever.

I had a baby.

I fell in love again.

I did it all without Patrick, which was inconceivable this time last year.

A full year.

Derek is the only one who knows what I had planned for today, so I'm not surprised when he texts to check on me.

I'm okay. I watched it. I survived it, and I even enjoyed it a little.

Can I do anything for you?

Come see me later?

I'll be there, sweetheart.

I've been told year two can be harder than year one, as unfathomable as that is. From what the others have told me, all the "firsts" are over, and gritty reality sets in. I wish I could avoid the pain I know is still to come, but if I avoid the pain, I'd also have to avoid the love, the joy, the good times sprinkled into the relentless grief.

So I carry on.

Year two, here we go.

Twenty-Six

Derek

The Wild Widows are in high spirits when we arrive at Bethany Beach, which is mostly deserted this time of year. That was kind of the point of doing this retreat in the fall. We wanted a peaceful time together without the crowds, and the price was right, too. Our group overtakes two huge houses with ten bedrooms each, located right next door to each other.

Gage brought enough wood to keep a bonfire going all weekend, and that's where we find ourselves after dinner on Friday night.

Roni has Dylan bundled up in a cute fleece outfit, and he's in good spirits as he's passed around from one set of willing arms to another. He's an easygoing kid with an affinity for people, which is why the others were fine with us bringing him to a no-kids event.

Roni quietly marked the one-year anniversary of Patrick's passing last week and attended a Mass his parents had in his memory. We talked about whether I should go with her and decided I shouldn't. There would be time enough for his family to get used to us together. The anniversary of Patrick's death wasn't the time. After a quiet few days immersed in memories and grief, she seemed to rebound this past week and was excited about the trip.

I've been thinking about this night and this weekend for weeks. However, now that go time is upon me, I'm frozen to my chair by the fire as Roni carries on an animated conversation with Joy, Kinsley, Lexi and Iris.

They put us in one of the first-floor suites, which I suspect was Iris's doing. She's the only one who knows this is the first time Roni and I will share a bed. The others think we've been getting busy for a while now, and we've never bothered to set that record straight. We've kept the inner workings of our relationship mostly to ourselves even as much of it has unfolded amid the Wild Widows.

Because it's important to me that I have a chance to talk to her before bedtime, I reach over to nudge her arm.

She looks over at me, fresh-faced and gorgeous in the firelight.

As I gaze at the face that's become so familiar and important to me, the anxiety inside me settles, and all I see is her, the answer to every prayer uttered deep in the pits of despair.

"Are you okay?" she asks.

"I'm great. Can we take a walk? I want to talk to you."

"Oh, sure. Let me just see if Iris will take Dylan." She leans over Kinsley to speak to Iris. "Can I leave him with you for a minute?"

"Absolutely. He's keeping me warm."

"He's a furnace," Roni says, laughing as I help her up.

"Don't get lost in the dunes, you crazy kids," Joy says.

"We'll try not to." I hold on to Roni's hand as I lead her away from the group toward the water. The full moon lights up the beach and the water with a bright glow.

"Where're we going?" she asks.

"Down here." I lead the way to a place I scoped out earlier—out of the sight of our friends, but not too far from home base.

"What's down here?"

"You'll see."

We walk to the spot where I stashed a blanket and two lanterns earlier. "Close your eyes."

"What's going on?"

"Just do what you're told for once, Veronica."

"Okay, Derek."

Have I mentioned that I adore her? I spread the blanket and light the lanterns before I go back for her and lead her to the blanket. "Have a seat."

"Can I look?"

"Yes."

"Oh! Is this where you went before?"

"Maybe."

"This is so nice!"

"I'm glad you like it. I wanted to talk to you when it was just the two of us, before we spend the night together for the first time."

"Is everything okay?" she asks with a concerned expression.

I can't have that. I kiss the wrinkle between her brows and the slight frown off her lips. "Everything is perfect since you found me and decided to stalk me."

As always, she laughs and hides her face. "I'm never going to hear the end of that."

"Never, ever. In case you haven't realized it by now, finding you has saved my life—and Maeve's. We both love you and Dylan so, so much."

"We love you, too," she says softly. "I never imagined it would be possible to love Patrick as much as I always will and to love someone else just as much. But I do. I love you like I loved him. If you told me a year and a half ago that I'd be sitting on a beach with a man who isn't Patrick and professing my love to him, I would've thought you were crazy." She uses the sleeve of her sweater to wipe away a tear. "But then, life happens, and you were there and so perfect and..."

"And..." I kiss her then, the way I've been dying to for almost as long as I've known her.

Her arms curl around my neck, and her mouth opens to my tongue.

I'm completely lost in the bliss of kissing this woman I've come to love so much. Before I know what's happening, we're reclined on the blanket, kissing each other with months' worth of pent-up desire. I almost laugh when I remember her wondering what we'd do if we were a bust in the bedroom. Suffice to say, that's not going to be an issue.

As much as I want to keep kissing her, I need to talk to her first. I slowly end the kiss and gaze down at her. "That was well worth the wait."

"Uh-huh. More please."

"It was really important to me that I ask you something before we spend tonight together. It's something big and life-changing and might be more than you're ready for, but I wanted to ask you before we sleep together so there would be no doubt in your mind that I'm asking you for all the right reasons."

She rolls her lip between her teeth and looks up at me with love and admiration and grief and happiness and so many other emotions reflected in her expressive eyes. "What do you want to ask me?"

"First I want to tell you something." I caress her face and kiss her again. "I love you, and I love Dylan. I love your parents and your family, and I love the way we've built the most amazing friendship I've ever had with anyone."

"I love all of that, too, especially the friendship and the patience you've had in letting me take the time I needed to be ready for this, for us."

I kiss her again, because how can I not? Now that I've had a taste of her, all I want is more.

"That leads me to my question." I kiss her forehead, the lids of her closed eyes, the tip of her nose and her lips again. "Will you, beautiful Veronica, at some point in the future when the time feels right to us, marry me and help me raise Maeve and be her mom and allow me to raise Dylan as my own while respecting the memory of their late mother and father? Will you make a life with me and the children we already have as well as the others we might have together?"

"Yes, Derek." Tears slide down her cheeks as she reaches for me and gives me another kiss. "Yes to all of it."

"Hold that thought for a second." I manage to prop myself

up on one elbow and fish the ring I bought for her weeks ago out of my pocket. Reaching for her left hand, I slide it on her finger. "You can decide when you're ready to wear this ring, to tell the world what we plan to be to each other. We're on your timeline, but I couldn't ask you without having a ring."

"It's absolutely beautiful."

I went with a square-cut diamond surrounded by smaller diamonds. I wanted something unique and special, like she is. I loved Victoria with all my heart, but I never felt like I completely knew her. After she died, I found out why. This, with Roni... This is different. There're no secrets between us, no hidden agendas or nefarious plots. We're just two people who've seen the worst life has to offer who were lucky enough to find each other.

When I once told Iris that I didn't know how to go on without the love of my life, she very gently said it might be hard to fathom after such an awful tragedy, but Victoria might not have been the love of my life. It was possible I might one day meet someone else who would wear that title. At the time, the notion seemed preposterous. But for a while now, I've realized Iris was right.

Roni is the love of my life. She's the one I'm going to grow old with, God willing, and who will be by my side for all the highs and lows still to come. I hope to be that for her, too, even if I'm aware that another man she loved had to die to make her available to me. It's all so freaking complicated, but also the simplest thing.

I love her.

She loves me.

We love each other's children.

She gives me hope for a future filled with laughter and joy after the two most difficult years of my life.

"Do you want to tell the others?" I ask her.

"There's no way I could keep this secret all weekend." She reaches up to straighten my hair. "I want you to know that it means a lot to me that you asked me before we spend the night together for the first time."

"I don't know why that felt so important to me."

"This might be TMI, but with Patrick, we were all sex all the time for the first couple of years. I mean, don't get me wrong, we did other stuff together, too, but that was definitely the focus."

"Vic and I were like that, too. We spent entire weekends in bed when we were first together."

"That was great, but the way this happened is, too."

I waggle my brows at her. "Now we get to the fun stuff."

"I might... you know... I've only ever been with Patrick. I might be emotional about it. Are you prepared for that?"

"I'm here for anything and everything. I'd be surprised if you weren't emotional. It's a big deal to do this for the first time with someone else."

"Were you emotional when you did it?"

"I was disgusted. It was a random hookup, and I felt sick afterward. I should've waited for you so we could do it together for the first time."

"Tonight will be a fresh start for both of us."

"How soon do you think we can get to that fresh start?"

She laughs and kisses me again.

I can never get enough of her laughter or her kisses.

"I need to get Dylan settled for the night, so we can use him as our excuse to retire early."

"I like how you think."

"Thank you for making this so special for me."

"Nothing but the best for my fiancée."

"Fiancée," she says, as if trying on the word for size. "I was Patrick's fiancée not that long ago, and now I'm yours. Some people never get lucky enough to find love once, let alone twice."

"We're very lucky that way and spectacularly unlucky in other ways. If you ask me, we deserve every bit of hard-won happiness and joy we can find together."

"I couldn't agree more."

I reach out a hand to help her up. "Let's go put Dylan to bed."

Roni

DEREK totally surprised me with the heartfelt proposal on the beach, and I truly love that he did it before we sleep together for the first time tonight. It means a lot to me that our relationship started first as a rock-solid friendship that found me at a time when I most needed it.

I won't lie, though. As Derek and I walk hand in hand back to the gathering of our friends, I feel a tiny bit disloyal to Patrick by wearing another man's ring on my finger.

Silly, I know, but there you have the dichotomy that is grief.

I'm thrilled to be taking this step forward with Derek, but still feel the twinge of guilt that I'm "cheating on" my late husband. I give myself a minute to feel that emotion before I stuff it into a box inside my mind so as not to let it detract from an otherwise perfect night.

Patrick loved me with all his heart. He would've liked Derek, and I take comfort in that.

When we return to the fire, each of us carrying one of the lanterns and with the blanket tossed over Derek's shoulder, the others look at us with curiosity. My gaze goes immediately to Dylan, who's asleep in Iris's arms.

"What goes on, lovebirds?" Joy asks with her typical irreverence.

"Oh, nothing much," I reply before extending my left hand. "But he did put a ring on it."

They erupt into cheers and excitement that rouse Dylan from his slumber.

I hand my lantern to Derek and take the baby from Iris.

"Congratulations, girlfriend," she says. "You got yourself one of the good ones."

"Thank you, and yes, I did."

As I soothe Dylan, I accept congratulations from the other Wild Widows.

"When's the big day?" Gage asks.

"Oh Lord, I have no idea." I glance at Derek. "Can we get back to you on that?"

"You bet." Gage kisses my forehead with the older-brother

sort of affection I've come to expect from him. "I'll have my dancing shoes ready."

"I'm jealous," Adrian says with a grin when he hugs me. "Y'all are rocking this Chapter 2 thing, while the rest of us are still trying to figure out how Tinder works."

Laughing at the face he makes, I say, "It just sort of happened between us. We certainly didn't go looking for it."

"And that's the best way for it to happen. When you least expect it."

"I hope you know, that you all know, Derek and I are going to be here until every one of you finds your Chapter 2."

"We're counting on that," Kinsley says.

"Um, one other thing, guys," I say, glancing at Derek. "Could you keep this between us until we have a chance to tell our families?"

"Of course," Brielle says. "Our lips are sealed."

The others nod in agreement.

"Thank you. Well, I guess I'm going to go feed this little guy and get him down for the night." I glance at Derek. "You want to help?"

"Sure."

The others groan.

"Subtle," Lexi says.

"Stay away from the first-floor suite tonight," Christy says.

"If that suite's a-rockin', don't come a-knockin'," Wynter adds with a cheeky grin.

It's a good thing there's a fire to explain why my cheeks feel red-hot. "On that note, I bid you all good night."

Derek says good night and follows me up the path to the house.

"That was mortifying."

"We knew it would be," he says, laughing. "You want me to take him for you?"

"Sure." I hand him over to Derek. "He's a load all of a sudden."

"Our little boy is growing up."

Our little boy... There it is again, that twinge of guilt to color

275

the joy. Patrick should be here to raise our little boy, but since he can't be, Derek is going to. "I've been thinking about what he should call you."

"He can call me anything he wants to."

We stomp the sand off our feet and enter the house through the sliding door and close it behind us to ward off the night chill.

"I was thinking I would refer to Daddy Patrick and Daddy Derek. I always want him to know he has two daddies."

"That sounds perfect to me. I'd love to be his Daddy Derek."

"He's a lucky boy to have you in his life."

"I'm lucky to have him, too. I've loved watching Maeve become a big sister."

"Me, too."

In the bedroom, I notice a bottle of champagne, two glasses, a pair of scented candles, a lighter and a note on the bedside table. "What have we here?" I ask Derek.

"I have no idea. That wasn't my doing."

I open the note and read it aloud to him. "'Congratulations to two wonderful people on your beautiful and well-deserved Chapter 2. You've been an inspiration to the rest of us with your dignity and your resilience. I'm so happy for you! Love, Iris.' That's so nice of her! Did she know you were going to propose?"

"She did. I asked her whether she thought it was inappropriate for me to ask you while we were on a getaway with our widow friends, and she said absolutely not. 'We've watched you two fall in love,' she said, 'so it's only right we should be there when you make it official.' She also said it gives the others hope that they might find new love again someday."

"She's so lovely. I hope and pray it happens for her."

"I think it will. She's very open to the idea, which is the most important step."

"True."

"If you want to rinse off the sand, I'll change Dylan and put his pj's on."

"That'd be great. Thank you."

"No problem."

I've become accustomed to caring for Dylan mostly on my

own, and we've found a good groove, but it sure is nice to have a partner to help with him. When Derek is with us, he always pitches in to help with Dylan. My heart aches for Iris, Brielle, Adrian and the other single parents in our group, some of whom lost the partners who were helping them through it from the start. I'd imagine it's harder to adjust to not having help when you've had it all along.

In the shower, I start to feel nervous for the first time about what's going to happen tonight. After waiting forever to finally do it with Patrick, I was amazed at how good it was from the beginning. He was all about me and my pleasure before he ever took any for himself.

I remember telling Sarah that, and her saying, "Marry that unicorn."

The memory of that makes me smile, even as I mourn the loss of her friendship. Despite the rift, I'm able to remember that moment with a smile now. She's been faithful about checking in, asking about me and Dylan and telling me she's thinking of us. I may have to forgive her at some point for not being as strong as I wish she could've been when I needed her. My year as a widow has taught me that not everyone has that well of inner strength to draw from that's been so instrumental to me.

I'm going to need that inner strength now as I make love with a man who isn't my husband for the first time. Until Derek, it'd been more than a decade since I kissed anyone but Patrick.

After my shower, I put on the pale blue silk nightgown and robe I bought to wear this weekend, put on scented lotion, and brush my teeth and hair. I'm as ready as I'm ever going to be to take this next step with Derek. I emerge from the bathroom to find him sitting on the bed with Dylan propped on his knees the way he was the night he was born, pumping his arms and legs with enthusiasm.

"Someone is full of energy, I see."

"He's waiting for Mommy and her magic milk to put him to sleep." Derek looks up at me and takes a long, greedy look. "You're beautiful."

"Thank you."

"If you want to take over with the little man, I'm going to grab a quick shower."

I settle on the other side of the bed and take the baby from him to feed him while Derek showers.

Before he gets off the bed, Derek says, "Hey."

I look up at him. "Yes?"

"Don't get in your head about this. It's you and me. It's gonna be awesome because it's us."

"How did you know I needed to hear that?"

He shrugs. "Just had a feeling." He reaches out to run a fingertip over my cheek. "Whatever happens between us tonight will be among the best things to happen to me since I lost my wife, even if all we do is sleep with our arms around each other. Don't worry about anything, okay?"

"Okay." His sweet words put me at ease the way nothing else could. From the beginning, his understanding and support have been the reason our relationship was able to rise like a phoenix from the ashes of our shared grief.

Twenty-Seven

Roni

By the time Derek emerges from the bathroom wearing only a pair of basketball shorts, his hair wet from the shower and his face freshly shaven, I've fed Dylan and put him down for the night in a portable crib. Derek and I laughed earlier about the ridiculous amount of equipment required to take one tiny being away for two nights.

"Is he out?" Derek asks in a whisper.

"Like a light."

"Can you have a sip of champagne?"

I haven't been drinking at all while breastfeeding. "I suppose a few sips won't hurt anything, and we are celebrating."

"Yes, we are." He takes the bottle and glasses into the bathroom to open it so the popping of the cork won't wake Dylan and returns with two glasses.

I purposely took the side of the bed that was Patrick's because I want everything about being in a bed with Derek to be different.

He settles on the other side and hands me my glass. "To us and the start of our second happily ever after."

I touch my glass to his. "To us."

The flavor of the wine explodes on my tongue and gives me a rush after so long without alcohol. "That's good."

"Yep."

"I can't stop looking at my ring. It's absolutely gorgeous."

"I'm glad you like it. I agonized for weeks over which one to get you, but I kept coming back to that one. I'd never seen one quite like it before, and I liked that it was unique."

"It really is. I've never seen one like it before either." I look over at him. "I was thinking about the first time I got engaged and how two seconds after we told our parents, we made it Facebook official."

"You can tell people if you want to. I'd be fine with that."

"I know, and thank you, but I'd like to wait a bit. I was thinking maybe we could host Thanksgiving and tell everyone then?"

"That sounds like a nice idea. It would give them a chance to spend more time with us as a couple before they know we're making plans for forever."

"Exactly, and I'd like for us to spend time one-on-one with your parents, mine and Patrick's before then for just that reason."

"I like that idea. I've already told mine that we're looking for a place together for after the first of the year."

"Mine know that, too. I need to talk to Patrick's parents about it."

"What do you think they'll say?"

"I'm not sure, but they know I'm determined to live my life as I see fit, not how they see fit. I think we came to an understanding this summer, and I've been making an effort since then to talk to them more often and make sure they see Dylan whenever they want."

"You're a wonderful daughter-in-law to them, Roni. I've seen that myself on numerous occasions. As long as we continue to show respect for them and Patrick's memory, I have to believe they'll eventually accept me as part of your life."

"I hope they will, but even if they never do, that changes nothing for me."

"Is that so?" he asks, his lips curving into a sexy smile.

"That is so."

He takes my glass from me and puts them both on the table next to his side of the bed. When he turns back to me, I'm filled with anxiety and anticipation and... Well, just about every emotion I've ever experienced shows up to make itself heard.

"Relax, Roni, it's just me, and I love you." He tips my chin up to receive a soft, sweet, easy kiss. "Remember, if all we do is sleep, that's fine with me."

He's perfect for me, and I love him, too, which is why I want to do more than sleep with him. I reach for him and draw him into another of the kind of kisses we shared on the beach—the deep, tongue-twisting variety that makes me forget everything that isn't him and this moment that belongs only to us.

One kiss leads to two, which leads to six, or is it ten? I lose count of how long we make out like two teenagers who've finally gotten a minute alone after a long, long wait. The thought makes me giggle.

He pulls back from me. "It's not good for my fragile ego to have you laugh while I'm kissing you."

"This reminds me of being a teenager."

"What kind of teenager were you, young Roni?"

"The kind who had a boyfriend that my parents watched like a hawk, so we had no time at all alone together until we'd been dating for, like, a year."

"Kind of like us, huh?"

"That's why it's funny."

"I'm going to need to kiss you a lot to make up for all the times I wanted to but couldn't."

"I can get on board with that."

He tugs at the belt to my robe. "What's going on under here?"

"You wanna see?"

"Is that a rhetorical question?"

I didn't expect to laugh, but I should've known I would. He always makes me laugh, and I *love* making him laugh.

I go up on my knees to remove the robe and toss it aside.

"I'm going to need a minute to take a good long look at you."

"You can look for as long as you want."

"Am I allowed to touch, too?"

"Please do."

He was right. This is easy because it's him. It's been easy with him from the beginning, which is why we're in a bed together tonight.

As he rises to his knees to put his arms around me, I link my arms around his neck and decide to share that thought with him. "I couldn't have gotten to where I am with you right now with anyone else."

He's busy kissing my neck. "I sure hope not."

Laughing, I poke his side and make him grunt out a laugh. "You know what I mean. The way this happened... It was just what I needed."

"Same for me, sweetheart. It was perfect from the beginning."

"By 'beginning,' do we mean after the stalking or during?"

His silent laughter makes me smile. "All of it. Every single thing."

After that, there are no more words, only more kisses, caresses and desperate desire. I had no idea how much I'd missed the touch of a man until Derek reminds me. He moves slowly and carefully, and his respect for the fact that this is the first time for me after Patrick only makes me love him more.

My gown disappears over my head, and his greedy lips find my nipples, sparking a rush of need that converges between my legs.

"Do I need a condom?" he asks, raising his head to look at me.

"I, uh, got a prescription for this nonhormonal gel that I can use while breastfeeding. I, um, took the liberty of applying it..."

"Well, aren't you full of surprises?"

"I wanted to be ready for this."

"And do you feel ready, sweet Roni, in all the ways that matter?"

I nod. I'm as ready as I'll ever be to take this next step in my journey and feel blessed to be taking the step with a man I love and respect.

"First things first..." He kisses a path down the front of me.

"Don't look at my stretch marks."

"I don't see anything but a sexy woman."

"Well played, Mr. Kavanaugh."

"You're beautiful, Mrs. Connolly." That reminds me of something else I want to talk to him about, but not now. Definitely not now as he proceeds to prove to me with his lips, tongue and fingers that we suit each other in bed, too. I put a hand over my mouth to muffle the sounds that come from the first orgasm I've had in longer than I can remember.

"Mmm. Told ya."

"I knew you were going to say that."

"When I'm right, I'm right. Ready for more?"

"Yes, please, but first, I should take care of you."

"Next time. Look at me."

I gaze up at him and find him looking down at me with those lovely golden eyes gone hot with love and desire. "Keep looking at me, okay?"

I nod and gasp as he pushes into me.

"Still good?"

"So good." It's good and wonderful and terrible and lovely all at the same time, and yes, it's possible for it to be all those things and so much more.

"I love you. I love Dylan. I always will."

"I love you, too, and I love Maeve. Always."

The words, the pleasure, the love, the desire... It's all there, everything we need to make a meaningful life together, and I'm just so damned grateful for him. Perhaps even more so than I was for Patrick, before I knew how quickly it could all end, with no warning or time to say goodbye forever.

Our bodies move together like we were made for each other. Derek makes sure I have another orgasm before he takes his pleasure, reminding me of what Sarah once said about unicorns. How lucky am I to have found two of them in one lifetime?

He comes down on top of me, breathing hard, and puts his arms around me. "So damned good. I love being right. I plan to be right a lot, just so you know."

"Thanks for the warning, and yes, you were right."

"Are those happy tears, sweetheart?"

Nodding, I say, "I'm just so thankful for you, for this, for a second chance, for Maeve and Dylan, for all of it."

"Me, too. Gratitude is a big part of my life these days in a way it never was before, not like it should've been, and I'm extremely grateful for you, Maeve and Dylan."

"When you called me Mrs. Connolly before..."

"Sorry. I said that before I took a second to think about it."

"No, it was fine, but it reminded me that I wanted to tell you I'm probably going to keep the name Connolly so Dylan and I will have the same name while he's growing up. Is that okay with you?"

"Of course it is. What would you think of Roni Connolly Kavanaugh? We can be the Kavanaugh-Connolly family."

"That'd be perfect. In case I forget to tell you every day, I love you, and I'm extremely thankful for every minute we get to spend together."

"Same to you, love." He raises his head off my chest and kisses me while giving a subtle push of his hips to remind me he's still inside me—as if I needed the reminder. "You want to do it again to make sure I was really right, and that wasn't just a fluke?"

"We probably ought to make sure before we shackle ourselves to each other for a lifetime."

"I love a girl who's thorough."

Epilogue

Roni

Over the next month, we spend most of our time at Derek's house. We bought a new bed and had it delivered there until we're ready to move to our new place, a townhome we bought together on Eighth Street, one block from where Sam and Nick lived before they moved to the White House and a block in the other direction from where I first saw Derek. I insisted on splitting the cost of the house with Derek, who objected strongly, until I told him it was important to me that we share in the cost of raising our family. He might always make more than I do, but my salary isn't shabby, and I want to be a partner to him in the same way he's been one to me.

Dylan and I spend most nights with Derek and Maeve, and we already feel like a family of four, slipping into a nice routine that works for all of us. It's been amazing to me how easy it is with Derek, and even though I still have my difficult days when grief reminds me I'm not in charge, for the most part I'm doing okay.

I've had to attend a couple of hearings in the case against the man who shot Patrick, which always sets me back for a couple of days, but Derek is there to support me on the good days and the bad. Arnie Patterson and the case against him and his sons has been back in the news again, which has been tough for Derek. Hearing about the man who orchestrated a massive deception and murder that took Victoria from him and Maeve makes him quiet, moody and remote.

I let him know I want to be there for him the way he is for me, and he's doing better about sharing the tough times with me. He's always so concerned about adding his grief to mine, but I want him to share everything with me.

We ride to work together, like we do every day, on the last Friday before Thanksgiving. Dylan is in the back seat, hitching a ride with us to his nanny at the White House. I love our morning routine of getting Maeve off to her daycare and then commuting across town with Derek and Dylan. Every morning, Derek still goes to the coffee shop to get coffee and hot chocolate for us.

I'm taking off all next week to prepare to host twenty people at my place, which has the larger dining room. Since I've never done Thanksgiving dinner before, I've recruited my mom and sisters to help me prepare.

Patrick's mom is bringing pies, and Derek's mom is making stuffing and green bean casserole. My sisters are also bringing sides, so I'm mostly responsible for the turkey, gravy and mashed potatoes. Easy enough, right?

Gulp.

I want this day to be perfect and have rewritten my grocery list at least ten times. I'm studying it again on the way to work.

"You're going to make yourself nuts, Veronica. It's all going to be fine."

"Easy for you to say. You're in charge of booze. No one can screw that up."

He laughs. "True, but your mom said she'd supervise the turkey. You've got every base covered."

"I guess."

"Can we talk about what you're really worried about?"

I look over at him. "What do you mean?"

"You're freaking out about telling Patrick's parents we're engaged. So why don't we take a ride down to see them this weekend and get that taken care of so you can enjoy the holiday?"

The thought of that makes my mouth go dry. As many times as I tell myself I've done nothing wrong and have no reason to feel guilty about my love for Derek, I can't for the life of me picture telling Susan and Pete that we're engaged.

"Or, we put it off until it feels less terrifying to you. I've told you before—I'm not in any rush. As long as I know that we're in this together for the long haul, the rest is just details to me. If we get married next year or in two years, that's fine."

"Have I mentioned today that I love you for understanding me so completely?"

"Not yet, but I'm always up for hearing that you love me." He takes a right turn into the entrance to the White House and is waved through after we show our IDs to the agent working the gate. When he parks in the spot designated for Mr. Kavanaugh, Deputy Chief of Staff, he shuts off the engine and turns to me. "Let's just wait, Roni. You've built this holiday up in your mind as some sort of launching point, and it doesn't need to be that. Let's just have the turkey with our people and keep the rest to ourselves for a while longer."

"You'd be okay with that? Really?"

"Absolutely. I can't stand to see you stressing about this. There's no need for it. We're not on any kind of deadline to move forward."

"In that case, I think I'd like to wait a bit, even though I want to be wearing that gorgeous ring for everyone to see."

He kisses the back of my left hand, where my ring finger is devoid of bling. We stashed the ring in the safe at his place until we're ready to go public. "We have a lifetime to spend together. Let's not sweat the small stuff, okay?"

"Okay."

With his hand resting gently on my face, he leans in to kiss me. "Feel better?"

"I do. Thank you."

"You don't have to thank me."

"Yes, I really do. For the friendship, the love, the sweet daughter I gain by loving you, for being there for me and for

Dylan, for getting me and the struggles that go with this widow journey, for all of it."

"If you're thanking me, then I need to thank you for bringing the light back into my life. Until I met you, I was just existing. This is so much better for me and for Maeve. Everything is so much better with you."

"I like the way happiness looks on you."

"I like the way it feels. I'd forgotten."

"I guess we'd better go to work."

"Probably so, but we'll continue this conversation later."

"I'll look forward to that all day."

MY TURKEY COMES out juicy and delicious. Our families gel like they've known each other for years. Patrick's parents are in good spirts and seem pleased to be with us, which is a huge relief. They're leaving after dinner to go to Pete's brother's house, so we have them for only a little while longer.

When my mom suggests we play her annual thankful game, in which we go around the table and everyone says what they're most thankful for that day, I start to think about what I want to say as Derek, sitting to my left, starts.

"I'm thankful for the family and friends who've been such a tremendous support to me and Maeve over the last couple of years, and," he says, glancing at me, "for new friends who've helped bring the joy back into our lives."

Under the table, I give his hand a squeeze.

"I'm thankful for old friends and new ones," Derek's mom, Ruth, says, "and for the smiles on the faces of my dear son and his sweet daughter. I'm thankful for Roni and Dylan and the chance to spend this day with the new family you're making together. We're so proud of you both and love you very much."

"Thanks, Mom," Derek says in a gruff tone that indicates an emotional response to his mom's heartfelt words.

"Thank you for making Dylan and me so welcome in your family, Ruth," I add.

"We love you both," she says.

"I'm thankful for this wonderful meal that my daughter-in-law made," Susan says, "and for the opportunity to spend this day with all of you. I'm thankful for my wonderful son and for all the joy his Dylan has brought to our lives. Thank you for having us today, Roni, and for keeping us close to your heart since we lost Patrick."

I blow her a kiss and put my hand over my heart to let her know what her words mean to me.

As each of our loved ones focuses their gratitude on us, I start to feel a sense of calm come over me. These people love us. They want the best for us, and there's no sense in keeping our plans a secret for their sakes.

When it's my turn, I take a second to get my thoughts together. "Last Thanksgiving, just over a month after I lost Patrick, I honestly thought my life was over, too. I couldn't imagine having to live every day of the rest of my life without him with me. I still wake up every single day and have to accept all over again that he's really gone. Even after all this time, that still takes me by surprise. Without the support of all of you, I'm not sure where I'd be right now, so I'm most thankful for the people gathered here today, as well as my sisters, my brother and a bevy of new friends for getting me through this year. I'm thankful to my sweet Dylan, who has been such a joy to me and all of us. I'm thankful to my darling Maeve and her daddy, Derek, who have given me, well... everything. After I first lost Patrick, I honestly thought I'd be alone going forward. I, um, didn't expect anything like this to happen... But over months of warm, genuine friendship, through all the crushing lows of new widowhood and the soaring highs of new motherhood, Derek... You've been my rock, my friend, my love. I love you and Maeve so much."

"We love you, too," he says. "You and Dylan."

I look at him when I continue. "Last month, Derek asked me to marry him, and I accepted."

The news is met with gasps of surprise.

"We... We weren't going to say anything for a while yet, because we know some people will think it's too soon or too this or too that, but for us, it's just right. Our relationship has given us both something we needed very badly after our tragic losses, and that's hope for a future that's full of love and joy and happiness. We can have those things even as we continue to grieve the loss of Patrick and Victoria and honor their memories while we raise the children they left us. I... I hope that you all can be happy for us and be part of our new life together, that we'll celebrate many more holidays just like this one. And, well... That's a very long way of saying I'm thankful for life and love and second chances."

My dad clears his throat as he raises his glass. "To life and love and second chances."

The others chime in, touch glasses and celebrate our news.

I'm still a tiny bit on edge waiting to hear what Susan and Pete think of it.

"If I may," Pete says, "I just want to add our congratulations to you, Roni, Derek, Maeve and Dylan. Our son... Our Patrick... He loved you so much, Roni, and you made him so very, very happy."

"Thank you," I whisper, using my napkin to dab at tears.

"After getting to know you, Derek, Susan and I feel confident that our son would've liked you, and he would've appreciated the way you've cared for Roni and Dylan. So, on his behalf, we thank you for that, and we wish you both a lifetime of well-deserved happiness."

"That means so much to us, Pete," Derek says.

I appreciate him speaking for both of us, because I'm contending with a giant lump in my throat.

"It'll always be important to us to honor and remember Patrick and Victoria," he adds, "and to keep them alive in the lives of Maeve and Dylan."

"We can't ask for anything more than that," Susan says tearfully.

Their blessing means everything to me—and to Derek.

MUCH LATER, we're snuggled up in bed at his house with our children sleeping close by. My engagement ring is back on my finger, and I'm more at peace than I've been since my life was suddenly turned upside down.

"How are you feeling?" Derek asks as he runs a hand up and down my back.

"I feel relieved that I didn't burn the turkey."

His low chuckle makes me smile. "The turkey was fantastic."

"Otherwise, you know, just another day."

"Right," he says, giving me a playful pinch to the bottom that makes me jolt. "Just another day in which we took a giant step forward toward getting the rest of our lives together."

"Oh, that. Well, yeah, that was cool, too, but not burning the turkey was definitely the headline."

Laughing, he rolls on top of me, looking down with such a fierce look of love that I'm reminded once again of how truly blessed I am to have been loved that way by two extraordinary men.

"When are you going to marry me?" he asks as he kisses my neck and makes me shiver with desire.

"How about next summer?"

"Do I really have to wait that long?"

"It'll be here before we know it."

His low groan rumbles through me. "I guess I can wait that long as long as I get to sleep with you in my arms every night."

"We can make that happen."

He makes love to me with an all-new reverence that comes from knowing our future together has been secured, that nothing and no one is going to stand in the way of our happily ever after.

"I wish you knew how happy you've made me, Veronica," he whispers in my ear when he's deep inside me, his body joined with mine in an almost holy alliance.

"You've made me just as happy."

"This is just the beginning for us. We're going to have it all. I promise."

Life has taught me that we all make promises we intend to keep, even if the universe often has other plans for us. Putting my faith in Derek and in his love for me and Dylan is a risk I'm willing to take if it means I get to spend the rest of my life with him.

THANK you for reading Roni (and Derek's) story! I so hope you loved this introduction to my new Wild Widows Series, a spin-off from the Fatal Series. If you haven't read Sam and Nick's story yet, you can start with *Fatal Affair*. Derek and Victoria's story unfolds in book five, *Fatal Deception*.

In preparing to write this book, I've probably read a dozen widow memoirs and thousands of Instagram posts from young widows. Their stories inspired my desire to write about the unique experience of young widowhood and its many challenges. To those who have walked this journey, you have my undying respect and admiration for your courage and fortitude. Thank you for sharing your stories.

From the moment Roni showed up in *Fatal Reckoning* after her young husband's sudden, tragic death, I wanted to know more about her. I'm not sure why her story resonated so deeply with me—and with Sam—but I couldn't wait to write this book. From the outset, I had the idea to pair her with Derek after she sees him in the neighborhood and thinks, at first, that he resembles Patrick. I loved the idea of bringing these two wounded people together, first in close friendship and then as something deeper.

The idea for the Wild Widows came later, as I read more about the many ways young widows and widowers support each other through the uniquely difficult losses of their soul mates and life partners far too soon. I love that there's such a robust community that wraps its arms around young widows and helps them find the way forward, and I can't wait to write more about the group we met in this book.

A word about the timeline for this series... Because the Wild Widows each begin their widow journeys at different times, the timelines won't be linear. Please don't try to match up this book with the ongoing First Family Series, as it won't align neatly. The timelines may jump around a bit, and I've decided that's okay for this series as I try to tell a wide variety of stories and experiences that take place over various time periods. One widow's timeline won't match another's, which is true to life. Some of their stories will happen simultaneously, and others will overlap, which is why I've decided on a nonlinear timeline. I'll do my best not to make it confusing, but the goal is for each story to stand on its own under the series umbrella.

I'm looking forward to the journey this series will take us on, and I hope you'll come along as our Wild Widows look for their Chapter 2s. Keep reading below for a hint of Iris's story in book two, *Someone to Hold*.

Thank you to my beta readers Anne Woodall, Kara Conrad and Tracey Suppo, for being the first line on all my books, and to Linda Ingmanson and Joyce Lamb, editors extraordinaire. Thank you to Sarah Hewitt, family nurse practitioner, for her assistance with the medical stuff and allowing me to take some liberties for the sake of the story. To the Wild Widows beta readers: Karina, Viki, Jennifer, Jennifer, Juliane, Gwen, Gina and Marianne, thank you for your input and enthusiasm for this first book in a new series.

And to my husband, Dan, and our kids, Emily and Jake, thank you for the daily joy and laughter as well as the never-ending support of my career.

To my readers, who follow me wherever the muse decides to take us, you honor me with your commitment, your trust and your excitement for every new book. I appreciate each and every one of you more than you'll ever know.

xoxo

Marie

Meanwhile back at the Bethany Beach fire pit...

Iris

As I watch Gage put more wood on the fire, I notice the way his muscles bulge under a fleece pullover with every move he makes. Well-faded jeans cling to his ass, and I wonder what he'd think if he knew I want to climb him like a tree, a thought that makes me giggle madly to myself while I take another sip of wine.

What would he do, I wonder, if I crawled in bed with him this weekend and wrapped myself around him?

Would he be horrified or happy?

I haven't the first clue, which is what will keep me from doing it. For now, anyway...

As far as I know, Gage hasn't been with anyone since he lost his wife and daughters in a drunk-driving accident two years ago. If he's getting busy, he's not sharing that with us, but I suspect there hasn't been anyone.

He was so devoted to Natasha and their girls and has struggled to carry on without them. His daily Instagram posts that succinctly summarize the young-widower experience are like catnip for me. I devour them with my coffee each morning, looking for further insight into the enigmatic man who's captured my attention so completely.

The best part is that no one knows I have a thing for Gage. I haven't told a soul, and I've been very careful not to give anything away in our group. For whatever reason, I suspect any sort of public declaration would drive him away faster than me snuggling up to him in his bed during this blissfully kid-free weekend during which anything seems possible.

What would happen if I just did it?

God, I want to know...

Read Iris's story in *Someone to Hold*, coming soon!

Also by Marie Force

Romantic Suspense Novels Available from Marie Force

The Fatal Series

One Night With You, *A Fatal Series Prequel Novella*

Book 1: Fatal Affair

Book 2: Fatal Justice

Book 3: Fatal Consequences

Book 3.5: Fatal Destiny, *the Wedding Novella*

Book 4: Fatal Flaw

Book 5: Fatal Deception

Book 6: Fatal Mistake

Book 7: Fatal Jeopardy

Book 8: Fatal Scandal

Book 9: Fatal Frenzy

Book 10: Fatal Identity

Book 11: Fatal Threat

Book 12: Fatal Chaos

Book 13: Fatal Invasion

Book 14: Fatal Reckoning

Book 15: Fatal Accusation

Book 16: Fatal Fraud

Sam and Nick's Story Continues....

Book 1: State of Affairs

Book 2: State of Grace

Book 3: State of the Union

Contemporary Romances Available from Marie Force

The Wild Widows Series—a Fatal Series Spin-Off

Book 1: Someone Like You

Book 2: Someone to Hold

The Gansett Island Series

Book 1: Maid for Love *(Mac & Maddie)*

Book 2: Fool for Love *(Joe & Janey)*

Book 3: Ready for Love *(Luke & Sydney)*

Book 4: Falling for Love *(Grant & Stephanie)*

Book 5: Hoping for Love *(Evan & Grace)*

Book 6: Season for Love *(Owen & Laura)*

Book 7: Longing for Love *(Blaine & Tiffany)*

Book 8: Waiting for Love *(Adam & Abby)*

Book 9: Time for Love *(David & Daisy)*

Book 10: Meant for Love *(Jenny & Alex)*

Book 10.5: Chance for Love, *A Gansett Island Novella (Jared & Lizzie)*

Book 11: Gansett After Dark *(Owen & Laura)*

Book 12: Kisses After Dark *(Shane & Katie)*

Book 13: Love After Dark *(Paul & Hope)*

Book 14: Celebration After Dark *(Big Mac & Linda)*

Book 15: Desire After Dark *(Slim & Erin)*

Book 16: Light After Dark *(Mallory & Quinn)*

Book 17: Victoria & Shannon (Episode 1)

Book 18: Kevin & Chelsea (Episode 2)

A Gansett Island Christmas Novella

Book 19: Mine After Dark *(Riley & Nikki)*

Book 20: Yours After Dark *(Finn & Chloe)*

Book 21: Trouble After Dark *(Deacon & Julia)*

Book 22: Rescue After Dark *(Mason & Jordan)*

Book 23: Blackout After Dark *(Full Cast)*

Book 24: Temptation After Dark *(Gigi & Cooper)*

Book 25: Resilience After Dark *(Jace & Cindy)*

The Green Mountain Series

Book 1: All You Need Is Love *(Will & Cameron)*

Book 2: I Want to Hold Your Hand *(Nolan & Hannah)*

Book 3: I Saw Her Standing There *(Colton & Lucy)*

Book 4: And I Love Her *(Hunter & Megan)*

Novella: You'll Be Mine *(Will & Cam's Wedding)*

Book 5: It's Only Love *(Gavin & Ella)*

Book 6: Ain't She Sweet *(Tyler & Charlotte)*

The Butler, Vermont Series

(Continuation of Green Mountain)

Book 1: Every Little Thing *(Grayson & Emma)*

Book 2: Can't Buy Me Love *(Mary & Patrick)*

Book 3: Here Comes the Sun (*Wade & Mia*)

Book 4: Till There Was You *(Lucas & Dani)*

Book 5: All My Loving *(Landon & Amanda)*

Book 6: Let It Be *(Lincoln & Molly)*

Book 7: Come Together *(Noah & Brianna)*

Book 8: Here, There & Everywhere *(Izzy & Cabot)*

The Quantum Series

Book 1: Virtuous *(Flynn & Natalie)*

Book 2: Valorous *(Flynn & Natalie)*

Book 3: Victorious *(Flynn & Natalie)*

Book 4: Rapturous *(Addie & Hayden)*

Book 5: Ravenous *(Jasper & Ellie)*

Book 6: Delirious *(Kristian & Aileen)*
Book 7: Outrageous *(Emmett & Leah)*
Book 8: Famous *(Marlowe & Sebastian)*

The Treading Water Series
Book 1: Treading Water
Book 2: Marking Time
Book 3: Starting Over
Book 4: Coming Home
Book 5: Finding Forever

The Miami Nights Series
Book 1: How Much I Feel *(Carmen & Jason)*
Book 2: How Much I Care *(Maria & Austin)*
Book 3: How Much I Love *(Dee's story)*
Book 4: How Much I Want *(Nico & Sofia)*

Single Titles
Five Years Gone
One Year Home
Sex Machine
Sex God
Georgia on My Mind
True North
The Fall
The Wreck
Love at First Flight
Everyone Loves a Hero
Line of Scrimmage

Historical Romance Available from Marie Force

The Gilded Series

Book 1: Duchess by Deception

Book 2: Deceived by Desire

About the Author

Marie Force is the *New York Times* best-selling author of contemporary romance, romantic suspense and erotic romance. Her series include Fatal, First Family, Gansett Island, Butler Vermont, Quantum, Treading Water, Miami Nights and Wild Widows.

Her books have sold more than 10 million copies worldwide, have been translated into more than a dozen languages and have appeared on the *New York Times* bestseller more than 30 times. She is also a *USA Today* and *Wall Street Journal* bestseller, as well as a Spiegel bestseller in Germany.

Her goals in life are simple—to finish raising two happy, healthy, productive young adults, to keep writing books for as long as she possibly can and to never be on a flight that makes the news.

Join Marie's mailing list on her website at marieforce.com for news about new books and upcoming appearances in your area. Follow her on Facebook at www.Facebook.com/MarieForceAuthor and on Instagram at *www.instagram.com/marieforceauthor/*. Contact Marie at *marie@marieforce.com*.